Caeia March was born i~~~~~~~~~~~~~~ up in industrial South Yorkshire. She came out as a lesbian in October 1980, and she has two grown-up sons aged 22 and 20. She lives in Cornwall. She thinks of herself as a countrywoman now and is a very keen gardener. She has published poetry, short stories and non-fiction articles and is widely known as a tutor of women's studies and creative writing. She is also the author of three other novels, *Three Ply Yarn* (The Women's Press, 1986), *Fire! Fire!* (The Women's Press, 1991) and *Reflections* (The Women's Press, 1995). She is currently working on a new novel in the form of a ballad.

Also by Caeia March from The Women's Press:

Three Ply Yarn (1986)
Fire! Fire! (1991)
Reflections (1995)

THE HIDE AND SEEK FILES

CAEIA MARCH

First published by The Women's Press Ltd, 1988
A member of the Namara Group
34 Great Sutton Street, London EC1V 0DX

Reprinted 1995

British Library Cataloguing-in-Publication Data
A catalogue record for this book is available from the British Library

ISBN 0 7043 4096 8

Printed and bound in Great Britain by Cox & Wyman Ltd,
Reading, Berks

Acknowledgments

This novel was started in June 1984 and was finished four years later. Thank you to the staff of the Fawcett Library, the Feminist Library and Goldsmiths' College Library where I did the research for the early parts of the book.

Thanks to all the women who told me that they enjoyed *Three Ply Yarn* and to those who wrote to me – your encouragement gave me confidence in writing this novel.

To all the women in the groups I have tutored – your commitment to your writing and to each other, and your sense of humour, has been an inspiration.

To The Lesbian Archive for enabling lesbians to do research and to keep records of our lives now, so that lesbian history will not be as hidden in the future as it has been in the past.

To Margaret Marshment, freelance editor, for hours of supportive feedback, ideas and detailed editing; and to Jen Green of The Women's Press for being one of the best editors with whom I could wish to work.

To Pat Angove, Sandra den Hertog and Elizabeth Carola for typing the manuscript.

To Sandra Anlin, Nancy Diuguid, Annette McQuillan, and Nola Parke for reading early drafts and for feedback; Judith for constructive criticism and friendship; Penny Holland for fourteen years of close friendship and for entertaining me and my two sons often with storytelling; Hania Dolan and Keri Wood for the fun of sharing our writing and going dancing. To both my sons for loud music, life and times of young people in the eighties.

Lastly I would like to thank my lover Keri Wood for talking, listening and bouncing around of ideas; for photocopying the re-writes, and for growing a wild flower garden.

Book One

One

Overhead the sky, black, shining black and reflecting light like her favourite new black boots. Stars like bright silver boot buttons.

Her name was Moss. It was 1920: she was sixteen, headstrong and determined. Moss in the lane.

No regrets. It was six strides back to the front door. Six strides too many. She would not go back inside. So she gave a brief typical nod of her head, checked the right-hand deep pocket of her skirt for the four £1 notes, almost the entire family savings, more than most Darlington families, patted her old canvas shoulder bag with the new boots in, and started to walk.

Without looking over her shoulder, she gave another nod and shrug, as if to say a silent goodbye, throwing off the ties of her younger brothers and sisters.

Above her, Cassiopeia. She knew all the names; had learned them from her younger brother Ronnie. He shouldn't be having to go down the pit. He hated to be indoors, to have an under-earth future. How he'd fought against it. But her dad would not give in.

The lane rose away from the pit village and she swung inland towards the hills at a steady rate. She loved walking. She reckoned on 10 miles a day. That would not be exhausting. It would give her time to find barns to sleep in and rivers to wash in. She must not allow herself to look bedraggled. She hoped the June weather would hold out, and the money. Prices had soared high as hawks since the end of the war. She would buy only bread, cheese and apples. At least in the country there was always plenty of water to drink. A loaf cost a shilling, and was still going up.

The wild night air carried the quietness of farmland. But through the night silence there whirred the familiar cabling buckets, louder now that they were not part of daily noises.

Moss was not ignorant, merely uneducated. She knew that. She would have stayed on at the Elementary and become a pupil teacher if she could. But being next to eldest, after Daisy, she'd had to go to drudge at The Hall on Mount Pleasant, after her twelfth birthday. Hands red raw with washing, straining her back lifting buckets of coal and water ten times a day up the house of a thousand stairs. That was Daisy's name for it. There were times when Daisy had a bitter way with words.

In Moss's deep left-hand pocket was the map she had 'borrowed' from The Hall under the pretence of dusting the shelves in the library. So she knew where she was heading. Had planned for success. Failure meant return, when there was, matter of fact, nowhere to return to. She shrugged again. She did not intend to fail.

It was the best time of the summer season. Ronnie would say this sky was covered in fine silk 'like of which you'll never wear, Mossie'. Black silk above, sewn with diamonds. She had never seen that. Her ladyship in The Hall took more to pale lavender. Ordered her clothes from London and thought nothing of paying fifteen guineas for a tea gown trimmed with lace. But woe betide a maid who ruined a cap or apron and had two shillings to find a replacement.

Real silk. Moss shuddered. Who was it had told her that they boiled the silkworms before they wound the silk off them?

There had been nights like silk though, under the rhododendrons. With Florence. Enough to remember. Did all girls go through that? No regrets. She'd believed in love at first sight, then. Though there was not much romance about the first meeting with Florence. They had actually been peeling 23 pounds of potatoes for one of her ladyship's banquets. On their own. Daisy was doing the hearths. Fifteen hearths. It had been so bitter cold last February. The skivvies' hands all but froze under the running cold water in the scullery.

That's how Florence came to miss the potato and cut her thumb. She'd gone on peeling, though. There wasn't time to stop. Moss could never have finished them all on her own in time for Cook. So they simply washed the blood off, half giggling, hoping it'd poison the lot of them.

'All down in one fell swoop,' laughed Florence. She liked to be called Florence. Said it made her feel older. Everybody but Moss called her Flo.

Such nights they'd had in April. Enough to remember. No regrets.

Just their luck to be found there by his lordship. Out for a midnight stroll with his brother and the pedigree Airedale dog. Stupid brute. Had come snuffling into the rhododendrons wagging its tail.

Then suddenly the softness was gone.

4

There was only herself and Florence thrown apart by the two men, to be taught a lesson they'd never forget. And all the minutes that it had taken, for the men to mount them as if they were cattle in the fields, that damn dog had lain there, still snuffling, thumping its tail wham wham on the ground. All the while the men cursed them, names Moss had not heard before, would never forget and never repeat. Names the two men said were too good for girls that did that, with one another.

Hardness was the word that stayed in Moss's mind.

The hardness of the ground, that before had not seemed hard, the hardness of the male bodies that cracked her young body open, so that she thought her hips would split in two, the hardness of their words, of their hatred. The hardness of learning that hard lesson.

Now she swung along, her old boots soft, familiar. Fighting against bad memories, and against new fears, of being jumped on, of having the four pounds stolen, of not finding work, of not getting lodgings.

Back in the house, Daisy would still be asleep. Snoring lightly, in the bed they shared with Janey, aged five. Daisy was the final cause of Moss's decision to leave.

'As God's my witness, I've done my best. Keeping guard out for you while you was out philandering. I'd like to kill him, your young man, and I would if I knew where he'd gone. I never thought you'd let us all down so, Mossie. I knew you was courting. But you wasn't just courting was you? You was letting your fancy man know what no man should know, not before he's wed you. And look how I lied for you, Mossie, and how have you repaid me? Tell me that?'

Moss couldn't. For if she did, Daisy would not believe her. And besides, she could never reveal how she'd felt about Florence, or what she'd done with Florence. That was forbidden, when it was known. Moss did not learn that in Elementary. It was something she and Florence just knew.

Florence would not reveal their secret.

Florence was gone where there were no more beatings, no more lessons.

Florence had run from her father, her brothers. She weighted her pockets with coal and waded into the fast river.

Her body was washed up against the weir, four days later.

Moss had had hysterics. She had flung herself on the bed almost passing out with the shock of the amount of weeping. If Moss's dad had been the beating sort, he might have beaten some of the truth out of her. No one would have gained from that. But the family all mistook Moss's tears for the shame of her lost virginity, and the grief over the death of her 'best friend'. They never connected the friendship with the truth, because they never recognised any of the truth. In their minds she'd been out courting and deceiving them and now she was pregnant. That was almost enough to explain the hysterics. Her friend's unexpected suicide obviously aggravated Moss's plight. No wonder she had to sob some of it out of her.

In Moss's family there wasn't usually much time for the two older daughters to indulge in crying. Either they were at work in The Hall or they were at work at home. Things had to be extreme before anyone older than Janey gave up time for a few tears. There was laughter, and large dollops of anger too. The usual response to anger was to rush out to the coal shed, slam the door shut to keep out the others, and wham the shovel hard against the wall till the mood wore off or the others lost patience with the din. Moss's mum's response was usually to shut herself in the privvy but even then she'd been known to take the latest baby in there with her and sit there pondering with it on her lap or at her breasts. If *she* ever felt hysterical, no one ever knew.

Moss thought about her mother as the stars moved and the night turned cold. She quickened her step, to keep warm, to give herself the power to face the memories of her mum.

Pregnant brides were no new thing in Moss's village, nor indeed in Moss's family. Her mum was pregnant with Daisy when she married their dad.

So the scandal was not that Moss was pregnant, at least not to anyone except Daisy, who had her own reasons for being scandalised, as Moss well knew. No. The scandal was that Moss refused to name the father, and would not help the family to vent their rage on the lad's parents and make them force him to marry her. That was the known pattern. The way things could and should be done. Moss ruined that.

Her mum cried and said she could stay. Her dad ranted at her, calling her a silly hot young bitch, and a selfish young filly, but said she'd better stay.

Daisy did not. She used the only power she was ever likely to have. Her fury at the injustice of her own life boiled over, as the earth flung itself into flames sometimes, rebelling at the men and women who depended on her. Then pent-up impatience broke the earth open, casting aside wagons and pit props, maiming and hurting people and ponies, in the uncontrolled bursting through. Moss's grandfather and two uncles had been lost in one of the earth's outbursts. She herself was the receiver of Daisy's.

'I lied for you. I went to chapel every Sunday and said I was sorry to God because I was lying for you. All those evenings when I said you was working late. You couldn't resist it, could you? It is a sacrament, Mossie. But you could go and get it when you wanted, couldn't you? I needed you, Mossie. How can I get married now, make a home for *me*? Have my own children? I thought we was in this together, you and me bringing up the others. How can I get my life now? Martha's only ten, she's too young to share the work. I'm not staying here just to bring up your brat. I'm not having your brat in the house. You go or I go.'

Moss stood there as if in place of her silent ladyship, decked out in her latest £30 furs, just delivered from London, while Daisy threw at Moss all the insults that she wanted to hurl at her ladyship's bosom and could not.

Moss intended to walk mainly at night. Days were warmer for sleeping. She was less afraid of being alone at night, while she was awake. She would not be likely to meet unwelcome people on the road.

She moved her body steadily towards Richmond. The lanes were quiet. An owl shrieked. She passed a field of cows, higgledy-piggledy, humped forms breathing with heavy animal sleep. She had done a twelve-hour day at The Hall. She envied them. Even if they were going to be milked dry all their lives, lose their calves, and end up as shoe leather on somebody's feet, being walked to a second death after death. Moss knew women who had been walked to death. She hoped she herself was walking towards a new life.

In the hedge bottom something was in a hurry. She tried not to be afraid – it was, after all, only trying to survive and it was smaller than she was.

The moon began to slide. A long arching slide. Giving her time, and company. She was already lonely. She hadn't expected that. Had thought of the miles as adventure. Had longed for time to herself. Now it was here. There was perhaps going to be more of it than she was ready for.

She stopped.

She was in the middle of a lane, one of a series that led, rising very slowly, towards Richmond and the Dales. There was no work in the Dales. She would bypass them, Swale Ure Nid Wharfe Wensley. Her destination was the coalfield south of Leeds. She knew coal, didn't she? Coal was money. Where there was money there were shops, and larger houses for managers, for vets and doctors, and some wanted servants.

She stood very still trying to breathe calmly, as steadily as those cows half a mile back towards Darlington.

Moss was suddenly very frightened. The first burst of activity, the leaving, the sense of direction, had been temporary. Had not lasted even until the first dawn. The moon was sliding but there was no light yet back to the east. She had no idea where to find the barn she planned to sleep in. And no real plan for buying food. She found that, from fright and relief at having been brave enough to carry through that leaving, she was now tired to the end of her fingernails. Every part of her was a small ache, and they all linked to each other. It wasn't romantic.

It didn't even seem brave, clever or adventurous. It just seemed long.

And would get longer if she stayed there in the silent quiet lane, where even her own breathing seemed larger than life. She fancied she could hear the trees growing, which perhaps they did at night. She didn't know. But the thought amused her, and against the odds she grinned. It broke the fear. Count three and start walking, she said inwardly.

So she did. And as she set off she remembered a game she played with Janey. They used to stand out in the lane, when Moss had a day off work, and Janey would yell one – and fling her arms forward; two – and fling them back, and then three – and fling them forward for Moss to catch and swing her round till Janey squealed 'Lemmego lemmego lemmego, Mossie, *please*' but not afraid at all, and Moss would swing her down to the safe ground again. There was not often time for games. The ones they had had time for she started to remember and the memories brought hot tears down Moss's face, where they steamed off, into the layers of night-time.

She looked up at the stars and chose two and decided to walk until the moon moved from one to the other. She thought of that as a game.

It worked. The lanes were dark green; the cold bit lines in her skin, like thin teeth. So she started to hum hymns inside her head and to see how many she could get through before the moon reached the second star.

Her feet followed each other and without thinking about it she discovered that they kept time with the rhythm in her head. In spite of Daisy's and God's anger, Moss was glad that she'd been to chapel, to learn those hymns. They were helping her do this, a foot at a time.

Rich man at his castle; poor man at his gate: God made them high and lowly and ordered their estate.

She ignored the words that she'd often thought were silly. Poor men didn't have gates. They used them for firewood when times were hard. And only rich people found that all things were bright and beautiful. But that did not stop poor people from knowing about beauty.

Moss and Florence had known about beauty, with each other. Moss felt now at the age of sixteen that even if life brought her no more of that ever again, she had had those experiences and no one could ever take them away.

She realised she'd stopped singing, and when she searched the sky, she found that the moon was almost there. So it was now time to find somewhere to sleep. She would give herself the luxury of eight hours, untimed. She never ever had eight hours. It was more than the nights ever had time for. Sleep in the day was only for the rich, or the dead, and now, as an exception it was for herself, alive and going forward.

She noticed a faint smudge of light coming up behind her. Good. There were several farms on the map between here and the town, and all she could do would be to choose a remote one, bed herself down (out of sight so that should she be so unlucky as to have any farm workers come near they would not find her), and give into the craving to close her eyes and drift away.

She walked on. Checked two signposts with the map, just about able to make it out now that the smudge was increasing.

The birds started. Ronnie knew all their names.

They woke the cockerel. Lazy sods, thought Moss. The grin again. Smudgey like the sky, she was so tired. But if she could grin she would win. She was doing this. Doing it. She wanted to crow like the cockerel. Scream her newness like him. Her old newness, that came from starting life over again against your own will.

Cockerels meant farms. She walked towards the sound. The barn was much too near the other buildings. Moss was too tired to care. She climbed the five-bar gate that led to the field behind the hay barn, walking away from anywhere that there might be guard dogs. She had had enough of dogs to last for ever.

The hay barn was half empty. If anyone came they'd come to the front, thought Moss, and pulled aside two bales in the far back corner. The sky was glowing pale cream and butter colours where the sun was starting to come up. Moss squatted away from her prepared bed, relieving herself and covering the mess with extra straw, and wiping herself with the least scratchy handfuls. She would love a drink and a wash but would wait. First a sleep.

She checked again that the bales really did hide her, and that none could topple on her and smother her. Hannah Swaith had been killed like that three years ago on Haywards Farm. She was only nine. Moss shuddered. She did not need such pictures to come up, and she didn't need the sun up either for that matter. So she shoved the memories that she could control, back into her head, and ignored the sun, which she could not control. She stepped out of her long skirt, which she folded neatly beside her; and took her new boots out of her bag so that she could use it as a pillow; and then she closed her eyes.

Barbara Imogen Farley was eight years old when Moss was born in 1904. Biff was a mistake. A love child born from her mother's affair with a young man that she'd met through union politics. Her mother was a Lancashire mill worker, living at that time in Manchester, and was widowed. Both Biff's sisters, Sara and Lucy, were unmarried and in their late teens. They also worked in the cotton mill, where their mother was an experienced bobbin mistress.

When Biff was thirteen, in 1909, her mother and sisters started to try to unionise the other women in the mill, and Biff's real education began. She had learned almost nothing in school, where she hated stitching samplers, and was not allowed to touch the globe that hung above everyone's head showing the British Empire. Years later, Biff still had the underdog's view of the empire, which she said came from looking up at it from under Antarctica every day. It was never lowered to the children's eye level that Biff could remember, and she was absolutely certain that she *would* have remembered that.

Biff had three mothers. She saw that as an advantage because of all the huggings and because of having no father. Her life was entirely lived with women from the day she could comprehend other people. The disadvantages were hard to find, and came only from having all those adults above her, sometimes as far above as the globe in the school room.

Biff learned everything at home that was worth learning. She was taught that bosses are powerful and that bosses are usually men. Her sisters said they had no need for men. Her mother had a need every so often, hence Biff's existence. As Biff grew older she was aware that from time to time her mother had a young man to love, but her sisters took that as the only disadvantage to having a flamboyant, loud-spoken, brash and lovable woman for their mother. Biff was not

10

supposed to know all that. She became skilled very young in the art of eavesdropping. It was her way of climbing an inch up the outside of a slippery greased globe.

By the time that Biff was thirteen, the Women's Social and Political Union had been in existence for three years and her sisters had become active among its working class membership. Their friends in Manchester, including much better-known activists like the Kenney sisters, were round at the house many nights of the week and at weekends, talking till late about the struggles ahead.

As a young woman Biff was extremely tall, with a keen, intelligent face. She had a proud carriage and walked without stooping, so that people were aware of her height. Her thick light brown hair was pinned back in a simple style. She had grey eyes that lit up as she talked, and large hands and feet.

In her own way Biff was beautiful, and she was very popular with the mill girls, although she didn't seem at all interested in the opposite sex. She never went in for gossip about who was courting who, who was engaged, who'd made a mistake and had to get married, which the other mill girls loved to talk about. There were others like her in the mill, and she was often the centre of a crowd discussing news and views about what was happening in Manchester and the world beyond.

Biff was slim built, flat chested and athletic. From very young she'd taken to cycling, hitching up her skirts and borrowing the local lads' bicycles whenever she could. As a young woman she bought knickerbockers and her own bicycle and could be seen anywhere around the mill, riding like a boy.

Biff's sisters, Sara and Lucy, were not typical mill girls, because they were not interested in the young men. But they were well known at work, and they had built up years and years of trust in the eyes of the other mill girls by just being there working for that length of time. Time is what trust is all about, they would say.

Biff did not always understand the twists and turns of the talk. Sometimes she was too tired to eavesdrop and once or twice her sisters had found her fallen asleep in a little heap outside the parlour door, where she'd been listening in. Then they would carry her up to bed, one holding her under the shoulders and the other under her knees. They'd take off her boots and apron and dress and slide her in between the sheets before she'd had time to make a sleepy protest.

'Why not let her join in?' said the visitors. 'She can do less harm on the inside. Curiosity killed the cat, you know.'

11

Biff especially loved Aggie, who especially loved Sara. Aggie would let Biff sit on her knee at the kitchen table meetings, and on a pouffe by her feet at the front parlour talkings. If Aggie went to make the tea in the giant pot that they used for 'the meetings' then Biff followed her, whispering 'Can I carry the tray please, Aggie?' Biff recalled later that Aggie always nodded and winked. Biff fell in love with the wink and tried it in front of the bedroom mirror, but try as she would, she couldn't make one eyebrow go up and keep the other one level and turn her head just so all at the same time. She had a crick in her neck for months practising but it remained Aggie's wink, not Biff's.

Larger meetings which her sisters sometimes called 'planning meetings' were held in larger houses owned by larger people.

They seemed larger in every way. Biff wondered if maybe it was their expensive clothes and the heavy fur collars; or maybe it was the puffed up hair that was made into huge rolls around their heads.

Lucy and Sara liked to follow fashions, and sometimes did their hair in puffs too, but not every day, because there wasn't enough time on account of the hours they had to work in the mill.

Lucy slept in bed with Biff. Sara slept with mum. But occasionally mum stayed out somewhere, with another young man, and sometimes Sara went over to Aggie's. From time to time Aggie came to stay the night with Sara.

In those days Biff recalled later, amused, it was quite a common thing for working girls to stay overnight with each other, after meetings. No one thought anything funny about that at all. It was very, very unusual for any working girl ever to have the chance of a whole bed to sleep in on her own.

In the two-up, three-down in Victoria Street, where Biff lived, there were sometimes two or three young women sleeping on the parlour floor too, on account of another late planning meeting.

Lucy was the younger of Biff's older sisters, born a year after Sara. It was from Lucy that Biff learned to go every weekend to the public library to read the newspapers. And it was Lucy who told Biff that until all mill girls could read and write, there would be no chance for them to become leaders in the campaigns for Votes for Women.

'Words is what matters in this struggle, our Biff. You mark my words. You don't get far reading Marx if you fink filosofy's spelt with an "f",' she said laughing. She wrote down philosophy for Biff to spell, and bribed Biff to learn philosophy by letting her come to meetings provided she did her lessons at home.

Lucy loved words and would have loved to go to college like Christabel Pankhurst but was never bitter about Christabel, nor about the other Pankhursts.

'You can't afford bitterness in the class struggle, our Biff,' she said, and she looked at Biff with her clear almond-shaped eyes that were like green leaves in summer.

One day, as Lucy was tucking her into bed, Biff put up her arms and whispered in Lucy's ear: 'Would you like somebody special Lucy, like Aggie?' The green eyes went wet, like leaves with rain on them.

'What's matter, Luce? Why you cryin'?'

'I'm not,' said Lucy, and Biff knew she was lying, 'I've got enough somebody specials. I'm all right. Now go to sleep. It's too late, really it is.'

'Too late for you, Lucy?'

'No, too late for thirteen-year-olds to be going to bed.'

Then Lucy kissed Biff and put out the light, and Biff fell asleep wondering if she would ever understand her older sisters.

The next day Biff sidled up to Sara, and asked her why Lucy didn't have somebody like Aggie to stay over.

Sara looked down thoughtfully as she buttered the bread, and for a couple of awkward moments Biff wondered if Sara would let slip with the bread knife. She seemed in another world, standing there thinking. She put down the knife then and carried the pile of bread and the teapot to the kitchen table. There were only the two of them in the house. Biff sat still as a full cat not even twitching her whiskers, watching Sara.

Sara decided.

'Biffy, if you ever tell Lucy what I'm about to tell you don't ever try to be my friend again. Do you understand me, Biffy?'

The still cat's eyes grew huge.

It barely nodded. Sara saw.

Sara said that Biff was now old enough to understand that it was all right for her and Aggie to love one another. She asked Biff if Biff *did* understand that. Biff, still being a cat, twitched whiskers to say yes. Cats can't talk but they know everything.

But then Sara explained that outside, in the mill and in the posh houses too, there were lots of men and plenty of women who thought that it was sinful.

'Do you already know that, Biff?'

Biff nodded.

Lucy was very unlucky, Sara continued, and then described for Biff how Lucy's friend had gone on a scholarship to a college for ladies and had met a gentleman friend there and next month, they had heard, she was going to come home to Manchester to marry him. They were going away after that to live in London, and they would be rich and successful. It was going to be hard for Lucy in the next few weeks because the wedding would be in all the newspapers, since everybody knew the family.

'Our Lucy's very upset, Biffy. So we've got to be kind and not talk about it to her.'

'Yes,' said the cat. 'Can I have my milk now?'

From 1910 to 1913 Biff secretly pledged herself to the suffrage cause. She gloried in her sisters' accounts of street meetings, was allowed to go sometimes to hear them, tagging along the edge of the crowd with other young girls, listening, watching the heckling, and admiring the ways the women speakers dealt with it. First, they'd put on someone inexperienced to draw the crowd, then, just as she was becoming nervous, facing the jeers and sneers, there'd appear the trained women, who knew, like Biff's sisters, how to make their points, without boring people, or making them violent.

Biff hung on to the edges of meetings at home, and began to go to those in local halls. She talked to her mum about the mill unions and the women there. Women who were banding together, gaining strength. It was an exciting time.

In 1912 Biff's mother was arrested and sent to prison. She had been caught throwing a brick at a shop window, on one of the visits of the women to London.

By now Biff was a mill worker. Her job every day was to mend the broken threads on the bobbins, under the guidance of a bobbin mistress.

That year was intense from the first day to the last. In the same months that Biff's mother was in prison, refusing to eat, Biff met Emily, who had also just started at the mill. She was not famous like the other Emilys. She was not to become a martyr either. Emily was local, ordinary and unusual. She was funny and sad, plain and beautiful, silly and sensible. She loved Biff back with the steady recognition that they, the youngest suffragettes, would have to learn to become leaders when the others were imprisoned, ill or exhausted.

Biff's mother endured forced feeding.

In April 1912 the doctors made a technical error on Biff's mother.

14

They put the tube of warm liquid into her lungs by mistake. She was released with pneumonia to be nursed at home. She had three months of her sentence still to serve. In May she was considered to be well enough to have to go back to finish that sentence.

She died on 10 June 1913, eleven months after her release from prison. No one could prove that the doctors killed her. Biff hated doctors from that time onwards.

By day Emily and Biff went to the mill. By night and on any days off they poured acid into pillar boxes; arranged for fleeing prisoners to be transported to safe houses, wrote tracts and manifestos, read newspapers and filosofy (Biff refused ever to spell it with 'ph'. And it was not a word she found that she used when writing); and they read history and economics and argued and discussed and made love.

They called themselves the backstage girls. The ones behind the scenes working getting things done. They loved each other with the passion that came with understanding filosofy, and they joked and raged and worked.

As all the campaigns escalated, and more shop windows were smashed, more acid was poured into pillar boxes and more doorstep letterboxes were set alight, the campaigns became split into groups around the type of violence, and the aim of it and the amount.

In the mill Emily and Biff talked, talked and talked, turning the issues inside out and upside down. They knew they were important to the campaign, because of the deep divisions of class which threatened the trust between the mill women and women who had been educated, had money, or time, or both.

Emily and Biff kept their passion alive for nine months, and then tried to watch and still love each other as passion changed into friendship.

Biff could not give Emily the time that Emily needed. There were meetings every night and work all day almost every day. It was hard enough to find the time to be alone together, unless they went into the woods in the hills from which the millstreams had originally been tamed.

'I don't want it to fade out like this,' Emily had sobbed. But it was already faded, and it was already too late in the pacing of the suffrage campaigns for them to be able to go back and rebuild in a slower world.

'You know that I love you,' Biff cried, and the tears were real tears mingled with the grief over the politics, and the grief over her mother, the grief of all political women for whom time is an enemy.

Their time was not women's time. It belonged to men. It was measured then, as Emily realised too, by the men who denied women their citizenship, and who fouled the air over Manchester with fumes from the mills, and who destroyed women's bodies and called it medical knowledge.

The gift that remained between Emily and Biff was rare. It was the gift of loyalty, wrapped carefully in everyday life so that somehow they managed to carry on seeing each other at work, and to work side by side for suffrage.

Through 1913 they remained loyal to one another, aged as if they were already in their twenties by the intensity of the two years since they met in the mill.

They did not have the luxury of growing up slowly with holidays and ponies, theatre visits, dinners and dances. But by the time the men declared the First World War, Biff and Emily at the age of eighteen were fully-fledged politicians, trained and experienced.

During the year 1913 the suffragettes came under vicious treatment if they were caught by the police. Women had their hair pulled out, their noses broken, their legs and breasts kicked, their shoulders beaten with truncheons, and they returned often from police stations looking like soldiers from a battlefield.

Lucy and Sara kept records of the working-class cases told to them in confidence, taken down by Aggie, sometimes in shorthand which she had been to night school to learn. The written records filed and stored were hidden in the cellars and attics of some of the less well-known houses in Manchester.

In November 1913, Biff's home was ransacked. No arrests were made, because no incriminating evidence was found.

On 11 December, Biff was caught with Lucy pouring acid into a pillar box. In the police station Biff was threatened with rape unless she co-operated with names and addresses. She would not co-operate. She was severely manhandled but not raped. She was released with Lucy, pending the trial.

On 13 December, Sara was taken to the police station accused of conspiring with Biff and Lucy. She was kept standing there for eighteen hours. When at one time she fainted, she was revived and propped up again. Later she was released pending the trial, which was set for the New Year.

On 29 December, some Manchester people returning from a late party found the bodies of two women who, it seemed, had been thrown from a motor car on to the pavement. They were identified as Sara and Lucy.

The coroner issued a verdict of death by misadventure. There had been no witnesses.

Emily feared that it would be Biff's turn next. She invited Biff back to her house one night after work.

In Emily's house they lit the fire and made some tea. The armchairs beside the fireplace were full of folded washing, Emily's mother's work, so they sat on the hearth rug side by side.

'I'm scared for you, Biff', said Emily. 'If you'd been at the party with Lucy and Sara you'd have been killed too. They'll get you, you know. They're watching you. They're on to you. You're not safe no more.'

'I know. I'm not sleeping at nights, keep waking trying to work out what to do.'

'We was stood there, me and the girls at work, talking about you . . . '

'About me?'

'We can't give you no money, Biff, but we're not short on ideas.'

'Oh aye?' Biff carefully placed small pieces of coal on the fire with the fire tongs.

'There'd be no union in that mill if it weren't for you and your sisters. The girls owe you a lot, they all think so. Don't go shaking your head at me. Just listen to me will you? I'll tell you what we thought.'

They sat talking quietly, leaning forward by Emily's hearth, hugging their knees and concentrating on every detail.

Emily said, 'You're as tall as a lad, aren't you?' Biff gulped. 'And you've big hands and feet.' Emily rushed on before Biff could get too upset, 'Don't get me wrong, I think you're beautiful and every bit a woman, if you know what I mean, but there's a way for you that a smaller lass like me couldn't take. What we thought was – it'd be so easy to get trousers and shoes, the girls'd all ask their brothers; and Aggie's sister, she's a hairdresser, she'd cut your hair off and you could pretend to be a lad.'

'Give over! Me as a boy? I've never wanted to be a boy in me life. Though I do like boys shoes . . . ' Biff trailed off.

'Aye well, getting girls' shoes for you was always the problem, wasn't it? And as the others said, you do wear knickerbockers already, to ride your bike.'

Biff was trembling as she rested her chin on her knees and looked into the fire. It leapt and hissed. Like tongues of dragon fire, thought

Biff, as tiny blue flames began licking along the edge of a lump of coal. Disguise is one thing, she thought, but what do I do when I've got one? The fire crackled and she knew the answer. It was a lonely sort of knowledge.

As if reading her thoughts, Emily said softly, 'Think about it, Biff. No one knows your nickname outside the family and friends. To the police you're Barbara. You could change your name to something fitting and then,' Emily reached her hand out for Biff's and held it as she continued, 'you have to leave Manchester, don't you? You're not at all safe here. It's been so bad for us already, losing your mam and then your sisters. Think what they did to your mam. It'd break us and the campaign if they started that on you too.' Emily tried hard to keep her voice steady. She was shaking and she struggled to gain control of herself again. 'You do know they are getting nastier, don't you? You'd be on some prison bench,' she swallowed and her eyes were wet now, 'tubes and clamps and torturers . . . that's why you have to go. For our sakes as well as for yours. The girls are all exhausted, morale is low. It'd give us such a boost to know we'd got you out of here, helped you escape.

'We've not had something to lift our spirits for such a long time. The girls and me, we want to do this for you. We're supposed to be saving lives, trying to make lives better. That's what it's all for, not letting them kill us off, one by one.'

Emily let go of Biff's hand, reached in her skirt pocket, pulled out a piece of soft cotton and blew her nose. Biff took the pins from her hair and let it down. She shook her head a few times, feeling the weight of her hair. Soon, if she did as Emily was asking, this would be a memory. For the duration of her disguise she would have her hair cropped short. She put her hand to her throat, trying to imagine what a collar and tie would feel like, day in, day out. She turned to Emily, and saw that her face was wet with tears in the firelight.

'Explain the rest to me, please.'

'You could cycle over the Pennines. Find work in one of the towns or cities the other side. As a lad. It would have to be unskilled work. They don't take lads in the mills. So not much use trying Bradford or Leeds. Try further south. You'd be in danger if you went as a girl, of course. But there's always lads on the move. We've got a bike for you. Yours might be recognised. It's only an old thing but it's being mended. It'll last you a fair time. And the hardest thing of all is you mustn't try to get in touch with us. Or you might put us in danger. The police are busy, what's one young suffragette to them?

They'll search here for a while. We'll put it about that you've gone to London.'

'You've gone to so much trouble. You all have. This takes more than one person. Clothes, bike, plans, rumours to spread. I will do it. And I'll never forget you.'

'I love you, Biff. It'd break my heart to think of you being tortured.'

'I love you too.'

'You'd best stay here tonight. God knows how you'll find happiness when you've gone, but at least you'll have life.'

'And you, will you find happiness? I want you to. Whatever way you can.'

'Life is enough for the moment. Happiness can wait for a while.'

In the New Year of 1915, having spent a year on the move in search of a safe place to settle, Barbara Imogen Farley arrived in the mining village of Herton disguised as a young man, presenting herself as Bernard Ian Ferguson, otherwise known as Biff.

Two

When Moss awoke the sun was high and the shadows short. She lay wide awake, training her ears for the sounds of the farm. She could hear pigs somewhere, and hens. Far away there was the sound of machinery, but she couldn't decide what it might be. She couldn't hear any voices.

After a few minutes she cautiously peered over the barrier bales, and looked around. Everywhere was green, and there were two fields of ridges with leaves. Potatoes. There was no one near this barn. She was sure no one could see her and that she could walk quickly back to the gate to the lane as if she'd been on any normal country ramble.

So far so good. She peed and put on her skirt. Then she let down her hair and fished her hairbrush from the right foot of her new pair of boots. In her left boot she had a piece of towelling and a sprig of fresh mint. She needed a wash, and to clean her teeth. She ate some mint and her mouth felt better.

She brushed at her hair, careful not to lose the pins in the hay. Then she pinned it up as quickly as she used to when rushing up to The Hall for 6 a.m.

It was a dry warm day. 'Just hold out for me to get where I'm going please,' she half prayed to the sun. She didn't know why, but she hoped anyway.

Then, checking the outlook again, she left the hay rick and, with her hairbrush and mint back in her new boots, and them safely in her bag slung jauntily over her shoulder, Moss sauntered across the field towards the gate. She climbed it and jumped down.

She had slept well and felt strong. The wind had warm honeysuckle in it. What a day. Life was all right, really all right.

She stepped out along the lane and went in through the farm gate. The dogs set up a row. A small girl appeared and shouted at them, then to Moss, 'Hello, who are you?'

Moss smiled and said hello and told the child her name, and said she'd come to see her mum.

A thin woman appeared from the back of the house.

'Hello,' smiled Moss. 'I'm on my way to see my aunt in Richmond. I wonder, do you have any bread to sell. I'd love to take her a nice present. She always says she's too busy to bake her own, bless her.'

The woman asked Moss if she was walking. Moss chatted on, saying that she'd just come from down the lane; that she often did this on her day off. 'She's used to me. I love walking, and I'm ever so fond of my aunt. I miss her ever so since she moved away from us.'

'Oh dear,' came the reply. 'Yes, I do so miss my sister you know. She went to York right after the war, it's just not the same without her. Do you want a drink, dear? You look quite thirsty.'

'Not to be any trouble,' said Moss.

'No trouble. Doesn't take a minute. You sit right here on these steps, nice and warm they are, been such lovely weather this month hasn't it?'

The child stood, fingers in her mouth, watching Moss and her mother, who disappeared indoors to return with a glass of milk and a loaf of new bread.

Moss thanked her and tried to drink slowly though she was parched. The dogs had quietened. The pigs smelled terrible, drowning the honeysuckle. The bread was wrapped in an old thin white cloth.

'How much is that please?' asked Moss, but the woman shook her head and said she had plenty and she was pleased for Moss to take it for her aunt.

The unexpected gift troubled and pleased Moss. Northern people had a reputation for generosity, but Moss was no beggar, and wanted to pay her way, out of pride. Yet she knew she'd have done the same if she had plenty. Times were not easy for any working people, and this woman looked thin and tired. So Moss looked in her eyes and smiled, and the smile that was returned was genuine.

'This,' Moss indicated the bread that she was now holding, 'is so kind. I don't know what to say except thank you.'

'Take care, and mind how you go. I'd say take the short cut to the Richmond road across the fields, but the bull's in there today so you'd best go the long way round.'

'Thank you. Thank you very, very much.'

Moss grinned at the child, who just stared, no smiles. Moss wondered if there really was plenty of bread around.

According to Moss's map, which she looked at once she was back in the lane out of sight of the house windows, it was 4 miles to Richmond.

So she would be there mid-afternoon, and that was time to buy cheese and apples and leave the town before dark.

She was glad to leave the pigs behind. Funny how last night's wind had not carried the smell. Moss was glad she'd been ready with the story of her aunt. She marched along, munching on a crust torn off the loaf. In Richmond there would be a public drinking fountain where she could quench her thirst which was encouraged by the bread.

You had to be careful drinking out of country rivers. You never knew when there was a dead sheep or something upstream. But according to her map she would cross the Swale by the road bridge about two miles outside Richmond. If she stopped there a while and followed the river downstream, she would be able to find a place sheltered enough to have a quick wash.

In fact the river came up sooner than Moss expected and she realised that maybe she had been wrong to plan to walk only at night.

Walking now in the afternoon she found she could enjoy the countryside; and could be more sure of finding food and washing places. She needed to stay clean looking. That way, the aunt, always in the next town, would be believable. Whereas if she missed being able to wash, or if she walked too fast and became dishevelled and sweaty, she'd soon start to look like an unemployed vagrant. It was that that Moss wanted most to avoid.

So she washed and did her hair slowly, to be on the safe side, and then continued the walk, at a leisurely pace, into Richmond.

Anybody who had an aunt who lived in Richmond had to be all right, thought Moss, wondering whether there were any poor people in that wealthy place at all. If there were they were well hidden out of the sight of the well-to-do who liked their town to look like the gateway to the northern Dales. The large farms in the area had been passed from generation to generation, and the shops showed the types of customers.

Moss obviously looked the servant of someone, as she bought her cheese and apples; as someone's servant she was not asked too many questions.

Besides she was shopping with a £1 note, and that in itself showed the shopkeepers that she was not beggarly, needy, or otherwise undesirable in that very civilised community.

She also found an ironmonger's shop and bought a small tin mug. She dare not afford a toothbrush though now that the war was over, the new ones were coming into the shops. At home they all shared the same one. They felt themselves lucky to have one.

There was no one near the fountain, so she drank out of her mug.

She left Richmond as the public clock chimed four.

By this time tomorrow she wanted to be half-way to Ripon. So she walked into the evening, on the road south to Bedale.

She had grown up in the country and she wanted to live in the country. Her home near Darlington had been in lovely countryside, and she appreciated that, even when she was too tired to enjoy it. There was always the possibility that the day off would be clear and bright, that even in winter there would be things to see, and to watch out for. So she used her eyes now as she walked to tell her what this land would be like next month, next season.

On the road to Bedale, with the sun slowly curving down over the Dales to her right, which was in the west, she saw green blackberries, tight, just coming on the brambles where the white flowers had finished. She saw meadowsweet and cranesbill. But the cranesbill reminded her too closely of the delphiniums which had lined the south-facing wall of The Hall beyond the rhododendrons. She shivered, and realised that blue was a spoiled colour for her now, because of those memories. Then she saw dog roses and the word 'dog' was nasty.

She sighed and walked faster till she was past the roses. It wasn't their fault, but the memories would take a long time to fade. Longer than the wild roses. She would call them 'wild' from now on.

The road was lined, like so many North Yorkshire roads, with miles of dry-stone walling. Hours of work must have gone into them. Some needed patching, where the wind and storms had unsteadied them. No one had been working on these walls for all the years of the war. These days no one had jobs. What a mess.

Moss knew that finding work would not be easy, even though rich people were still hiring servants. Things had changed since the armistice. Many of the women had had to give up their work for the soldiers who wanted their jobs back.

The sky was reddening now. Red at night, shepherds' delight. There had been a lot to learn about farms and farmers in her home village because all around the colliery was lovely rich farmland. Land that Ronnie ached to work with. He said he wanted to put things into the land, not tunnel under it. But her dad remained firm, because there was more chance for Ronnie to make a living under than on top.

Ronnie did not own land, so he could not choose. But that did not stop him, nor Moss as his dearest closest sister, from calling the land beautiful. Together they had discovered where to find scarlet pimpernels, and wild anemonies.

Once she had a secure job, Moss would write to Ronnie. One day she would hope to see him again. If her baby was a boy, she'd call him Ronnie. Moss wanted to live somewhere just like her old home.

North Yorkshire was wild, as Moss had known it would be. Her dad's cousin's older son had become a preacher, moving from village to village, and from town to town. When he came by he brought news of the outside world, and would take Moss on his knee telling her about the Dales and the cities south of the Dales, in the West Riding. He hated the cities. It was a slow death for poor people, he said, to live in a city. Pit villages were toil and struggle and sometimes death and dust. But out of the open door you could still see past the tip to the woods.

'In this house you can leave your door on the latch all night, Moss, but you couldn't do that in a city.'

South of Bedale Moss found a barn and slept from just before dawn to the early afternoon again.

From Bedale the route led to Ripon, and from there she would turn east to avoid going through Leeds. She had taken in cousin Don's warnings. She feared the people she might meet in the city. Feared the men who lived off 'immoral earnings' and feared even the women who had to make ends meet by making their living like that. Moss had much more fear inside her than she recognised when she started, and she felt years older than her real age as if each day's walking added five years to her experiences and to her feelings.

She also worried that her old boots would wear too thin for the whole journey. She was not used to walking without boots and so she dare not try in case she blistered; then she would not be able to carry on. She needed her new boots to look smart at the end of her journey, so that she could find work.

On the road to Ripon, Moss saw the faces of the poor. A family was walking. Father, mother carrying a baby, and two small boys about five, Janey's age. Moss knew about unemployment. The man was one of the half million, or was it three quarters, on the government registers. The government was proud, the papers all said, of the fact that unemployment had dropped a bit this summer. Moss nodded as the family passed her. She didn't feel like getting into conversation with them. The family had pinched lines from their noses to the edges of their mouths. Those were the giveaway signs. Her dad said you could see despair in people's eyes. To Moss it seemed that the bottom part of poor people's faces was even more revealing. Perhaps the father was a returned soldier, returned to the Land Fit For Heroes. Perhaps the new baby happened after he came home, and perhaps that's why the others were Janey's age. If she'd been a newspaper reporter, Moss would have taken a picture of them and written a story. She wondered whether newspaper reporters had ever known what it felt like to be poor.

Cousin Don had said there were very terrible slums in Leeds and Bradford. Some people actually lived in basements and never had sunlight coming down inside their homes. Their beds were wet whenever the drains could no longer cope with the heavy rains. There were no chimneys and no fireplaces in the basements so the families almost froze in winter. And cousin Don had scowled and said that even this was not as bad as Liverpool and, of course, London.

Moss had no desire at all to go to London. She was north country born and bred, and though her family also had Indian blood through her grandmother's line, Moss considered herself northern and intended to stay in the north. But not, if she could possibly avoid it, in one of the hell-on-earth cities. She felt in her deep pocket. There were four half crowns and three £1 notes and a few coppers. The map was still safe in the other pocket. She was on her way, and unlike the family whose faces would not leave her, she was not desperate and destitute. When she had a job and had lodgings, she would save and save however hard it was, and send the £4 home. She had left a letter in the toby jug on the mantelpiece to say so. She hoped that they would believe her.

Two days later she came to Wharfedale, at the easternmost end. So she would spend her fifth night in Linton-in-Craven. She was tired of barns, tired of walking, tired of the aloneness. She had reached the halfway stage. She wondered about calling at the inn and yet she dare not risk being asked questions, perhaps even being sent to the parsonage and then the police. She didn't want her money squandered on a bed and hot water, though she would have loved to have a proper pillow.

So she stood on the small green, and the church clock said three and she thought of home and Florence and Daisy and everything past and present and was overwhelmed.

That was when she had her first piece of miracle. Miracle was hers and Daisy's name for something much better than luck. Moss suspected that Daisy actually did *believe* in miracles. Moss did not. But the name stuck and the next few moments almost made her agree with Daisy's faith. In miracles anyway.

A motor car pulled up on the green and out stepped two women, laughing together. They were upper-class, from the motor, their clothes and their voices. But. Usually Moss had no buts when it came to the upper crust.

They took out a map and laid it on the car bonnet and were heads together, discussing, tracing out a route as Moss stepped off her stone seat and walked towards them.

'Excuse me,' said Moss politely, 'I am later than I expected' – she was talking her best talk – 'and I'm on my way to see my aunt. Would it be all right for me to have a lift with both of you, please?'

Moss could not remember afterwards what they said or even how they said it because she was so dazed at her own actions, outspokenness, and sheer bluff.

They put her in the back seat, where the wind nearly blew her head off and they dropped her later 30 miles away to the south of Pontefract. It was to be Moss's only ride in a motor car for the next ten years. She made the most of it, watching the green fields and villages whizz by. It was strange not being able to touch the land as she travelled on it, so to speak.

The two women laughed and talked to each other, but not much to Moss who wouldn't have been able to reply anyway, because the wind would have stolen her words and dumped them in rivers.

The entire 30 miles was spent by Moss in a mist of clear excitement that she tried not to show. The women were on holiday. They lived in London but Moss was not stupid, and it was clear that they did not come from slums and if there was trouble they could just drive away from it. They probably shopped at the same places as her ladyship back at The Hall. Moss shuddered. The women lent her a warm rug to keep around her shoulders. They were not haughty women. They were kind and thoughtful. But to Moss they came from, and were returning to, another life than hers, in another world. She did not know how it felt to have holidays. Time that did not have to be paid for, in one way or another. Half crowns that did not need checking every hour to make sure they were safe. Boots that were part of 'a wardrobe' such as her ladyship had had.

In the back seat of the motor car Moss had a funny daydream. Funny because it was new and it felt peculiar. Possibly it might have been funny to laugh at but that wasn't the sort of funny she felt as she dreamt it.

Florence was alive, and rich, and had a new motor car. Florence could drive it, and had leather driving gloves so her fingers did not become numb with cold. Florence invited Moss to drive away from Darlington, for a holiday. Florence had found a house in the south of England and was going to live there and wanted Moss to come too, and they would share Moss's new baby.

On the road south of Pontefract the two women stopped, let Moss out, exactly where she wanted, and waved goodbye. One of them wished her a good journey on to her aunt's. But the other one, the one with the clear honest eyes, and driving gloves, held out her hand and shook Moss's and said, 'Good luck, Moss. Una and I shall remember you,' and then drove off.

So it was in a barn near Pontefract that Moss slept on the fifth night of her journey.

One of the effects of 'the miracle' was that Moss was suddenly placed in a new kind of countryside without the long slow changes that she had planned for.

This countryside was green and dotted with farms, but it was not wild, not by any stretch of Moss's imagination. The change was from moors to gardens, as if the little fields were sewn together with hedges, and the effect was a quilt in greens and browns with black bobbles for the slag heaps. There was not the same dry-stone walling between Pontefract and Sheffield as there had been north of Ripon.

The villages were dirty, some of them, and they smelled terrible when the coke ovens were working if the wind was in the wrong direction. That was how Moss experienced the journey from Ponte-fract to Conisborough which she walked in two more days. She was nearing her destination. Her money was lasting very well. What wouldn't she have given for a Sunday dinner with her mum's good gravy? She tried not to remember. To keep her mind set forward in the direction of her feet.

She was feeling fit because of the walking, though bone tired of barns. She had a choice of places between Conisborough and Shef-field and she had enough money left. She was glad she had not given in and eaten too much or bought hot drinks with it.

She was 3 miles from the village of Herton, and about 15 miles out of Sheffield, when a stranger fell in step beside Moss. This was the first time anyone had harassed her and she was at that moment unpre-pared. She had counted four families and about twenty different indi-viduals on the road since Pontefract, all searching, it seemed, for work and lodgings. Times were obviously bad here in the south York-shire coalfield. But the rich women on holiday were not the only rich people in England, and even in this part of England there were the owners of halls and other posh residences who still wanted maids, though they were cutting back on attics full of servants. Even the rich were economising, in their own fashion of course.

The person by her side was not, however, harassing Moss. This individual was tall and thin as a beanpole, pleasant and clean shaven. Used to working as Moss could tell from the hands. Not a down-at-heel soldier, then?

'Name's Biff. You been walking long?'

'Hundred miles. People call me Moss.'

'That's a mighty stretch, Moss.'

Moss nodded. Biff asked nothing. Moss ventured nothing. Biff was not one for conversation by the looks of it.

'Times are hard,' said Biff presently, looking down at Moss sideways. 'I was a stranger, too, to Herton, five years past, in the war. Times are hard,' Biff repeated, 'for them as lived through it that is.'

Moss couldn't think of a reply, so she stayed silent. She felt all right. There were buttercups in these hedgerows, and hawthorn and many kinds of grasses. No footpaths. No traffic at all. Moss's left ankle rubbed, a dull raw rub that went half-way up her calf. Some of the stitching was worn loose and the quarter inch that had come away was on the inside. She saw three cabbage white butterflies, the first of the summer. She realised that she hadn't noticed any butterflies along route. Must have been there but maybe she'd been thinking and missed them. Moss liked the steady easy stride of the person beside her, and the silences in between Biff's statements.

Then it seemed to Moss that if Biff had not something worth saying Biff said nothing. So Moss thought perhaps she'd better not jump to too many conclusions concerning the tall stranger walking along beside her.

Walking along beside Moss, Biff noticed the hedgerows, the colours, green, brown, yellow and purple, and white flowers on the May bushes.

'I've been lucky in Herton,' said Biff slowly. 'Came here like I said, five years ago; thought maybe the grocer would know everyone. Called in there, asked if anyone might have a room. Never dreamed *they'd* offer me one. They needed the rent money, being wartime. Trade was not good. Frank's dad was ill. Frank's the first person I met in Herton. Only son. Him and his mother were trying to keep the business going.'

'How come you weren't called up?'

'I was,' Biff lied smoothly. The same old lie. 'I was wounded.' Biff did not say when. And if Moss was confused about that, she did not say so.

'Oh, I'm so sorry. I'm so nosey sometimes. Always was.'

Biff shrugged to show no offence taken and wondered if there would ever be the freedom not to lie. Something about Moss attracted Biff. The character of Moss's shoulder perhaps; courage to not look back, turn back. Biff speculated what Moss was walking away from, or walking towards.

'Frank's dad is dead now. His mother died last week. That's why I been out walking. Clear my head. She was like a mother to me. You could call it a grief walk.'

Moss was silenced, ashamed of her prying, her brashness. She realised how lonely she was, having been used to a large family. 'Cacophonies of sound' her dad would say. He learned those words from his own grandfather, Moss's great grandfather. Moss didn't dwell on the Indian heritage at this moment, though all the family knew it and were proud of it. She wondered if sometime there might be a chance to get to know Biff. Then she would be able to tell Biff the story, all its twists and turns.

She grinned. It usually confused people. You had to toughen up when you had a proud heritage that no one else respected. Likely as not people would snub you before they would listen.

28

As Moss remembered the cacophonies, she heard Daisy's voice, 'For God's sake, Moss, put wood in t'door; we don't live in a stable.' And her mum shouting back, 'No, Moss, you leave that damn door open, open I say, or I can't see what Janey's getting up to; Daisy you leave our Moss alone, alone d'you hear. Ronnie come back this minute, this minute, and fill this scuttle.' And so on and so on. Repeated like the buckets, cabling, cabling.

Moss's neck and chest tightened. She felt as if the canvas bag were strung around her neck, lying on her bosom with a brick inside it. She wondered if she would ever let herself cry for them all. She knew about grief walks. Too late to turn back now.

Biff could tell that Moss had been through plenty of distress, and for once Biff wanted to see the future, to be certain of life as well as death. Biff wanted to be sure that hope followed despair as predictably as morning came every day even if the nights had been lonely.

If Biff had not been on a grief walk, and had not met Moss, then Frank would before too long have advertised for a housekeeper. A new person, to replace the work of his mother, a new woman with her own hopes and fears, to come and live in at the grocer's.

But, as Biff had just found out, death always brought emotions out sharper. Biff had learned that before, through the death of her mother and through Lucy's and Sara's murder. Murder that had gone unchallenged in the coroner's court.

The intensity of hopes and fears that reach unusual heights following the death of those closest to us was not new to Biff. But recovery required that the intensity faded because if it did not it would lead to madness, and so Biff, going on the walk, was going through a repeat of the grief cycle. It was not less intense just because it was a repeat. It was familiar, and Biff knew it would fade, given time, but met Moss while at the height of the extra aware stage.

It was in that chance meeting in that particular emotional state, that Biff saw Moss not just as a good-looking woman with black eyes and almost black hair in a country lane, but also as a possibility, an opportunity not to be overlooked.

Presently, about a mile and a half out of Herton, Biff asked, 'You need a room then, Moss?'

'Why?' Wary. Was this a proposition? Who was this stranger after all?

'Frank's back room's spare now, that's all. We need a housekeeper.'

Biff and Moss came into Herton from the east, along East Lane passing by Ryelands Farm on their left and Hennet Farm on their right. East Lane ended at the Square and from there the land sloped down in front of them.

In the nineteenth century this would have been an English farming village still with its hall where the squire would have lived, and its church called St Stephen's, its pub, and its farm labourers' cottages.

But now facing Moss was the square of a thriving mining village, in which this new friend, her first since leaving, had settled.

Ryelands Farm had originally belonged to the squire, explained Biff as they stood at the high ground on the south side of the Square.

'Are you interested in this, Moss? I don't want to bore you.'

'Oh, you're not boring me, Biff. I'd have liked to stay on at the Elementary and be a pupil teacher. My mother was a pupil teacher but she had to give it up when she fell in love with my dad. Mother taught us lots of history. I'll maybe have a chance to tell you some, sometime. No. You're not boring me. Please go on.'

'Oh good. I love history and, well, I don't get much call for telling it usually.' Biff laughed. It was the first time Biff had laughed since Frank's mother had died. 'Well, behind those trees there' – Biff pointed to their left – 'that's the old Hall. Only there's no squire now and the vet bought it and he has his own golf course. That road at the far corner diagonal that is Church Lane, well, you can see why it's called that.' Moss grinned and nodded. 'It goes downhill steeply so it isn't a bus route at all. Then it curves round by the pond and goes back behind the pit. That part is mucky but if you carry on it's lovely country a mile or so and then you can walk for hours, no interruptions.'

Moss could see that on the north side of the Square down to her right was St Stephen's which Biff said went back to Norman times when the whole village was a manor, with a lord (Moss shuddered thinking of The Hall) and all the fields in strips and everyone paying tithes. Biff was a walking history book. Moss was fascinated.

They turned to their right down through the Square passing to the right of St Stephen's and into the High Street which led downhill for about half a mile. They walked a few hundred yards, between rows of higgledy-piggledy small shops, a tiny post office, a draper's, three sweet shops, a men's clothiers and a wool and baby shop and came to a road running off to their right. Looking down that road Moss could see some new terraces of houses half started before the war but left unfinished, and behind them were open fields.

The High Street opened out then into the market.

'On Fridays,' said Biff, 'you can meet anyone and everyone just by coming here. This is really the market town for all the smaller villages for miles around. We have 150 stalls all packed with goods on Fridays. You can get anything from boot buttons to a teapot here.'

Beyond the market was a Victorian two-storey building which looked like a library.

'That is my favourite place in Herton.' Biff laughed again. 'Come and take a look, then I'll take you ten yards further to Frank's shop. Oh, I'm sorry. Are you exhausted, Moss? P'raps you'd rather go straight there?'

'I am tired. But I'd rather see your reading room first. Then, could I have a cup of tea, Biff? I'm thirsty.'

So they just looked in quickly to the library, but Moss could quite see why someone like Biff would take to it so.

The reading room was a light square room on the side of the main library. The centre of the reading room had a table about 10 feet long and 6 feet wide with portable stands on it for magazines. Around the walls at about waist height for men, slightly higher for women, were more sloping platforms and a few old people were standing there, reading the daily papers. The platforms met the walls just below the windows which went full height up to the ceiling.

They stood together looking up at that ceiling, which rose gently from all four walls to a central point and was made entirely of green glass leadlights.

'Whoever designed that ceiling was inspired, eh Moss?' whispered Biff.

Moss nodded and smiled at Biff. She was glad she'd seen that room. It mattered to Biff. Moss could see that Biff was someone who needed to be able to spread a bit of hope around. At least, that's how it felt to Moss, nodding there silently. It would have seemed silly to tell that to Biff, because Moss would have to get to know someone before sharing those kind of thoughts. Beside, it would take so long to whisper it and talking any louder than a whisper wouldn't seem right in this room. Moss could imagine, though, that this room was a real comfort in winter when it was cold outside, and she noticed that they had a good variety of magazines as well as the daily papers. The only problem was how you'd find the time.

Three people said hello to the tall figure and one old woman produced an apple and pressed it into Biff's hand.

After that they didn't linger, but went quickly out of the library and across the road to Frank's shop which was about two minutes' walk away. No wonder Biff came there often.

'Any friend of Biff's is a friend of mine,' said Frank, extending his hand across the shop counter as Biff explained that they had met on East Lane, and that Moss needed a room for a few nights and was looking for work.

Biff's loyalty to Frank impressed Moss deeply. There was no expectation that Biff had the right to employ Moss, before talking in private to Frank.

Frank Smith was as boring as his name, and without any sense of his own worth, Moss decided before the first evening's meeting was over.

He was a good, kind, honest man and hardworking. A shadow of what he could have been if only he had left Herton, his parents, the shop, and gone out to see the world. He was forty-six.

Moss's main emotion for Frank was pity. She came from a noisy family, each character jostling for recognition, each person sure of being a real person, warts and all. (Ronnie actually did have warts. They were a right nuisance to try to get rid of.) A formidable family from the inside or the outside.

Moss might describe her parents as the salt of the earth. Frank Smith, she would describe as clay. Solid, could make something out of it, but none of the bite of salt.

The possibility of working there, and the fact of finding a room for a couple of nights, in this easy unexpected manner, sent Moss's head spinning fantasies. But Moss was too practical to expect life to turn up good fortune without some kind of price. It never had for her family. Likely it never would.

So she took the room, possibly for a few nights, at a shilling a night, not including food, and waited. She was not kept waiting long.

Frank was married to the shop. On closing days he was bored silly. He was up each morning at 6.40 for delivery vans, and then he brought down the awnings, put out the OPEN sign and cigarette signs, and then stacked and sorted and refilled. The routine, and the shop which gave him the routine, were Frank's whole life.

He missed his mother's presence. He felt he was the sort of man who needed a woman around, to mother him. That feeling did not worry Frank. Nothing much worried Frank, about people, because he had found that if he just waited, people came into his life and stayed there, as Biff had done.

Frank missed his mother's work. He liked his shirts hanging there, all seven of them, on hangers in his wardrobe; his pants stacked, not a quarter inch out of line, in his drawer; his socks folded in pairs, right side out; his bed sheets bleached white, and ironed and aired.

He liked his work coats, the knee-length khaki ones with four buttons down the front and deep pockets, to be ready for Mondays, all three of them, hanging on coathangers in the lobby at the back of the shop.

Without his mother, whom he loved and had been kind to, these things were not possible. If they were not possible, then his appearance in his shop would not be what he was used to, what he expected, what he wanted, what was good for his trade.

Frank thought for two days about Biff's idea for Moss to stay on in the small back room in return for housekeeping. He realised Biff's loyalty for the umpteenth time, and his mother's unpaid labour for the first time. He had always appreciated his mother. He saw that she had worked very hard, they all had, the hours, the spick and span standards. But Frank had never put a price on his mother's labour before, until Biff faced him with Moss as a prospective employee.

Frank suggested a month's trial to see how they all managed.

Three

Sunday lunch in Herton was the high meal of the week. Yorkshire pudding first, plenty of gravy. Then the meat and three veg.

Moss served lunch, tensing herself for the showdown. It was September 1920; she was almost five months on. Agonies for days, preparing. To be thrown out, moved on. Homeless, destitute. Away from two friends. Would they still be friends once they knew? They sat at the table, with the leaf out, laid just like Frank's mother would have done, napkins and all. She was a right one for standards.

Moss was determined not to cry. Only once she'd cried at Sunday lunch. Back home in Darlington.

So now she braced herself lest she let the tears slop off her face into the gravy, messing the Yorkshire pud.

They could tell from the catch in her voice that she was going to tell them what they already knew.

'You've been good to me, both of you. I've got something, er . . . to tell you. I . . . er . . . I'm almost five months on. I'm sorry. I should've said to begin with. I . . . er . . . I shouldn't have let it go on. I'm really sorry I didn't tell you, for all our sakes.'

Frank put down his knife and fork. He leaned back, slightly. 'Marry me, Mossie?'

Biff went grey white, staring at Moss.

Moss choked on the pudding. Biff looked as if the floor should open and swallow them all.

'What did you say?' asked Moss, trying to swallow and talk at the same time.

'You both heard.' Frank looked from one to the other. 'I want you to stay here, Moss. With us. I want you to marry me.'

'Excuse me.' Moss fled. Grabbed her coat off the back door hook, against the September chill, and ran. Through the High Street into the Square, out along East Lane, the way she'd come into the town.

Out in the lane she sped along, letting the wind rip at her hairpins. She still had shoulder-length hair when it was let loose. She'd never thought of marrying Frank. It was a sensible answer, a solid suggestion, from a kind man. Mrs Frank Smith, grocer's wife. It made sense, and didn't. To marry Frank would secure a hearth and home, a place in this town, food for the baby, for herself. To marry without love. When pity and familiarity were the only emotions. To do that to the wild girl inside her, who'd slept in haystacks and talked with Biff into the night by the kitchen fire long after Frank had gone to bed, about the government, unemployment, housing, politics and history.

She wondered then if Biff would stay. What was it about Biff that intrigued her? The turn of the head, the laughter they were beginning to share in this unusual household? She realised then, that she had feelings she'd not named before. That she felt it should be Biff asking her, not Frank. Never a hint or gesture from Biff had given Moss any clue as to Biff's deeper feelings. Biff worked, laughed, was friendly. Rode out every day on the delivery bicycle, loaded with boxes up and down the hills of Herton.

Moss slowed down, found her hedgerow seat, where the old oaks met the corner of a field, and was full of bitter resentment.

*

Frank ate his Yorkshire pudding slowly. Biff hadn't spoken. The silence could have cut the meat in paper-thin slices. Moss's cold food was congealed.

Frank thought what he'd said was no great earth-shaking surprise. Moss must already know that he'd come to rely on her. She was a good cook, competent housekeeper. He liked her laughter. She was light to have around the house. Marriage was what he could offer. He liked the idea of children, had guessed that Moss wouldn't have left home in the first place if she hadn't been in the family way. She'd see reason. She didn't have many choices. He'd offer marriage again when she came back. He was surprised that she'd run out, but even his mother had done that now and then. All the best women in the world, the steadiest, had to explode now and then. He didn't feel the need himself, but then he expected women to be that much more emotional, all things considered.

Biff ate in silence. Desolate. To offer marriage to Moss was impossible. One day there'd be freedom from the lie. To leave, if Frank asked for that, would mean breaking away from these two people, whom Biff needed, relied on. Love of Moss consumed Biff. Lying awake at night, thinking of Moss, knowing what a love there could be, if only. If only. Such a small massive block to loving Moss, marrying Moss, bringing up children with Moss. Of course, Moss was pregnant. Biff had always guessed. It made Moss more lovable, not less. 'As vulnerable as I am,' thought Biff. 'It's all about vulnerability, and hiding. Keeping up those defences, to get through another day.'

To stay, if Moss married Frank would be to live with yet more lies. Biff, trapped in disguise. Moss, trapped in bed with Frank, lying there before and after, not knowing what passion could really be.

Biff ate in silence, with an ache in the heart and loins. An ache that could only be soothed, released, turned into a wild goose flying, by the return of Moss's own passion. No hint from Moss had given Biff any hope and, in any case, Biff had learned years ago, after fleeing in disguise from Manchester, to live without that kind of hope.

Biff ate as much as possible but was becoming sickened by the meal. Biff's plateful stood for all the times that Moss had cooked for the three of them since her arrival eight weeks ago; it shouted silently that they'd come to a major change. Biff felt the lack of emotion in Frank, as a great hole for dinners to pour into. However well fed or hungry was Frank, the same lack would be profound.

To begin with, and for the five years till Moss came, Biff responded to Frank's lack with calmness, almost verging on relief. No one knew, nor asked, why or how Biff had arrived in Herton. Frank's lack of curiosity was part of Biff's protection, coupled with Frank's fastidious privacy which was matched by Frank's parents when they were alive. Frank's mother was a stickler for standards. (Privately, Biff called them rules.) But she was also very warm, and she laughed a lot. She was the heart of the household, and its head too after Frank's father took ill and died. So Biff knew, in the heavy silence of that fateful Sunday lunch, that it was no coincidence that Frank accepted Moss's unique vitality, providing that she kept the household as impeccably as his mother had done.

To Biff, Frank had been an older brother, an unusually kind-hearted one, not given to bullying. Biff now realised how little Frank needed to bully anyone, given that Frank had everything he asked for, when he asked for it. He hadn't even bothered to look for a wife. He'd found Moss through his friend, without lifting an eyebrow or a finger.

As Biff tried to finish the plateful, the ache inside intensified, until Biff could stand the tensions no longer.

'I'm going out. Up to the hills. It's a bit of a shock. Need time to think.'

Frank looked surprised. 'On your bike, Biff?' was all he said.

'Aye. I'll be back after dark, Frank. There's nowt to do for t'shop is there?'

'Not till morning. Mind how you go, Biff. See yer later on then?'

' 'Course, Frank. Be seeing yer. T'rah then.'

Frank heard Biff shut the back door and clatter the 'pride and joy' out of the shed. Frank had a twinge of his mother, who'd named Biff's new racing bike. His mother's voice seemed clear in the room. Frank was surprised by that. He'd never believed in such things.

The backyard gate latched up then down, as the wheels of the pride and joy clicked smoothly through, and Frank heard Biff turn the bicycle into the ginnel past the side of the kitchen and shop towards the High Street.

Frank sighed at the upset in the routine. He usually liked Sunday afternoons playing cards with Biff, sometimes doing a spot of decorating, very occasionally, after Moss had washed up, going in a threesome out along East Lane into the woods for a long walk. To Frank, Herton was a good place to have been born and bred. A busy village, almost a small town, plenty of work, on account of the good deep coal seams. Herton Black was famous throughout the area, even as far as Barnsley, where it was known as Barnsley Black. Only thirty miles by bicycle up into the Pennines. That was Biff's thing really, especially since Biff's old bicycle got beyond repair and Biff had saved up for the pride and joy, but Frank liked a spin now and then and kept his father's bicycle well maintained for that purpose. Biff once or twice hinted to Moss she should get some trousers and try it out. She laughed her light high laughter. Like bells. Frank hoped she'd come home soon and, regarding the congealed mess on Moss's plate, and the unfinished untidiness of Biff's, he sighed again and started to clear the table. He didn't do the washing up. That was women's work. But he scraped the plates, and seeing the waste, wondered if he might buy a dog, sometime.

Anyone watching from the air would see us as termites scuttling from the anthill, thought Biff, cycling up the High Street, turning right into the Square past the church, and free wheeling west down Church Lane, as the wind whipped past.

A fine September day, but Biff was not in the mood for appreciating red berries on the hawthorns, nor the dahlias in the scattering of miners' gardens at the bottom of Church Lane by the colliery. Most miners lived in the griddle, and in villages around Herton, to the north. The north side had the wind and smells from the slag heap and coke ovens. No one rich lived that side. Rarely, a rich man's daughter might fall for a miner's son. Occasionally there was a shotgun wedding. Then she'd move north, to the griddle or beyond, and would change geography and lifestyle altogether.

Biff's thoughts sped round with the wheels. The climb began, as the colliery was left behind. Not an even upwards journey. The hill undulated, long slow upward slopes, that made Biff's calf muscles ache to match the ache inside; steep sharp downward escarpments deceptive, dangerous. Biff was acutely concentrating, aware that breathing mattered on the up hills, and the road surface was crucial on the downs. The slightest unevenness could jolt the front wheel and send Biff headlong over the handlebars, into concussion, at the least.

The concentration was important. It left no room for fears, hopes, or jumbled emotions. It was the concentration of the athlete, the coal miner, the artist and the suffragette. It clarified the essentials, and Biff knew that thirty miles of this to the Derwent Valley would strengthen both heart and resolve.

Biff propped the pride and joy against a rock outcrop, and stood looking out over the stones and wild moorland.

Finding shade from the afternoon sun, and wind, Biff flung out, resting, thankful to be horizontal after the effort.

It was time to consider the role she was playing as a woman hiding in men's clothes in Herton.

Whereas Moss had lost her family, through becoming pregnant, Biff had lost hers through politics.

Lying in the shade, Biff couldn't hide from the memories, letting herself weep and longing to cover the memories over with Moss.

In the woodlands, just south of East Lane, Moss watched two grasshoppers coupling on a tuft of grass. Life would at least have been simpler as a grasshopper. Live, couple, breed, die. She had no idea how long lady grasshoppers expected to survive.

For herself, she had to make decisions. Marrying Frank meant bedding with him. She looked on that with distaste, although she was no puritan, but she craved passion and women and she did not want more babies.

Florence's elder sister, who was married, had not let Florence grow up ignorant. She had told Florence how to use pieces of sponge soaked in vinegar to prevent babies, and said there were rumours around about rubber caps. Rich people had them before 1900, reported Florence's sister. 'But I've not found out yet how the likes of us can get 'em, even if we had the money, which we haven't.'

Moss realised her choices were limited, as far as birth control went, and she realised that if she was already considering all this, she must be taking Frank all too seriously.

She pondered many minutes, with the grasshoppers still stuck together, about Frank's naked body on top of her in bed if they married, and about Frank being so unconcerned about loving.

He'd be reliable, kind to the child. Children. Moss corrected herself. She'd have to give him one child of his own, possibly two. He had a right to that. That meant three. How could she possibly conceive, carry, and nurse three children, when one was born from rape and the others from boredom?

In this town, the grocer's wife's position would be a safe one. The shop was not many steps from the market. People came in for a look, a chat, to linger. They came on market day, Fridays, to meet each other, to share a joke. There was plenty of laughter.

If Biff stayed (if only Biff would stay), life could be made tolerable. Before long there'd be new friends. Already some local women greeted Moss by name, after it spread along the gossip grapevine that a housekeeper was in residence in Smith's. Customers dreamed up things they'd run out of, just out of curiosity.

Everyone would guess the dates; they'd know it wasn't Frank's child. She'd need another soon after to make him respectable. Herton people were not much different from back home, thought Moss. They'd squeal scandal, loving it, glad it wasn't them, then the novelty would wear off and they'd settle down.

Thinking this didn't help Moss's state of mind at all. She wanted a reconciliation with Daisy, and with her mother, who knew how to cope with scandal. The fury about Moss's baby could have been overcome, they all knew that, if the family could have afforded to feed it. To lose her family on account of money sparked Moss's anger deeper than any of Daisy's resentments or her mother's shock. It was as if Daisy had said, 'If anyone's going to have a kid the wrong side o' the blanket, *I* am, not you Moss. It's *my* turn, for God's sake, when is ever anything in this house going to be what *I* want.' But Daisy's brat if ever she had one could no more be afforded than mine, thought Moss sadly. She missed Daisy snuggled up in bed with her, Janey the other side.

She found herself horrified at the thought of sleeping round Frank's body every night, not Daisy's. Daisy had been so soft, affectionate. She pushed the thoughts away. They didn't suit full-grown women. Full-grown women sought affection in marriage didn't they? Fleetingly she saw herself curled around Biff. It would be good to kiss Biff just below the ear. Fascination with Biff was leading nowhere fast. Moss forced herself to push away thoughts of Biff.

If she married Frank, if, then she could let herself have the three children straight off. That way at least she could postpone worry over birth control. She must find out more about the rubber things. She had a feeling she could ask Biff, even about personal things. Biff wasn't starchy, and knew what was going on in the rest of the country.

Moss resented Frank's freedom from all this worry. He'd no more know about the rubber things than he'd know the names of stars in the heavens. He'd never see the sky as a black silk dome either.

'So I am going to marry him then?' she asked, or rather told herself, nodding at the one grasshopper now resting on the tuft. 'I should think you do need a bloody good rest after that, what a performance. You poor little bugger.' She laughed crudely, stood, shaking out her skirt. 'Goodbye, Moss Stratton; hello, Mrs Smith.'

Moss's marriage to Frank was a small affair, in the sombre quietness of the Methodist Chapel.

Biff wore a new suit, dark charcoal grey. If the stitches could have burst with frustration, they would have, in sympathy with Biff's feelings. But they held together, twisted around each other, keeping the pressed cloth in place around Biff's pride, a suit of soft armour between Biff and the woman who walked steadily down the length of the small chapel, her hand on Biff's arm, to be given away. 'Not mine to give,' thought Biff, with no one to share the thought. Biff hoped that the hurt and grief would come through on her face as toughness, making her look more manly, so to speak, on this public viewing of herself in disguise. She need not have worried. The only people in the chapel were a few of Frank's oldest customers, who'd last been here for his mother's funeral, and a few children who'd crept in at the back of the plain building to gawp.

The gathering in the Methodist Hall which adjoined the chapel was larger. Many more customers were invited, wives, husbands and older children. There were sandwiches and cakes, beer and trifles; Frank was not a wealthy man and the spread was seen as him doing his best to be generous in the circumstances. After all, everyone in Herton knew by now that Moss Stratton had nothing to bring except her child and her work to this union. Moss was calm rather than beautiful. Not exactly the radiant bride, but thought of with some affection in Herton because of her laughter and willingness to work. There would always be the holier-than-thou brigade. Every mining town had its stalwarts. Pillars of the Church of England. Let them gripe about this chapel wedding if they liked; the company that collected in the hall that Saturday went away satisfied that Frank had always been a good man, and saw it as his duty to do the best for his young, happy-go-lucky housekeeper. He'd made his bed and no doubt he would comfortably lie on it.

Biff stood apart from the assembled small crowd, drinking her beer, aiming the occasional joke at the lads of her own age, whom she met down the Colliers' Arms from time to time. What the future held for her in terms of love, warmth and passion she couldn't help but contemplate. Her suit itched, her legs felt dead, her chest weighed more than a sack of potatoes. She wanted her sisters, Lucy and Sara, with their hatred of men and chapels. They knew what was what. She wanted their laughter, their analysis, their clear eyes on this mess. She wanted to hear them saying, 'Be brave a while longer, Biff. He'll get his comeuppance, you'll see.' Instead she was alone, apart slightly from the celebrations that weren't really celebrating.

Looking back on that decision in later years, Moss wondered how she could possibly have seduced herself into believing it would work out.

From the first night in bed with Frank she realised it was the disaster she'd most feared. With crudeness formed from despair, she formed the words in her mind: 'In out shake about take it out and wipe it.' That was as much as Frank would ever understand about pleasure, his or hers.

Biff, trying to sleep two doors away, listened with dread for bedsprings rattling, and hearing none she snapped awake, wetness saturating the pillow as she let herself silently cry for the waste of both women.

As a man in Herton Biff could walk about at night, and sometimes after the shop closed, while Moss was having a bath or talking to Frank, Biff would take a stroll towards open country, without hurry or fear of who she'd meet on the way. This she could not have done had she been dressed as a woman, living as a woman. Although Herton was not a place for violent crimes such as were reported from the cities, there were girls and women with a story to tell, or to hide, about men's demands after dark. This made Biff angry. She felt disgusted at being seen to be part of a male world where women were taken advantage of; a male world where men had rights and women had duties. But the same world protected her, giving her the freedom of the roads by day and by night.

Biff's favourite trousers were her corduroys, with deep pockets. She had developed a habit of standing with her hands in her trouser pockets, her jacket unbuttoned, revealing a knitted pullover. She carried a diary in one pocket, her wallet in the inside pocket of her jacket, a clean handkerchief in another. This still left spare pockets for loose change, and a notebook and pencil for the jottings she made whenever she could pop into the library.

Biff was restless with the need for politics. She scoured the papers daily in the reading room for news of the women's campaigns, picking up what she could on international news, economic measures back home, the rebuilding of Germany, the reviews of books in the *Manchester Guardian*.

Often, she felt trapped locally by her disguise. She couldn't initiate a local branch of the Women's Labour League, because she wasn't a woman. She dare not break through the patterns she'd built steadily and with care to protect herself. So she fretted and rested alternately, dissatisfied in new ways with the tedium of the day in, day out sameness of the grocer's shop routines.

Moss became tired. The day began with the baby's feed at 5.30, too early to start the day, too late to go back to sleep before Frank woke at 6.30. She always sat with him at breakfast, after which he went through to the shop where he was sorting, unpacking and tidying by 7, ready for opening at 7.45.

With the end of the war, local shops like Frank's had been granted off-licences for beers, wines and spirits in spite of remonstrations by the Temperance Leagues. Moss always marvelled how easy it was for Frank to put his morals in a drawer and lock it tight when his own beliefs conflicted with his desire to make a profit. It was the same with the marriage. Frank was unperturbed about gossip because people needed what he had to sell, and no one else could supply like he could. So he'd gone ahead, and it had, so far as the public and sales were concerned, proved him right. And it was the same with the off-licence. Strict temperance members of the chapel might complain and bully as hard as they pleased, but when Frank's mind was made up around business, there was no shifting him. So he went for the licence, and lo and behold, the stars from the east settled over the shop and sales boomed, temperance ladies or not.

Moss could see that for Biff and Frank it meant more work and sometimes heavier work with the lifting and storing of the crates and hoisting up and down into the cellar. But Moss acidly recognised that each time the till pinged, Frank sent an arrow prayer of thanks up to the Lord above.

Frank took no interest at all in Sadie, and Moss knew why. Frank's sole concern would be with the next baby, which she fell for when Sadie was four months old.

That was the time when Biff began to harass Frank about the changes needed in the household.

It began over the simple matter of washing up the evening dinner dishes. Usually in the evenings Frank and Biff ate in shifts while the other one stayed on in the shop. Biff could see that, what with the house, the men's meals and feeding Sadie, Moss was doing an eighteen-hour day. But whereas Biff and Frank *sat* for lunch and for their evening dinner, Moss barely had time to, because she was preparing, serving and clearing the dishes, bringing in the pudding and clearing that away as well. It was women's work, which Biff, as a woman, wanted to be part of. As Frank's delivery boy and spare hand, she couldn't cross that barrier without a complete upheaval in the way the household was run.

It was all very well when Moss had been six and seven months pregnant, but now that Moss had Sadie to care for and another pregnancy, Biff feared for Moss's health. She was thin, pale and drawn with her black eyes losing their sparkle and a beige pallor about her face. Biff had often wondered about Moss's black eyes, and straight luscious black hair. She'd never dared ask Moss the origins. Biff was reminded in Moss's looks of three Indian sisters she'd known back in Manchester. Moss said she came of mining stock from Darlington, so Biff asked nothing, but sometimes wondered all the same.

Biff had not liked or wanted sameness in her friends in the suffrage movement. She'd looked to the Kenneys for a lead on difference, especially class difference, but the rows between Annie and Jessie on one side, and Biff's sisters on the other, had deepened, and Biff as a younger sister, a small insignificant spectator, had not been able to ask the questions that she wanted to. Sometimes that was because she'd had no words. The questions were unformed, and uninformed, in the back of her mind. It was a physical sensation. As if the part of her brain just at the top of her spine was a place for forming questions, but the questions never quite escaped. Jessie Kenney had then gone off on her travels with Emmeline Pankhurst, to Russia on the Mission for Serbia, then to America as a freelance writer.

Jessie was now working for the Red Cross in Paris and they had all lost touch. It was a shame, thought Biff. Jessie had been the closest in age, and the closest in background to Biff. Biff didn't even know if Jessie loved women, the way she loved and wanted Moss. Perhaps Jessie never would. Sexuality was rife all through the suffragette discussions, but they weren't written down. Biff did not know how to move forward.

Of course she'd followed in Herton library editions of *Women's Dreadnought*. There at least her working-class sisters had had a voice. Yet . . . There was always the word, yet. The split had also been around the work with men or independent of men. The East End Women's Federation worked sometimes with men, which Biff and her sisters had not agreed with. So now she was stuck in a grocer's shop in Herton, loving hopelessly a woman whose life was being timetabled around washing up, washing sheets, washing baby clothes, washing shirts; washing; washing. Cooking breakfast, lunches, dinners, washing up, cooking, washing, washing up. Biff felt they were all in the lunatic asylum sometimes. It was only lunatics, or men, who could possibly organise women's lives like this. Something had to be done. Moss had made a choice. What choice?

Biff went over and over in her mind the events of the Sunday when Moss had declared her pregnancy, when Biff had the chance to speak out, of love, longings and passions, that no woman was allowed to speak. So she hadn't. Now she lived daily with the consequences of that.

Biff's challenge to Frank was made in the shop while they were very quiet in the middle of a Tuesday afternoon. Frank was half-way up a ladder arranging packets of Farley's Rusks on one of the higher shelves. To get them down for the customers he used a pole with a pair of 7-inch blunt pincers on the end, that his mother and father had used before him. But to place them on the shelves was a two-person task. So for once Frank was up the ladder and Biff was at the bottom passing up the boxes of rusks.

'Frank, can I have a word?'

'What's up, Biff? Summat troubling you?'

'It's Moss. I'm worried about her.'

'She's not said owt to me. What's up?'

'That's just it. She's hard-working and she doesn't say much, but she's worn out with the household, looking after us and Sadie.'

'Aye, she is that,' said Frank unexpectedly. 'But we all work long hours Biff. Specially since we got the licence.'

'I'm fretting that she'll lose your baby if she goes on.'

Biff knew that this would touch Frank. He loved Moss in his own way, and he did care. It was just, thought Biff, that Frank was still at heart a real Victorian.

Frank came down the ladder. He leaned on the counter and stared at Biff. He asked then if the midwife had said anything. Biff shook her head.

'I'd like to help her a bit in the evenings, Frank. She's been up by then from 5.30 when Sadie wakes. She's doing actually longer than both of us. I'd like to clear up in the evenings when I'm off work.'

'She came here to be a housekeeper,' said Frank.

'I know that. And she came here pregnant too. I'm not saying nowt agin' all that, Frank. I'm just saying that now she's having this second one I'd like to be some help to her. I don't go on all this women's work thing like you do. Times are changing, Frank. You have to change with the times.'

'This is my house and my shop,' snapped Frank. 'And you are here to work in this shop, not to nursemaid my wife.'

'I am not nursemaiding anyone. But I'm warning you, Frank. If you don't watch Moss's hours you'll be having no child of your own, because she'll lose it and you'll lose her. Have you seen how thin she is these days? No mill girl ever worked the hours your wife works. 5.30 in the morning till 11.30 at night. Come on, Frank. See reason will you?'

'You're a good worker, Biff. I'll say that more'n once. Moss knew what was what when she married a grocer. If you want to give up your time off to play housewife's help then I'll not stand in your way. But don't expect me to sympathise. She's working no harder'n any other wife in this town.'

'I know. Pity the whole town didn't go down under zeppelins if you ask me.'

'I'm not asking you. Now, if you don't mind, you can finish these boxes while I start on that coffee.' He looked at his watch. 'Moss should be in with the tea in a minute.'

'I need the privvy,' snorted Biff and left the shop.

She was seething with frustration. It was true what Frank said. Wives did twenty-five-hour days every day in Herton. Small wonder Biff's sisters had declared they'd never marry. 'Oh, how I want to take Moss away from here. From Frank's bed and from his house and shop, and never return.' Frank had nights off when the off-licence was closed, and so did Biff. They both had Sundays free. Moss did not. Her shifts never ended and the workload would increase again when Frank's child was born.

In the shop Moss brought the mugs of tea. She had Sadie under her right arm, straddled across her hip bone. She carried the tray with the mugs, left handed.

'Here's your tea. Where's Biff?'

'Stormed out. He's concerned 'bout your health. You told me you was all right.'

'I'm tired, that's all.' Moss shrugged. 'Sadie doesn't sleep nine hours yet. You know that.'

Frank looked at her stomach. 'Biff thinks you'll lose this baby.'

'I'm bleeding a bit, Frank. I told Biff late one night, when you'd gone to bed. Biff's concerned. He thought you'd be too, I expect.'

'He wants to do the clearing up after dinner.'

'That's nice. I'd appreciate that.'

'It's not what Biff's paid for. You know how I feel 'bout women's work. Washing up's no job for a man.'

'Times are changing, Frank.'

'I don't go on these new-fangled ideas, Moss. You know that. My mother'd turn in her grave, God bless her soul.'

'I've no doubt she'd have appreciated some help too. Have you thought about that?'

'She was proud to be a woman, Moss. Proud.'

'You don't think I am?'

'I don't understand you, Moss. You're changing.'

'No, Frank. I'm not. You just never knew me before. That's all. Drink up while it's hot.'

Moss swept out just as Biff came through. They exchanged glances but Frank didn't see. He was already bending down to a box containing tins of dry mustard.

Frank went to bed each night at 10.30. Moss did not because Sadie seemed at her hungriest at 10.15.

Moss was trying to persuade Sadie that a nine o'clock feed would last till 5.30 or even 6. She tried leaving Sadie to cry but Frank wouldn't have that; said he needed rest if he was going to keep the off-licence open each day for the full hours.

Moss would sit in the armchair in the kitchen almost asleep over the sucking baby, and Biff sat with her.

'You go to bed, Biff. I'm all right, really.'

'I wish I could feed her for you, Moss.'

They both laughed. Biff's breasts ached. She wondered how other women in disguise had got away with posing as men. She'd heard some taped their breasts back. P'raps they had to if they were big-breasted, but that must have hurt. She was relieved she was flat chested. It made that part simpler. Nothing else was simple. Her monthly rags she bundled into newspaper and hid in her saddle bag, to be dumped on the rubbish tip down by the pits. She'd even buried some up on the moors. Thank heavens for that bicycle. Plenty of the mills north of Herton sold rags, useless odds and ends of stock, wrongly dyed or woven. Getting rags in the mill areas was no problem. She wondered how women in other towns and cities managed when they couldn't wash them as Moss could. Possibly they used sponges. She'd tried that but washing them out wasn't always easy. Better to manage with rags. At least she wasn't a heavy bleeder. That was something.

'I want to help you round the house, Moss. I've been thinking. I don't see it as women's work. I can't bear it, you getting tired out like this, waiting on me. Frank's another matter. Another generation p'raps. I'm not, er, saying he's . . .'

'You don't have to, Biff. I know what you're saying. I don't know how I let myself marry Frank Smith. I should have left. I didn't want to lose your friendship, Biff, but you don't know quite what you're letting yourself in for do you, until you've done it? There aren't enough hours in the day for mothers. We can't afford any help. Lord knows I don't want servants, some poor girl skivvying under my guidance. I couldn't be doing with it, but I think I'm going mad. Mad from this need for sleep. I shouldn't be saying this, Biff. It's not loyal, not loyal to Frank. I don't know why I'm letting this out. I suppose I'm just so tired I'm beyond thinking about loyalty. Seven months from now there'll be two babies. Where's the laughter gone, Biff? You and me. We used to sit up here talking politics, setting the world to rights. I haven't seen the *Daily Mirror* for weeks, don't know what's happening in the world, I'm almost past caring.'

Moss did not cry. The tears were locked away like Frank's imagination in a drawer. Someone had thrown away the key. She felt she might never have time to cry again, and anyway she was too tired. Even crying takes energy. She looked up at Biff and with the directness that came from despair she said words that Biff never expected to hear.

'I love you, Biff. There's something strange about it all. I don't know what the hell is happening to me. I have a child. I want love and passion. There is none to be had. This is too hard, I'll never be able to say it all again if I don't say it all in one fell swoop. I've a child, another on the way. I'm worn out and worn down and I'm eighteen. And I love you Biff like I never expected to love anyone again. And I don't understand it, and I don't know what to do with it.'

Moss looked over the bald head of her daughter, at the person of Biff sitting opposite. She had no other words to explain the strange chemistry that worked and didn't work all at the same time. No patterns to help her break out of this madhouse, but she knew that there was more to the rest of her life than bedding with a boring grocer and having a child of his every year until she died in childbirth too tired to push out the tenth, eleventh or twelfth. She had thought there might be a decent gap between Sadie and Frank's first child. But the terrible truth was that she'd had one bleeding, and missed the next. With that kind of luck she was going to be filled with children till she died.

Biff faced the precipice. It happened sometimes up in the Pennines. There was one place she knew a few miles from Ingleton where you'd be walking along on clear open turf, and then suddenly, there in front of you, the land plunged down into an open cave. There was a desire then to fling forward, into the open cave, falling like the river on the far side, down, down, to the nothing at the foot of the drop. The water disappeared underground, and people would vanish, lost for ever from being so foolish as to not know where they were treading.

The words she longed to know from the woman she loved most hung there in the mouth of the open cave.

Her first impulse was to speak. To fill the air between her and this new love with words, building a wall of defences that Moss would never again try to climb over, through, round. To talk about friendship and trust. Marriage to Frank. Loyalty and support. To talk about reorganising the household so that they all had a share in the household duties, which Frank would never agree to anyway.

Biff resisted speech like she'd resisted arrest.

The silence opened up, filled instead with the sucking of the baby on Moss's right breast, where she'd shifted Sadie three minutes ago. A place where Biff wanted to be.

Then Biff sat beside the chasm, aware of her own voice doing the speaking, her own heart taking risks, as if she wasn't part of the risk at all. She watched and listened to herself, wondering again for the hundredth time if her mother had survived the terror of tubes and clamps in the women's prison by detaching herself like this. She wondered how long she'd take to get back safely from the ravine, and what Moss would do to her when the full story was out, and the cave became deeper between them as Biff approached dangerously close to the edge.

The voice that was hers spoke very quietly and Biff listened to it, quite surprised at its courage. Meanwhile Sadie finished sucking and fell asleep with her fist in her mouth and her face still against Moss's bare right breast.

'I'm not a man, Moss. I never ever have been. I don't know if you've ever thought that the strangeness of loving me might be that I'm a woman.' (Moss's right arm was round Sadie. She put her left hand up to her face, watching Biff's face all the time, thinking of Florence, with her black eyes taking in the words, sorting them out, re-sorting them, trying to make sense of the new unexpected shift of knowledge.) 'It's not new to me, Moss. I knew it through my sisters. They both loved other women. I just grew up knowing. Sleeping in the same bed with them, other women coming to the house, mill girls. It was known. I just learned from being very small that wherever there are sisters, girls sharing beds together, that kind of love is possible. I expect lots of girls never take it any further. Just passes. They get married. They might even blank it out, forget it. But I met

Emily, in the mill. At first there were plenty of chances for us. We used to go out to the woodlands. It passed off. We had to let it grow into a friendship.

'It's funny how I met you, Moss. You looked so bedraggled. Trying to be proud. I felt for you. Usually I'd go out on the bike, but I had a puncture and I didn't want to spend the time mending it that day. So I went out there on that grief walk, and life brought you along. I have loved you since that time, Moss. I can't offer you marriage. I can't give you babies. But I want to love you, to share a bed with you. I can give you love and passion. But I don't think I'd ever have risked telling this to you, if you hadn't spoken first.'

Moss was crying now. As if the drawer had a secret spring, that jumped open, pushing against any further locks. Perhaps it was the unexpectedness. The sudden explanation for why the feelings had been strange. Perhaps, she thought afterwards, it was the openness of her body through the baby lying there obviously contented. Perhaps the shock of the emptiness every night with Frank, whose nearness she felt invaded her. She could go on perhapsing for years.

She looked at the vulnerable soft line of Biff's neck below the ear, and she wanted then to touch every inch of Biff's skin, to be awake to this newly discovered woman. She wondered whether other married women had gone through these feelings too. Had there been others like her, who had rediscovered this kind of love? What had happened to them? Where were they now?

Biff didn't have much idea what response to expect from Moss. Biff hesitated, still ready for the double act, self and not self, glory and joy or loss and grief. Mixed up with hope and an open future. Having to leave this place if Moss was furious. How to stay on, if Moss was indifferent. There were no possible ways of knowing how Moss might react, except that Moss's eyes were huge, and searching all over Biff's face, and were wet with drops running down. Was that a sign of despair or hope? Biff waited, listening for Moss to reply. Moss said two words. She said, 'Kiss me.'

Biff leapt back into her body and glowed.

The clock on the mantel shelf chimed 11.15. Biff leant forward, and as she did so the antimacassar slipped down the back of her chair crumpling itself behind her. It was a soft sound, and the kisses were soft sounds too. Sadie was sucking at her fist as she slept. Moss unbuttoned Biff's shirt, and kissed her breasts as Biff leaned over.

Moss made small laughing sounds in her throat, and felt the kiss go down to her knees, under her skirt where Sadie was curled asleep in

49

her lap. Moss had a memory, that had obviously lain half buried from early childhood, of running out in the field, and feeling that each of her bones was alive, that each bone could run a long way, joined to the other bones. A feeling that had been lost under long skirts and Florence's grave, and had returned, and would stay.

Biff felt that it was an historic moment. A moment that her sisters would have wanted for her, and her mother too. She was sure about that. She thought of Emily, and how they had wanted each other to find happiness. She bent her head and kissed Moss's mouth.

Four

In Herton in the twenties it was unheard of for mothers-to-be to buy the clothes they needed for the layette. Moss was no exception. Instead the women bought the patterns. Weldon's usually. Then they cut out and stitched the baby clothes themselves. Sometimes they sewed by hand, but some women like Moss were lucky enough to have been handed down a mother's or mother-in-law's sewing machine. Moss had Frank's mother's Singer which was a treadle.

Moss tied a piece of string from the treadle wheel to the rocker of the crib and so while Sadie slept she snatched a half hour here and there between her household tasks to make the new baby's layette.

The details of everyday life varied only a little from day to day. On Tuesdays and Fridays Biff cycled around Herton with the weekly and half-weekly orders. Biff was the darling of the old ladies who could not work out why such a nice young man had not been snapped up quick on the local marriage market. The Friday delivery was especially helpful to those who could not walk as far as the market, for cut-price eggs or soap. Instead they relied on Biff who had worked out the route to please everyone's timing and could rely on a cup of tea and bread pudding at 11.15 at Mrs Dundy's and tea with a potato cake at 3.25 at Mrs Hines'.

Mrs Dundy had two sons both in the pit, who had married twin sisters called Grace and Mercy.

Since both Dundy brothers had two of the better-paid jobs at the coal face, the Dundy women had a securer standard of living accordingly. On Thursday afternoons Grace and Mercy called in to see Moss. It was a two-hour break, the highlight of her week. She had fought hard for the time off. Frank had agreed on condition that none of the housework was slipshod or left aside. This had a shunting-on effect which made Wednesday nights later because Moss finished the ironing before she went to bed. She kept the sheets in the top cupboards that were almost at ceiling height and were part of the black-leaded framework built all around the open fire and the bread and the meat ovens. The fireplace took up almost the whole living-room wall. There was no fireplace in the scullery which housed the sink and the copper for hot water.

There were many miners' families that would have liked a fireplace with airing cupboards above it like Moss's. She appreciated it herself when the sheets came out so warm and flat, but cursed it on black-leading days. Many of the miners' wives had to boil the water for washing in galvanised buckets over the fire. They had a hob that swung over the coals and away again. All day long the kettle would hum on the hob, behind the waist-high fireguard.

The fact that Thursday afternoons were Moss's only negotiated time off, and that by three o'clock she and Grace and Mercy would be busy sewing, talking and looking after four toddlers, did not free Moss from having to make tea and provide scones for Frank and Biff in the shop. Biff had offered to get them but Frank was not having that. So Moss settled for the quiet life and stopped at a quarter to four to get Frank's refreshments. It didn't seem odd to the visitors. They were used to taking orders like that. They saw themselves as the heart of their households, but they were answerable for every penny and for every part of their routines to their men, even when their men were at work. They received their housekeeping money on Friday nights. But neither of them had any idea exactly how much their husbands earned.

Moss, on the other hand, knew exactly how the accounts were going because Frank said that when he died she would be able to take over. He did not want an ignorant wife as far as the shop was concerned. Moss did not have her own money, and was not able to buy even a pair of new drawers without asking Frank's permission. But she knew what the weekly takings were, the overheads, and the outstanding debts.

It was Moss who taught Grace and Mercy to use the treadle

machine and it was through both sisters that Moss came to hold sewing classes in her back kitchen on Thursday afternoons.

The other topic never far below in importance was what could be done by wives in this town about the conditions down the pits. There wasn't a month went by without an injury underground. The women lived within earshot of the pit hooter and although it blew only for a serious disaster, no one ever slept at night without some kind of thanks that it hadn't gone off during that day. It was like living on the side of a volcano, as Grace Dundy put it. Wives were always aware of the possibility of being widowed and their children rendered fatherless.

Moss sometimes felt ashamed of the lie that she was living with the Thursday mothers' group. She longed for open talking about women's friendships but she might as well long for men to land on the moon, or for a visit to the Milky Way.

She would lift the crocheted cloth and the vase of fabric flowers off the large living-room table, take off the velveteen cloth, and cover the polished wood with oilcloth. Then out would come the patterns and scissors, pins and cottons as the women cut out, snipped, talked, pleated, tucked, gathered and smocked together, the weeks becoming months, and the various confinements coming closer. Miss Brookes, who ran the town's wool and baby shop, supplied Weldon's patterns, and the Friday market supplied the Viyella and the trimmings.

They used to joke about Miss Brookes, estimating her age and her bygone romances. But after sharing her love with Biff, and finding herself deeply involved with the longing for Biff's body, as a woman, Moss began to see women like herself everywhere. Everywhere included Miss Brookes.

Miss Brookes lived with another spinster called Miss Field who ran the infant department in Herton elementary school. Miss Brookes and Miss Field did not wear corsets. They had never worn corsets according to Grace and Mercy who said their mother held up the two spinsters as targets of respectability and ridicule too. It was typical of Herton that the two contradictory labels went side by side. Herton people relied on those contradictions as plovers fly around the fields to lead you astray so that you won't find out the true facts of the situation.

The women of Herton were proud of their ability to look after the men and the children; to mend and patch, to design and sew, to knit, and to keep their places spotless against the dirt that seeped in on to the window ledges and splattered the sheets and nappies with soot.

The coal was the wealth of the earth, that put the meat on the table on Sundays and the bread the rest of the week. But the women were the salt that flavoured the food, and the yeast that made the bread rise in the big white bowls beside the hearth.

Thursday morning Moss made cakes, scones, bread pudding, and Frank's favourite, a weekly cut-and-come-again cake. Usually it had raisins in it as well as currants. For festivals it also had candied peel and chopped cherries and a dose of sherry. On lean weeks it had just currants. If she could afford it, she spiced it with cinnamon. But if the babies had colds or Biff was getting winter snuffles which might turn to cold, then Moss kept the cinnamon sticks, in an airtight jar, and grated them into hot water and made everyone drink it. It was a trick she had learned from her mother who learned it from her mother who brought it with other remedies from India.

It made sense now to Biff that Moss looked the way she did. It fell into place why Biff had been reminded of the Indian sisters she had known in Manchester. Moss's grandmother was Indian, and had come to England with her brother. They were then split up. Her brother was sent to boarding school in Yorkshire and Moss's grandmother was boarded with a well-to-do English family who had spent thirty years in India before returning to take up farming in the Dales.

'You know, Biff, if we think we're on our own, loving each other, like we do, just imagine what it was like for my grandmother. She was well educated but treated like a beautiful pet over here. The people she lived with used to invite their friends round just to meet her. More like to gawp she said.'

'So how did she get to be your grandma?'

'She ran away, joined a circus. She'd been riding since she was five. She'd been very wealthy in India. Upper-class I suppose we'd call it. Anyway, she was not going to let them marry her off to some English snob, though she had plenty of offers. Even as an old woman she was stunning to look at. The tales she told. Well, believe it or not, Biff, the circus came to Durham, to perform, tent and all. My grand-dad was all of seventeen, been down the pit a while, and he saw her and fell in love. She was married to him within four months. His family threw him out, and they moved to Darlington, there was plenty of work. People got used to them after a while. There were always travelling folk up north.'

'What about the Dales people? Didn't they care? Why didn't they go after her?'

'She had been warned often of the peat bogs on the moors.

Everyone had told her to be careful when out riding or walking, especially in the twilight. You know how the shadows play tricks in the twilight. So she borrowed one of the horses and trekked up on to the moors. She left her hat and cloak near the edge of the bog; by the time they were found they'd be filthy and tatty, and her tracks would have been covered over. It was wild weather. It can blow branches around like matchsticks up there sometimes . . .

'Soon after she left there was a terrible storm. She wasn't stupid. She knew they'd search. But the circuses were always good at hiding people. Jugglers and clowns. You'd never guess at the lives that some have led. Escaped prisoners, debtors, debutantes, orphans, as well as the real circus families that have gone on, you know, for generations. Grandma told us stories that would make your hair curl.'

'You followed in her footsteps in a way, Mossie. Leaving like that.'

'She wasn't pregnant.'

That was all Moss told Biff on that night. The bitterness of how Moss came to lose her own family sometimes bubbled through, like stray bubbles in a vat of wine. Herton women made their own elder-berry wine sometimes. If Biff was very lucky, Mrs Hines gave her a glass and a Shrewsbury biscuit. She made wonderful elderberry wine. She told Biff that the minister was most partial to it. You could watch the bubbles rise off the yeast and break on the surface. Then Biff would think of Moss, and about how much their love was the yeast that made it possible to rise above their everyday existence. Biff feared sometimes that in older age she might turn vinegary, watching Frank sup Moss's good youth away.

Moss's two children were born within fifteen months of each other. She called her son Ronnie.

She then began to resist having any more and to talk to Grace and Mercy Dundy about how to stop it. They were all three at their wits' end although they successfully avoided pregnancy many times. They had tried cotton wool soaked in vinegar on a small string. They'd tried falling asleep before their husbands came in. They'd tried getting up straight after 'it' and douching. Moss rid herself of her third child with two bottles of gin and a hot bath in Grace's house in the spring of 1924. Grace came round with Mercy to Frank to say that Moss had tripped over in her back yard and was now bleeding terribly. Could Frank please, please hurry? She said she'd given Moss some brandy to bring her round. Of course, the brandy was really to disguise the smell of the gin. Frank asked how Moss was, was told she was asleep now and in bed at Grace's, and replied that he would close up at closing time and come round afterwards. Mercy stayed to look after Frank's children.

Biff shook, with fear for Moss and with anger at Frank's lack of passionate concern. After all, wasn't Moss his wife? How could a man keep to his routines when his own wife was bleeding in a strange bed in a strange house?

Moss had warned Biff that if she ever became pregnant a third time she would get rid of it. Now she was bleeding its life away in Grace's house and her own life possibly as well.

'I'd like to go and see her,' said Biff trying to keep a steady voice.

Frank looked at Biff, who was leaning against the counter, both hands clenched into fists. For once Frank wondered if Biff was going to lash out. Frank thought of Biff as a gentle fellow, usually. There he was, young, strong and athletic, cleanshaven and tidily dressed as usual, but on fire, tensed and angry. With a hard-set jaw and sharp-angled shoulders, Biff's body reminded Frank of one of the old squire's race horses. His own father had taken him to see them paraded in the Whitsun gymkhana.

Frank didn't usually spend much time thinking back to his own youth. What was the point of that? He was a secure married man with a family. But there stood his young friend, grey eyes turned to bright steel, cutting through Frank's thoughts, until he felt sliced to pieces. Really, thought Frank, Biff is stepping too far out of line. That is my wife he is getting angry about. He ought to pull himself together, calm down and get on with his day's work. He's altogether far too emotional sometimes. And it won't do.

'There is not an emergency. She's having a miscarriage and women do that sometimes, Biff. My own mother had one when I was fifteen. Moss is young and strong. She's not the first woman in Herton to be losing a baby. She won't be the last. They do not close the pit for a miner's wife who is in labour or in a miscarriage, and I shall not close this shop.'

'I need to see her, even if you don't. I am going to her, Frank. You can stay open if you like, and you can sack me. But I am going to see Moss. She must have us near. She must.'

'If you leave this shop against my orders, when we are supposed to open, you are breaking our contract with each other.'

'If you leave Moss and she dies, you are breaking your oath. Have you thought of that? Your conscience is your property. Mine is mine.'

'My God, Biff, anyone would think this was your child not mine.'

'That's a hell foul thing to say about your wife. She is loyal to you even if you're not loving to her. I'd rather you sacked me now if it comes to that. She might die. She wouldn't be the first wife to die from bleeding in this place. Or from too many children, or childbed fever. My God, Frank, I don't know what makes you stay alive but it most certainly is not your heart. And this I do assure you, you ungrateful sod, is *not* my lost child. I wish to God it were. That I do.'

Biff raged into the back room where Mercy was now rocking Ronnie who had colic and would not sleep. Sadie was asleep upstairs.

Biff, the woman in hiding, looked at Mercy, who had no need to hide, and was jealous of the chance to be a woman. Biff had no desire whatsoever to be the wife of one of the Dundy brothers. But to stop hiding and openly be Moss's close friend and companion, life long, was a dream beyond all dreams.

'I'm going round to see Moss,' declared Biff, aggressively, brisk to the point of being brusque.

'I'll never understand Frank Smith. I'll never understand men,' sighed Mercy, putting the baby face down over her knee and rubbing his back round and round, like Biff wanted to rub Moss.

'Nor will I,' said Biff, leaving Mercy surprised, still rubbing the baby.

Until Moss 'miscarried', Frank Smith had not given much thought to the relationship between Moss and Biff.

Frank was not prone to thinking much about people. He was not at all interested in politics like Biff, and would never let Biff draw him into discussions about unemployment, growing industrial unrest, and the publicity for the Labour Party. Frank was above politics. He did not need change, and did not welcome it. But he could not avoid the changes in his wife, and he had been uneasy as to where they originated. It never occurred to Frank that he might have anything to do with those changes.

He had been touched at first to see the younger man championing his wife. Frank did not like Biff to be openly challenging, but had had to admit to himself that, providing Biff didn't ram politics down his throat, so to speak, the household did run very smoothly now that Biff helped Moss out from time to time.

Then Moss tripped over in Grace Dundy's back yard and Frank's doubts came to the open air for the first time. Doubts which had been there a long time, he now realised.

He had had a good training adding up and making things tally. Now he applied his lessons to his wife and his shop assistant (who was also delivery boy and handyman).

Frank decided that two and two made four.

Moss had been resisting him in bed. Not that he, Frank, made many approaches. He didn't usually feel terribly interested, in fact it was quite difficult to summon up much enthusiasm for it at all. But that was what married people did, he assumed, even if not all that often. And, of course, they did it if they wanted to have children.

Moss had been reluctant ever since Ronnie was born. She said she was tired, or having her time of the month, or that the children were wakeful and she didn't want to have to get up in the middle and therefore to upset him. Moss had often said it was better not to bother. So if she was pregnant, then unless a woman could get pregnant just any time, which Frank thought was most unlikely, then . . . Frank Smith came to the conclusion that two plus two equalled Biff.

Then Frank began to doubt that Moss had tripped over in Grace Dundy's back yard.

Frank Smith had not been able to make the off-licence stocks tally: there were missing two gin bottles and a small brandy.

Frank went through all his accounts again, late Saturday night. He said nothing to Moss or to Biff about how he felt. He would sort out his thoughts by himself, just as he had when he had decided to marry Moss in the first place. He realised he was not really cut out for marriage and family life. Children needed playing with and talking to. There simply wasn't time in a man's life for them. It was a woman's task to raise children whatever Biff might mutter about.

He missed his mother for the umpteenth time. She hadn't needed sex like his wife did. He'd had more room in his bed, and more time in his life. A mother was so much better for a man than a wife. Especially a young and beautiful wife who turned the heads of his customers (they adored Moss, who made them laugh), and his delivery boy. From the point of view of trade, his wife was useful. People came into the shop to see her and lingered and tried out new lines as if to please her. It was the little ones that were disrupting the household and heaven knew how many there might be if Moss had a shine for the younger man.

Frank Smith had always thought he would die young. Before fifty. He had been glad that Moss would inherit from him. She was good with money, and he loved her in his own way. The will was made. He could see no reason to go back on that. All that work should rightfully go to his son one day and he would of course see

Sadie all right. It was she who had brought Moss into his life, to carry on the line.

Frank Smith had no time for grief over lost delivery boys. There had been grief in the past over his mother, and before that, over his father. But they had been his own flesh and blood. Biff had been a good friend while they had worked together just the two of them, but now it was time to think again. He, Frank Smith, was a married man, of reasonable standing in the town. He had shown strength of character to marry his housekeeper when she needed a husband, and now, he thought reluctantly, he ought to show the same strength in asking Biff to leave. But he needed more time to think about it. It would mean finding an elderly housekeeper to do Moss's work and mind the babies, so that Moss could be out in the shop with him where she would get the training she needed and, he added, almost too quietly to hear his own thoughts, 'where I can keep an eye on her.' He decided to deal with it all very slowly. He would get Christmas over with first. He did not like to be hurried.

Five

It was a dark December evening just before Christmas 1924, and Frank had gone to bed early with a heavy cold. The children were both asleep and the shop had been shut half an hour, when there came a loud persistent knocking on the back door.

Moss had just finished her supper, and wiping her mouth on the corner of her apron and smoothing her skirt in an unconscious gesture, she went to the door and opened it. Her smile leapt suddenly as Albert, Grace's older brother, and several of his first and second cousins, some barely out of their teens, opened up with 'Oh Come All Ye Faithful'.

'Evening, Mrs Smith, we're collecting for the children.'

'Am I going to get me money's worth? The last lot as called here managed one feeble verse and straight into "Figgy Pudding" and "Gi'us The Money".'

'Come on then lads, let's be having yer,' called Albert. 'The lady wants a fine rendition.'

'An aria from the *Messiah*'ll do,' laughed Moss as they all roused into the spirit with 'God Rest Ye Merry Gentlemen'.

'No merry rest for us ladies, then?' Moss quipped and called over her shoulder into the room, 'Come and lend your ear to this, Biff, some fine Herton voices on our very doorstep.' Then turning to Albert she added, 'Hang on Albert while I get me purse. It's a good cause.'

Biff reached the doorway and joined in 'Figgy Pudding'.

'Come and join us then, Biff-lad,' said Albert.

'And a nice beer or two down Colliers' Arms when we've done,' said Georgie, one of the younger cousins, 'Come on, Biff, tha's a fine voice as I remember from last year. Tha sings a lovely tenor that tha does.' So, to the sounds of 'Aye, come on Biff, show a leg,' and 'Tha can't refuse can tha when it's for the brats,' Biff left the kitchen and joined the singing throng.

The crowd made its way through the town up and down the back streets with Biff singing her lungs out and her throat dry until an hour before closing time they arrived one and all at the Colliers' Arms.

Biff rarely went pubbing with the lads and men. But about three times a year, and one of them was usually Christmas, she was, like tonight, hard pressed to avoid it, lest she seem mean, unsociable, hen-pecked and downright strange.

She bought a round: for Georgie who was now nineteen and a hard drinker, a young miner who had been down the pit since leaving school; for Albert, who was much older than Grace and who lived in the next village; and for several of the cousins and second cousins who lived locally and with whom she was on nodding acquaintance. They all had Herton names. They were Dundys and Jacksons, Fields and Gibbses. Biff knew them all by sight, several by name.

She perched herself by the bar, mindful to sit like a regular male drinker shoulders relaxed and knees wide, one foot hooked on the cross-bar of the bar stool.

She told herself not to over drink, to watch her words, her gestures, her small mannerisms, but she realised after a while that she needn't have worried. They were all so used to her being a man, acting a man's part in a mining town, that anything she did was taken to fit in as part of her self, her male self.

She listened, nodded, and watched. The jokes started. One of the cousins was getting married in the New Year. His fiancée was one of the most attractive women in the town, an older woman, a widow, ten years older than the young man whose name unfortunately for him happened to be Henry.

'Sup up then, Henery the Eighth,' said Albert in the middle of the group and making as much mileage as he could. 'My round. And Biff-lad tha must have a double brandy for the festive season. Tha's not going all night on beer tha knows. Not wi' a wedding to celebrate.'

'Aye, sup up Biff,' said Georgie, who being several years younger than Biff had the common sense not to say Biff-lad like Albert. Biff always wished she looked older on these occasions. She did not look her full twenty-eight years, and for a young man she was seen to be fresh-faced, which made her the darling of several of the old ladies to whom she delivered Frank's orders weekly.

' 'Tis months since I seen yer in this pub,' remarked Henry, 'and I'll never know how tha goes all night without a leak. Tha must have a bladder like a camel.'

'I have that. And tha's not getting me on the brandy this time.'

'Tha say, does tha,' said Albert, nudging Biff and winking hugely. 'Tha'll have what tha gets and be thankful, eh lads. Like our Henery.'

Albert paused, theatrically, enjoying every minute. Much shoving and gesturing accompanied all Albert's repartee, and there was never such an audience as the carol-singing one, hoarse and intending to get well oiled.

'Brandies all round, Gloria, please love. Make 'em doubles and line up alongside the pints, there's a lass. My tha looks a fancy sight in that frock. Don't she, lads. Eh, Gloria, if I wasn't a married man I'd be popping the question.'

'And what answer might tha be expecting then, Albert?'

'Gloria in Excelsis, a man can live in hopes. Here y'are, Henery. Here's thine. There now Biff-lad, get that down yer. That'll warm the cockles of yer . . . '

Biff's protest was drowned in warblings and yodellings of 'Henery the Eighth' from Henry and everyone else joined in. Biff sang along, hoping to avoid actually supping the brandy.

The toilet for the men was the open sort with no cubicle. There was no lock on its door. Only a few of the older women came into the Colliers' Arms, sitting separately in a little room the other side of the bar, and the younger women never came. There was no toilet in the pub for women, and most of the place was meant for men only, with the drink and talk for men only, except Gloria who was seasoned and whose husband, the publican himself, used to be a professional boxer. So no one gave Gloria much trouble.

'I'm Henery the Eighth I am, Henery the Eighth I am I am. I got wed to the widder next do-or, she been wed seven times be-fo-or. Every one was an 'Enery, she wouldn't have a Willie' (much winking) 'or a Sam . . . '

Albert slapped Biff heartily on the back and she choked over her pint, having surreptitiously placed her double brandy where someone else might pick it up, with the others awaiting drinking on the bar.

'Come on, Biff-lad, sup up, gerrit down yer. Henry's turn for a round. Tha's plenty more beer to get through and a dozen double brandies. The night is still young. Drink and be merry, lads, for tomorrow we die.'

With Albert standing over her, Biff finished her pint and picked up her brandy as if to sip it. But Albert saw through this tactic immediately and joked her through the double brandy, almost forcing the glass empty and placing it on the bar with a flourish. Next was Henry's turn to push a double brandy on her, and down her, for quite clearly she had to be a man, drink up, and not be churlish or half-hearted about it. Not to drink was to insult Henry whose marriage was talk of the town, and whose night it clearly was, despite Albert's centre-stage performances.

Soon there was a line of alternating double brandies and bitters waiting along the side of the bar which had been commandeered by the Albert-Georgie-Henry gang. And hangers-on. As the men worked their way through the drinks, and Gloria washed the empties and replaced the orders, Biff realised she was on her fourth pint, was desperately needing the toilet, and must have therefore downed three double brandies.

Henry was singing ever more loudly, raucously and part-harmoniously, through his entire repertoire and had reached the lines of 'Ilkley Moor': 'Then we's'll all have etten thee, then we's'll all have etten thee.' He wasn't near the bar so he fished in his pocket and passed another note to Georgie who did the honours, ordering more double brandies for everyone.

Biff's head was reeling from the smoke, the red-striped flock wallpaper, the red lampshades which cast pools of blood-red light and shadow, the jostling over by the dartboard, and all the swirled confused layers of talk, guffawing and singing. Smoke drifted, blood red, as Biff supped her fourth double brandy and felt fire creeping along her arms and down the backs of her knees. She shifted uneasily, now cross-legged, on the bar stool wishing away the desire for the toilet.

'Oh, Mother,' she prayed, 'Mother, are you up there? Lucy, Sara, you there? Help me to keep me mouth shut. Don't let me blow up the pub or me life in Herton. Keep me and Moss safe.'

'Here you are. Here. Eeh, lads, this fellow's no drinker. Look at him. Pink as me mother's corsets after four brandies.'

'My drink's beer,' said Biff weakly.

'His drink's beer,' repeated Albert, slapping Biff on the back again and winding her. 'All on us's drinks is beer. 'Cept for weddings. If it weren't for our Henry and his lovely, lovely bride, we'd all be supping beer. Thank heavens for Henry's lovely bride. Long live the beautiful, the bee-oo-ti--ful Mary Swithinbottom.'

'Long live Mary Swithinbottom.'

'Here's to the lovely Mary.'

'Here's to the lovely bottom.'

'Merry widows of Herton town.'

'Oh gawd. Prop him up,' said Albert as Biff swayed on the high stool. 'Lean him against 'bar. Here, hold his head while I help him sup this bitter.'

Between them the men got Biff through her next pint of bitter. The empty glass was placed on the bar.

'What he needs is another double brandy,' said Albert. 'Two more'n he'll get through it. Out t'other side.' He held the brandy to Biff's mouth and held Biff's head as she sipped it.

'Thanks-shalbert,' slurred Biff. 'Thassh better. Me headssh a bit funny, thasshall.'

'Biff-lad, tha should come here more often, then tha'd be all reet. Tha's in need of more drinking, I can tell.'

'Aye, for a man what works in Frank Smith's offie, he's the driest fellow in Herton, is Biff,' remarked Henry. 'Isn't that so, Georgie?'

'Leave the man alone, all on yer,' said Georgie. 'It's all right for you, Albert and you, Henry, but I live right near me auntie Grace and my auntie Mercy. You'll have me in t'soup, all on yer.' Georgie regarded Biff who was by this time right out of it. 'And what about Mrs Smith? She'll go stark staring mad she will. Have you thought on that all on yer?'

'Aye, look at t'state of him,' added one of the cousins.

'He's a bit on t'pink side, I'll say that,' said Albert, amidst some shoulder shoving and arm nudging from the other cousins. But Henry wasn't to be silenced so easily by Georgie's late-off-the-mark concern for the grocer's assistant. 'Aye but his boss's wife is second-best looking woman to my Mary, in this town. I wouldn't say no to a cosy late night supper by t'living-room fire. I've heard it said she's got passionate blood. She came from them gypsies what went over by Pontefract, tha knows.'

'Nay, it weren't, it were Doncaster.'

'No wonder he don't come out pubbing then, eh lads,' observed Albert, striking up with his own version of history: 'Oh-oh, Old King Cole was a merry old soul and a merry old soul was he. His wife were hot and his daughter bold, as any lucky man could see.' He looked at Biff who was propped against the bar, eyes closed, bright fuschia pink, and ad-libbed, 'and a very lucky man is he.'

The night wore on, behind closed doors, after opening hours. Closing time came and went. Biff didn't know.

A commotion down the ginnel leading from the front of the shop, down the side to the back yard, signalled to Moss that Biff was coming home. Funny that she could not actually hear Biff's footsteps. Moss listened, wondering now whether it *was* Biff or maybe, maybe thieves. There'd been a spate of burglaries in the town in recent months. Surely there wasn't going to be an attack from a marauding gang? The Hawsley brothers had been in court. One had been sent down for robbery.

The knocker on the back door clanged loudly. Moss heard Georgie's voice.

'Mrs Smith? Mrs Smith, are you awake?'

Moss didn't expect the scene which met her as she opened the door. Four men, all the worse for wear, and Georgie being one of them, were carrying a large thick tartan blanket. It was like something from a spy film which they sometimes had down the High Street at the Curzon. Moss loved spy films.

'Here y'are, Missis,' began Albert. 'Lost property. We found it in t'pub. Believe this belongs here.' They deposited the snoring heap in the blanket on the ground like a sleeping pig from Ryelands Farm.

'Well don't just leave him there. For God's sake, bring him in.'

Moss looked quickly over the floppy form. Trousers intact, zip done up. Dry, hadn't wet itself or needed changing. Shirt still buttoned, tie slightly loosened, just the top button undone, for breathing space. Thank heavens for small mercies. The gang of four stood sheepishly. They all reeked of brandy.

'Which one of you's done this? He don't drink, only beer. And he stinks worse'n you do. Brandy coming out his ears. Who did this? He didn't do this all on his tod. Oh no.'

All eyes turned on Albert who blushed, mumbled and shifted

uneasily from foot to foot. A naughty schoolboy who'd been found out, thought Moss.

'I'll have you for this, Albert Gibbs. You do your family no fine favours. Your family name'll stink like brandy if you carry on like this. I'll have you for this, that I shall.' She was a tiny figure beside them, but taller than any of them each time she used her voice. 'Now then, all on yer. Tell me what he's been saying. What gossip have I got to deal with. What's he been saying?'

'He didn't say nowt, Mrs Smith,' said Georgie who by now was wondering how he'd dare come face to face with either of his aunties, both of whom were Mrs Smith's close friends and had a great liking for the grocer's assistant. Georgie went on, 'He didn't say nowt. He were reet out of it. Five doubles and he were gone weren't he, lads?'

Moss ignored Georgie and turned on the two cousins. 'And what are you two standing there for like lemons? Got no tongues in your heads? I want to know exactly what has been going on. This man here cannot afford no hangovers. He has to be at work in my husband's shop at six. On the dot. You got me? We don't run no charity show in this shop.'

'Honest, Mrs Smith. Our Georgie said you'd be wild. Mr Ferguson he didn't say nowt. He went pink and blotted out, missis. We neffer meant no harm.'

'Oh, you've got tongues then? Or are you just a pair of throats to pour brandies down?'

'Henry's getting married, Mrs Smith,' began Georgie. Albert was silent, regarding Moss who at that moment seemed to him to be far more beautiful than he'd ever before noticed. Henry had been right about that. Moss had black flames flashing from her eyes. Albert resisted the temptation to blurt out, 'My but you're lovely when you're angry.' He contented himself with sewing his mouth up lest he land himself and the lads in yet more trouble. Many's the time he had thought that the women ran this town. Now he knew it.

'I know Henry's getting married. And if Frank and Biff and I have *all* recovered we shall all be at the wedding. At least you brought him home. Thank you for that. Have a nice Christmas, all on yer.'

She stood, a tree rooted now in Herton soil, firm and unflinching in the winter's wind and frost. They left, bidding her a happy Christmas.

Moss left Biff on the floor, went upstairs for a pillow and three blankets and checked that her husband and children were still sleeping. Returning she removed Biff's tie and unbuttoned several more buttons of her shirt, shoved the pillow under her head and covered her with the blankets. Biff sounded like an orang-outang with terminal bronchitis.

Once more Moss tiptoed upstairs. She stood in the dark on the small landing listening intently at the three sleeping people. She was thinking fast, about the fact that the one thing Biff dreaded about pubs was that there was no toilet she dare use: If I leave her downstairs all night she might pee on the kitchen floor. There'll be no way to protect her real identity if that happens. In the dark, Moss reached into the cupboard on the landing and felt for the bedpan they had used for Frank's mother. 'You never know when that will be needed,' Frank had said, and wouldn't let Moss throw it out. It was wedged under the spare pillows. Moss tugged. The cupboard door creaked. She stopped. None of the sleepers stirred. With some difficulty, in the dark, Moss released the bedpan, without clanking its cold metal against the frame of the cupboard.

She stepped steadily down the stairs, avoiding the one that creaked.

Back in the brightly lit kitchen, Moss wedged the door with a chair, just in case. She rolled the covers up, freeing Biff's legs and bottom, unzipped her trousers and yanked them down, followed by her underpants. She couldn't help glancing over her shoulder towards the door. She reached for the bedpan, thinking that when she had potty trained Sadie, she'd often had to hold her over the cold china chamberpot, last thing at night. The sleeping child had barely woken, had relieved herself, and fallen back asleep. It must be the feel of the cold rim against bare skin, thought Moss. But I never thought I'd be doing this for you, love. She shoved the pan under Biff. It worked like magic.

When all was completed, and Biff was neatly done up in her trousers and covered up again, Moss removed the chair from under the handle of the kitchen door.

Moss then made herself a pot of strong tea, and drank two mugs full, both scalding hot. Then she poured herself a double brandy from the bottle they'd been saving for Christmas. She swirled it in the glass, and then sipped it slowly, wiping her eyes and shaking her head. She was laughing and crying at the same time. 'Oh Biff,' she whispered to the snoring shape on her kitchen floor. 'I love you.'

Six

Biff had made a plan, as the spring of 1925 became summer. She would talk things over with Moss, and would leave the shop. The tension was acute between Biff and Frank now that Frank had made up his mind that Biff was some sort of young stud.

Biff longed to take Moss away. Set up home and live happily ever after. It was impossible. The job market was worse than it had been for many years. It was rumoured that the unions were going to boil over before long, and the long-term effects of that could only be guessed at.

Biff's passion for Moss was increasing, and the physical need was overwhelming. They snatched at their loving behind closed doors whenever they dared, between 11 and the early hours, but every chance was a risk and now that Frank had put two and two together and made three and a half, it was becoming well-nigh impossible. The next pregnancy might kill Moss if she tried to end it, and would chafe Biff's heart if she didn't. Another child of Frank's would be beyond toleration.

The problem was how to earn a living when all Biff knew was working for Frank Smith. At least, she told herself, she had faced up to him being her boss. Had stopped hiding inside the friendship and cordial atmosphere of her first few years with Frank. They had been good for each other then. She regretted what was lost but it was time to be realistic, tough minded, to come out of hiding from herself and face herself as a woman who would always love women, be attracted to women and therefore would probably be alone. She had been hiding from the police, but had left behind the need for that. Was probably missing presumed dead on police records. They didn't go on hunting for ex-suffragettes for ever. It was also time to look at her own politics squarely. She did not regret having hidden. It had given her time to breathe, to become adult in years to match the adult experiences she had lived through before being adult enough to endure them. Yes, she had hidden. She would not hide any longer. She would leave here, go to London. Would work in a factory and study at night. Would train to be a radio engineer like Jessey Kenney. Her mind was made up. She would talk it over with Moss.

Biff did not know how or when she would see Moss. She hoped that one day Moss would leave Frank. But it could not be guaranteed. Hadn't her own sister Lucy loved a woman who had left her for a man? What guarantee was there that Moss would leave?

Biff had had enough of posing as a man. She would find it very hard to go back to women's fashions but times were changing. There were no more long dresses that made winter days and rainy weather impossibly difficult. Fashions were getting shorter and women wore breeches now for cycling. She would be a woman in women's garb, but unusual with it, setting some trends. She let her fantasies run on.

Moss made some decisions. She would ask Biff to take her away from Herton. If she stayed here she would die from the next miscarriage, and if she stayed and became pregnant again, she would go mad. If she stayed Biff would leave, and life without Biff would be intolerable. Listening out for the footfall in the passage; the heavy pedal noises of the old delivery bicycle as Biff arrived home from doing the rounds; or the clink of the 'pride and joy' as Biff took off to the hills. That was rarer these days now that Biff was helping at home.

Moss had things to do with her life. She could not do them with Frank and had been foolish from desperation in marrying him. She was calm about that. Total error. One of life's hard lessons, learned too young but not too late. She would reverse the decision.

She was Moss, granddaughter of Varsha, and she loved a woman called Biff. She had no idea who else in her own family had loved like that. However, through Biff she had knowledge that this was not terrible or even unusual. It was simply not open, and therefore it was not counted among the future plans of most young girls. It was also simply best. But. To stay with this grocerman that she had married was to deny Biff's feelings as well as her own. Biff was obviously approaching the end of her tether. They had not talked yet, but Moss knew Biff well by now and if she, Moss, did not broach the subject soon, Biff would go alone. Biff would go not knowing how Moss felt. Biff would be alone and betrayed. Biff would live the rest of her life wondering if what had seemed so powerful a force linking them together had been just a passing fancy on Moss's part. When in fact it was the bread which Moss ate from every day. The bread of loving.

For a few pence you could buy bread and a bar of soap to wash the lies out of your mouth. But you couldn't buy enough glue to stick back together the broken pieces of a lover's trust, when once her lover had stayed with a man instead of walking away to a new life. You could pay rent for a roof over your head, if you could find work; but you couldn't guarantee to find again the love which you had to hide.

When she and Biff left with Sadie, they could go so far away Frank would not find them. They would start a new life somewhere, together.

But they would have to go without Ronnie. Frank would set the police on her if she took his son and heir. He would leave no stone unturned. It was one of his main reasons for having married her in the first place.

To reject her own baby was a desperate thing for any mother to do. She loved her son, had named him after her own dearest brother. But she could not get away with stealing him from his father. All hell would descend. Leaving Ronnie in Herton was the price they would have to pay. The minimum price, Moss agonised to herself, for freedom from the grocer and his anger at such betrayal.

It was half past eleven on the night they decided to talk. Moss was going to tell Biff that she wanted to leave with her. Biff was going to tell Moss about her own decision to leave.

Frank had gone to bed when the sound split the living room open.

The Herton Colliery hooter blew.

It was the sound of hellfire and brimstone. The sound of the hounds that eat the dead. The sound of flood, fire and devils. The sound of earthquakes; and fingers being eaten by 20-foot rats that live in the heart of Hades.

For the wives it was the sound of bones crushing and brains spewing. For the children it was the noise of a hundred daddies screaming.

It woke the grocer and he leapt into his clothes. He was out of the bedroom and down the stairs in time to hear Biff grabbing the pride and joy and pounding its pedals to the pit. The grocer followed on his father's old bicycle, arriving five minutes after the delivery boy.

All was the confusion of those below a dam; those who live in the shadow of dormant volcanoes; who live in the polar regions where the ice can crack; or in the alps where an avalanche can threaten.

Orders and screams covered over the moans from beneath the coal. It was the night that Gallery 3 was flooded.

All able-bodied men gathered, awaiting instructions. There had been a cave-in of the shaft caused by the pressure of water in Gallery 3. The plan was to approach Gallery 2 where some of the men who had been about to enter Gallery 3 had been trapped. There were thought to be twenty-two men trapped in 2, and fifty-seven dead in 3. The water level was rising steadily. There were no more than thirty-four minutes of air left. As an estimate it sounded accurate. It gave the rescue teams some hope. The experienced miners were put in charge of volunteers like Frank and Biff who would shovel as ordered. 'No initiative' was the instruction. Initiative was inviting another disaster in Gallery 2, to match the tragedy of Gallery 3.

When the roof above them caved in, Frank fell, screaming. Trapped with her foot under a beam, Biff lay beside Frank thinking, 'Why do we always leave it too late to say the things we most want to?' She imagined Moss at home, and she came to a decision. 'Why did I even think of leaving? What would I do without Moss? Wouldn't I rather cope every day, posing as a man, so that I can continue to love Moss?'

Out loud Biff called, 'Frank? How're you doing?' Frank didn't reply. Biff couldn't tell if he was unconscious or dead.

At home Moss paced, fuming her frustration at being a skirt-wearing mother, not a man-poser like Biff. She wanted to be there by Biff's side.

In the Herton pit disaster of 1925, Grace and Mercy Dundy were both widowed, and their children rendered fatherless. Of the twenty-two men who had been trapped in Gallery 2 for whom there had been hope of rescue, fourteen were brought out alive. Of those, three lost a limb through crushing.

Of the rescue teams who were caught in the second cave-in, twelve men died, and three suffered severe spinal injuries. Frank Smith lived. He was paralysed from the armpits down. His delivery boy, who gave his name as Bernard Ian Ferguson, was unhurt except for a crushed ankle which caused a permanent limp.

The national daily newspapers made it a two-day wonder. It was a scoop for some young journalists, a lucky break for others.

The people of Herton paid for a memorial which was placed in the main square. It was impossible to go anywhere through Herton or out of Herton without seeing that memorial. So, for the people who lived in the sight of the colliery, the event was not a two-day wonder but a living tragedy. Years later, two young social workers, keen and fresh-faced in their desire to reveal the history, talked to the old folk in the local authority home, built on the edge of the town in the progressive sixties when there was still money to spend on items like 'the elderly'.

By then Moss and Biff were living down Church Lane. They heard of, but were not part of, the oral history project. They were hopeful that the social workers meant well. Kind young ladies with safe jobs and hearts of hope. They rushed into and out of Herton in the short space of nine months. The same time it takes to birth a baby. They birthed some unhappiness. Rejuvenated memories that the old people could manage best by hiding from. Memories of the nightmares of children who know that fathers are buried in a heap under coal and water, gone all soggy. There were children who slept for over a year with the light on. Wives who took lodgers for rent money and slept with them for humanity. Lovers left pregnant who would have been respectably married, just in time.

So the social workers published their thesis, and became a two-day wonder themselves. And when they had gone, the old folk were left, with memories, until the beam fell and crushed them.

At first after the disaster, Frank sank into a morose depression, bitterly rejecting everyone's efforts to pull him through it. He would be wheeled in his special chair into the shop, and sit there complaining. If the customers came to talk to him he would go over the events that he knew like a rehearsed speech. People who used to call in to see how he was began to go to Naylor's at the other end of town. Trade began to fall.

One evening when the shop was empty, Moss said, 'Biff, why don't you get supper tonight? I'm going to have a talk with Frank. We'll stay out here in the shop. I'm just closing up.'

'Want any help?' asked Biff, indicating the things to be brought in from the pavement.

'No thanks. I'll do it.'

'She can manage,' grunted Frank from his chair. 'Not that I'm much use these days.'

Biff went into the kitchen, and Moss brought in the sign, shut and locked the shop door. Then she pulled the customers' chair over to Frank and sat facing him. She reached for his hand and held it. 'Now then Frank, are you listening to me?'

' 'Course I am. That's all there is to do isn't it, listen?'

'Right. I'm glad you're listening, because what I've got to say isn't easy. You, Frank Smith, built up this shop with your parents. It was pretty run down when they took it on, as I remember you telling me. Am I right?' Frank sniffed. 'We are losing custom on account of your bitterness about your situation. And I have got a few ideas about it that I want to share with you.' She squeezed Frank's hand. 'There is absolutely nothing wrong with your head, Frank Smith, and there is no reason why you shouldn't pull more weight in the running of this shop. I am not having you sitting there like a pudding, in the corner, gone all sour and doing us all no good at all. You are going to work for your keep like the rest of us. Why? Because I've had to work all my life and so has Biff and I don't see why you shouldn't as well. If you think you are going to get sourer and sourer for the rest of your life you've got another think coming. I'm not putting up with it.

'So I have arranged with Biff for a new young delivery boy to work here, one of Grace's young cousins. Second cousin twice removed she said. There, that made you grin. That's a change. First time you've smiled in weeks.

'His name's Stanley and he'll take his orders from you. Biff will make you a table just the right height and you can rest your arms on it while you're sitting there, and you can write the orders out, and do the books for the deliveries. Then you can give them to us at the end of the week and we can tally them with the main orders. But you have got to work. And I don't want to hear about how you are, what happened in the pit, any of the details. You are stuck in a rut but we don't have to be stuck in it with you.

'I may sound hard, Frank, but my feeling is that it's work that'll bring you out of this depression. We've tried everything else, till we're all going barmy with you. What do you think?'

'No harm in trying, I suppose.'

'Right then we start tomorrow. Come on, let's take you through for supper. But first how about a nice cup of tea?'

When death takes seven years instead of seven minutes or seven hours, the person who is going to die makes every minute of life calm if possible.

Frank had always known he would die young. He had not known that he would take seven years. He did not want to last that long. Would have preferred that the doctors' prognosis had been more accurate: he had been told five years. But because he, Moss and Biff knew that, and because he had worked side by side with Biff digging out Grace Dundy's husband, who had died seven hours later, there was a death and life bond that linked the three people at the corners of an equilateral triangle. Frank was wheeled each morning into his shop which was run by Moss and Biff. He became the order person and the book-keeper. Moss and Biff served behind the counter and Stanley was the delivery boy as planned.

Frank said that he would like to sleep downstairs, alone. Sleep was physically painful. He would wake in a sweat with the stiffened muscles of his back unbearable. He told Biff that he realised that the younger man had won. That he could not give any wife any longer what she needed. He asked Moss to divorce him and to marry Biff in case there were babies.

'There will be no more babies. I give you my word,' said Moss, and stayed married.

To Biff she said, 'I am going to make his last years alive content and worth living, or I shall roast in hellfire myself.'

Biff did not challenge Moss on the idea of hellfire. The pit disaster had taken away the resentment in them both, of life as lovers having to hide their love, of life as women without votes, of life in the working class. Biff had lost her fantasies. The disaster was real. She had knelt beside Frank as the pit prop axed his back, trapping her own right ankle. The sear of white-hot pain through her leg sensitised her to the degree of Frank's pain. So, having shared that and come through it alive together, she too wanted his death to be the end of a calm time of security in his family life.

No one taught the three of them to prepare. They did it because the alternative was family war.

But Frank's suffering with poor circulation in his feet and legs below his knees and the daily threat of gangrene if he was bumped or bruised when they were helping him into and out of his bed in the living room, all of that made them value his life.

'Do you think it is only by understanding closeness to death that we understand the meaning of life?' Biff asked Moss one night when they were in bed.

'I'm not sure about that,' Moss replied. 'But I do know that I was right not to follow Florence into that river with coal in my pockets; and that when Frank is gone I shall at least be able to feel that I've done my best. I get exasperated sometimes, when he has his difficult days. Then I think how he could have been alone and bitter, if you and I had walked out. And then I'm sure it has been better for all of us this way. He was very good to me when I needed him. I don't want him to suffer. I'm doing what I can now for him. He knows his shop is going on even if it is only leasehold. That's a real relief to him. And now that he's working again trade's picking up.'

Abandoned by his own body, Frank Smith had to come to terms with other people washing and dressing him, changing his bag, and clipping his toenails. He was almost forbidden from becoming a sour old man with rigid routines to hide his own shortcomings. Instead he had to look at the needs of those around him, especially his children. He had to learn to give.

He was no fonder of politics in those years than he had ever been. He failed to understand the General Strike nor the ways it was fought, nor the ways it was lost. But the children talked non-stop about the world around as they knew it, and he couldn't remain remote from their feelings or ideas.

'That man will be larger when he ends his life than he ever was while he had his whole body,' declared Biff. It was true. Frank was almost able to understand the meaning of the word happiness, by the end of the five years. After that for the remaining two years every day was a bonus. He had not lost his earlier friend, known to him as Biff. He still had attention from his wife. He had all his customers coming in and out, bringing him news and titbits, not to mention tittle-tattle – there was plenty in Herton but he never before bothered with it: it was just something people did, and he had failed to see it as the sound-track of a moving film.

Most of all he lived with the satisfaction that his wife was happy. He thought that no one outside the house knew why. But Herton people were not stupid. They gossiped and created rumours, just as they always had done.

Moss and Biff each kept their own rooms. But many's the night they slept together, and since they were both up and working at 6, long before the children woke in their bedroom at 7.30, they were not intruded upon nor found out. As far as Frank was concerned, Moss had discreetly made sure there were no babies. That was what he had asked for. He honoured himself for his decisions, and respected her for keeping her side of the bargain. It appealed to his tradesman's sense of a balanced account.

Frank was also clearer to himself just why he was not bitter about his own condition. There were seventy-seven good reasons why. Their names were chiselled into the stone memorial in the square.

Frank Smith died in June 1932. His gravestone said: 'Here lies Frank Smith, dear departed husband of Moss. May he rest in peace.'

Book Two

Seven

It was in the seventh month of 1953, the year when her daughter Lindsey was seven that Sadie was seven months pregnant, and this was to be her seventh child. She had known since being tiny that seven is a magic number. That, of course, was why they had at last been given a flat, this marvellous fifth-floor flat, on the Peabody Estate, in Covent Garden.

They didn't mind the shelves of concrete stairs up and round the fifteen landings, even though it took thirty-five minutes from the bottom to the top with all the children and the shopping. They didn't mind because before that they'd had two rooms with high small windows, dark and gloomy and filthy dirty that couldn't be opened far enough to be cleaned. Two rooms for the eight of them, not counting the almost-ready new baby who would make nine.

Now they had a living room-cum-kitchen and three bedrooms. It didn't matter that they couldn't afford curtains: nobody could see in and there was nothing to spoil the view over rooftops and old trees and part of the market itself.

The smallest bedroom was 7 feet by 7½; big enough for Sadie and Sam's double mattress on the floor. The girls had a bedroom, the boys another. The children were small and slept two to a bed; Estelle had a cot.

Sadie was a spirit who longed to live in the sky. She felt she would nearly die of the dark if she spent another winter in the old place, where her youngest three children had been coughing, and the baby, Estelle, was bronchitic.

Sadie needed to try to save the older ones before it crept towards them, starting with tiredness, weakness, wheezing and difficult breathing, and then the cough.

Sadie hadn't thought of having another baby. Six was plenty. Sam was working his heart out on the market, up and out of the flat at four in the morning. She herself didn't get in until six a.m. from her job as an orderly at Charing Cross Hospital, known locally as 'The Cross'.

She could walk to and from there now in a few minutes. It was so easy, though she was slower at seven months pregnant than she had been at the beginning. She carried easily, gave birth quickly. A pain in the back and so simple. Except for Lindsey, being first born. Sadie hadn't known how to birth a baby. Lindsey had had a harder time than the others, which made her special. But then she'd always had the edge on the others, being first, and Aries, a fire sign.

Sadie loved all her children, but she favoured Lindsey. A wonderful, sensible girl but painfully thin, not tall enough for her age. No harm had come to the younger ones because Lindsey kept an ear for them from the time her dad left to the time her mum, Sadie, returned. Sadie would creep in:

'That you, Mum?'

'It is. It's only me. Tuck in, lovie. You can go back to sleep now.'

Two hours on her own at night, at seven.

Sadie hadn't wanted to leave Lindsey in charge like that. None of the women who worked nights in the hospital wanted to leave their children. But they had to, wages being what they were. The wireless kept on about post-war boom; people getting comfortable; wives staying home. But as Sam and Sadie knew, it didn't mean their sort of people. Their sort worked and loved and survived, best they could. What worried them day and night was not only bronchitis from the damp in the old flat, but also whooping cough, reaching epidemic levels in London. At the hospital there was talk, too, about an increase in tuberculosis amongst the poor.

Sadie had been seventeen when she left Herton to find work in London. There was plenty of work on offer and she wrote home often about the people she was meeting and the places she worked. Most of her jobs were low paid, cleaning in hotels and working in hospitals.

During the war she had stayed on, living in the YWCA where she had made friends. She was reluctant to leave the busy city. To Sadie, Herton had nothing to offer compared to London, even in wartime. She wrote to Moss and Biff that this was the best thing she could have done. Then just as the war was ending, she had met Sam at a dance, and within a couple of months she was married and was expecting Lindsey. Sam worked as a porter at Covent Garden fruit market.

Sadie wrote to Moss saying that she had found the man she was looking for. They might never have much money, she had said, but at least they would be happy, and they both wanted several children.

Lindsey took after Sam. Practical, reliable, completely wrapped up in family and devotion to the younger children. They tumbled through life despite the creeping cough brought on by their old damp rooms and lack of sunlight. A united jumble of individuals, the way families were meant to be, according to Sadie.

Sadie named her sons after the Kings of England, her daughters more haphazardly, on the whim of the moment: Lindsey, seven; George, five and a half; Charlie, four; Mary, three; Jimmy one and a half; and the baby, Estelle. 'The nearest I can get to naming her after one of the constellations, that's going a bit too far.'

They were all black haired and black eyed after herself and her own mother. Sam called them 'me blackeyed bunch' and could be heard around the flat: 'Come on me blackeyed bunch, here's yer dinner, get to it.'

It was growing up with a dad like Biff, after having a dad like Frank, that gave Sadie her definite opinions on the sort of man she wanted as a father for her children, a husband for herself. Sam, like all his family, was nondescript to look at except for his laugh and his wild blue eyes. Sky eyes. She'd been on many a flight in those eyes, and a reward for flying showed in each of her six marvellous children. She knew there was no family like it. They were the best children in the world without a shadow of doubt. 'If it wasn't for some religious nut in the sheath factory sticking pins in the things to please God,' Sam said, 'we'd have a few less rewards and a bit more money.'

But when the children couldn't reach the toilet chain in the indoor toilet in the bathroom (they'd not had a proper plumbed-in bath before) it was Sam who tied on an extension string and passed it through a hole in a huge five inch potato he brought home off the market, so the children could grab the string resting their hand on the potato, and pull the thing and make it work. It was such a novelty that Lindsey and Mary each took their doll into the room to see it; and the children climbed on and off the toilet, pulling the chain and lifting on the youngest ones for a whole morning; and Jimmy had to use two hands pulling down each side of the potato, till Sadie cried with laughing.

From each bedroom window the sky made different pictures. Spires and steeples and cirrus clouds and cumulus. Sadie taught her children the names for the sky. All except Jimmy (and Estelle of course) could have a go at telling the weather from the clouds. How high, what shape, what colour, how dense; and the wind scudding and wisping crystals of ice along the edges of the cirrus horses' manes.

The family who had rented the flat before Sadie had known. Known about the sky. Watched the birds on the rooftops, in the trees.

'Isn't it funny, Sam, not knowing who painted these?'

'Must've been a painter 'n decorator, should think, or how'd he get the paints, uh?'

There was no wallpaper in any of the rooms. Sadie and Sam couldn't afford to do the place up. No matter. Every wall was covered in pictures of birds, drawn and painted, and every one was going somewhere different or doing something different. No two were identical, anywhere. They'd been round, checking. Birds preening, swooping, rising, falling, floating, wings stretched. Someone knew their exact lines. Someone who loved them. Someone who could draw.

The children's favourites were the parrots in the toilet. Red, blue, yellow, green; touches of dark blue; and even one with fluffy purple feathers. Pecking parrots; peeping parrots; prying parrots; preening parrots.

'Good job the things can't talk,' said Sadie. 'What with six children and nineteen parrots the place'd be a riot. They might be busy, 'cept for the one asleep with its head tucked underneath its wing, but at least they're quiet.'

In the girls' room there were sparrows, blackbirds and budgies; in the boys' room were starlings and swifts; and in hers and Sam's room an owl, an albatross and four penguins contemplating their toes in a group. 'Union meeting,' said Sam.

'Better'n watching them making babies,' Sadie replied.

Jimmy squealed, as he sat on the floor of the living room. Lindsey ran in to see what was happening. The little boy was sucking his big toe, and crying loudly.

'Here, Jimmy, let me see. What's the matter? What've you done?' Lindsey took Jimmy's foot in her hand and examined it closely. Blood was dripping from a gash caused by a long splinter from the bare floorboard. He was the third child that week to hurt his feet on the bare boards, so Lindsey knew what to do. She found Sadie's wool bag and pulled out a darning needle. She lit the gas flame on the cooker and quickly passed the long needle through it. Jimmy was crying, sucking his toe again. He had his back to Lindsey and didn't see the needle until Lindsey came towards him with it. I wish Mum was home, thought Lindsey.

'Here we are. I'm going to get it out for you. Like Mummy.'

Lindsey sat on the floor and grabbed Jimmy who was trying to wriggle away. He started screaming. The screams brought Mary and George to the door of the living room.

I wish Mum was here, thought Lindsey again, but she knew that Sadie would be a good while longer, because she had gone to the jumble sale with Charlie and the baby to get them some new clothes. 'Shhh, Jimmy. Now sit *still*. Come and hold him,' Lindsey called to Mary. 'I have to get this thing out or it will go bad. Come *on* Mary, we have to.'

'Don't want to,' said Mary standing by the doorway, horrified at the thought of Lindsey poking into Jimmy's toe with the long needle. 'I don't like needles.'

'Get your body over here this minute,' ordered Lindsey, and Mary came reluctantly forward. 'Now sit down here and hold his hands out of the way. Stop screaming Jim, you're making it harder.'

'I want a carpet,' said George loudly from the doorway. He thought he wouldn't have to help, but he was wrong.

'Come here, take his other foot,' called Lindsey. He obeyed in case she hit him. She had a heavy clout for such a skinny girl; and whenever she slapped him, it stung. He didn't want a slap from Lindsey, so he took Jimmy's other foot.

'Now I'm going to get the splinter out, Jim. I'm sorry. I'm going to hurt you, but if you wriggle it'll hurt more so keep still. Hold him tight, Mary.'

'No, no!' Jim wailed, but Lindsey persevered. Blood was seeping all around the long wooden splinter making it harder to see what was going on. Lindsey hated hurting him. Mary was white and trying not to shake. George said: 'I'm going to be sick.'

'No you're not. Big baby, it's not you that's got the splinter.'

'It was last time. I want a carpet.'

'Carpets is for rich people, stupid. And we're not rich people. So don't go on and on. And don't tell Mummy or you'll make her upset. She hasn't got any money for a carpet.' Lindsey dug harder with the needle. Jimmy writhed and let out a high-pitched yell. Lindsey wrenched with the needle. The splinter was out.

Lindsey hugged Jimmy who was sobbing. 'There now. It's all right. It's all gone. We'll have to put your socks on. Oh we can't, can we? I forgot. They're still wet. You'll just have to have shoes.' Turning to Mary, she said, 'Get me that piece of flannel on the sink and the soap please.' I wish we had another pair of socks, each, she thought.

80

Lindsey washed Jimmy's toe and wiped it on a piece of towel. She found the bandage that George had finished with from last week and bound up the sore toe. Then she carried Jimmy to the bedroom and put him on the bed, where he curled up still sobbing.

Lindsey went to the window and looked down into the street. She couldn't see her mother anywhere. Perhaps there were some good things at the jumble sale after all. Her mum had said, 'It's a shame people don't throw out carpets, that would be too much to hope for. But it would be a lot better for the little ones if we could find some nice pieces of lino.' Lindsey sighed. She'd better go and peel the potatoes for dinner. She could hear Mary and George coughing in the living room.

Behind her, Jimmy had stopped sobbing and was sucking his thumb. 'There you are Jimmy,' she said. 'You have a sleep. Then when you wake up your toe'll feel better.'

One day, thought Lindsey, we're going to live in a flat with some lino.

It was Sadie's night off. She slept soundly until Sam woke at three-thirty. He reached for her, held her close.

'When you leaving?'

'I've to give a week's notice. Give it another fortnight, then I'll tell them.'

'Can you carry on that long?'

'Case of having to. Shan't be back there for a while. Lindsey can't have much more time off. School Board man'll be round again. I teach her what I can here at home, but s'not enough. She's got to get to school.'

'Have you writ to Moss and Biff yet?'

'No. Not yet. I can't bring myself to think about it. They'll have her, you know they will. First I've to get the birth over with, make sure the new baby's all right. You never know, Sam. The others are lovely but there's not a mother in the world doesn't worry, check it's got everything, you know. Mary at work reckons them chemicals in the war got a lot to answer for. No, I'll wait a bit 'fore I write.'

'How you going to live without Lindsey, when she's gone?'

'Gone? Oh God, Sam, I don't know. I just don't know. I love her. In such a special kind of way. She means me and you starting off, making a life, remember?'

''Course I do. The others came along soon enough. It'll break me in bits, sending that child to your mum's.'

'Well, your mum can't take her and somebody's got to save that child's life. I know that I shouldn't have favourites. No mother should. But Lindsey's my first born and she's never given me a moment's trouble. She never complains about all the work and she works far, far too hard for a little girl her age. We can't let her go on like this. I've seen other little girls like her in The Cross. All working at home with dozens of brothers and sisters just like our Lindsey has to. It breaks me up to see them little wizened things, old before their time. It always falls hardest on the eldest. I can't let my Lindsey go on getting worn out. She'll be so run down she'll have no resistance left, none at all. Heavens knows how she's escaped bronchitis so far.'

'You'd think it was the first world war not the second, the conditions people live in. Thank God we got this flat.'

'Yes. We got ourselves out of those terrible rooms. And now we've to save our children before it's too late.'

'I told you I'd sleep separate, Sadie. We've tried everything else. Time of the month, everything. I'll sleep in the living room. We can't go through this again. We can't afford another after this one, can't clothe the ones we've got.'

'You're not sleeping separate, Sam. That's the start of the end for married people. We're short of things, of course we are, but we eat all right on account of your perks, thank God for the market. I'm fretting about Jimmy, his toe's festering. I'm taking him back to the doctor's on Friday. Let them take another look at it.'

'You're doing all you can. It's *me* not doing all *I* can. If we have any more, people'll say I don't love you, a right selfish bastard, that Sam Abbotts.'

'Hush. Let'm say what they will. Tongues talk, anyroad. No matter what we do or don't. I know what I've got. I've got you. What I want. Nobody could love them kids more'n you do. But we've to stop the bronchitis getting any worse and we've to save Lindsey before she gets it in the first place. We can't let it happen to her. We can't.'

'Well, when me uncle and me brother get settled, they can sponsor us.'

'Oh no, not that again, Sam. No. Not Australia. I haven't seen me own mother for six years, what with the two hundred miles. How'm I going to get home from Australia?'

'I'd have a job, a good job, prospects. Meat. We could afford meat. No more bronchitis. It's a new country, it still is. Jack says so. He writ me in his letter. You read it. You know.'

'Not Australia, Sam. We have to find a different answer.'

82

Eight

It was August 1954. Lindsey sat in the train holding Grey, talking about her nanan and grandad, and pointing them out from the now battered photograph which they had sent. The wheels of the train sped over the tracks with a steady soothing rhythm.

Going to Nanan Going to Nanan Going to Nanan.

'You'll be all right there, Grey. They'll be ever so kind to you.'

The huge velvet elephant did not reply but Lindsey knew that she was listening carefully, in her own way. Lindsey set her mind on getting to Sheffield Midland without crying. It was silly to cry, now that she was eight, she told herself. And besides, it was just for a long holiday, and she'd be able to have a bedroom of her own, like a princess. Except she would share it with Grey, but that was different.

It had been a long train journey and she would soon be arriving. She went with Grey to the toilet, returned, made sure she had her case near by, and was at the window again when the lines began to meet and part, ready for the run in to the platform.

She saw them immediately.

'Look, Grey, that's my nanan, the one in the nice green coat; and that's my grandad. He's the tall one with the brown hair. Wave.'

With her free arm, Lindsey waved, and she noticed that her nanan didn't look old like she'd expected. She had black hair parted in the middle and pinned in a knot softly in the nape of her neck, and she was smiling and waving back. Her granddad had a sports jacket on and grey trousers. He looked kind and he had a little bit of grey in his hair. He was nearly sixty after all and that was really old, according to Lindsey.

'Doesn't my nanan look like my mum and like me, Grey. Oh, the train is stopping; come on.'

The young girl with her nose pressed against the window of the arriving train was so like Moss's daughter Sadie that she could have been Sadie herself.

Moss ran forward. The child had seen them and for a moment was gone, obviously reaching for her suitcase, as with a final whistle and jolt, the train arrived at Sheffield Midland.

Biff's limp took her unawares for once, and she stumbled and halted for a moment as she watched Moss greet her grandchild.

'Lindsey? I'd have known you anywhere, love.'

'Are you my nanan?'

'I am, love. I'm your nanan. You can call me Moss if you like, or Nanan. I don't mind, love. Here's Biff. Biff is always called just Biff, all right?'

She was not a pretty child, nor even good looking. Her mouth was slightly too wide, her jaw a little too square and determined, and when Biff looked closely, she discovered that, like most people's, Lindsey's face wasn't quite symmetrical. Her almost black hair was neatly tied into two thick plaits, and her hands were large for a girl her age, square and with the nails bitten.

But when she talked her whole face moved and changed, never still, like a thousand faces in one. She had the sort of mobile expressions that an actress could use, or a public speaker, reminding Biff of some of the suffragettes on the bare planks of wooden carts, addressing a crowd and holding the attention of each man, woman and child. Lindsey Abbotts was the kind of child you could love, with a face that people would fall in love with over and over again, drawn to it irresistibly.

' 'Lo, Biff. It was you sent me Grey, wasn't it? I love Grey. I talked to her all the way here so as she'd not be scared.'

'Did she cry?' asked Moss, as Lindsey held out her hand to be held.

'She did a bit, Nanan. I told her she'd to be good as gold at your house, so we'd not get sent away. I'm eight. I wasn't crying. Grey cried and cried, so I joggled her over my shoulder.'

'So then she stopped.'

'Oh yes. Because I'm good with babies. I told her we was coming to you for a long holiday so when Mum's got some money and Estelle and Jimmy and Mary have stopped coughing and Dad's got a better job, we can go home again. So then she stopped and I told her stories out the window. I'm glad you sent her to me, well Biff did really I know, and I'll never leave her. Do you want to hug her?'

They both hugged the large felt elephant, telling her she'd done just fine. Biff took the suitcase and Lindsey had Grey under her spare arm. They started the walk to the bus station and with it Biff·felt transported to Darlington, into Moss's family when Moss was eight.

This was what it might have been like, knowing Moss during her childhood.

In fleeting moments Lindsey looked exactly like Moss. Then something would happen, the glance change, and the resemblance go. Lindsey was white-skinned whereas Moss was not, though she would pass for white in Herton. It was something Moss rarely spoke about although Herton rumours had reached her in the early days, that the grocer's housekeeper had what Herton called a touch of the tar brush.

Herton's prejudice seeped up through the floorboards sometimes, like the smell from the sewers when they cracked in a hard winter.

'We thought you was one of them tinkers,' Mrs Johnson had come straight out with, and Mrs Croysen, who was with her in the shop, added, 'Yes, we ran them tinkers out of town. Them with their wild children giving our little uns all kinds o' notions about skipping school.'

'So what if I was a gypsy?' snapped Moss, 'I'd as soon not settle where I'm not wanted, thank you all the same.'

'Hoity-toity. You want to watch her, Frank Smith. She'll be getting ideas above her . . . '

'No porridge oats until tomorrow, Mrs Croysen, when the delivery comes. Now, Mrs Johnson, did you still want that little bit o' Wensleydale I saved you? Or did you come into my shop for a gawp and a gossip, eh?'

'Now don't take offence, Frank Smith. We meant no harm. She just looks well, a bit different, that's all. We're only interested. If she works hard that's what matters in this town, eh?'

'She works hard.'

'Well that's all right then. Good day. We'll be in for the porridge oats in the morning.'

'Please yourselves, ladies. You know where the shop is, and they're the best prices in this town. After eleven tomorrow then.'

It had all been said in front of Moss as if she hadn't been listening. It passed through Biff's mind, as a newsreel of memories, during the walk from the station to the bus stop, and on the bus ride to Herton. Home.

In Herton, Lindsey was freed from drudgery. She didn't have to do the family wash, soaking it, rinsing it, using the mangle for hours, and ironing the lot when it was dry. Nor did she have to scrub the wooden floors nor feed the babies and dress the toddlers.

She became a child herself. With a skipping rope and a bicycle.

On Sunday afternoons, if Biff's leg wasn't playing up, they cycled together down Church Lane, away from the colliery, along the valley bottom and up the far slopes to the end of the rough track where it met an old stone curved bridge, beyond which it was too steep to ride.

There they would pause, on the packhorse bridge over a tumbling tributary, where the stream dropped down with perfect timing, the water pouring like continuous sand from an egg timer that would never run out.

On clear days when the sky was wide and there was no wind, they could hear, beyond the rush and bounce and leap of the falling water, the steady whirring of cables and buckets across the valley. But sometimes the wind carried the sounds of the distant view away so that from afar the landscape was silent, the houses clustered around the colliery deserted, leaving the buckets switched on, endlessly cabling up, tipping, righting themselves and returning to a ghost town.

On those days the bridge became the only real world despite its musical waters and spell-wishing trees. Trolls lurked under the bridge; branches creaked overhead; and Billy Goats Gruff owned the secret paths from the packhorse bridge to the hill meetings where miners had trekked with lanterns by night, to plan the first unions; and where women had gathered to pass messages over the Pennines, to the Pankhursts.

Biff would sit on the low stone wall atop the bridge, with Lindsey perched on the flat coping stones beside her, leaning against her shoulder. Lindsey would hear the first tale, the next, and the one after that. The overhead canopy scattered green sunlight from the sky; and Biff turned each leaf on each sapling into one sentence; each branch one paragraph; each tree one character, growing stories long and slow and deep and high. They came from the same source as Biff's love for Moss and her lovemaking with Moss. Telling them to Lindsey, Biff occasionally had images in her mind from times when she had flown with Moss over woods even greener than these woods, and could long to make a child, this child, from those tangible moments of happiness. No one except Moss would ever know those thoughts. But, keeping pace with the seasons' changes and the need of the growing child, Biff retold and re-imagined myths and legends, history and heritage, to root Lindsey in Herton – its land; its people; its past, present and future.

In Herton Juniors, Lindsey was a new girl. An outsider. When the novelty of her voice wore off the others stopped asking her to talk to them, and the groups and gangs settled down again without her. If it hadn't have been for one other girl, Rita Jackson, Lindsey would have spent her first weeks alone.

Rita had been in hospital for the whole of the first year juniors, so, although she was a year older than Lindsey, she now had to make up the time in Lindsey's year.

'I thought it would be horrible coming back. Not having a best friend no more. Joan was mine, but when I got sent away to the isolation ward, she got fed up. No one to go round with. So she made best friends with Lynne. I hate Lynne. Stuck up cat. Just 'cos her mum's school nurse at the secondary mod. What's so big about that, anyroad? My mum's better'n her mum anyroad. They have to eat thick bread. Ugh. You know, the sort the crusts take ages. I went round there once. Ugh. I like thin sliced best, do you?'

'Yes,' lied Lindsey to keep in with Rita. 'And I like my bacon with tomato sauce just like you.'

'I changed to Daddies sauce now. Do you have that?'

'Oh yes,' lied Lindsey. 'I like that too.'

Rita stuck to her new friend like glue to the Christmas calendars they all had to make each year for their homes. Rita was the middle of five Jacksons, and was Brenda Jackson's daughter, Grace Dundy's granddaughter. Her eldest brother, Tommy, was courting and worked down the pit. Eddie had just started in the pit and was trying hard to start courting; not much success. Rita told Lindsey in confidence it was because he had pimples. After Rita there was a long gap until Philip, five years younger, and then Neil who was just a year old.

'D'you know something?'

'No, what?'

'Rita Jackson, stop whispering behind your hand this minute. Get on with your long divisions. You're behind enough as it is. You chatter faster than your dad digs coal. No more talking or there'll be trouble.'

'Sorry, Mrs Lewis.'

'What?' whispered Lindsey when the teacher was the other side of the room, untying someone's long plaits from the back of a chair and scolding Jimmy Hawsley for the hundredth time.

'There was this pop star on the radio in hospital. He said he was on his back like me for a year when he was exactly the same age.'

'Go on, s'all right. She's not looking. She's putting Jimmy Hawsley in the corner.'

'He said that's when he decided to make his mark on the world. So I am too.'

'How can you be a pop star, Rita? You're just a girl. You haven't even gotta guitar.'

'No, not a pop star. Summat different. Dunno yet. But I am. I'm going to make a mark on the world.'

'Yes, but how? Oh, watch out, here comes Pooey-Lewey.'

They worked on Saturdays, delivering for Biff, who paid them each two shillings. That was high wages, enough for comics and sweets and a trip to the pictures.

'Mrs Thompson gave us Tizer and gingerbread men,' said Lindsey to Moss. 'Miss Field gave us some home-made Shrewsbury biscuits and old Mr Schofield gave us pear drops. You won't tell will you?' Moss shook her head. 'Only his granddaughter brings them because she thinks he likes them and he don't so he saves 'em so as he has something to give us.' Biff came into the kitchen as Lindsey was finishing the anecdote. 'Here, Biff, you try one. You won't split will you? Cross your heart, cut your throat and hope to die.'

'Cross my heart, cut my throat and hope to die,' said Biff, keeping a blank face and doing all the actions. Lindsey was convinced. 'All right then. Do you want another one for after? Aren't they scrummy? Can I go out on my bike now?'

'Scrummy. Yes. Back before teatime, mind.'

Lindsey had an unexpected and terrible temper that could sweep through the skies like splits of white-hot lightning, tearing open the clouds until they roared and the earth under her feet could tremble. She loved animals and hated anyone that was cruel to them. She would fling home from school sometimes, the thunder clouds tight inside her body. She would slam the back door shut, and leaning against it, she would let out the screams inside. Moss and Biff in the front shop would hear her, and one would hurry through to find out what had sparked it this time. It was something Sadie hadn't warned them about.

'I'll kill him, so I will. I said I'd tell and I'm going to. I'm going to kill him so's he can't do it again.'

'Hey hey, what's all this?'

'Jimmy Hawsley. He's got three day-old chicks in a box. Up a tree and they're going to starve. I'm going to kill him. Beast.'

'Now stop that yelling, Lindsey, and wash your face. I'm not having the whole of Herton listening to you screaming in my shop.'

'I'm going to kill him. I'm going to kill him.'

'I said go and wash your face. Now. Now do it.'

Lindsey hardly ever heard Biff speak in that tone and she fled to the sink and put her face under the tap. Biff passed her a warm towel from the cupboard over the fire.

'Here. Wipe it. Now sit down and don't you dare scream again in my home. I will not have it. The whole world will think we're beating you to a pulp. Whoever heard such a noise? Now tell me where this tree is, this box.'

'Down the market.' Gulp. 'You know.' Lindsey sobbed, more quietly. 'Those big trees down the backs. All tied up, sort of hoisted up, waving about in the air. Three. He's got three.'

'Boxes?'

'No, not boxes, stupid.'

'I beg your pardon. Do you want me to sort out Jimmy Hawsley, or shall I put you in your room?'

'Sorry. Chicks. Three chicks from the farm. He thieved 'em when he was playing there.'

'Did he?' Biff paused, wanting to slap Lindsey hard for calling her stupid, and made herself hold back. She was getting used to these outbursts. Not frequent but very unpredictable. Lindsey's eyes were swollen, her jaw set, and her heart torn round its edges because the chicks couldn't protect themselves.

'Go and get a barley sugar, and go to the toilet and blow your nose, then we'll go out to investigate.'

Lindsey loved Biff going out to investigate. Her granddad had an air of such quiet, strong authority. He'd sort out Jimmy Hawsley. Remorse set in for daring to call her granddad stupid, and for screaming all that noise. But she felt better. She couldn't scream at Jimmy Hawsley because he had his gang with him, and there were four of them. So she'd run one way and Rita the other, and she knew Rita was shaking too. If Joan, Rita's friend from before she went into hospital, had been with them, Lindsey was sure the three of them would've stuck together, waded into the gang and all hell would have been let loose. Joan was taller than Jimmy Hawsley, tough and very strong and she'd already kissed two boys. Joan could have sorted them out all right. But Joan had a job after school, delivering for Naylor's shop, the other end of Herton, and the chicks would be dead by tonight if somebody didn't get them down and take them indoors. Lindsey sobbed and sniffed, trying to stop. Rita had gone to get her dad if he was home, and then there'd be so many people that Jimmy Hawsley would have to give in.

The lads had fled before Biff and Lindsey arrived. Rita was coming through the back alley behind the market with her dad, who was between shifts. He had a huge stick and he looked like he meant business. Rita hadn't screamed or cried. She always stayed calm when these sorts of things happened and Lindsey wished she could too. But when the anger started in her belly it came up and up, threatening to burst open her head if she didn't yell. So she usually yelled blue murder, and sometimes she'd not stop shaking until after she'd had a sleep.

'It's up there, look.'

'I can see it, Arthur, but I'm blowed if I can reach it.'

'Can you climb up there, Dad?'

'Aye, I reckon. What about if I get up on yer shoulders, Biff?'

'Righto.' Biff bent over, pressing both hands against the trunk of the tree. Her lean body and toughened muscles prepared for Arthur's weight.

'Ready then, Biff?'

'Hold tight, Biff, or Rita's dad'll slip.'

Biff grinned. 'Never you mind Rita's dad slipping, what about my poor shoulders?'

'Be careful, Dad. Oh he's got it, look, Lindsey. Dad, you've done it.'

Arthur had one hand on the box. He grabbed the nearest branch with the other hand. Biff's face was red, growing deeper red as she shouldered the weight of the man. Arthur unlodged the box and called down. 'Rita, I'm going to have to drop it, love, 'cause I need me other hand to keep me balance. Can you catch it?'

'Hey wait,' shouted Lindsey. She took off her coat, held it out to Rita, and they made a fireman's blanket like they'd seen on television, at Rita's gran's house.

Arthur dropped the box as gently as he could. Panting, he crouched down and half-slid, half-leapt off Biff's shoulders. Biff was purple with the effort.

Rita opened the box. There were two stiff balls of yellow fluff and one live chick.

Lindsey filled up and spilled over. Biff held her close and she cried, but the screaming had gone. Fast and temporary as a storm Lindsey's lightning usually seared her and spent itself out. Rita didn't cry. She sniffed loudly but only a couple of drops of tears squeezed through.

She envied Lindsey who could weep enough to fill the Ladybower after a summer drought.

'Thanks, Arthur. Bloody louts, eh?'

'Like father like son, Biff. They've always been a bad lot, them Hawsleys.'

'Never a dull moment, eh, Arthur?'

'You can say that again, Biff. I was in me bed. Me lass here comes flying in like a bat out of hell, eh, our Rita? Now then our lass, you'd better both of you bring that poor thing back to me loft, not that I hold out much hope. But I've rescued a few exhausted pigeons in me time. How's yon shoulders then Biff?'

'Your Brenda's Yorkshire pud showing its weight, I'd say.'

'Aye she's a damn good cook, for sure. Haven't seen you down the Colliers' Arms for a few weeks back, Biff. How about a pint after shop hours?'

'You're on, Arthur. I'd better be getting back to me shop. Now then, our Lindsey, you going on this mission of mercy then, to Rita's house?'

Lindsey nodded and hugged Biff whispering 'Thanks. I'm sorry 'bout all the screaming, Biff.'

''Sall right, our lass. Go on with you. I want you back home 'fore dark.'

'T'rah then, Biff,' called Arthur, and Biff returned through the market to take up the day where it had been so rudely interrupted.

Nine

Sadie sat at the scrubbed deal table, working her way through the pages of the notepad she'd bought for the letter. Around her were the scatters of her earlier attempts. Her neighbour's youngest child, David, batted them around, tottering after them, sometimes dropping to his bottom, in his funny sideways crab crawl which he'd not needed to do for months but still liked doing. Lindsey had moved like him, half on her bottom. But Lindsey was a grown girl of eleven now. Sadie sniffed and rubbed her sleeve across her eyes. She wore a cotton shirt-waister dress which she'd made herself. She was a thin woman, her face lined and tired.

If only we had the money, she thought, I could go up there, talk it over with her. The coach was cheaper than the train, but still no chance.

Sadie could hear Estelle, Jimmy and Ronnie, her seventh and last child, playing under the beds where they'd made camps and tunnels. Sadie's trained ear was tuned in to the voices of her children, and she recognised play not war, and she tuned out again. David had started to chew on one of the screwed-up scribbles. 'Stop that. You're old enough to know better, you big baby.' She picked him up, hooked the soggy mess from his mouth with a well practised finger, despite his protests. She hugged him and set him in the huge wooden play-pen with a wooden spoon and a cardboard box. Now, except for the din he made beating the box up in disgust at her, she was free for five minutes.

The prisoner looked out from behind his bars. None of her children had liked that playpen. Neither had she. They looked like the penned up rabbits in the condemned cells behind the butcher's. Playpens and Brussels sprouts, hated equally by all.

Sadie began again.

Dear Lindsey . . .

She sucked on her new biro. They hadn't long been invented. What if Sam had been a biro inventor, then they'd not be in this two and eight. Rumours were spreading that Covent Garden was to be uprooted. To the other side of the river. Outer Siberia. And no tube. Never mind the fares. Porters like Sam feared massive lay offs. People feared the changes, enormous and remote; posh phrases like re-development and urban decay and such like. Bran tubs of posh phrases, pay your money, take your pick. Likely as not she and Sam'd get booby prize.

Sadie regarded the rubbish all over the floor left where she had tossed it or David had shuffled it. Resigned, he was now curled with his old blanket like a cat, sleeping when there was no chance to be let out.

Do town planners tear their hair out over their plans, like me with this letter? she wondered. Never seen inside a planner's office, or an architect's. How do you turn a hope into a letter? An idea into a drawing? A neighbourhood into a wasteland? What about the people whose lives are chucked away, cast aside and forgotten, because someone drew a picture of a new market, or wrote a stranger's letter to a faraway child, words from the other side of the sky?

Whose idea was it to move the market anyway? People were saying it could take years to come about. That was a lot of waiting and seeing, thought Sadie. You could die or starve waiting on• an architect's plan. Or your heart could wither. Hearts don't break, said Sadie aloud, quietly, they crumble, waiting. She listened to David snoring, coming through the bars like bread through a slicer. All her own children were snorers except Mary. Bright as a button was Mary, and didn't stand a chance, unless the family fortunes changed, were made to change. Chance for what, exactly? thought Sadie.

She didn't move lest she wake David. She sat very still silent now, noticing that her heart was beating too wildly, feeling the tears running on her face.

By itself the rumours about the moving of Covent Garden market were not enough reason to uproot the family, and call Lindsey back from Herton. But from Sadie's point of view they were one more insecurity, on top of all the others.

Thankfully, none of the children had become fatally ill in the whooping cough or polio epidemics, though Jimmy and Mary had both taken a long time to become really strong children.

The real reason to leave Britain and move to Australia was that Sam's parents had gone out there to join his brother and were doing well compared to Sam back in London, that Sadie had slowly come round to Sam's way of thinking about emigrating.

The thing that held her back for many months after she had finally agreed that the move was a good idea, and had admitted that she was no longer against it in principle, was that Lindsey was settled and happy and thriving in Herton.

To write to her eldest daughter asking her to come home and live in London was one thing: to ask her to leave England on a one-way ticket to the other side of the world was something quite different.

Sadie herself had loved both her adoptive father, Frank, and her mother's live-in common-law husband, Biff. She knew from Lindsey's letters that she adored both her grandparents; that she thought of Biff as her real granddad, though she knew that he wasn't actually her granddad; that she had made close friends with girls of her own age in Herton; and was getting along well in school.

There wasn't a day went by without Sadie thinking of Lindsey and missing her, sometimes feeling that the umbilical cord had never been properly cut and that they were still joined together. She loved her too much to want to turn her world upside down again by breaking her away from Herton and her beloved grandparents, after she had successfully recovered from being torn from her family at the age of eight and sent to Herton for her health and well-being.

Sadie picked up her pen and once again tried to draft a letter to Lindsey.

Herton in the late fifties was slow and steady. The buckets cabled up and down, tipping slag on the heap that grew imperceptibly week upon week. Over a decade it might seem higher, rounder, dominating the landscape of farms and woodlands, streams and paths. Like Herton's post-war generation of children, it grew, inch by inch, until from time to time someone might realise that a month, a year or two had crept past. Rita's older brother Tommy was married, and his wife became pregnant; her other brother Eddie, found a girlfriend. Her younger brothers started infant school. Winkle-pickers and teddy boys arrived and stayed. Young people started smoking and passing for eighteen and going to see 'X' films. Lindsey's holiday had stretched to two years, then three, until 'the letter' came.

Dear Lindsey   4th May 1957
   Your dad has been to the place to book our tickets and we are going to Australia in eight weeks' time with the little ones.
   Your dad can get a better job out there and we need the money. We can get assisted passage. That means they pay most of the fare now that your dad has a job to go to. Your dad's aunty is going to find us a place to stay till we get sorted out. We love you a lot. Do you want to come too? Or do you want to stay in Herton at your nan's? I would come up there to fetch you but I haven't got enough money for the fare. I am writing to your nan same post.
Love from Mum.   xxxxxxxxxx

Lindsey and Rita cycled out of Herton with the letter in Lindsey's anorak pocket.

It was their last Whitsun holiday from Herton Juniors. They were due for the eleven plus exam, their futures unknown as they planned how to make a mark on the world. Plans, great ones, are catching, like scarlet fever. But childhood and its epidemics was almost over. Come next spring, they might even have kissed some boys. Lindsey's hair bobbed behind her in a pony tail as she cycled. The girls raced towards the white-painted milestone which stood solid in the grassy verge a few feet from the steep track up to the packhorse bridge.

Determined, Lindsey shot forward, taunting Rita over her shoulder as she flew past to the winning post.

Red-faced she arrived, turning, laughing, with Rita only three yards behind.

'I'll get you next time. So there, Lindsey Abbotts.'

'Two to me. Two to me.'

'Okay, okay. You won. No need to crow.'

They parked the cycles and shared out the Tizer, extra fizzy from the shake-up. Then they walked, following the track as Lindsey had done a thousand times with Biff.

It never disappointed them, the view from the bridge.

Lindsey took out the letter, tore it to pieces, and threw her mother's words into the water.

She watched the pieces floating and tumbling down the hill. She didn't dare think what life would be like in a place so far away. If they really wanted her to go with them they'd have come and fetched her, no matter how much the fares cost. Surely they knew she wouldn't leave Nanan and Biff. Not even to go back and live in London. There was nowhere on earth as beautiful as Herton; she wasn't leaving till she fell in love with somebody. And that was years and years away. Until then, Herton was her home, and Nanan and Biff were her family now. She dare not think about missing her mum and dad and all her brothers and sisters. She'd got over all that. She'd had to. It was three years ago and three years were like for ever when you were eleven.

The late afternoon light moved around the shop, touching the edges of silver biscuit tins; red metal round tins of cocoa; green glass family hair shampoo bottles; blue green and silver bubble gum wrappers. It recoiled from the hard cruel circles of steel on the bacon slicer; stroked the imitation mother-of-pearl handles in the cheese display, avoiding the sharp slopes of the cutting edges.

As the angles changed from the southeast to the southwest window, Biff served and gossiped, commiserated and commented.

Most of Biff's attention was on the job. Livelihood. Biff could cut cheese to within a quarter of an ounce, amazing the housewives who went away delighted, and who would have been more amazed had they realised what a clever woman Biff was.

It was Biff's intention that they would never know; and that they would return again and again to buy from the shop; so Biff served quickly or slowly according to the need, mood and preference of whoever was buying.

The very old people did not want to be served fast. They liked the chair by the counter to sit on while they waited. They appreciated the company, and the reason for getting out of the house. Biff's shop was safe, familiar. Not overwhelming like some of the new-fangled stores.

Just like the village green behind the Church, the surroundings in the grocer's shop hadn't changed for years. The sun played cricket in the afternoons, bowling the sunbeams on to wooden shelves that held each day's delivery of crusty white bread; they batted it to the glass counter over the cheeses, where it was fielded by white marble slabs, caught, returned to glass jars in the windows, finally coming to rest on the rounded edges of small sets of wooden drawers, soft, brown and old, holding packets of cinnamon powder for colds, tubs of baking powder, and boxes of whole nutmegs.

But a part of Biff's mind was up in the hills. Each turn of Lindsey's wheels was followed. Each pedal's rise and fall was filmed, as if Biff had a hidden silent camera suspended from an invisible dragonfly, a soundless miniature helicopter.

In the kitchen behind the shop, Moss scraped the pastry from her fingers, glad of the ordinary daily action. Small, soothing, dependable.

She scrubbed her nails and cleaned the final scrap of dough from under her ring. Biff had bought her a decorated gold band which she wore now in place of Frank's wedding ring. People who had called her Mrs Smith, now called her Mrs Ferguson. But something, she wasn't sure what, stopped her from abandoning Frank's ring. That could be tempting providence. So she still wore it, but on her right hand. In memory of the man who had given her a roof and a table, a place in the world when she had least expected it. She wasn't the only common-law wife in Herton. Whatever people felt, or whispered behind their backs, to a woman's face they'd say Mrs, and the new name that she told them.

She dried her hands and reached for the half eternity ring that she always hung on its own hook by the sink when she was baking. It winked just like Biff. She kissed it and eased it on to the ring finger of her left hand until it nestled against her decorated gold band, like herself and Biff in bed.

She whisked the first batch of tartlets from the oven, remembering last night's passion with Biff when the same fingers long, slim and pale brown inherited from her Indian grandmother, had touched every inch of Biff's skin.

The first batch was smelling wonderful in the oven. Moss kept it sparkling bright. Many's the time she had run a clean finger over its cold smooth shine. Like all new gas ovens it had cost a small fortune, though people said they were coming down now with the post-war mass production, and it had to last Moss for years.

She wrapped her clean right hand in a fresh tea towel before lifting a steaming kettle from the gas towards the sink. No more messy fire places, no ashes that had to be carted off to the allotment. Behind her Moss could hear the filaments of the gas fire clinking and clanking. They sounded like talk, but her mind was too full of her own thoughts for them to get their words in edgeways.

The steam misted up her new glasses. Her eyes had been bothering her for some time. The glasses had cost a bomb. Bomb. Moss shuddered thinking of Hiroshima. America had dropped the atom bomb in August '45. It had gone down the same day that Sadie had written saying she was pregnant with Lindsey. Now Sadie had written a different letter.

Moss washed the pots and then washed her hands in her favourite buttermilk soap. Actually it was second best, but sandalwood was too expensive except at Christmas and the last lot Biff had bought her was finished.

They loved one another's cleanliness. Had done so from the first. The longings, clingings, warmth and tenderness were still there. Long gone the days of youthful urgent fumblings, equally passionate, with Florence under the rhododendrons. Moss thought of the angry dogs, the men, the loss of Florence, the birth of Sadie. Tears slid from behind Moss's glasses; down her cheeks and she licked them away.

She rarely gave herself time for tears. She knew anger, laughter, grief and survival, and the few times when she allowed moments of quiet deep bereavement came with Sadie's letters. Few and far between.

Moss didn't regret having had two children. Ronnie lay at peace somewhere, at the bottom of the Atlantic, her twopenny son who had been wasted in a war that had cost millions of pounds, measured by men in bags of bodies, like coins in a bank vault. It was a century of discardable people, their lives old news next week like headlines tossed in the gutter when the fish and chip papers were empty. Take care of the pennies, her own mother used to say, and the pounds will take care of themselves. The women zipped their purses so carefully but the men seemed to rip open the sacks willy-nilly, pouring Ronnies, tens of thousands of them, into the sea.

Sadie was almost a stranger now. Gone away to live. Alive, but her life caused almost as much grief as Ronnie's death. Sadie was capable of swinging the scales of loving up and down recklessly, without a thought for balance. Moss stopped crying and cleaned up her glasses. Confounded things but practical. There were always several truths. Never one problem with one solution, one question with one answer. Always complexities. She blew her nose on one of Frank's old soft hankies, washed out until it was a comfort. And God knew, she needed some comfort. Sadie's letter had tipped her world off its axis.

'This poor child,' she had said to Biff last night. 'Sometimes I blame myself. If I hadn't been with Florence and we hadn't been caught . . . '

'You wouldn't have had Sadie and she couldn't be doing this now to her daughter.'

'How come you know what I'm thinking?'

'Don't we usually?'

'Yes, but . . . '

'But this isn't Sadie's light drizzle. This is one of her force-ten gales. She flings rocks down river. Rocks you thought would stay up valley, where they should be.'

'I try to prepare for her letters, even this sort. But she enters me and leaves me, as she always has done, raw and vulnerable.'

'If it wasn't for Sadie, we wouldn't have Lindsey. And perhaps you can't get a thunder and lightning child, if you don't have a few storms, eh?'

'I don't want any more talk tonight, love, I want bodies.'

'I love you, Moss, every day. And I love you wanting me.'

'I need you. Shhhh, you'll wake Lindsey. But I love to hear you laugh a little, like now. I need it.'

'So do I. And I like laughing too.'

'You're incorrigible.'

'So are you. I love the way your mouth turns up, just before the laughter comes back.'

'Almost as much as I love this little bit of your neck.'

With a jolt, Moss realised that she had been daydreaming. The second batch would burn if she didn't hurry. Quickly she opened the oven door and removed the hot tray. Easy does it. Hot. Life was hot. Too hot, sometimes.

She should have kept a journal like Virginia Woolf, she thought. But there wasn't time. She would have loved to have been Virginia writing *Orlando* for Vita. How she and Biff had revelled in that book. Hints and innuendos. They'd read it aloud to one another, taking the voices, at night by the gas fire. Four times through. Biff should have been an actress. She could imitate Vita's voice from the radio, because they knew it from the gardening programmes.

'I bet they did it a few times behind those old brick walls.'

'Yes, but what about the servants, Biff? Me and Florence knew everything about them upstairs when we was at The Hall.'

'Paid to keep quiet I suppose. No shortage of money for that class of women.'

'That's right. Take that Una and the other posh one that gave me a lift. I've pondered on that quite often. I'm convinced it was Radclyffe Hall. Missed my chance there I did. I'd have had a whale of a time as *their* servant. I should have asked for a job not just a lift.'

'Well now, Mrs Frank Smith, if this life with Bernard Ian Ferguson isn't good enough for you, you will have to cast your net a little wider.'

'There may be plenty more whales in the ocean, Barbara Imogen Farley, but Herton is a tiny backwater, my love, and I doubt that women in this town are queueing up to make love with the late grocer's wife.'

'Then you'll have to make do with this old plaice.'

'Oh, Biff love. Even poor old Frank could pun better than that.' Moss kissed her and kidded: 'You make me feel sixteen, give or take the odd birthday and a sprinkle of grey hair.'

'You're as young as your heart feels. And everyone knows that grey hair means good sex.'

Ten

Herton Hall was sold in the summer of 1957. Miss Field and Miss Brookes were told categorically that a retired bishop was coming to live there. Grace Dundy overheard the cinema usherette saying that it was going to be turned into a country club. Mercy Dundy's cousin had everyone believing that it was going to be a home for ex-prisoners and a petition went round to try to stop it, until the local paper published an interview with the man who had bought it.

He was a London businessman. An antiques dealer called Pierre Mullière. He was married and had three sons at Eton. He himself lived most of the year in Europe where he collected things. His flamboyant, red-haired wife, Harriet Mullière, would run an art school and picture-framing business from Herton Hall. They had rebuilding to do, especially the stables and mews cottages above the stables.

'Huh. Whoever heard of such a thing?' Grace declared whilst gossiping in the shop with Moss and Biff. 'Artists. In Herton Hall. The place will be overrun with strangers, painting pictures of buckets cabling and cows in the foreground and turning the town into a public gawping place. Huh. I'd leave if I could. It's the worst news Herton's had in all the years since the war.'

'Oh come on now, Grace,' replied Moss. 'Don't exaggerate. They probably won't come into town at all. It's too ordinary, too mucky. One whiff when the coke oven's in its element and they'll dash back to London, you mark my words. And they'll never stand a Herton winter. Besides, if they do venture out of the grounds, which I doubt, we could do with a bob or two from one or two well-lined pockets, right here, in this till, couldn't we, Biff?'

'I should say so,' agreed Biff. 'Fear not, Grace, for they bring us good tidings of great ha'pennies.'

'That's just like you, Biff. And Frank before you. You're all the same, you shopkeepers.'

'And where would you be without us? Do you want these beans or not?'

'You're wrong, Biff,' Grace replied. 'I don't want this town invaded by a bunch of artists from London, sniffing out so called local interest. They'll turn this place upside down. Then I hope they'll get bored, pack up and go. That I do. One and thruppence, then.' Grace handed Biff a two shilling piece with a wry smile and waited for change. She still gave off angry sparks like a firework in someone's back yard, but with Grace they never lasted long.

'Anyway I can't stop no longer much as I do like a natter with you two. I've got me sheets out and it looks like rain. I'll be seeing you then.'

They laughed as she left.

'She's a case. There's never a dull moment in this shop, Biff, and we've missed tea break. I'll go and put the kettle on. Cut us a slice of ham, will you? I've got new bread baps out the back.'

After the builders arrived Herton Hall was guarded by three white bull terriers with dark pink eyes and sharp white teeth. Jimmy Hawsley was bitten and had to be rushed to the doctor's surgery. The doctor gave him a hard time for trespassing, which set Jimmy's mum's teeth on edge. She started a rumour that the doctor was bribed, which was a lie. So then it was passed around that he'd been invited to Herton Hall for cocktails, which was true.

The builders finished mid July. School finished one week later. Herton Hall attracted children from the town like iron filings to Mrs Lewis's huge magnet, which she would take ceremonially out of its strong cardboard box, and pass to the nearest child to touch. No one would speak, not even to ooh and aah. All the pairs of eyes brown, blue, grey and green, with glasses and without, would shift and change as the chain of attracted pieces, paper clips, rusty nails from someone's pocket, safety pins from someone's dress, even forbidden razor blades, would overlap and dangle.

Just as silently, Herton's children avoided the pink-eyed, white-bristled, sharp-teethed dogs, shinned the three-feet-high dry-stone walls, skirted the rose bowers and advanced upon the outbuildings, the first week of the school holidays.

Herton's children were usually a hard-working bunch. They had coal to shovel from the free loads outside the miners' council house gates, into the coal holes out the yard; they had outside toilets to whitewash in the holidays; they had windows to clean and errands to run; babies to mind and allotments to weed. Whatever time there was for trespass and adventure they had earned. So most mums and dads didn't forbid raids on the Hall. They just didn't ask the wrong questions about raw knees or scruffy jumpers, grazed shins or scuffed toe-caps. A few of the granddads and nanans were told tearful tales and sworn not to tell the mums. And more than a few mums found rose thorns caught in woolly jumpers; and brick dust on the hems of summer dresses.

Two weeks into the holiday the fiesta was ended by the arrival of Mrs Mullière and the first batch of artists. The Herton Foundation for the Visual Arts was launched.

Lindsey and Rita had made a secret cave in the deep tangle of branches under the most remote fir tree on the edge of the grounds. The dogs were restricted to the town side of the house where the stone walls allured the other schoolchildren. The east side was almost impassable because of dense woodland that lay between the grounds of the Hall and the grazing fields belonging to Ryelands Farm.

There was never anyone else in the quiet woods. This was the place where the snowdrops drifted, and wild violets grew, and sweet briar roses.

The camp was hidden and safe. Two years ago the girls had made swings for the fairies and an old biscuit tin filled with water and half sunk into the ground had been the fairy queen's lake with a leaf boat for a ferry. Now they felt they were outgrowing the fairies, but neither of them removed the swings or the tin.

It was the second Tuesday since the Art Foundation began, and Rita and Lindsey were reading a comic, when the silence in the girls' camp was shattered.

A twig cracked in the direction of the Hall. They put fingers to their lips, eyes rolling, their secret about to be discovered. A branch next. It was dry. It broke like the sound of a trap firing. The girls were always careful of poachers' traps on the way to the cave. Their fingers tensed around each other's hands.

Lindsey wondered if a man might be approaching. 'Never talk to strangers,' Moss had warned. Lindsey didn't know all the facts of life, but she knew men shouldn't go near girls. She shivered and felt cold sweat down her back. What if . . . ? Another crack. Swish of a fir branch.

No barking, Rita realised. Whoever was coming hadn't got the dogs. She couldn't hear dog noises. She should have brought her own along, but the silly old thing always wanted to chase the cows and that was *really* trespass. You could get taken to the Juvenile Court for causing that. Swish of another fir branch. No calling. No talking. Whoever it was was alone. Rita was dying to have a pee and began to worry she might let it go from fright, and wet her knickers. At her age. What a terrible thing to happen. She clenched her thighs and hung on hoping the person would skirt around the fir tree, not notice the cave, make for the grazing fields and go off down the valley.

'Aah!' Lindsey let the word slip from terror. 'It's just a girl,' she exclaimed as the branches parted.

'Oh, heavens, you scared us silly. Oh, I must go out and have a pee. I can't wait.' Rita scrambled out while Lindsey returned the stare of a girl with dark curly hair, more than a year older than herself. Athletic-looking, in shorts and T-shirt, short socks and tennis shoes, she seemed slightly taller than Rita.

'You should't be in here,' said the girl. 'This is my aunty's place. What're you doing here?'

'Same as you, so there.'

'I'm exploring.'

'So're we. And we was here first. We live here. This is our cave. We found this two summers back and you're not invited.'

'I can come in if I want. It's my aunty's.'

'There's a spell on it. You don't know it. It's our spell. It's protected. 'Gainst trespassers like you.'

'I won't tell. If you let me stay too.'

Rita came back, flustered, with the tie of her dress caught in the band of her knickers, so that it hitched up at the back.

'You've got your dress caught up,' said the stranger.

'So what?'

'So I won't tell about you in my aunty's wood if you let me come here too.'

Rita and Lindsey regarded each other, like they'd seen Rita's mum and dad do when Rita asked a favour before they, the grown ups, had had a chance to 'talk private'.

'I'm Lerryn,' the stranger said. 'My Aunt Harriet, I call her Aunt Harry, owns the Art Foundation. I stay with her in the holidays sometimes.'

Lerryn watched their reactions and she knew she had them then. She had always been able to talk her way into things, and out of things. Her mum said she could sell stones to a quarryman and come off smiling. So she knew when they didn't interrupt her she might as well carry on. In for a penny in for a pound, and she was terribly lonely in Herton and they might want to stay at the cave and be friends.

'Aunt Harry's my mum's older sister. She lets me paint. I want to paint like her. More'n anything in the world. What do you want to be when you grow up?'

Caught off guard Lindsey said, 'A mother, with four babies.'

'A nurse,' said Rita. She wanted to add, 'And I'm going to make a mark on the world,' but she couldn't because Lerryn was a stranger and she'd only told Lindsey.

'Pooh,' said Lindsey getting her nerve back. 'Who wants to be an artist anyway. Silly job. Only posh people do daft things like that. Real girls grow up and get married and have babies. Maybe a little shop,' she added thinking of her nanan, 'and some factory work if there is any. To pay the rent and get nice things. If your husband's not very rich.'

'I'm never getting married,' said Lerryn.

'Your aunty-posh-pants got married. Or she'd never have started her silly Art Foundation.'

'I'll tell my aunt. I'm off then,' Lerryn turned to go.

Rita grabbed her arm. 'No. No wait a minute. We're sorry. Being rude 'bout your aunty. You stay.'

Lerryn sat down. Rita could see in the dim sunlight that she was trying not to cry. Remembering the isolation ward, her return to Herton, her fear of being all on her own in the juniors with no best friend, Rita came across more gently, 'If she's your aunty, then what's *your* name, your mum and dad, I mean?'

'Trevonnian,' Lerryn spelt it out, saw the girls relaxing a fraction, and took her chance with the rest. 'My aunt wrote off to this place in London that wanted extra girls working there, and she sent a photo. Well she's very pretty, was, she's middle aged now, but then she was just sixteen and they must've really admired her for her nerve. She's a real character. I really love my aunt. She got the son of the family firm to marry her. I don't know all the ins and outs. It was a huge firm, all to do with paintings and antiques.'

'You talk funny. Sort of singy and round.'

' 'Course I do. I talk like Cornish people and I'm proud of it. Aren't you proud of talking Yorkshire?'

'Never thought about it,' said Rita. 'I'm Rita. That's Lindsey, by the way. Do you want to be friends then?'

'Do you?'

'You're not to tell about the cave,' warned Lindsey.

'I won't.'

'Cross your heart, cut your throat and hope to die.'

'Cross my heart, cut my throat and hope to die.'

'Now shake on it,' said Rita, and they did. 'We'll all come here tomorrow morning if it's not raining.'

Herton Hall opened its doors to the girls because they were friends of Lerryn. Rita and Lindsey minded their Ps and Qs and took everything that was on offer. From the pantries to the attics the threesome spent the summer together. They made up plays about smugglers and turned the blue carpet into an ocean theatre; they took poster paints into the rose garden and made birthday cards for everyone they could think of; they sawed logs in the woodshed, and baked scones in the oven of the wood stove. They picked raspberries and strawberries and armfuls of flowers to take home in the long light evenings.

Lerryn was in her element. Looking out from the Hall window at night after she should have been asleep, she made out the shape of the hay ricks in the south fields and the apple trees in the orchard. The stables hid the tip, though nothing in Herton hid the sound of the buckets cabling, and as they whirred Lerryn imagined the men underground and on the sea. Although she was holidaying in Herton, Cornwall and the sea in all its moods would never leave her.

Until that summer, Lerryn had only had crushes on her women teachers. This time she had fallen for a girl, someone she could love who was nearly her own age. She never said a word to Lindsey, who seemed so happy, shining with pleasure at now having two friends devoted to her, and Lerryn wanted to kiss her. She daren't. It would have blown everything. There was no one at all to talk to about it. She had always known she would not get married. One look at her mum and dad, or at Aunt Harry with Uncle Pierre, made Lerryn's flesh creep. She daren't write it in her diary in case one of the cleaning ladies that Aunt Harry had employed from Herton chanced to find it. But Lerryn was sure. She knew that meeting Lindsey was important. She knew her feelings for Lindsey were 'taboo'. She'd heard that word discussed by many of the artists who were trying to break taboos in design and form. She loved the words they used when they were talking about their work; she longed for someone to tell her she was old enough to be a real artist; and she planned and schemed to be part of their world when she was independent.

She was almost thirteen. She felt it was too soon to tell all her hopes and dreams to her aunt. but she understood that she had her aunt's blessings because she was the daughter that Aunt Harry had longed for. So she hid the fact that at her age she knew what she wanted and what she didn't want; because it was supposed to be too early to know.

'You spend too much time with adults, Lerryn. Try making some friends of your own age,' her mum had said repeatedly before this trip to Herton. 'I wish your dad and I could give you things like my sister does. I do. I really do.'

'You do give me things, Mum. Just by letting me go and stay with her for holidays. I'm no trouble at any of her places. I do just what Aunt Harry tells me. I don't make any mess and I always tidy my room.'

'I should think so too. I wouldn't let you go if you didn't. I don't want my sister telling me you're a nuisance, now do I.'

'I won't be, I promise.'

'And try to find some nice girls your age to play with. All work and no play makes Jack a dull Boy.'

Lerryn thought, Well that's a bit silly if I'm a girl, but she replied, 'I'll try really hard, Mum. I'm sure there's lots of girls to play with in Herton.'

'I hope so. I don't want you to be lonely in that barn of a house and your Aunty's got her guests to entertain. She can't be with you all the time.'

Lerryn leaned her face against her arm, on the window ledge, as she watched the moon rising over Herton. Her arm was bare and slightly goose-pimpled from the night air. It was salty from the day because she hadn't had a bath. She licked the salt off her arm. When it was just her normal skin under her tongue she carried on licking, slow quiet tongue strokes from her wrist to the inside of her elbow. Thinking of the Cornish words for thunder and lightning, *taran-lughes*, her secret words for Lindsey. She had found them in the library in one of Aunt Harry's books. Her tongue spelled out the letters of the magical, spellbinding names. *Taran-lughes*. She was in love with a girl, though she was too young to be in love with anyone and it should have been a boy, anyway. But it never would. She didn't care. She'd found, in the library, a book called *The Well of Loneliness*. It was about rich women. It wasn't a happy book. She daren't tell anyone she'd read it. She'd been drawn to it by its title. It was how she felt. At the bottom of a well, but some wells came from underground streams and, letting her tongue stay wet on the inside of her arm, Lerryn imagined breathing in clear deep water, swimming through from the bottom of the well, into a crystal-clear underground river. She would swim and dive, no fear of the cold water, strong and sleek like a seal under the ice caps. She was following the stream until it joined a tributary, and flowed towards the open air. It would emerge in a patch of sunlight in a young woodland where primroses flowered in springtime in soft creamy butter clumps. She had some drawings of them. 'You spend too much time on your own Lerryn, with that damn sketch book.' She remembered her mum's voice. But it was only because her mum cared, really cared, wanted Lerryn to grow up with lots of friends and get married and be happy.

She would wade in the stream, clamber on to the bank, and run the rest of the way, skirting the lacy ferns around the furry banks of grass, through the wild garlic. Then she'd hear it. The sea on the pebble beach. Pulling and sucking. Pulling and sucking. Licking the pebbles just like she licked her own arm. The sea a mouth, her mouth, soft and wet and wanting to cry out from all the secrets hidden deep.

She returned to Cornwall with a promise from Lindsey to be pen-pals; and from Aunt Harry to take her again to Herton next summer.

Compared to Herton Hall, home did indeed seem poor. Her dad's wages as a hospital porter were so low, her mum worked as a cleaner for a wealthy family, many hours a week. How could they possibly understand me wanting to be an artist, sympathised Lerryn, who loved them both dearly. The most they can do is see it as my hobby, like Dad's fishing, or Mum's patchwork.

The following summer, longing to go to Herton, Lerryn found that waiting was easier if she took herself to her favourite place along the coast path.

Lerryn slithered slowly on her belly, on the soft turf, until she could peer down into Catherine's Cove over the edge of the cliffs. Head and neck in wild salt-smelling air, shoulders, arms, body and legs splayed on the firm turf. She knew and understood the danger of each inch along these cliffs only a few miles from Land's End. They were hers. This was the perfect ledge to enjoy the sound of the water vibrating on the rocks with a steady reliable rhythm. Here the old strong grey granite was firm, having withstood the weathering throughout time. It would last another few minutes, just for her. Here she could catch time and water and moments of danger as easily as the gulls, as they dropped into the sea barely splitting its surface, aiming for their prey with deadly accuracy. They fished, streamlined, their speed carrying them forward invisibly under water, until they emerged, bobbing white blotches of feathers, so far away that it seemed impossible.

Here were the best clumps of clinging mesembryanthemum, the flowers almost frolicking over the cliff face, defying height and salt; here in every crack and crevice tiny clusters of granite-loving sedum flowered in white pink and yellow, different from the varieties further around the coastline. Here the shocking-pink dianthus opened its tiny jagged petals revealing soft brown centres, and she loved the thin bluish green leaves, such a contrast. How did they survive here in the wind and the sun and the rain?

Deep breaths, seaweed and salt spray. Happiness. She mustn't stay too many minutes, like this. One deep breath too many, one moment of dizziness or lack of concentration and she'd slip, splat, lost in pieces on the rocks below like the remains of some sea monster's picnic. She used her knees and elbows, as usual, to inch back to safety, sat for a moment back on the warm grass, to gain her balance and then stood up. Keeping to the track she very carefully walked to her stone seat.

Far out to sea a mist was gathering. Like Merlin's cloak of invisibility in the legends of King Arthur and Tintagel, the mists were playing tricks with the horizon, washing it into the sea. They were taking the curve away, so the world was flat after all and unwary fishermen wouldn't know and would certainly drop off the edge. Lerryn was making her own cloak these days, to protect herself from her mum's questions about boyfriends, or rather the lack of interest in them.

Lerryn thought of Lindsey who had hardly bothered to answer her letters, and wasn't giving anything at all away. She seemed pleased that Lerryn was returning for this, their second summer together, but that was all. Lerryn had covered over her disappointment, telling herself she had been too enthusiastic again, probably overwhelming Lindsey with her ideas and details of this to do and that to do.

The sun warmed for a while and the mist lifted, playing light and shadows as the clouds moved, so that Lerryn half expected the lost land of Fair Lyonesse to rise from the water in shapes of hills and castles, and fields of flowers.

Until she had had Mrs Tindern for Art and for History, Lerryn hadn't thought much about being a Celt or the language or the legends. In junior school they'd 'done' King Arthur but that seemed as far away as Noah's Ark, and just about as likely. Then the magic woman had arrived. She encouraged Lerryn's mind like silver paint on drab canvas, touching and lifting, emphasising and discovering.

Lerryn had once let slip at home about Mrs Tindern and the Friday afternoon folk-tales. Her mum had been furious. 'How some teachers do earn a fine living off the rates while the rest of us are working our bones down.'

After that Lerryn kept her excitement, and her enjoyment to herself. Besides, how could her friends help falling asleep in class when they'd been up working on their families' farms since dawn, and had more hours to do after supper? Mrs Tindern knew what she was up to. Lerryn loved her for it. She always closed her eyes when the teacher started talking, her soft west country voice was so good, and she knew everything, or so it seemed. Lerryn could imagine the bal maidens, the girls and women who had worked the pit tops, hours and hours for just a shilling. And she half believed in the knockers who tapped out rhythm on the best lodes down the tin mines for their favourite miners, the ones who remembered to share their lunch each day with the other folk, the Pobel Vean, who lived on the astral plane. Woe betide the mean men, and the ones who simply forgot. For the knockers were the cleverest of the underground piskies and they could tap out a false rhythm too, leading the men astray, into danger.

Aunt Harry, on the other hand, said she didn't believe in piskies. When Lerryn had conveyed this to Mrs Tindern the woman teacher had raised one eyebrow which made her look just like a piskie, so Lerryn thought, and had said you didn't have to have an education to believe in the fairy folk, and if you had an education all the more reason to want to go deeper into it.

Mrs Tindern had looked at Lerryn for quite a few minutes, and said, 'You just need to love Cornwall. One day there'll come a time when people can't get enough of Cornwall and the Celts. But you'll probably be middle aged yourself, Lerryn, by then and I wonder if you will still be as interested as you are now. I wonder.'

Two weeks and she would be off to Herton with Aunt Harry. She was so excited, wanting to carry memories of the coastline, to draw and to paint. Secure, in her armchair of stone, which soaked up even the weakest sunshine for her so was always warm and welcoming, she watched and waited patiently, her attention on the waves at the foot of the cliff. Green and grey, they arched and curved, breaking and retreating. Lerryn had the feeling, an old familiar feeling, that someone was under the water, stirring it, swishing it this way and that with enormous sweeping movements of a hidden hand and arm.

It was said that smugglers had arrived at the cove whilst Old Catherine was sleeping. They had been carrying huge oblong trunks, so large it took two of them to shoulder the weight.

Old Catherine was so angry at being disturbed that she conjured up a storm. The smugglers were drowned. The treasure chests were turned to granite and flung to the base of the cliff, higgledy-piggledy.

Lerryn waited an hour for a glimpse of the granite treasure chests, for the waves to suck back further, a little further. Then for a few minutes there they were, the ones that happened to have fallen on top, exposed again.

A few moments later, the waves returned, cobalt and emerald, white and foaming jade.

Spray flew from the lids in all directions, until the sea hid the treasure again. Lerryn wondered if Catherine were watching, and whether the sudden glimpse of the boxes and chests pleased her as much as it pleased Lerryn.

The sun broke through as if someone had painted warm yellow into the clouds. Lerryn leaned back against the stone seat, letting the rays fall full on her face, wondering if this is how she would feel if, one day, Lindsey Abbotts might want to be kissed in the sun.

Eleven

The shop was empty, but there was plenty of work to do. Moss was cleaning the small wooden drawers and replacing the labels and Biff was stacking the bottom shelves with tins of fruit from heavy boxes. As they worked they discussed the good fortune of two of Grace and Mercy's distant relatives, Peggy and Stan, who had been employed as housekeeper and groundsman to run Herton Hall.

'Peggy loves the new kitchen up there. Yards of formica tops and all the mod cons you could think of.'

'Best thing they could've done, selling up and moving in there. They'll not be sorry. To tell you the truth it was them going to work for Mrs Mullière that set me to thinking.'

'I thought summat was on your mind. Come on then, best be out with it.'

'The fact is, Moss, I'm worried out of my mind about *our* future. What happens when we can't run this shop any longer. Where'll we live, how'll we manage?'

'You are a daft thing sometimes, love. Look at you, all in a state. Fancy getting yourself worked up like this when you could've shared it with me.'

'It's been going round and round. Didn't know where to start. I'm sixty-two and I don't want to be fretting about this when I'm seventy, and the rent's going up again. Not to mention the rates.'

'Right. Now then. Tonight after supper we shall both sit down together with a pen and paper and see if we can't sort some of it out, all right?'

'Yes. All right. We have to face facts. We can't stay here for ever and it was Peggy and Stan moving that set me to thinking.'

'Mind you, they'll have the same problem as us when they're ready to retire.'

'They will. But that's a long way off for them; and it isn't that far off for us.'

'Do you know, Biff, I was convinced Peggy'd top herself when little Neil died of meningitis. She's pulled through something wonderful. Good luck to the pair of them, that's what I say. Was that a bicycle bell?'

'It was. Look who's propping her bike against the wall.'

'Lindsey's out the back with Rita. No time to call her,' said Moss, lifting the counter flap and going through to the customer side as Lerryn entered the shop.

Opening her arms wide, Moss gathered Lerryn into the welcoming hug. 'Lovely to see you. We've missed you since last summer. Lindsey wanted you to live here all year.'

'Hello, Mrs Ferguson. Hello, Biff. It's lovely to be back. How are you both?'

Lerryn was taller, filled out. As usual she was wearing shorts and a light-weight cotton anorak, with tennis socks and shoes.

'We're fine, thanks,' said Biff, smiling ear to ear. 'All the better for seeing you again. How are your mum and dad?'

'They're both well. They said to send their best to you. I've been looking forward so much to seeing you all!'

'Well then let's not be delaying you any longer,' said Moss, lifting the counter flap again. 'Come through this way and I'll put the kettle on. Lindsey's in the yard. She has some new pets out there.'

When she saw Lerryn coming into the yard, Lindsey felt half excited and half scared. She said a brief, warm 'hello', but it was Rita who did most of the talking, asking Lerryn what the journey had been like and then saying she wasn't stopping long because she was going out with her new boyfriend, Steve.

Moss called them indoors. 'Here you are. Tea and scones. The biscuits are in this tin. I'm back into the shop but let me know if you're all going out won't you?'

Lindsey at last found her voice. 'Thanks, Nanan. Lovely scones. I'll be taking my bike up to Herton Hall soon, is that okay?'

Lindsey felt good near Lerryn and she poured the tea and handed out the scones feeling sort of tingly, not like she felt near Rita. She couldn't talk to anyone about it, though both her nanan and Biff were

111

easy to talk to about most things. She didn't know what it was about Lerryn that made her feel like this. She put it down to excitement and going to stay at Herton Hall with Lerryn, because there was a lot going on there.

'In a minute I'll take you out to see my newts, Lerryn. I've got three. The most beautiful is a female. I called her Helen of Troy. Then there are two males – Houdini, he's the one who keeps trying to escape and Oliver Twist, who is always hungry.' Rita sniffed and reached for another scone. Lindsey added, 'Do you like newts, Lerryn?'

'Yes. Tell you what,' said Lerryn, pausing for effect, 'Aunt Harry's giving us all a pond. Everything in it, you know.'

'Water?' asked Rita, as sarcastically as she could.

Lerryn ignored her, wondering silently if Rita was going to make life difficult, get jealous, feel left out. She had been invited to Herton Hall too, but had refused the invitation. Well, thought Lerryn, I shan't leave her out, no good antagonising Lindsey and those two are best mates. If I want to be near Lindsey, I'll have to be specially careful not to ruffle up Rita. She said, 'Not just water, *moving* water. There's going to be this pump thing to take it all in a tube to the top and let it make a waterfall. We can make it ourselves if we want. I thought you'd like it.'

Rita poured more tea, didn't reply and continued to look aloof and indifferent, but Lindsey said confidently, 'I would.' She liked Lerryn, and her aunt, come to that. She remembered Aunt Harry in a wonderful black velvet two-piece, tossing her flaming red hair as she laughed. What an aunt for anyone to have, especially someone who was lonely, in a village with no other girls her own age, like Lerryn at Catherine-in-Penwith. She was glad that Lerryn had written pen-friend letters. She wished she'd replied properly but she wasn't one for letter writing and she couldn't ask Rita to help her, not in a month of Sundays. 'I really would,' she added. 'It'd make a change. Will you be having some newts? I love newts. I adore newts, actually. Mine are in a vivarium now.'

'Ugh, not newts,' snorted Rita, and turning to Lerryn she said, 'Mrs Kinton, our new librarian, went to your precious Cornwall for a stupid holiday and read about your stupid monster thing, Morgawr, like Nessie only in Falmouth Harbour. I don't know if you've seen it, he she or it, and I don't care. It's only a giant newt anyroad. Silly woman came home from her holiday with this idea for a project for the *kids*.' Rita emphasised the word, curling her nose. 'To grow newts, of all things. Now, my little brothers have got newts in the bath, newts in the basin, newts in the living room, newts in the bedroom. Ugh. I am sick', she touched her belly, 'of bloody newts. As for you,' she turned on Lindsey, 'I know you love animals and I know you're my best friend but I . . . don't . . . like . . . newts. And I'm not spending my holiday mucking about in a bloody pond. You both do what ever you like. I'm going out with Steve. My *steady* boyfriend. See you later.'

Rita swept out, the back way, slamming the yard gate loudly.

Lerryn felt her grip on Herton slipping and sliding, as if Herton was one of the cliffs at Catherine's Cove and her ledge on which she sat safely had become slimy. If someone didn't reach out to catch her as she fell, she might crash on submerged rocks and disappear under the sea, lost for ever.

'It's good to see you again,' Lindsey reached out, caught hold of Lerryn's hand and let go quickly. 'I wanted to write long letters but I never know what to say. I thought you might think I was silly, so I only wrote a bit, then I dried up.'

'What about Rita? She's your best friend.'

'Oh she'll come round, she always does, eventually. I'll tell you all about that, later on. Let's go and see my newts. I want to show you Helen of Troy. She's *so* beautiful. Then I want to dash back to your place to see your pond. Oh, I'm so excited! Come on.'

The workmen had dug an enormous hole between the sycamore trees and the rose gardens within sight of Lerryn's bedroom window. The hole dipped and curved with a ledge around the edge and had been lined with soft sand. The workmen were stretching a lining over it and placing heavy stones here and there at intervals to hold the lining around the edge. They were men from the next town, strangers to Lindsey, who knew the local builders. They left the lining in place and went off for lunch.

Aunt Harry came along the drive, wearing beautifully cut slacks and a matching casual jacket in a pale cream colour that looked stunning with her red hair. Like a large, beautiful opera singer on television, Aunt Harry gave a wonderful performance but wanted all the attention in return.

'Hello, Lindsey. How do you like the pond?'

'It's so big. It's smashing.'

'And are you taking part in young Mrs Kinton's newts project?'

'You bet. I love animals. Especially newts.'

'Would you like to bring your newts to live here in this pond? There's plenty of room.'

Lindsey looked surprised and Lerryn felt uncomfortable. She looked down at her feet, hoping Lindsey would stand up to Aunt Harry, who could be quite overwhelming sometimes. At that moment Lerryn realised that although Aunt Harry would help her make her dream come true, she really wanted to be independent, to become an artist by herself, far away from her aunt. Aunt Harry set the price so high. All adults did.

Lindsey meanwhile was speaking very calmly and firmly and being extremely polite, while it was Aunt Harry's turn to look surprised. 'It's very kind of you. Thank you. I'd like to think about it.'

Lerryn wanted to cheer but she kept right out of it.

'Quite right,' Aunt Harry was saying. 'Take all the time you want. I like a young woman with spirit and you certainly have that, Lindsey. We could do with lots more girls like you in the world. Now why don't you both,' she turned to include Lerryn, who was still very embarrassed, 'go and find Stan. He's in the end shed mending the lawn mower. I don't know what I'd do without him. He's so good with machines. Plenty of spare wellingtons in the shed. And surprise, surprise a tank full of newts. Mind you I had a job to get them. There's not a newt to be bought in the whole of Herton. I had poor Peggy traipsing round for a week. So I had these delivered from Sheffield this morning. Now off you go, and I must be away in a few minutes. I'll be back late tonight. Have a lovely time, 'bye now.'

With that she strode off towards the kitchen with a wave of her hand, her footsteps crunching on the new gravel drive.

The afternoon sun was hot on their backs as they began to fill the pond. They pulled off their thin summer jackets and, in T-shirts and shorts and wellingtons, they sprayed each other with the hose, and took turns to splash water into the lining of the pond.

When it was Lindsey's turn with the hose, Lerryn took off her wellingtons and socks and lay back on the grass, stretching her bare legs in the sun and putting her arms up behind her head as a head rest. She had almost everything she wanted and it seemed a perfect afternoon. She watched Lindsey, who was unaware that she was being watched as she concentrated on filling the huge pond, her movements happy and relaxed. Lerryn noticed that Lindsey's wet T-shirt was clinging to her body where her breasts were just starting to grow. A warmth filled Lerryn's belly, deep inside, not for the first time, and she longed to touch Lindsey but knew that she wouldn't. Lindsey was taller and her whole body was gradually changing shape, and her pony tail bobbed this way and that as she moved her arms and shoulders, working with the hose. Lerryn found her far more interesting than any old pond.

Lindsey worked on, unawares. She was thinking of Aunt Harry's offer about the newts, and was upset and angry, excited and disturbed all at the same time, though mostly she was thrilled with the afternoon, the pond, and the feeling of summer sunshine drying out her T-shirt.

She asked herself if she was just being childish (Rita was maybe right, and she was still a kid) not trusting Aunt Harry just because she had pots of money. Besides, thought Lindsey, spraying the stones the far side of the pond lining and returning the hose to the water level in the pond, Lerryn's own parents were very poor and if it wasn't for Aunt Harry, Lerryn would be stuck at home lonely, with no one to make friends with. The long summer holidays would be awful if you had to spend them all on your own (except for little brothers and everyone knew they didn't count). It's all too much to think about, she decided, watching fascinated as the lining took its shape from the sand and the weight of the water stretched it tight. The stones around the edge were so heavy that the pond lining held in place and the water slowly crept up.

Out loud Lindsey called, 'Do you want a turn, Lerrie? I'm going to wade in, before it gets too deep.' She began to pull off her wellingtons, letting the hose lie spurting on the grass for a moment.

Lerryn, running barefoot towards Lindsey, didn't see the wet grass, slipped, began to topple, and tried to regain her balance. Lindsey, with her wellies half off, tried to reach out to help Lerryn, caught her hand as she tumbled towards the pond, and was too late. Joined to Lerryn and unable to stand up in her half-wellies, she crashed into the water on top of Lerryn shrieking with surprise and scattering arcs of shining water and peels of laughter.

Stan hurried to the scene where the girls were having hysterics with Lindsey on top of Lerryn in the water, trying to pull off her wellies.

Stan, who had been primed by Peggy and Harry to expect such an outcome, roared with laughter at the pair of them, wishing he had a camera. 'Look at yer, completely soaked like a pair of drowned rats. Come on out 'o there, the pair on yer. Go on,' he added, 'as the two drenched girls crawled out onto the grass. 'Go on, get yourselves indoors. Our Peggy's got dry things for yer and hot soup. Yer can finish filling it tomorrow.'

That evening Lindsey didn't have to make do, as she'd expected, on a camp bed. Instead a divan had been placed in Lerryn's room for her and both beds were made up with fresh sheets and hot water bottles, because Herton Hall was chilly even in summer.

Snuggled in her own bed and with her arms around the hot water bottle, Lindsey said, 'Hey, Lerrie, did Aunt Harry tell you the badgers have arrived in these woods? Right near where mine and Rita's cave used to be. The new housing estates going up disturbed them; they had to travel here to find a new home.'

Lerryn spoke from the next bed, where she was curled, facing Lindsey, with her hot water bottle on her stomach. 'Aunt Harry says she's going to buy up some extra fields and woods, so the badgers can't get driven away again.'

She buys whatever she wants whenever she wants, thought Lindsey. I wish she'd buy a home for Nanan and Biff when they've to leave like the badgers. Out loud she said 'Good. At least they'll have somewhere safe. If I had pots of money like your aunt I'd have done that. Look out of the window, Lerrie. I'm glad we left the curtains open, the sky's on fire. We'll be able to see the moon when it gets dark. Do you like the moon as much as me?'

Lerryn swallowed. 'As much as you?'

'Yes, as much as I do?'

'Yes. I love the moon. Lindsey, did you remind Rita you'd not be home tomorrow?'

'Yes, but she doesn't come round to my house on Sundays any more, because she goes to his mum's for Sunday lunch. She says she's courting.'

'Courting?'

'Yes. Isn't she daft, starting so soon. Listen, Lerrie, can I tell you something?'

'About Rita?' Lerryn waited as Lindsey nodded, looking uncomfortable and guilty. Then she added, 'But Rita's your best friend and she feels bad already because I'm here. It puts her nose out. Perhaps you'd better not tell me anything.'

'I know. But she gets like that anyway. She has terrible moods sometimes. But I've got to tell somebody.'

'All right. I promise.'

'She lets him make love bites. I've seen them. And not just on her neck. On her *waist*. She showed me because she says having a boyfriend is what being a girl is all about. But it put me right off instead. I'd never let a boy do that, would you?'

'Me? No.' Lerryn held her hot water bottle closer, comforted by its furry cover as well as its warmth. 'Do you like boys, Lindsey?'

'They're all right, but I'd rather have my newts actually.'

They both giggled, feeling relieved for different reasons known only to themselves.

'Actually I asked Nanan and Biff about it. Not the love bites, I mean about boy friends, you know, just generally. Biff says I've plenty of time. No need to hurry up like Rita. There's lots and lots of time. For you too, Lerrie.'

'Me? Oh boys don't interest me at all. I'd rather have my painting. And I *love* coming here to Herton.'

Lindsey yawned and settled down to go to sleep. 'Night night, Lerrie. I want you to come here every single summer. I wished you lived here, all year round.'

Outside the window the sky was now dark and the sycamore leaves were like bats hanging, silhouetted.

Lerryn closed her eyes, and before the first bat had flown off in to the night she was fast asleep.

The problem of taking her newts to Herton Hall gnawed at Lindsey. One lunchtime, back home on her own for a short time, she decided to find out what her nanan and Biff felt about the idea.

'Biff,' she began in a tone that signalled squall and rainstorms, 'would my newts stand a better chance in Aunt Harry's pond?'

'Better chance of what, love?' Biff replied, cutting slices of cheese and buttering thick crusty bread.

'Well, I'm all upset and I don't know what to do and I can't talk to Lerrie in case she gets upset too.'

'Whatever's the matter, Lindsey love?' asked Moss, pouring tea and passing Lindsey a mugful.

'Well, you know Rita and me call Aunt Harry Aunty posh-pants?' Moss and Biff nodded. 'It's because she has got pots and pots and pots of money. She wants me to bring Helen of Troy and Houdini and Oliver Twist to live in her pond. And I don't know why she asked me. And well, I wondered if rich people are always so greedy. She's got a whole tankful of newts of her own, so mine would get mixed up with hers and maybe even get bullied or something. And she's very nice, she's a very, very nice lady and ever so kind to me. I mean she got me a real divan bed just for me to stay there. Not saving up for it like you'd have to. She's kind and very funny and I really like her, but I think she's got a real nerve wanting my newts as well. Is that selfish of me?'

'Now why would it be selfish, Lindsey?' asked Moss as gently as she could, yet feeling that she wanted to storm up to Herton Hall and thump Harriet Mullière for so churning up her granddaughter.

'Well, for a start, I'd be sharing my newts with Lerrie, and for another thing they might have more space, a better life. After all, it's a bit squashed out in our yard.' Lindsey thought of the Peabody flat and being sent away for a better life and she started to cry. Huge drops ran down her face and she wiped them on her sleeve. Biff fished a hanky out of her trouser pocket and passed it across to her. She always liked to borrow Biff's hanky. It was always a clean one, all soft and ironed. 'And for another thing, Helen of Troy mightn't fancy Houdini or Oliver Twist and then she'd not be reproducing.' Lindsey spoke the word slowly, having learned it from her newts book.

Moss and Biff exchanged glances; they daren't even smile let alone laugh, or the shower would become thunder and lightning, both of which were imminent.

'And why don't you want to take them there?' asked Biff.

'How did you know I didn't want to, Biff?'

'Because if you did it would be different and you wouldn't be so upset would you?'

'No. I wouldn't.' More tears. 'I always get upset when anybody's lonely. Lerryn's lonely and I'm glad I'm her friend. I think she's wonderful. So I thought it might help if I took my newts there. But she's going home in a few days and then my newts won't have anyone either. Only a great big lake of a pond thing and they'll all escape, you know what Houdini's like, and never find their way back to me. Then they'll be lonely and so will I without them, and Aunt Harry should have thought of all that, shouldn't she?'

They nodded and Lindsey broke then into pieces, sizzling and shuddering like an electric storm in the sky, and she put her head on her arms on the table, sobbing. Biff came round and sat beside her, and folded her into her arms.

'It's all right. All right. Come on now. You don't have to do anything you don't want to. Aunt Harry will understand and so will Lerryn, if you tell her.'

'I couldn't tell Lerryn. She needs Aunt Harry, so she can get to be an artist. Her mum and dad are really really poor. Much worse off than us.'

'We're not badly off, Lindsey. We've food and heat and a roof over our heads. The shop is hard work and long hours but we are doing all right, love.' Moss spoke quietly and wondered what Lindsey had overheard about their future plans and worries. They would have to be more careful if the girl was going to become so distressed. In an effort to calm Lindsey right down, Moss said, 'Take me outside and show me that vivarium again. Maybe we could make it a little bit bigger. Come along.' Determinedly, Moss stood up and led the way into the back yard. Biff put her arm around Lindsey and they followed Moss.

At the vivarium they stopped and peered closely at Lindsey's newts.

'They seem all right to me,' said Moss. 'What do you think Biff, love?'

'I think they're doing fine. But we could extend their home a bit. Look, there goes Houdini,' replied Biff. 'He *is* splendid, isn't he?'

Lindsey bowled a question at Biff faster than a Yorkshire cricketer. 'Could he possibly be a she? Could I have made a silly mistake? I know he hasn't a frill down his back and he's sort of in between to look at. I don't think he's ugly enough for a he, even for a newt. Were you good looking as a boy, Biff?'

'That's not for me to say,' Biff ducked instinctively.

Moss fielded spontaneously, thinking how on earth did Lindsey dream up that question at this of all times. Aloud she said 'I can't imagine you were ever not good looking, Biff, and I didn't know you as a boy. Come on, I shouldn't have interrupted lunch like this, let's all go and finish it or we'll have no afternoon left.' Moss turned to go indoors.

Biff let out a sigh of relief but Lindsey was oblivious, having recovered from the tempest, as always, as quickly as she'd begun it. Lindsey flung her arms around Biff and hugged fiercely. Then she ran in after Moss and once inside she kissed her. 'That's it then. I'm all right now. She's not having my newts. She'll have to make do with her own, won't she?'

'Now what about finishing your lunch, Lindsey?' asked Moss.

'I'm not hungry any longer, Nanan. Can I take an apple? I want to get back to be with Lerrie. She'll have finished her painting now and I want to go out on the bike. 'Bye. I'll be all right now. And thanks, I do love you both.'

Yesterday had been 5 September 1958, her fourteenth birthday. Lerryn, back in Cornwall, had been with her mum to Mevagissey but there hadn't been time to draw anything, so Lerryn kept her mind open like a camera, recording on to colour film; and now with coloured pencils, very good expensive ones in a tin from Aunt Harry for her birthday, she sketched uninterrupted. She was glad to be back, loved September at Catherine's Cove, loved living here so near the sea.

Herton had been landlocked, its secrets held in tight by the hills and fields which surrounded it. She had held her own in equally. Everyone seemed to be on about boyfriends, marriage, families, children. The men artists at Herton Hall on courses phoned home to wives and teenagers, wives and toddlers, wives and grandmothers in granny annexes, wives and babies, pregnant wives, and working wives. Wives wives wives. Rita talked boys; Peggy and Stan talked about boyfriends for Lindsey and Lerryn. Boys boys boys. There had been no way at all to escape the messages. The only person in Herton who seemed uninterested in boys was Lindsey, and Lerryn dare not breathe a word of what she had hoped, to the special girl she had hoped it with.

Now she drew yesterday's images, beginning first with Mevagissey harbour, full of boats at high tide. She had sat up on the hillside with her mum, enjoying fish and chips out of newspaper and a bottle of fizzy lemonade. Below them in the sparkling harbour, boats had been bobbing. Halliards had snapped and cracked against the masts; bells had been clinking and tinkling; and mooring ropes had tightened and slackened with the rising and falling of the tide.

Some boats were ready to leave, full of visitors about to be taken out of the harbour, paying by the hour to see the sea. Others were fastened as if they'd never be let loose, like Lerryn herself.

She wanted to be an artist. But her mother said it was only for posh girls, and that Lerryn should leave school at fifteen and start a hairdressing apprenticeship.

The boats had bobbed in sympathy with Lerryn yesterday, straining at their moorings, ready to be cast off, make new journeys. Beyond the harbour the wide open sea beckoned them. It had been calm, hardly a ripple, deep blue and darker under the cliffs where the rocks lay in sword-sharp splits, barely hidden under the sea's soft surface.

None of the images was lost on Lerryn, especially since her wonderful mornings with the tutor for water-colours, back in Herton Hall. Blending, deepening, layer upon layer, experimenting, light, shade, depth, texture. Waves of excitement as she learned the medium. Techniques cutting through the secrets of the sea, like the prows of fishing boats cleaving the water.

Lerryn recorded picture after picture with the pencils that were so exciting to bring to the cliffs because they could be layered and blended, so that she had scope even though she was crouched as usual in her stone armchair without paints or brushes, pots of water or rags to wipe the paints.

She had absorbed her day in Mevagissey enjoying the bustle of people in summer colours; the crowd which moved and changed on the quayside. People catching the last week of the school holidays. Bright clothes: pinks, blues and yellows. Reds, whites and all shades of orange, apricot and salmon pink.

Best of all she recalled and sketched the hats. Every description. Kiss me quick. I love Cornwall. I love Mevagissey. I'm with her. I'm with him. Straw hats. Canvas hats. Hats on babies in pushchairs; on old ladies in the sun outside cafés where even the table awnings looked like hats. Panamas for protection and boaters for fun. Hats hanging on strings dangled from shop fronts; hats around vendors' necks as they sold hats and newspapers at stands. Floppy and flippant; starched and prim. Hats with feathers; and hats with ribbons.

A couple of days from now and Lerryn would have to wear her school beret again, if she could remember which drawer she'd shoved it into. She would see Mrs Tindern, and some of her class friends from the other side of Penzance, and there'd be catching up to do. There were some she quite liked, they'd been together for all the years at secondary school, but she didn't look forward to the questions about boyfriends. She just wasn't interested, and she was sure she was growing up to be, well, she didn't dare name it even to herself, but it separated her from the other girls, who would have sent her to Coventry if they'd guessed.

She stopped her drawings and placed her pencils carefully in the right places in the tin. Suddenly it seemed a lifetime until next summer in Herton: and even that wasn't definite, depending on Aunt Harry's plans and expeditions. The sun had moved far to the right, and was slowly getting ready to dip towards the horizon. The temperature had dropped and Lerryn shivered.

Aunt Harry might trip and track all over Europe (she had been hinting at the States recently too) but her niece was not of the same line; did not go to a private school; would not know how to pay rent money to her mum, unless she left school at fifteen to work in the salon in the village.

She looked down the cliff, past the clinging flowers, blue, white and lovely shades of pink, yellow and cream, to the rocks slashed by waves, shaped by storms, and seriously considered letting herself fall, free-fall, one-flight, one only; a one way downward ticket. She gathered all her courage, stood up, and with her art materials safely in her shoulder bag, she carefully picked her way to the narrow footpath that led over the cliffs to home.

Twelve

'I want to go to London.'

The statement rang loud as the pit hooter through the house behind the shop. Moss put down her knitting. Biff stopped in the middle of washing up the Sunday lunch, turned and looked across to the table. Lindsey was staring into the tea mug. She loved a strong cuppa after lunch. Outside it was a clear wide open day and Biff had been about to suggest a bus ride up into the hills . . .

'I suppose it pulls me like it did my mum,' added Lindsey. It was August 1963; she had been seventeen in April.

Moss swallowed, and fought back a tear behind her glasses. Lindsey saw it and rushed on. 'You won't be losing me. But Rita's off to Leeds to start her training. Peter's going to London to study geology. He says I can share a flat with him. I mean, we've been going out for the past two years anyway, and we don't have to get married, not these days.' Pause. Then into the thick silence, dense and heavy like day-old Yorkshire pudding, she challenged, 'You haven't and you've both been happy. It's love and commitment that matters. Not getting married. A bit of paper won't keep us together. We don't need it.'

'It's not about the bit of paper,' began Moss, 'it's about *us* facing the end of a small miracle.' Moss's arthritis was troubling her. She momentarily thought, as she eased herself out of the chair, that if they spent as much on medical research as on the H bomb they were surely clever enough these days to find a cure. She edged over to the table and held herself upright by resting both hands on the back of a dining chair. 'We couldn't stop you, we wouldn't even if we could. You have only been on loan to us, and you've brought us more than we could ever have hoped for. We both knew this was coming, you've been giving us the signs for months.' Lindsey sat back in her chair taken by surprise. 'Biff and I both left home at your age. If you're going we'd rather you went out without any hurt or upset. It's just that . . .'

'That the time will never be right for us,' added Biff. 'It's *your* timing. It has to be. It's *your* life. There will be changes here soon anyway. We're ready to retire. We've been to see about that house to rent in Church Lane.'

'The one just down from the Vicarage,' interrupted Lindsey, adding, 'It's a lovely little house, Biff. Will there be . . .'

'A room for you. Of course. Herton's your home. Come back whenever you want to.'

'I love you, Biff, and you, Nanan. I want to go but I'm scared. It's such a long way. If Peter was going to Sheffield University, I'd not think twice. I could come home weekends and see you. But London's so far. But I've got to do it. I don't want to be in Herton without Rita.'

'We know that, Lindsey, love. We've talked late at night, haven't we, Biff?'

Biff nodded, unable to speak for the tightness around her throat. She felt strangled as usual by her collar and tie. She wanted to scream out to Lindsey to find a woman, love a woman, not run off to the capital of England with some whipperty-gipperty boy of eighteen, however nice a local lad he might be. Unconsciously she pulled at her tie, a gesture that Moss had come to recognise over the years whenever Biff was trying to get out of her disguise. Moss had never mentioned it to Biff. To anyone else the gesture was ordinary, barely noticeable and certainly not a symbol of despair.

'Come over here away from that damn sink, Biff,' chided Moss, 'you look as if you should have a ball and chain round your foot.' As Biff hesitated, she she added, 'Your granddaughter's in need of a hug more'n that damn sink is, and so am I for that matter. There's nothing like a hug at times like now. Now, come on love, hobble across this two yards of carpet for goodness sake, and let's be giving our Lindsey a right and proper send off.'

It was mid-September when into the grocer's shop in Herton there strode a young woman carrying an artist's portfolio under her left arm. She wore her dark brown hair short and curled and was dressed to kill in black corduroy slacks with a bright white jacket and black shirt.

If that girl's not a lesbian, I'm a man, thought Biff immediately, surprised at the word that came into her head.

'Do you remember me?'

Recognition, because of the sing-song voice.

'Lerryn, what an amazing change. We often wondered what happened to you. That last summer you came here, and a few letters to Lindsey, then nothing till now.' Biff extended a hand which Lerryn shook warmly. 'Hang on a minute while I call for Moss.'

Biff limped to the lobby and Lerryn stood waiting, enjoying the sameness of the old-fashioned shop, which reminded her, as it had always done, of the village store back home. Cornwall had changed too in the intervening years, accommodating to the new demands of the sixties' visitors, altogether more sophisticated than the fifties' families had been.

Moss hurried in, followed by Biff, and she lifted the counter hinge and came through to the customer side. She opened her arms and so did Lerryn as they stood hugging and grinning with a sense of belonging.

'Oh this is wonderful. One door closes and another door opens,' Moss said over her shoulder to Biff. 'Isn't that so, Biff?'

'It certainly is,' replied Biff and in answer to Lerryn's look of slight bewilderment explained, 'Lindsey left for London last month. It has been so empty here. It's wonderful to see you and . . . '

'She left for London?'

'Look. It's nearly closing time. I'm going to do something I never do. I'm going to shut up shop a bit early. Come through the back, and have some supper with us, then we can all catch up.'

'Oh yes. Yes, please,' Lerryn nodded, about to start shaking with disappointment and determined not to show it. She suspected Lindsey's granddad of guessing, he'd always been a perceptive soul, and as men went she was fonder of him than most, so she followed Moss thankfully into the back kitchen.

Biff pulled down the awning and took in the 'OPEN' sign that said bread and dairy products, fresh daily. People would have missed it if Biff hadn't put it out each morning, and would have known something was wrong. Friends would have knocked to make sure Moss wasn't ill, her arthritis being much worse this year; or would be wondering if Biff had gone down with the flu that was decimating the old people in Herton. No one needed to know what Biff sold, and they all took it for granted the products were fresh daily. Frank Smith's reputation was unsullied and Mr Ferguson's prices were just as good as Frank's had been, given that this was 1963 and everything was going up, and up.

Mr Johnson saw Biff taking in the sign, and hurried over, looking at his watch. 'You're shutting up shop early then, Biff?'

'I am. We've got a most unusual visitor and I'm making history. It's the first time I've done it and no doubt if it's up to you it'll be the last. Can I do owt for you, Mr Johnson?'

'It's the wife's migraine again. Me daughters is all over to Sheffield today, gallivanting as usual. So there I am managing the missus on me tod and run out of marge. You got time for half a pound?'

'Half a pound coming up, Mr Johnson.'

Biff found it quicker to get the half pound than argue the case with

Mr Johnson and by the time he had gone, the clock in the shop said closing time.

Biff sighed ruefully. So much for getting away with it. There'd been no one in the shop for the last hour, but it was always the same. Toast falls butterside down, except for Mr Johnson's. He had marge.

'The girls were really sad when you didn't come back to Herton the next summer, Lerryn. I think they missed the good life up there at your aunt's place. Lindsey was all for being friends with you summer in, summer out.'

'You'd have been good for our Lindsey,' said Biff quietly.

There was an awkward silence. Biff thought, I'm right. I'm sure I am. She came back because she loves Lindsey.

Lerryn thought, Biff seems *so* sympathetic. So does Moss. If they only knew how I really feel about Lindsey, would they understand? After all, Herton people are set in their ways, just like the people back home.

'More ham?' asked Moss

'No thanks, Mrs Ferguson, I couldn't. You've given me such a feast. It's very kind of you.'

'So what's been happening to you all these past summers then?'

'Well, nothing much, really. My parents, especially my father but not only him, mother too, they thought, or rather decided, that I was getting ideas above my station at my age. All the art stuff.'

'And were you?' asked Moss, gesturing to top up Lerryn's tea mug, and receiving a smile and nod.

'I suppose so. You think you know everything at thirteen. I was pretty unliveable with at home. The only time I felt like my real self was when I was painting and I could only do that fully when I was with Aunt Harry. You see, my side of the family, my father and mother, they're not used to money and they don't trust any of the ideas that people with money have. They think of me as betraying them and my home, by wanting to be an artist, and that's because I can't be one if I stay there. I could go to evening classes and have it all as a hobby. But not seriously train or anything like that. Actually, it makes me laugh to think back because the first time I told Lindsey and Rita about it they said the same as my parents. That was before they had a chance to paint outside in the grounds . . . '

'Birthday cards. We've still got them.'

'Have you really, Mrs Ferguson?'

'Call me Moss, dear. Now you're a young woman it seems more fitting.'

'I always think of you as Moss. Because I liked your name so much when I first heard it, and Biff's. Where did your name come from, Biff?'

'Oh just a nickname from the full name. Years ago. I can barely recall it.' Biff pulled at the collar and tie, and Moss patted Biff's arm and said, 'Put the kettle on again, will you, love? I'm dry as a bone with all this talking.'

'I'd better be going.'

'Don't be daft, Lerryn. We don't get that many young visitors. We're delighted.' Moss realised she'd made a bit of a gaffe, and tried to put Lerryn at ease. 'Are you on holiday here now?'

'Not really, Moss. I, er, I had a chance to join one of the courses and I, er, I thought it'd be good to meet Lindsey again after all this time. I'll never forget her or Rita, or anything about those summers in Herton. They were important to me. Herton's a special place.'

Lerryn noticed the look and smile that passed from Moss to Biff and back again. They were suddenly much younger. Like teenagers in love. A fleeting moment, then gone, hidden under grey hair and tired bones. She noticed Biff had a habit of tugging at his tie. It was quite endearing.

They waited for her to continue, eager it seemed for a link with someone of Lindsey's age. She realised they all wanted to be near Lindsey so it brought them closer to each other.

'I did as my parents asked and started a hairdressing apprentice-ship. They had several rows with Aunt Harry about it, but she couldn't offer me anything better. She lives in all her different places up and down this country; that's when she's not on the Continent travelling with her husband's family. Besides, I really love my home. I finished the apprenticeship in three years, then I made myself get through the next years there until I was nineteen. Now I'm going to stay at my aunt's place in London, and get hairdressing work. She has contacts in all the top salons as you'd expect. It's strange, straddling so many different worlds, but I can do some induction courses at night school, and then I hope for the Slade.'

'Aiming high.'

'Yes. I want to be excellent at my art, Biff. I want the best training I can get. I always have.' Lerryn shrugged and grinned, embarrassed at having talked so much, revealed her hopes and dreams. Some of them.

'Well if you're going to be in London, you can get in touch with Lindsey there. She's working in a factory near Old Street, sewing gloves, bless her. She'd only been in London two days when she started. Peter's only on a grant so they're very short of money,' added Moss, trailing off as she and Biff saw Lerryn flinch and recover, maintaining her poise and struggling to keep hold on dignity. The flinch told them what they'd both guessed. They each wanted then to take Lerryn in their arms and comfort her, telling her she wasn't alone, that they were women who loved one another, but they had to stay silent. Separated from the young woman who needed them; isolated from the new generation of women growing into a world of fast-changing attitudes and opinions. Where a Lerryn could dare to dress like a Lerryn, and come searching for a 'friend' like Lindsey.

'Who is Peter?'

'He's a young man from Herton, who asked her to go and live with him, while he studies geology and geography there. His parents disapprove. But we felt she should make her own decision. She was very determined. You know her. She can be thunder and lightning if she's made up her mind.'

'You amaze me, saying that. I thought I might be the only one who thought of her like that. I've always had exactly that image for her. We have a Cornish phrase for it.'

They didn't ask her, not wanting to pry further. She was shaken and sad, they could see that. It grieved them. Moss scribbled Lindsey's address on a piece of paper for Lerryn, but she was certain that the young woman would not contact Lindsey in London.

Thirteen

In July 1966 Lindsey was travelling home to Herton with Pete to tell Moss and Biff about the baby. She and Pete had married quietly and quickly as soon as Lindsey knew she was pregnant.

Pete had surprised Lindsey by being delighted about the pregnancy. It was she who was disturbed by its unexpectedness, not he. Now that his degree finals were over, with an upper second in geology, he had landed exactly the job he'd wanted and been working towards – a good opportunity with the Derwent Valley Water Board. So now he wanted everything else too. A wife, a family, a home and a wide circle of friends to share it with.

'Anything could blow us apart,' he said, when trouble escalated in the Middle East.

'How, when we love each other? It's all so far away, Pete.'

'That's not what we all thought when we went through the Cuba crisis, or the assassination of Kennedy. I have this feeling sometimes that we shouldn't wait for any chance at being happy and settled. Live the life we want, the way we want to.'

'I love it that you want what I want, Pete. I always have. There aren't a lot like you.'

'Oh, unique am I? Well you're pretty wonderful yourself. Times might be changing fast, but love's still love isn't it? I love you, Lindsey. I know we'll be happy in Yorkshire again.'

'Are times really changing that fast, Pete? I dunno. I didn't see much change in the glove factory . . . Hours and hours for low wages. That's no different from Nanan and Biff.'

'You don't have to do that any more, love. Not with me getting this job. This is what it's all been for. Beautiful country out there by the Ladybower; rented cottage. We'll be happy. All three of us.'

'I hope so. I shan't miss the hours but I shall miss the company . . . I had a lot of friends in that factory by the time I left, Pete. I don't know what I'm going to do all day.'

She paused, thinking about the glove factory, while Pete concentrated on his driving. They always used the M1 when to-ing and fro-ing to London.

Turning to look at Pete, Lindsey saw a resemblance to her granddad. She loved Biff, and it had always been Pete's similarity in temperament to Biff that had attracted her to him.

She thought of all the ways in which Biff was considerate, and smiled to herself, remembering Rita's comment: 'Your granddad never leaves the toilet seat up. You are lucky. In my house the toilet always smells awful because of my little brothers, and I'm the one that has to bleach it. And they never put the bloody seat down. Nor does my dad. Mum's always on at him and Philip and Neil. She might as well talk to the wall. If I lived with a nice man like your granddad I'd think I was so lucky.'

Lindsey had asked her nanan, 'Nanan how did you get Biff always to put the seat down? Rita wants to know, 'cos she's so fed up with her dad and her brothers.'

128

'Biff's easy to live with, that's all. We've never had a bother with it.'

So that had been that. It had taken a bit longer to work on Pete, but he liked a quiet life, so he'd given in. No bother at all, like Nanan said. They must both be lucky with the kind of men they'd found. But there was no doubt that once she'd lived with a man like Biff around the house, she'd had high expectations about the ways men should behave at home. And, so far, Pete had come through quite well. Of course, Lindsey thought to herself, keeping quiet while Pete was driving, it was hard for a man, any man, to understand things from a woman's point of view. She was sure that if men could get pregnant things would be very different. Even for the considerate ones like Pete, they didn't have to think every time they had sex that this might mean a baby, growing inside their own body. She looked sideways at Pete's stomach. They'd often joked about him getting pregnant. If only he could their future would be secure. They could sell the story to the *News of the World*, exclusive, make a fortune and live comfortably ever after. Then she could get pregnant in the normal way and there would be no problem about money or nannies. It would all have been taken care of.

She had written some hilarious letters to Rita about it, and had felt happy and comical when she'd read out Rita's replies. She wrote that Steve was thinking about it. Maybe they could be the world's first foursome with both their men pregnant. Even more fame; even more millions.

Lindsey missed Rocky and Maureen, her two close friends from the factory.

Rocky was thirty-seven. She was a Black woman, thin and warm, with a graceful manner and a little grey in her hair. Lindsey always thought of her as one of the most neatly dressed women at work. Summer and winter, Rocky liked to wear pleated skirts and a blouse and cardigan. As Rocky talked she used her arms and shoulders. It was like ballet. Lindsey sighed remembering her. Rocky had been so kind; and Maureen was especially good for a laugh. Maureen was small, round, and blond, she had Black foster brothers and sisters, and many Black friends. She and Rocky had got on well together for years.

There were rumours round the factory that Maureen really fancied Lindsey but it had never been a problem. Lindsey sighed. Live and let live, she thought. She kept those thoughts to herself. She had other things to voice.

'And what if we get snowed up out there in the winter? They do out there. It used to be all over the local news. You know it did. Branches blew round like bus tickets out there in the wind. Biff and me used to see the remains of it all when we took the bus out to Ladybower in the spring.' When Pete didn't answer, she continued, 'Mind you, you're right. It is a lovely place. The scenery is paradise. I'm just not sure about the people, I mean lack of 'em. And there's a lot of money in those parts. We'll be a bit down market.'

'Hang on a minute.'

Lindsey went silent as Pete indicated right, overtook a car in front that was weaving all over the road.

'Sorry 'bout that, love, looked as if he was drunk. Let's see how it all works out. If we don't like the rural life we can move back into Sheffield. I'll travel.'

'Make a long day for both of us, Pete.'

She went quiet again as he had to overtake another car that kept changing lanes without signalling. Lindsey felt the baby stir in her belly. She wondered if it knew it wasn't a hundred per cent welcome. She had always wanted children. Four. So did Pete. One of the things she loved about him . . . But she hadn't wanted to begin her new life away from the factory in rural Yorkshire with a baby already on the way. She'd wanted one more year before starting a family. Perhaps some part-time work; and time to get to and fro from Herton because Rita was getting married at Christmas and was working in the local cottage hospital.

As if reading her thoughts Pete said, talking ahead as he kept his eyes on the road, 'Think positive, love. Baby'll go in a carrycot in the back seat. We don't have to let this baby cramp our style. Nor any of the others.' He winked. 'We've always wanted children. And now we're starting. It's an adventure. I'm good with kids so you'll not be on your own. Remember when I was the only boy who used to babysit for his sister's kids. The others might've taken the micky, but it didn't stop me getting me exams, finding you, going to London. I loved those kids and now I'm having me own. It's bloody wonderful.'

'Yes, but . . . you make it all sound a bit too ideal, Pete. You might not feel so cheerful if the baby was inside you right this minute. You might be ready and the baby might be ready, but it took me by surprise. It wasn't what I wanted right now. I don't want to upset you, Pete, but I really don't think you listen to what I'm saying. It's my body this is happening to. Your body doesn't have to do anything. You are just exactly the same and all you have to do is sort out your feelings. But I've got much more than that to *do*. Every hour of every day until the baby arrives my body has got to get on with this, and *do* things. It's a busy time for my body, and I wasn't ready for the new job. It's like they said to you, "Never mind taking finals, just leave all that and start your new job." You wouldn't have been *ready*. I feel as if I'm talking to the wall like Rita with her brothers.'

'That's not fair.'

'I said I didn't want to upset you. I am getting on with the job, and I'm doing quite well. But I feel as if my body's gone to the Olympics and I haven't even started training.' She started to laugh and he did too. They laughed as he drove, and it freed her from her worries, for a little while.

Twilight came and with it new hazards. A fine sleet was gathering into shimmers on the road surface. No one was taking much notice. Cars overtook at seventy-five, going on eighty. The juggernauts were solid trundling up the inside lane, and fast saloons whizzed into the outer lane, sometimes sending a fine spray up from their back wheels.

Lindsey felt the baby stir. I was being so careful too, she thought to herself, caps and creams and gawd knows what else. She whipped round to look at Pete, astonished when he answered her.

'Well when we've got the four we want I'll have the operation. Then you won't have to worry. Green light,' he winked.

She laughed, because it seemed thousands of light years away and it was all suddenly absurd; and because Pete often took her by surprise, tripping her into laughter till she felt better. She could tell he was pleased to hear her laugh. He'd pressed the right button after all. He gave her one of his sideways looks, and patted her knee quickly, returning his hand to the wheel.

She felt wanted, loved, and confident that he wanted the same things from life that she did. It was a lot to know at twenty. Behind them an articulated lorry pulled out from the inside lane and came on to them fast and heavy. The driver flashed his headlights for Pete to move. Pete couldn't. There was a steady stream of red tail lights ahead in his lane; and he couldn't pull out into the overtaking lane because there was no safe space in the frantic splash and zoom of white glares in the wing mirror. One after another they strobed into and out of his view. Behind him the lorry flashed again.

'Big bully,' exploded Lindsey. Pete nodded. 'What you going to do, Pete?'

'Not a lot. I can't change lanes.'

'But he's only ten feet behind us.'

'Hasn't heard of breaking distance.'

'What if the one in front has to stop?'

'Close your eyes love. It'll be all right. We've had it far worse than this coming up and down. We've been all right before. That guy behind us'll get bored sooner than we will. He'll see sense in a minute. That's it. You close your eyes.

'She's coming round.'

It was light, white. Yellow blotches. She swam in hot liquid. Cold. Hot. Lights. White hard lights, yellow blotches. Dark.

'Yes, she slipped back but she's coming round.'

She swam in liquid. Floated the other side of nothing. Voices: Biff's. Nanan's. Where was Pete? She opened her eyes. Closed them quickly against the brightness. The liquid swirled, everything moved. A familiar face, blurred. For a moment it seemed to be a woman's face but then it cleared, and it wasn't: it was the dear familiar face of her granddad. It was Biff.

In the strange, white, yellow-bright room Lindsey let her eyes move around the walls, the silver tubes and clamps, the window shaded by a venetian blind. She realised this was hospital. The bed had a beige and white thick cotton cover over the fresh white sheets. The other familiar presence was Nanan, talking quietly to her on her left side.

'You've done very well. You're going to be all right. And your baby. It was touch and go for the baby but its heart is fine, fine. You're both going to be all right.

Lindsey listened. Moss seemed miles away. Her voice echoed, and it was hard for Lindsey to keep her attention on it. She closed her eyes against too many questions, too much recognition. Why weren't they telling her how Pete was? She realised she couldn't move her arms, heavy against her sides, but on top of the cover. She looked down her nose towards her arms, and discovered they were filled with tubes and the tubes escaped through bandages to link up to drips and clamps. Why didn't somebody tell her about Pete?

'Where's Pete?' Lindsey asked turning her head a little to look at Biff. Then in rising panic, 'Where is he? Tell me where Pete is.'

Biff swallowed, about to speak. Lindsey interrupted, 'You can't say it can you? You can't because he's dead, isn't he?'

She had half a second to see Biff nodding, before she faded into nothing.

When she came round again the window had been blanked out.

Somebody must've been in and flicked the blinds shut. It must be night. It was night and she'd been unconscious, and was now awake and Pete was dead. She remembered the lorry, the flashing head-lamps, and Pete's voice: 'Just close your eyes.'

She closed her eyes and could see the motorway, the red tail lights, the glaring and fading of the overtaking saloon cars. She was breath-ing but dead. Had become one of the living dead, like the people in horror films, buried alive. She fought against it. Tomorrow she would wake up after a long sleep and it would be normal again. Life. Her and Pete, the cottage, the new job, the lovely reservoir, the wind in the trees, the heather up on the moors. She slept.

When she woke it was light again, and she felt fine, ready to see Pete and have the baby.

'Nurse.'

A head came round. 'Tell my husband I want to see him now please. Tell them to bring him to see me.' The nurse looked startled, and nodded and left.

Another nurse came to her, patted her shoulder, checked all the tubes and drips.

'I said to bring my husband in, Nurse. Tell them to get him. I'm ready to see him now.'

This nurse was more senior. She sat by Lindsey, and reached for her hand. Lindsey couldn't move her hand, but the nurse covered it with her own, and Lindsey felt the warmth. It was a strong hand.

'Mrs Shepherd. Can you hear me? He was called Peter, wasn't he? He took the full impact, Mrs Shepherd. It didn't cause him any pain, you know. It was instant. If he had survived, he'd have been a vege-table. I know it's terrible for you. Are you listening? Nod to me. That's it. Yes, that's it. Let it come.' The nurse waited as Lindsey cracked. First the salt tears that poured, then the choking moaning sounds. She kept hold of Lindsey's hand and used her free hand to wipe Lindsey's face and mouth. 'He is dead. You are going to live. You will be able to walk and use your arms too. You have a lot of internal injuries. They had to take out your spleen. Do you understand?' Lindsey nodded. 'You have both legs broken and your left arm. You will be in here about two months, and then we shall do a Caesarean for the baby.

'Nurse. I don't want the baby. I want Pete,' Lindsey sobbed. 'I don't want the baby. I *don't want* the baby.'

'I'm going to give you something now, Mrs Shepherd, to let you sleep. Your grandparents will be here when you wake up.' The nurse wiped Lindsey's face again. Then she fed her a sip of water from a spout on a beaker. Grateful not to think any more, feel any more, Lindsey let the drugs take her back into thick falling feathers.

The hospital room was beige and white with pale green walls like her old bedroom in Herton. From where Lindsey lay she could watch the clouds in the sky outside the window. She came to rely on that square, reading the changing shapes for messages. A cloud one day would be Pete's profile; another his back and shoulders. One day two clouds meeting and parting were herself and her mother on the platform and the deep grey shadow passing across the other was her elephant who had comforted her on the journey north to Herton. Longing for something to hold on to, she searched the changing clouds for the pack-horse bridge but it eluded her.

Sunlight became her close friend. It kept irregular visiting hours, often taking her by surprise entering via the window, with a bunch of flowers. It talked and danced, amusing her endlessly. It was a powerful ally.

On sunless days Lindsey watched the blue, white and grey patterns outside the glass square. On those days the sky was framed, the edges of the window as hard and unyielding as the oblong metal frame of her own bed. She was framed too. Then she despaired and lay picturing herself, lying there in a white nightdress in white plastercasts with a beige and white cover on the bed. Outside was a sky full of clouds, like a crowd of unhappy people waiting in a forlorn queue. Then the queue would change and the people disperse. The sky would become a wide blue bedspread and the sunlight pour into her bones making her strong again.

In the long narrow garden behind the house in Church Lane Biff eased the dahlias on to sticks, and dead-headed the roses. The plot was a blaze of September colour, but Biff was short changed on joy and hope, because Lindsey didn't want the baby.

Biff tied the last remaining dahlia, a full-blown white star, cream and pink towards its centre, with one of Moss's old stockings. She fingered the dark green tooth-edged leaves, and straightened up. The September skies were clear and high, after an early morning mist. From the end of the garden near the greenhouse, which she had built from instructions in a gardening book, Biff could see beyond the top to the far side of the valley, and remembered with a pang the long cycle rides to the packhorse bridge with Lindsey. It seemed like centuries ago.

Sadly Biff put away the secateurs and garden gloves, lifted a mesh sack of daffodil and narcissus bulbs to a high shelf away from the damp floor, until she found time to plant them, closed the shed and made for the house. It was usually a thrilling walk back along the flower beds at that time of year, stopping by each blossom to check it for perfection, spotting the occasional daring weed and removing it, noticing a new rose about to burst, another dahlia bud on the turn.

But this September even the variety and changes in the pulse and life of the flower borders couldn't lift the spirits of the two women, weighted down by bereavement and shocked at Lindsey's rejection of the unborn baby.

'Why did you keep your pregnancy such a secret?' Biff had asked, the last time they had trekked to Chesterfield to the hospital.

'You won't like the answer, Biff. You know you won't. Why ask me when you won't want my reply?'

'Try me, love.'

'I didn't want it. I spotted the first two months anyway, so I just thought I was having a light period. I didn't believe it. Pete wanted to marry me, but I was quite happy going along as I was. He'd always said he'd marry me the moment I got pregnant but I didn't want to be pregnant, so soon after his degree. If I hadn't have got pregnant, I'd never have married him, and he'd be alive now.'

'What sort of nonsense is that?'

'It's true. This baby killed him and I don't want it. And who are you to tell me to have it? You never gave Nanan any. You are making me very angry, very very angry, all this pressure – I don't want it and I don't have to love it. It killed Pete.'

'Oh, Lindsey.' Moss spoke quietly from the other side of the bed. She reached out to touch Lindsey's arm, but Lindsey pulled away, hating everything and everyone.

'Not you as well, Nanan. I don't want to see you if you're going to make me want this baby. I can't stand it. I can't, I can't.'

'I know what it is like to have a child I didn't want.' Moss spoke quietly. She looked across at Biff, who asked without words if Moss wanted to be on her own, and when Moss nodded, Biff smiled sadly and left the bedside to take a walk to the Friends of the Hospital canteen. 'I'm going to tell you some of my story, about my life. I don't actually care much what you decide to think about me afterwards, or about this baby. It's your life and you're going to live it how you want. But Biff has loved me, in my life for these long years and I will not let anyone, you nor the Queen of England both, talk to my beloved like that. I will bring up your baby for you. I will love it and so will Biff, as we loved you. And you can return to London, young woman, and do whatever you can to survive and be happy. Things are never, never the way they seem in anyone's life to outsiders. Sometime in the future when you are out of this crisis, loved again, held in some-one's arms like I've been held and cherished in Biff's, and I pray to God it won't be too long till that happens, then you will remember me saying this. Things are never what they seem.

'I was young. I was a mere girl, self-centred and strong. I was a ser-vant in a rich man's house. No, don't look at me like that. I was not his mistress. Nor did he take me to his bed in his house. Oh no. I was in love with a girl. Her name was Florence. There was no one at all I could tell. Girls are not supposed to love each other. Yes, Biff knows. Biff knows everything there is to know about me . . . I was discovered with Florence under the rhododendrons by the rich man and his brother. So they taught us a lesson. And I conceived your mother. Florence walked into the river, yes just like Virginia Woolf. Only Florence is forgotten except by me, and I pray that Virginia won't be. Frank never knew the whole story. Only that I had been a headstrong girl and was expecting some lad's baby. He was good to me, but Biff is the love of my life. Your child was conceived out of love. And if you aren't going to love your child, I shall. I lost both my children, neither of them conceived in love. I was not to have any more, but Biff and I had plenty of love to spare. It was never on rations, or we'd not have taken you in. I shall love your child, while you go back where you belong now.

'You would never settle in Herton. London will always call you again. There are bells that chime for you there. Like your poor mother, worn down from work and pregnancy, bless her. Have the baby, then go. Go and work it out. There is something calling you back. You will come and fetch your child one day when you know that you're ready. I will not stop loving you, but you are not welcome in my house while you are consumed with hate.'

Lindsey's child was a girl, born in October 1966 by Caesarean. The baby had black hair and dark eyes, browner than autumn. It was put on the bottle, and after it had been in hospital two weeks it was taken home to Herton by Moss and Biff. Lindsey refused to name it.

'Shall we call the baby Rosie?' asked Moss. 'Do you remember, Lindsey, that was the name you said you wanted, when you were little and said you were going to grow up and have four?'

Lindsey shrugged. 'All right, Nanan. They're letting me out of here in two weeks time. I've arranged for Rhona and Sean to come and get me. Sean was Pete's best mate all through university and they've got money, you know, from his uncle. They've bought an old place in Hackney. I can have the ground floor till I'm stronger, then the attic.'

Moss swallowed: 'Do you want me to bring Rosie one last time to see you?'

Lindsey shook her head. 'I'm not ready, Nanan.' Lindsey started to shake. She reached her arms to her grandmother, and Moss reached out too and they clung as Lindsey sat up in the bed. Physiotherapy was making her stronger each day. She would leave the hospital, walking with a pair of crutches, and she couldn't wait to get back to Rhona and Sean's house, to be near people who had been near to Pete. Rocky and Maureen said in letters that they could get her a job at the factory any time. She would be sitting all day. She thought it was feasible.

'I'm sorry, Nanan. I didn't mean to hurt Biff. I love Biff. And you. I just can't handle it. But I will. I know I have to. I can't abandon Rosie. And I won't. I'll come and get her. I just need time, Nanan.'

'I know that, love. You need time and you need some loving. The sort that Biff and I can't give you. If we lived next door in London we'd help you. Your baby will come to no harm for a little while with us.'

'I love you, Nanan. I tried to talk to Rita on the phone but she can't bear to be near me. She won't even come and visit me.' Lindsey was crying over Moss's coat. 'I wanted to be friends with her again. I didn't expect such a reaction.'

'Time's a great healer. Let Rita get on with her own life, eh? Her marriage. You can't force these things. Biff and I really love you, we can't show it more than we are. You remember that. Hang on to that. And when you come through this we shall have a beautiful little girl for you.'

Lindsey nodded, unable to speak for tears. There was a bottomless feeling of water pouring out through her feet as Moss unwrapped herself and left the hospital, and Lindsey lay back on the bed, her weak legs feeling light without the heavy plasters, her muscles thin and wasted. Her skin from her ribs to her navel on her left side and across her pelvis was purple from scar tissue. She felt like an old vase, dredged in broken pieces from the bottom of the Mediterranean, mended but fragile, complete but empty.

It was Biff who tended Rosie in the night, feeding her, changing her and settling her down again. Moss took the early morning shift, bringing Biff tea in bed, though the stairs were difficult because of Moss's arthritic hip.

Moss waited tensely for Rita to visit. She wanted the contact for Lindsey's sake; but part of her wanted a respite from Herton's narrow attitudes, embodied in the sort of traditional woman that Rita had become.

On the walk to Moss's, Rita was deep in thought. It was just after opening time as she passed the Colliers Arms. Someone's voice called, 'Hi, nurse. Want to bandage my arm?'

'Gotta syringe of arsenic in me handbag.'

'Is that a friendly way to treat an old mate of Steven's?'

'Friendly enough. How you doing, then, Dave?' Rita laughed.

'So so. Tell that husband of yours he owes me a pint.'

'He's not my husband. It's a month till we're married. I'll tell him then. Can you wait that long?'

'Can he, more's the point? If I was him I'd marry you tomorrow.'

'That's bigamy, yer saucy bugger. Geron home to your wife.'

'Be seeing yer, Rita.'

'Be seeing yer, Dave.'

They both laughed and waved as Rita turned up the narrow lane which led into the main square. She waved to Mrs Denny the church caretaker who was at the bus stop. In one month the church doors would open for her and Steve. Herton would celebrate one of its daughters marrying one of its sons, the patterns repeated as they had been since the pit shaft was sunk over a century ago. Herton was slow to change. She liked that about it. You could depend on Herton.

Turning down Church Lane towards the vicarage and the terrace in which Moss and Biff now lived, Rita reflected that Lindsey had never really fitted in Herton. Running off to London with Peter Shepherd for example. The wild side of Rita secretly admired Lindsey for her nerve, but only in rare moments, now and then. Rita felt trapped inside her angry feelings towards Lindsey, and invaded too. She desperately wanted peace of mind, especially with her own wedding coming up.

She reached Moss's back door without even having realised she'd gone down the ginnel. Once inside the kitchen she felt edgy and sensed immediately that Moss was too. They went through into the livingroom at the front, where the baby was asleep in a carrycot.

'I brought these for her,' Rita began, holding out a parcel wrapped in congratulations paper with pink rabbits and bows on it.

'Oh you shouldn't have.' Moss opened the paper and took out a white knitted jacket with a matching hat edged in pale pink that she'd seen in Miss Brookes' and Miss Field's wool and baby shop. 'They're lovely. It's very kind of you, Rita, would you like some tea?'

'I'm glad you like them,' said Rita formally. 'Yes thanks, tea'd be nice.'

Moss went out into the kitchen and returned almost immediately with a tray with cups and saucers laid out prettily and a teapot, milk jug and sugar bowl. Obviously, thought Rita, she was rehearsed for this visit, just like me.

'Ready for your big day then, Rita?'

'Yes. No. Well, almost.' Pause. 'One sugar please. Thanks. Is there anything er, I could do to help you?'

'You could put pen to paper. Our Lindsey could do with a letter.'

'I tried umpteen times. Since she went back. But I can't seem to get the words right. I think I know what I'm going to say, then I get the pen in me hand and it all goes. I was so shocked, you see. Shocked she could leave a baby. I mean if it was Steve's, I couldn't do that. Flesh of my flesh. But I was hard on her. I wish I hadn't been.'

'Rita, can I ask you something?' Rita looked anxious but seemed to agree, so Moss continued. 'She was in hospital weeks before the baby, before you knew she was going to back to London, leaving Rosie for a while with us. So why didn't you go and see her then?'

'I don't know, Mrs Ferguson. I've asked myself that question dozens of times. I even wrote to an advice column about it. I think all my dreams were smashed around my feet: us as a foursome, even a double wedding. I had no idea Lindsey was pregnant – that she'd got married. We'd had a lot of marvellous letters about planning our families, but she never actually told me she was pregnant. So I suppose she was coming home to Herton to tell me, same time as telling you both. Surely you were angry too?'

'In my family, things were quite different from in Herton. When I was a young girl it was quite usual for girls to get pregnant before they married. And in the farming areas it was normal. What use is a farmer's wife who can't have children?'

'Oh my God. I never heard such a thing.'

'Rita, you are a nurse. I don't believe you.'

'I mean in my family, Mrs Ferguson. What other people do is different.'

'All right, Rita. But Lindsey was special to you, as you say. And you are upset about being split off from her, and so it's not too late to write and tell her. It's never too late if you know who your friends are . . . '

'I've got friends. I know who my friends are.'

'And are you going to abandon them too?'

'I didn't abandon Lindsey. I was being honest.'

'Good, that's all right then.'

'I wish I'd lied. That's all.'

'Lindsey would've known. She's no fool. Write and tell her.'

'I don't think writing would do any good. Might make things worse.'

'Phone her then. I've got Rhona and Sean's new number. They won't mind.'

'There's a box outside Steve's mum's. Perhaps I will. But . . . '

'But you're so angry inside that you think it might all spill out?'

'Yes. I am. I don't like feeling like this but I always do when anyone abandons a baby.'

'Rosie is *not* abandoned, Rita. She is living for a while with her great-grandparents. When are you going to stop being tied in knots inside Herton's rules?'

Embarrassed and anxious, Rita bent over the sleeping baby, gathering herself together, wanting a way of changing the conversation. The tension in the air was acute.

'Rosie's the image of you, Mrs Ferguson.'

'Do you think so?'

'Oh yes. Same eyes, same hair. I've only got to look at her.'

'Did Lindsey ever tell you about *my* grandmother, Rita?'

'Your grandmother?' Rita screwed her eyes up, thinking, then shook her head. 'Not that I can remember, Mrs Ferguson, why?'

'She was Indian. From northern India. When she came to this country she was in her teens. Hindu.'

'But I thought . . . er . . . You go to the Methodist chapel every Sunday.'

'That's right.'

'Oh!'

'It takes all kinds of people to make a town like this, Rita. This town should be for everyone. But people don't think until they're challenged. I am on the outside and the inside of this town, and so is Lindsey. She challenged you, and you rejected her. Because she doesn't quite obey the rules. In this town the rules are hidden until somebody breaks them, steps outside them.'

'That's right, Mrs Ferguson. And I like Herton, and its people, and I don't intend to step outside, as you say, and I would never never give away my baby, no matter what happened to me.'

'Maybe not, but you were an outsider once, after your year in the isolation ward, and you were glad of Lindsey then.'

'I didn't come here for a sermon! If I wanted one I'd go to the church.'

'Good. Because you didn't get one. You got the real feelings of a real person. Like I said already, I'm both an outsider and insider, and I know it both ways round.'

Rita hurriedly tried to finish her cup of tea, but she liked her tea lukewarm and it took her a couple of minutes. Moss was reminded of the cave up in the Pennines where they still had rope-making machinery. Long pieces of hard raw jute ran over pulleys, traversing the width of the cave, about three feet above the floor. It seemed someone had brought the machinery into Moss's living room. As the ropes stretched and twisted around and around one another, half inch needle-like jute fibres spun off, cutting the air and dropping to the ground. The handle was turning and sharp rope filaments were flying off at tangents too near to the sleeping baby; and twisted tense cables rubbed along Moss's arms giving her rope burns.

'Steve's on earlies, I'd better be going.'

'Just a minute then, and I'll write Lindsey's phone number for you.' Rita had the courtesy to sit and wait as Moss scribbled the number from the book on the mantelpiece and handed it to Rita. Moss didn't ask Rita to promise to phone; and Rita didn't make any promise.

The rest of their unspoken tension and anger hung around them in the air, like smoke from the coke ovens. Moss wondered if her very private thoughts were suspected as the seconds were passing, split seconds, splitting open the old wounds so that raw feelings were in danger of leaking out. Rita was deeply disturbed, deeply sorry and did not know how or when she would be able to speak about it. But she felt, in Moss's front room, that this was going to be one of those hurts about people's differences that would ulcerate, unhealed for a long, long time.

'Say goodbye to Biff for me.'

'Of course I will. And we both hope your plans go well for your wedding. Hope you will both be happy.'

Rita left. Both women knew then that the other was still angry. Both felt like crying, but neither of them cried.

Fourteen

Back in London, Lindsey recovered steadily from the car crash. As soon as she could walk without crutches, she began work again at the factory near Old Street. Rhona dropped her at the door of the factory on her way to work and after work she waited for Rhona to pick her up again.

At first she felt extremely tired and it was all she could do to eat dinner and fall into bed. She craved sleep, often having nine or ten hours a night. She didn't go out because she was exhausted, but she did hold down the job and was pleased with herself.

Most of all she was delighted to be back with Rocky and Maureen. 'You're like family,' she told Rocky.

'That'll be the day,' replied Rocky. And when Lindsey looked abashed she added, 'But I've missed you, and I'm glad you're back. And when you can walk properly, we'll do the markets, one every Saturday, 'bout time you had some new things, cheer you up. And me? I'm for a new hat, or maybe two.'

Rocky kept her word, and they would meet up for a couple of hours from time to time, shopping together, calling in at a cheap café for tea and doughnuts, Rocky's favourites.

Gradually, the ache inside her thigh bones eased as Lindsey ate well and slept well and she took up swimming, building from half a length to five, six and ten. With each length that she added over the winter months, she felt her muscles toning up and her body returning to its previous strength.

Physically, she was healing, but she knew that it would take more than a few trips to the market and the swimming baths to overcome the emotional numbness that engulfed her. Late at night, just before she slept, she would place her hands on her belly as she lay in bed, alone. Her fingers would trace along the scars; and once again she would feel like an empty vase, made of porous clay. Her feelings had poured from the vase, as if they were water; warm or cold, it didn't matter, they had gone, and she couldn't be bothered to try and bring them back. She would fall asleep, and dream of water pouring from an overhanging cliff in the Dales, flowing down into nothing, disappearing into the earth, going nowhere.

The canteen of the glove factory had high windows with wire grilles so that the outsides couldn't be cleaned. Inside, the place was tiled half-way up the walls and above that cracks and uneven patches showed through the peeling beige paint. At the top of the walls ran a railway line assembly of thin and thick water pipes, meeting and joining, linked occasionally with vertical pipes painted in tatty flaking grey. Overhead neon strips completed the bleak workhouse appearance, unsuccessfully designed, according to Rocky, to put the women off lingering over lunch.

Just before Easter, Lindsey and Rocky sat with sandwiches and coffee, lunching together on Maureen's day off.

'Come to church with me, Sunday.' Rocky looked Lindsey in the eye. Rocky was thirty-eight; for weeks she had watched her young friend, a widow estranged from her child. Like a cardboard tube in the centre of a roll of cloth. Shimmering blue silk; gold and silver brocade; warm strong worsted; thick green baize. Wrapped and rolled tight, an empty cylinder, inside layer after layer, so that Rocky grieved for herself at the same age, for the colours and textures she couldn't reach.

'It's not for me, Rocky.'

'You don't know till you've been. It's for whites as well. Not just us people.'

'I couldn't. My nanan's religious, but it's not for me. But you're very kind to me, Rocky. I'm all right, getting through.'

'No, girl, you're not all right. Why? Because you stopped dreaming. And if you can't dream you can't live. That's the trouble in the cities.' Rocky looked at the high windows that let in only deep grey daylight. 'No sky. Your dreams explode round you. No land. Nowhere to dig, plant them in rich soil see them grow. So you shout your dreams into thick air, die in exhaust fumes, and you die a bit inside.'

Lindsey stirred her coffee, thinking of the many hours they'd shared in this canteen, talking across this very table, with its plastic top all chipped and cracked, like her dreams. She could find no words, but she looked up and her face said, Don't stop, I need to listen to you.

'Choked. You come to the factory all day, whirr whirr, working the cloth with the other women, and you talk about shopping and friends. Maybe elections, Middle East. But you keep your dreams folded in a clean hanky tucked inside your bra strap. Keep 'em safe. You don't sew dreams where strangers can see your thread.'

Lindsey's eyes were luminous and Rocky knew she must speak,

speak, cutting words through Lindsey's stitches around Lindsey's protective roll of cloth.

Rocky went to the canteen counter, and brought back two steaming mugs of coffee. She stirred three sugars into hers, then, as Lindsey sipped the hot drink slowly, Rocky asked, 'Did you know I had to leave my baby, back in Jamaica?'

'You did? You never talked about it. Oh Rocky, which one was it?'

'Elizabeth. My baby that's a teacher, now. You snap your fingers, Lindsey, turn round, and they're done and grown right there.'

'Was she all right? How did you feel? Who had her? Did you grieve?'

'Hey, wait a minute, which question first?'

'All of them! All of them. I never met any other woman who left a baby. Not one. Is that why you kept an eye out for me?'

'Lord knows you need somebody to keep an eye out for you. I grieved. I worked. Each and every zip I counted until I could send for her. She was six.'

'Six years. Oh God, she didn't know you.' That's what I'm afraid of, Lindsey thought, Rosie won't know me. I'm that stranger who left her. Out loud she said, 'I've done everything to forget her. I can't sleep. I can't get her out of my mind. I'm obsessed, Rocky. Obsessed.'

'Go and get her. You got your lovely little attic place. I didn't have no place. One room. No children allowed. You gotta place. You go and get your baby. She'll bring love back to you. She'll surely bring you love. Lord knows you need it.'

'So do you. We all do. D'you want a jam doughnut?'

'Two.' Rocky spoke loudly, and heads turned. She didn't care. 'And another coffee. Roaring hot and three sugars. I like my life to be sweet.' When Lindsey returned with her laden tray, she felt excited, determined, weak and strong. She asked, 'You never went back to live there?'

'No work. Three more children born here. My youngest, Donnette, just fourteen. Earl and Danny in between. My brother's here now, in London. When Earl and Donnette's grown that's where I'll be, living with my brother. I couldn't live alone. Not again. Here's home, this cold country. Cold and grey. But it's home. And I've still got my dreams. Rosie'll have hers too, later on. Hidden from you. Like my children. Ask no questions, get told no lies. They got their own dreams, like I had. I get on, get by. But I never lost my dreams. Come to work dead beat, dog tired. Go home dead beat, worn down. The work here wears you down. And all for your young ones, give them hope. What you got if you ain't got your kids? What you got? Lost dreams, girl. You go and get that baby.'

Lindsey smiled, thinking of Rosie and of the image of the roll of cloth that Rocky had just given her, and for the first time for as many days as she could remember, she felt a layer of the cloth unwind. Jamaica and Herton. Homelands. She was young, exiled. Rocky was older, exiled. They were mothers, both. What you got if you ain't got your kids?

They drank their coffee silently, as close as if they were touching. Rocky was thinking of the time when she sent for Elizabeth, how it put the parts of her soul back together, and she had breathed freer carrying the burden of her child herself than she had ever breathed during their six year separation.

She wanted all her children to go to college. That was what she sewed gloves for. She would have liked an education too, but there was only Saturday and she couldn't cook and clean and shop and get an education all on Saturday. Leave the education for the young ones. She looked across and smiled at Lindsey, who was not as old as Elizabeth and was already a widow with a baby. Started young as she, Rocky, had done. She'd been called Raquelle in those days. She looked at the canteen clock. People said you had more time if you didn't have your kids with you. But you filled it missing them; they tore your heart strings out. 'Come on, Cinderella,' she quipped. 'Your pumpkin's waiting.'

'Wave your wand, Rocky. They might put the piece rates up.'

'That's not magic,' replied Rocky standing up, preparing to start the afternoon stint, 'that's miracles.'

Lindsey stood with Moss, Biff and the baby, on the bridge over Lady-bower Reservoir, saying hello and goodbye to the place where she would have lived; where Peter would have worked for the Water Authority.

It was April. Green soft fluff lay on each tree, hiding the twigs, but the branches wouldn't be hidden until May. The spring was young and so was she. A young woman with a young baby, her own.

I have come to claim my life and my child, she thought. To put the parts of me together, what did Rocky say, the parts of my soul. Take in everything, face everything, deal with everything.

'I've been overwintering, Biff,' she said out loud, 'like the plants in your garden.' Moss joggled the pushchair as Rosie stirred, and the baby slipped back into sleep again. 'It took me all those months just

145

going to work, coming back, seeing friends, going to sleep. Waking up, going to work. Day after day. All those months. Who'd have thought I'd be here now, looking at the water, feeling calm. I can hardly believe how calm I am.'

They nodded and Moss patted her arm. The water reflected the sky, clouds and trees. Grey and blue water, high on the banks because of the winter rains. The day was timeless, hours and minutes undefined. The water hung still in the reservoir, like a silent hand on a clock that had been stopped. There was only the movement of the sun and the slow turn of shadows to show that the world hadn't ended. Everything was quiet. Stones on the bridge were warm grey in the sunlight. The clouds in the water floated deep. By the bank a slow ripple caught the sunshine and curled it carefully in a steady spiral up the trunk of the overhanging tree.

'We trusted you to come and get her,' said Moss. 'We have known you since you were eight years old. Time was on our side, and on yours.'

'And Rosie's,' added Biff. The baby was waking up, sucking her first finger, with her thumb through the hole in a small crocheted blanket. 'She doesn't mind much what goes on so long as she's got Dees.'

'Dees?'

'She was in the high chair yelling her head off, about a month ago. I tried everything. Was she wet? No. Hungry? No. Hot? No. And in desperation I said "Oh here, have this." Gave her the blanket. She said "aaa Dees", went quiet as a mouse and won't be parted from it.'

Lindsey grinned and pulled faces at Rosie, who pulled faces back.

'You're going to miss her, aren't you?'

Moss replied, 'Of course we'll miss her. But she's *your* child and we're not getting any younger. And she's young enough to take the changeover. A few more months and I'd be worried,' continued Moss. 'I have been worried actually. About the timing of you coming for her. Biff gets twinges.'

'Now, then. I'm all right.' Biff put on a warning face.

'What's the matter, Biff? Where do you get twinges? What are you hiding from me?'

'Come on, let's walk over the bridge. There's a lovely view the other side.'

'I said . . .'

'I'm all right. It's just a bit of indigestion I expect.'

Moss tutted but Biff was adamantly silent. Moss and Lindsey

exchanged looks and shrugged but they knew better than to pursue the issue.

The bluebells weren't quite ready. Under the trees they were inches tall but tight and green budded. Everywhere leaves of all shades of green were uncurling. Ferns were thick at the base, almost a foot high, their tops like springs ready to uncoil. Grasses were unfolding, and there were nesting birds everywhere flurrying about with bits and pieces for home do-it-yourself.

The place was abundant with life about to open up, jump out, leap high, in a flight of leaf, feather and frond.

Moss trundled Rosie's pushchair, pointing things out, stopping to show things to her. She'd done the same for Sadie, the same for Ronnie. This might well be the last baby that she held closely, loved nightly. If Lindsey had others they'd be Londoners. Moss wanted Lindsey to return to London. London had opportunities and although she herself had never been the slightest bit interested in visiting it, she recognised that it was as much a magnet to Lindsey as Herton Hall had been to the triangle of young girls that had played there during the restorations and rebuilding.

Ladybower was a place of reflections. The long stretch of water, a mirror for the mind and soul. Moss turned with the pushchair to look back towards the stone bridge. It had been a good idea to make this journey. The grey and blue sky gave space for feelings, and it was feelings rather than thoughts that Moss had experienced during the whole expedition. Back to Darlington and Florence; forward through Sadie, and Ronnie who had died at sea. 'God rest his soul,' prayed Moss, as she always did when the war and Ronnie came into her heart.

Ladybower was also a place of the heart. The place where Lindsey would have brought up Rosie. But Moss was not romantically tied to any one place. She lived and would probably end her life in Herton. But she had begun near Darlington, in a tiny village in open country, and it was to the countryside of the North that she was attached. Having once had to uproot and replant herself, she had discovered that sometimes it was necessary and that it could be made to work out.

She let her heart dip into the reservoir, settle on the earth under the water, and absorb its stillness, drinking.

Fifteen

The Hackney hard-to-let which had been Lindsey and Rosie's home since 1967 was one of a dismal collection in an old block, with cracked concrete stairs swirled with litter and dog dirt, and the occasional alley fight which left the buildings and landings strewn with broken bottles. But Lindsey's flat was spotless and comfortable inside, like those of her neighbours. She was proud of her home, and had just finished decorating her kitchen in green and white, with a new roller blind on the window.

From half-way up the kitchen wall came a sound like mice with metal teeth, rasping their way through the plaster from the next-door flat. Scrape, scrape. The sound was repeated without becoming a rhythm. On her side of the wall the wallpaper stayed intact, although the noise was so insistent that Lindsey half expected a small pointed nose and whiskers to appear any minute.

She busied herself at the kitchen table which was covered in thick newspaper as she settled to shoe cleaning. Outside, the summer evening was light and bright. Inside, sunbeams with dancing dust in them made overtures to the pairs of shoes which stood to attention, waiting to be polished. The sunlight moved steadily across the silent pairs of leather toes; black, brown, blue, red and yellow. Lindsey hummed 'Blue Suede Shoes', as she worked, though her current favourites were not suede but new French blue leather courts with low heels.

Rosie, at four and a half, was in bed, probably dreaming of white rabbits and dormice, mad hatters and tea parties. The picture book version of *Alice in Wonderland* from which Lindsey had been reading to her lay on her bedside table. Lindsey buffed Rosie's red sandals and held them in her palms, admiring them. Old Hans Christian Andersen tales, red shoes, red knitting-wool, came into her mind. Then in trooped childhood, unabridged, and memories sharp as pins in pincushions. Young brothers and sisters with wearisome coughs and worn-out shoes.

Each child had had one pair of shoes; and one pair of socks. Lindsey's mother, Sadie, used to try to dry the washed socks overnight by the living-room fire. Once, Sadie had taken a pair of wet socks to work, to dry them on the hot hospital radiators. The head cleaner had found them and put them in the rubbish. Sadie had to beg for them back; Lindsey remembered that they had been Jimmy's socks, which was why he'd had a nasty incident with a splinter.

More memories: of her mother and father whispering behind the bedroom door, in the urgent tones that told Lindsey, eavesdropping, that once again the topic of the night was *money*. They thought that Lindsey couldn't hear, didn't know. But she had known: too much; and not enough.

Now, years later, she realised that whenever she had any spare cash, it was shoes that she indulged in. Enough shoes; too many shoes. Shoes for all kinds of walking, all sorts of weather. Paid for from her full-time wages from the glove factory where she worked with Rocky and Maureen. Maureen's indulgence was special food: gateaux with fresh cream and real fruit; expensive French cheeses with walnuts pressed around the edge.

Once, in this very kitchen, they'd talked about their 'treats'. It was a special conversation that returned to Lindsey in every detail whenever she was polishing shoes.

'Look, I got these in the sale,' she had begun. 'I've always wanted some yellow shoes!'

'What a colour! Shame I've stopped asking you out dancing.'

'They're for walking not dancing, and besides we got over all that. How's Tessa anyway?'

'She likes dancing. With me. We're fine.'

'How's your mum taking it, and Marissa?'

'Mum's all right. She came with us down Gateways.'

'She what? You're joking.'

'I'm not. I told you, Mum's all right. In more ways than one. Put it this way: there are six of us and she keeps in touch with some of her other foster kids as well as Marissa. Marissa's more family on account of how long she fostered with us. I'm lucky, I know. Some mum's'd go stark raving mad if their daughter turned out gay and took her girl friends home.'

Lindsey's eyes were wide with disbelief contemplating Maureen and her mum at the Gateways, not to mention her mum accepting her lover.

'And Marissa introduced you to Tessa, right?'

'You're a bit on the slow side sometimes, aren't you? Think back to your nanan growing up in a family where her mum was half Indian and her dad was white. Well?' Maureen waited for Lindsey to think hard, then she said challengingly, 'Well, my foster sister is Black and her friend Tessa is too. Tessa has two little girls and I love kids . . .

Marissa knew me and Tessa were both gay and lonely. And don't come the how-can-she-be-gay-with-kids bit again because I'm bored with trying to get your head out of a box.'

'I'm sorry. But you're lucky your family accept you being gay. Most families aren't so open about it.'

'Oh Lindsey, a big toughie like you talking such old fashioned rubbish. This is the seventies. Don't get me wrong, it's no bed of roses. Marissa's brother lived with us too and the police hate Black youths, loved chucking Chas like a piece of meat in the back of a police van after he'd been to a bop.

'Listen Lindsey, I'm a white woman and Tessa is Black and her daughters Sharon and Jean are Black and we all have to learn how to live together. We don't have to learn how to love. We already do love. It's the living of it day in and day out we have to learn – and we either will or we won't – but it won't be for want of trying. Not on my part or hers. Now that's enough about me and my true life romance, what about you? You still happy on your own?'

'Love it. Taken me long enough. Don't know what I'd have done without you and Rocky. I'm doing all right. I've got my kid, in there dreaming her socks off. And I've got you for my friend. I wanted you to find somebody like Tessa, not like me. Rocky says I'm still all sewn up in a roll of cloth. I think she's right. I'll unpick my stitches when I'm ready.' Lindsey had packed the yellow shoes back in tissue in the shoe box as Maureen cut them both a huge slice from a lemon layer cake.

'Here you are, I matched it to your new shoes. Tuck into that. A minute in the mouth, an hour in the stomach and a lifetime on the hips. You always were too skinny. Fatten you up a bit. You can keep the rest for Rosie.'

'You spoil us. I thought you were saving up for Aussie.'

'My famous trip down under? I've got seven pounds in the post office.'

'That'll go a long way. One day soon I'm going to take Rosie to see her grandparents.'

'Want someone to carry your suitcase?'

'No thanks. You can carry Tessa's. Besides, mine'll weigh a ton. Full of shoes.'

Lindsey stopped reminiscing and decided to break for coffee. She was just scrubbing her red and blue hands when she heard the neighbours knocking at her front door, presumably to return the wallpaper scraper that they had borrowed earlier.

Lindsey called towards the front door, 'I'm coming', as she hurriedly dried her hands on the kitchen towel and made her way down the hall.

She opened the door, fell down a rabbit hole and landed in the grounds of Herton Hall face to face with Lerryn Trevonnian.

For a few moments the two women stared at one another.

Instead of the young Lerryn in shorts and T-shirt by Aunt Harry's new pond, here was a tall graceful woman, wearing jeans and white leather lace ups and carrying a bunch of salmon pink roses. Lerryn wore an unbuttoned denim jacket with many pockets over a white linen open-necked shirt which offset her clear skin and short dark curly hair. She still had the same deep green eyes, of course, and now they smiled at Lindsey, taking in every sign of Lindsey's total surprise.

Lerryn was astonished too at the change in Lindsey. Gone was the carefree young girl with her hair tied back in a pony tail, her body light and quick moving. This woman was about five feet four, possibly a fraction more, which made her three or four inches shorter than Lerryn herself. Lindsey's thick black hair was cut short and stylishly shaped to the nape of her neck, swept back over her ears so that Lerryn could just see tiny gold earrings. Lindsey had put on weight and it suited her. She wore a summer skirt and her bare feet were thrust into soft brown leather sandals. The material of her skirt and matching shirt-blouse appealed to Lerryn: an abstract pattern of green and blues with sudden splashes of soft yellow. Sea and boats in Mevagissey harbour at high tide in sunlight.

'Lerryn!'

'What wonderful material! Hello, Lindsey.'

Lindsey's next words tumbled over one another in an effort to express a whole variety of feelings, 'Oh, thanks. It's so comfortable. Oh well, heavens you'd better come in. Come on in, you'll be taking root there on my doorstep.'

Lindsey hopped down the hall with Lerryn behind her as the burrow shrank several sizes, packed with people from the past. All the selves that made up Lindsey were followed by Lerryn and her full entourage of Herton connections, all jostling along dressed as characters from *Alice*; Aunt Harry as the Queen of Hearts; Peggy as the Cheshire Cat; Stan as the caterpillar smoking his pipe; Mrs Kinton, the Morgawr lady from Herton Library, as the Duchess; and a chorus of playing-card people all waving palettes and paintbrushes shouting 'roses roses all the way'.

Lindsey dashed around as white rabbit, squeaking. 'Sit down here. I'll clear these shoes away. Kettle's ready boiling. Lovely roses. Here's a vase.'

Lerryn looked around the green and white kitchen, and arranged the roses. All the carefully rehearsed phrases and sentences had blurred into a confused mass, like a ball of rubber bands which she had once made from old stock at the back of Aunt Harry's stationery cupboard. Mentally Lerryn picked at the rubbery ball for a loose end to start the conversation with, but not finding one, she chose to comment on the colour of the newly decorated kitchen.

'This is a lovely room. Did you do this yourself?'

'Mostly, and my friend Maureen from work helped me. I'd take you through to the living room but we can't use it right now. The plaster fell off the ceiling and we're waiting for the council to come and fix it. They take for ever. Where do you live now?'

'Finsbury Park. Near the tube.'

'Oh, in London. Is that council too?'

'No. It's a ground floor flat and it backs on to a garden. I'm a very keen gardener, like Biff. How are they? Are they both well?'

'Up and down. Biff still cycles. He's quite amazing. Well, I think so. So is Nanan, but her hip troubles her. I've been suggesting one of those new hip jobs but her doctor says her heart won't take the operation. I went and had a real set to with him about it actually.'

Lindsey caught Lerryn's eye, and for the first time she felt a deeper reconnection. They searched one another's faces for a moment as if to find a way of telling each other all the things that had happened to change them during their years apart. Lerryn had been fond of Moss and Biff; she felt some of the intervening years slip away. At the same moment the sun slipped behind the high rise blocks, and the room grew darker.

'I'll just put the light on,' said Lindsey, rising and reaching for a table lamp on top of the tall fridge, surrounded by spider plants that had multiplied down the sides, green and white. The lamp cast shadows around the kitchen.

'You were saying about the doctor?'

'Yes. I can't understand why they won't give Nanan a new hip and be done with it. She's not that old at sixty-seven and it would take away the pain. But he reckons it's something to do with rheumatic fever. Apparently she had it when she was nine. Weakened her heart. I wanted her to have a second opinion, because she hasn't had a whisper of heart trouble all these years. It's Biff who gets twinges, not Nanan, not that I can get *anywhere* with him. What a mule he can be! He's got this absolute thing about doctors. I do my best with them both but they close ranks on me. Nanan won't go for a second opinion. I dunno: it's their lives, but I don't like to think of Nanan in pain. She walks all right, just, and she can get upstairs to bed.' Lindsey sighed. 'I haven't given up yet, just biding my time.' She looked at Lerryn, slowly. 'It was good of you to ask me about them, Lerryn. I must admit I got such a shock when I saw you there on the doorstep. I'm only just taking it all in.'

'I was going to phone first but . . .'

'I still don't trust the phone. Funny that. I got it because of Nanan and Biff. Hot line, you know.'

'Yes.' Lerryn felt instinctively good about continuing with the Herton connection. She thought to herself, a bridge. We both need some sort of bridge. She asked, 'How often do you and Rosie get up there?'

'No special plans. Just as often as we can. Rosie starts school in September. So then it'll be half terms and holidays. Sometimes I take her up there at a weekend and I come back on account of work. We all have to pay the rent don't we? And then I go back in a week or so and get her. When she's a teenager I'll put her on the coach, but you can't do that with a four year old, can you?' Lindsey flinched, and Lerryn noticed for the first time the pain lines around her mouth and eyes, as if someone had suddenly stuck a needle in her. Quickly Lindsey seemed to regain control, and she smiled and asked, 'So tell me about the amazing redhead. How is Aunt Harry?'

'Older. A bit fatter, otherwise just the same. Oh and a few grey hairs, not many. Actually she kept me posted about you and Rosie because Peggy and Stan pass Herton news on to her. I've been wanting to see you. Losing my nerve each time. People change; and I realised I didn't know you at all, didn't know Rosie, and I'd done nothing about it and time was pouring itself into a hole in my paintings. Then Peggy told Harry that Rosie was due to start school. And I thought, my God, another five years have gone past. For me, life seems to slip away in blocks of five or six years.' Lerryn sipped her coffee, and Lindsey waited for her to collect her thoughts. Lerryn's manner had changed from the calm, confidence of the doorstep; now she was less assured, younger somehow, her voice was uneven, her sentences shorter and nervy.

Watching the changes in Lerryn, Lindsey felt a strange compassion. She wanted to reach across to Lerryn just as she would have done if it had been an older Rosie sitting nervously opposite her with something difficult to say. In that moment Lindsey did not mind being a mother to Lerryn, her main identity these days was as a mother. Her love for Nanan and Biff was about mothering too, because both of them in their own way had been like a mother to her. Biff himself had been so unlike a granddad; more like a grandmother: shopping, cooking and cleaning, changing the beds and comforting her when she was upset. She had never understood this, but she knew it affected the way she herself behaved as a mother to Rosie, and she didn't feel the need to analyse it beyond that. She waited for Lerryn, thinking of Nanan and Biff and Rosie.

Lerryn spoke quietly: 'Did your nanan and Biff ever tell you that I went to Herton to look for you just after you had left with Peter Shepherd?'

'No.'

'It was the first chance I'd had, money and all that. By then I'd done the apprenticeship in the salon in Catherine-in-Penwith.'

'I remember *that*. You were dreading it. It was terrible money, Lerryn. You'd have been better in my glove factory. Tell you about that in a while, go on.'

'Just that really. I went to find you, and you'd gone to London with Peter.'

'I'd have loved to have had a friend from the past, while I was first in London. Why didn't you contact me?'

As the words left her lips, Lindsey remembered Lerryn curled in bed in Herton Hall, watching the sky on fire, and saying, 'I'm never going to get married. Boys don't interest me. And I *love* coming here to Herton.'

Oh my God, thought Lindsey, Lerryn said boys didn't interest her. Is that why she can't answer me? Is it that *I* interested her?

Lindsey sat quietly, waiting for Lerryn to reply.

Lerryn drank slowly, unable to answer. She put her mug on the pine table, noticing how the reflections seemed to gather and burst like bubbles each time one of the mugs was moved. She couldn't possibly answer Lindsey. It was too soon. But she didn't want to lie. She hated hiding all her feelings, either from herself or her friends. She particularly didn't want to hide from this woman whom she'd finally come to find. She was at a junction in her own life, and she had questions to ask of Lindsey. Turning point questions, that were now clear to herself.

'Why don't I put the kettle on again?' said Lindsey. 'Tea or coffee?'

'Actually I'd love some tea. Is that Earl Grey up there on the shelf?'

'Yes. And d'you know what? It was Aunt Harry started me off with that all those years ago. Honestly. Nanan and Biff never had it at home of course. Good old British Rail special for them. But then years later Rocky, who I work with, brought me some; and every time I drink it it reminds me of your aunt. Wait till you see my best china teapot. It's the most fantastic teapot in this city. It was made for Earl Grey. Eat your heart out, Aunt Harry. By the way, do you ever eat frozen cream cakes?'

'As it happens, yes. Love them.'

'Good, because I've one that Maureen gave me in the freezer tray, and we haven't time to wait for it to defrost. There we go then. Tea for two.' Lindsey filled the kettle then opened a cupboard door. Turning she said, 'Now. Tell me I was exaggerating.'

She held out for admiration the worst monstrosity of a patterned teapot that could ever have been designed. Her laughter was young again and she could easily have been carrying a bunch of red clover and wild scabious from Herton's woods. Every shade of pink and purple had been used in the pattern and the crinolined ladies waltzing sedately round the pot looked like the *Come Dancing* competitors on the new colour television set in the pub which was never tuned in properly, red arms and green legs on a salmon pink dance floor.

'There you are, you see. You chose exactly the right colour roses. Now you just stay comfy there while I bustle about. Not enough room for two charladies in here.'

Lerryn watched as Lindsey moved around, taking care of the situation with the kind of generosity that Moss had always had. But Lerryn had seen the pain in her face for a fleeting moment. Finally Lindsey placed on the kitchen table a tray comprising the queen of teapots, the frozen cake on a matching plate, forks, a cake knife, mugs and milk.

'Help yourself,' she said, leaving the room for a minute and returning with a framed photo, which she stood beside the tea things. 'This is my daughter, with Rocky and Maureen from work. This is my child who I live with; and these are my two friends who get me through.'

After their first meeting three weeks ago, Lindsey and Lerryn had met almost every evening for a couple of hours, talking as if the rest of humanity had disappeared, leaving just the two of them, and Rosie, shipwrecked on an island.

But Lindsey suspected that Lerryn wanted more than a friendship; and this evening after dinner at Lindsey's flat, tension was beginning to build up. It was time for Lerryn to be making her way home, but she was not hurrying, to the point that her delaying tactics over the washing up were now obvious to Lindsey.

In the momentary lulls between the sounds of washing up, an old fashioned alarm clock, with a huge round face and a pair of bells on top, ticked the minutes of Lindsey's evening towards night-time.

Lerryn studied a Pyrex dish, carefully scouring the stubborn brown marks along the edges with a Brillo pad. Thinking that Lindsey hadn't heard her properly, she repeated her question, 'How'd you feel about me staying the night?'

Lindsey's footsteps to-ed and fro-ed across the vinyl kitchen floor as she dried the knives and forks, clattering them into the compartments of the cutlery drawer. She didn't want to sound aggressive but her tone was harsh as she replied, 'You think you can breeze back into my life and start a relationship with me? You've got more frontage than Marks and Spencer, you have.'

'Why not? I've loved you for a long time, Lindsey.'

'Lerryn Trevonnian, how can you say that? You don't know me. Me as I am now.'

'I love you. I'm sure of that. We've known one another a long, long time, Lindsey.'

'But I'm not sure about myself, as regards lovers, like you are.' Lindsey's voice made a tell-tale stumble then she retrieved her composure and carried on. 'I'm not at all used to the gay thing, let alone words like – lesbian. They don't come naturally to me.'

'But your best friend is a lesbian and your little girl plays with her lover's little girls. You're used to that. Rosie loves Maureen, you said that yourself, and she's completely used to Tessa and Tessa's kids. So you are familiar with it in that sense.'

'Pass us that tea towel. The red stripey one. And shush, you'll wake Rosie.' Lindsey shook open the folded cloth and started wiping the dish which Lerryn had rinsed and passed to her. Then she said, 'Rocky used to say I was all sewn up inside a roll of cloth. I think she was right and I've started to unpick some of the stitches, Lerrie, but it takes time, lots more than you seem to think. It's true that Maureen used to fancy me, and she waited around for a while, hopefully. But I was sewn up tight inside a thick white shroud, after the accident. And I was glad when Maureen found Tessa. They're happy together and it makes a family life for me with Rosie. But inside me I'm still half dead and I don't know if I'm ever going to come alive.'

Lerryn turned from the sink with her arms up to her elbows in soap-suds.

'But you did tell me about Maureen. If you didn't want me to know you wouldn't have told me anything. All you'd have said was that Maureen was a gay woman who was lovers with Tessa. Here, you wanted to wipe this saucepan over with a cloth. Hold this while I wring one out for you.'

'I'm slow to change, Lerrie. I've been on my own since Peter died. And I never gave a thought to a woman lover, even though Maureen fancied me.'

'I don't mind being slow. What I want is to start. I want to stay the night and be close to you.'

'But I don't want to lead you a dance.'

'Well we've done the veleta and foxtrot.'

'And I'm not ready for the tango or the quickstep. Three fast weeks and a few friendly hugs. And you want more.' Lindsey sat down at the table.

Lerryn tipped out the bowl of washing up water and ran a new bowlful. She squeezed the washing up liquid bottle, pushed its red nozzle under the water, and let it suck. She couldn't tell why she was taking such a pleasure in the noises, whether it was childish or aggressive or both. She attacked another saucepan vigorously. She said, 'Yes I want more. And I'm sure we've got potential, you and me. For something long and real and lasting. I want to share it with you.'

'There's plenty of ways of sharing, without leaping into bed.'

'That's not what you said to Peter Shepherd.'

'Peter was a person, a man I loved. You can rewrite my life as much as you like, but he was the father of my child, and I have been alone these five years since I became his widow. Either you start to recognise that or we've nothing to build on. You had my address by all accounts. But you were nowhere when I was going through all that.' Lindsey took a fork and began fiddling with the soil in the potted plant that Lerryn had brought her. It was in a beautiful ceramic plant holder.

'You're right. I was nowhere. I went searching for you and you'd gone straight, sodding off with a man. So where did that leave me, queer of the sixties? In a wilderness such as you will never know. They queue at your door, if I'm to believe you. Well, I should be so lucky. I've stood at Gateways, making my drink last ages, getting up the courage to ask, ask.'

'Perhaps you're spoiled. Too used to getting what you ask for.'

'Me? What on earth are you on about?'

'Aunt Harry. Fairy godmother always bailing you out. I'm in this hard-to-let with a child – but you've got your own studio, no rent, lovely garden, descended from on high five years ago, twenty-first birthday present. There is no one up there on cloud nine to hand out flats or gardens in my family. No one.'

'Now who's raising her voice? You'll wake Rosie. Watch out, that pot, you'll drop it.'

'Drop it? Drop it?' Lindsey picked up the pot and Lerryn froze, anticipating what was about to happen as Lindsey said, 'I'll do more than sodding drop it!' She hurled the pot to the skirting board under the window where it shattered, scattering soil and sherds. The plant lay shocked and collapsed without its tiny trellis for support.

'Oh my God. You bitch!' That was Harry's. You knew that was Harry's.'

'Harry, Harry, Harry! I'm sick of your precious aunt. I've wanted to retaliate ever since she ordered those bloody newts' (Lindsey smirked in satisfaction, remembering Rita saying 'bloody newts') 'from Sheffield.'

'Do what? I don't understand.'

'No, you don't. How do you think I felt? My mum had to give me away they were so poor, and your aunt can order newts to play with from Sheffield.'

'You colluded in that, like I did.'

'I was obliged to. To be grateful, delighted, say thank you, watch my Ps and Qs. I bloody had to like those newts.'

'All these years, you've resented them?'

'Like you said, we go back a long way. You get all of me or none of me, Lerryn. Package deal. Me, my daughter Rosie, and all my feelings, and I tell you, I've got plenty. Oh I could love you. I could love you to pieces, yours and mine. That's why I want it out in the open. All of it. Every last bit of unfinished business. I am a survivor. A real toughie. I have had to be.'

Lerryn wiped over the draining board, playing for time, and put the kettle on for coffee. She felt herself becoming larger, her tall body filling to full size, and turning, she faced Lindsey with her back to the kitchen sink. She thought, This is it, then. I am, as they say, back to the wall. Make or break. She said, 'What do you want? Line us up on a Richter scale, the wretched of the earth? We both know about aloneness. And loneliness. And work. Hairdressing is low, low pay for long, long hours. And yes, I do really live with loneliness. I've been like an open cave with the sea washing me each tide, for years. Even if I'd been a rock pool, there'd have been some anemones. Shells and lovely colours.'

' "Shells and lovely colours",' Lindsey imitated her. 'Oh spare me the poor little rich girl scenario. You had money to cushion you, not like Maureen or Tessa. Women who struggle with their gayness, against odds that you'll never ever begin to know. Oh I *know* I'm not taking myself seriously about loving women. I've a lot to learn and go on learning. That's why I'm still living on my own, sleeping on my own, making love with no one, no one at all. But let's get this clear once and for all, Lerryn. A woman like you with an aunt like yours will never go hungry, either for food or for lovers. You told me yourself that Aunt Harry introduced you to the wealthy Anna von what's her name.'

'Get it right. Anna von Schiller.'

'Yes, Thanks. Schiller. I'm not ignorant, Lerryn. I never will be. I'm merely shrouded. Lost inside a thick roll of cloth like Rocky so cleverly realised. But I tell you something. If I ever hear you whinge about your lifestyle, I'll show you the other side of that door faster than you can say Aunt Harry. I respect you for your hours of work. I do. I respect what you worked through to get to art school and do brilliantly; and I like the paintings you've showed me this past few weeks. But you've got it made, because you have a place to live and a studio to work in, such as most girls from the working class would give the coats off their backs for. And all because your redhaired gorgon of a relative prostituted herself to her boss and got him to marry her! Well, good for her I say, but don't forget where your good luck came from.'

'Strewth, you are one hell of an angry woman, Lindsey. Like you say, I'm rushing things. I'm sorry, but I am sure of loving you and wanting you and I'm sure that I've the right to ask for what I want. I am perfectly certain that part of your anger is fear of your own power for loving. Call it a shroud if you like. But many women do go through what you've been through and don't stay hiding for as long as you. There's more in you than you want to know about. And that makes me sad as well as angry. Because you were a powerful strong teenager, and surely you know deep down that you're hiding from your whole self?'

Lindsey opened her eyes wide and stared at Lerryn as if seeing her for the first time. She was used to people crumbling when she was angry, though she didn't get angry very often. But Lerryn was standing calmly at the sink, drying her arms on the soft kitchen towel, looking strong and gentle and in control, and Lindsey wondered then what Lerryn was like as art tutor with her students, with such a steady fire burning inside her.

She had been about to shout at Lerryn to pick up the pieces of the pot and stick them back together if she was so offended about Harry's pot being broken. But now she realised she had met her match. Lerryn was no soulful little rich kid scrabbling for handouts from Harry. She was indeed a survivor, making it in a competitive world, and making it successfully.

'Tell me why you didn't stay with Anna, will you?' she asked as kindly as she could.

'Because she wanted me to travel with her, on her terms. I told you already, though you are having a hard time understanding, that apart from the flat with the studio, I will not take anything at all from Harry. And the same goes from Anna too. I could have had an easy life, art materials, places to sell at, barons and baronets to sell to. I've met people who'd turn you purple with anger at their money and resources. But I am independent and that is how I'm going to stay. I did love Anna, and we are still friends. No doubt you'll meet her sometime when she is in London. But I had never found out what there was for you and me; and that was always unfinished business. I have been lucky in love now and then, but that isn't what I'm talking about with you. I'm talking about a woman who fascinates me, whom I love, and with whom I want something lasting.'

'I'm not marrying anybody.' Lindsey stood up, found the brush and dustpan and began carefully sweeping up the sherds and soil, without further hurting the plant.

'I didn't say marriage. I don't want copies of married men and women. I don't belong in marriage and I don't want what it offers. I said something lasting. Would you like some coffee, Linz?'

Lindsey looked up from where she was kneeling. 'The pot is gone, just like our teenage years, Lerrie. Gone. Broken. Finished. If I start with you now, I have to start as the woman I am now. And yes, of course I am afraid. I know how to stick the bits of me together when I am on my own. I don't know how to do that with anyone else around. You arrive here, full of light and colours and you want to hurry me through.'

'I didn't expect a soft little northern lass who likes animals. I've spent too long a time on the wing for that. But I didn't expect to find you quite so hard.'

160

'I'm no one's fieldmouse, Lerrie. Sit down a moment. I'll make the coffee.'

Lindsey was trying to get a union branch started at the glove factory near Old Street. There was Lindsey herself, Shanti, Joyce, Rocky and Maureen.

Lindsey told Lerryn, 'We're all experienced machinists, fast and accurate, so we don't think they can get us for shoddy work. Well, they could try, but we think they'd have a job of it. It's going to be uphill, we all know that. Rocky and me, we think we might try to get on one of them short trades union courses at the trades union college, something like that. Maureen's been pushing me for years to study this, study that, but it's not for me. Not like Tessa, slogging through the OU. I couldn't be doing with that at all. I know who I am. I'm a working-class lass from the north and I don't give a damn. That's who I am. I don't want fancy letters after my name. None of that. But I would enjoy going on a course with Rocky, even if we had to take time off for it, you know, in our own time.'

Lerryn was getting to know Rosie, who was due to leave play-school and start 'real' school, as she called it, in September. She had offered to babysit for her on the nights when Lindsey was meeting with her other friends who were keen on the union.

'You know I'd have Rosie for you, don't you?'

'Would you? I was thinking that if I could time a short course in the school holidays or something, I could ask Nanan and Biff. Rosie adores them and vice versa.'

'Sounds like you've got it worked out.'

'Well, it was Rocky started me off years ago. She set me thinking about a lot of things. Don't get me wrong: I've nothing against thinking. I just don't want to study formally.'

'I'm beginning to get used to you. I often wonder what's going on in your head.'

'Trouble usually.'

'Fancy a trip down Ridley Road market this Saturday?'

'I thought you'd got an art workshop?'

'It was cancelled, thank heavens. I hate working Saturdays. I'd much rather be with you and Rosie.'

'All right, why not? And Rosie could have lunch in the pie 'n mash shop. She'd love that. You like my Rosie, don't you?'

'We like each other, or hadn't you noticed?'

'Course I had, daft thing. Can't tell you what it means to me.'

'Anyway, you stay and have your meeting tomorrow after work. I'll pick up Rosie from the child minder's and stay with her until you get in. I'll make us a late supper.'

The next night, Lerryn was bathing Rosie, filling the bath with bubbles from a huge plastic dog with a red hat that screwed on and off. It was bright yellow with a green bow around its neck and one eye in a permanent wink.

Rosie was a tall child with long hair which was dark-brown, almost black, and the same dark eyes as Lindsey and Moss. She had cream-and-roses skin and was a tubby little girl, always asking questions. Her favourite games all included singing, which she did at the top of her voice.

'When I grow up, Lerrie, I'm going to be an actress.'

'Pass me that big sponge, that's it, bend forward, I'm going to wash your back. Why do you want to be an actress, Rosie?'

'Cos I like dressing up. And singing. I'm going to be in plays in real school.'

'Okay, stand up now, mind, don't slip, here's a nice warm towel. Arms up and I'll lift you out.'

'You going to come and see me in my plays?'

'Course I am. Wild horses wouldn't stop me,' said Lerryn, rolling her eyes so that Rosie giggled. 'Let's dry those toes, then you can put your pyjamas and slippers on.'

Rosie climbed into her pyjamas and held out her hands and began to sing, loudly:

'If you're happy and you know it
                              clap your hands
If you're happy and you know it
                              clap your hands . . .

You sing too, Lerrie. I'll show you. I'll sing it then you sing it. That's how we do it at playschool. But I'm too big for playschool now.'

And Lerryn sang with Rosie:

'If you're happy and you know it
                              and you really want to show it
If you're happy and you know it
                              clap your hands.'

'Can I have a story?' Rosie asked. 'And I've got to have a pee, Mummy says, so as I don't pee my bed. I only pee my bed if I forget to go last thing.'

Lerryn read from *Where the Wild Things Are*, Rosie's current favourite. By the time she had closed the book, Rosie was curled up asleep.

Lerryn put the book down and the bedside light off. She tiptoed to Rosie's door, and leaving it ajar, she peered back around it and could make out the child's sleeping form and hear her breathing steadily.

She stood in the hall for a moment with the light throwing her shadow across Rosie's half-open door. She wiped a tear from her eye and was surprised to find it. Returning to the kitchen, and preparing supper for Lindsey, Lerryn imagined what it would have been like to be a fourteen year old on a first date, if she had been that lucky at fourteen. Instead, at that age she had been alone on a Cornish clifftop where kisses were as far away as stars in the night sky; love was the floor of the ocean, and you had to be a mermaid to dive in that deep.

Tonight after supper, she would return to her studio, alone. She knew who she loved and who she wanted. In her late twenties she was coming into her body. Her skin surface was her own coastline; her shapes, its hills and valleys. Her breathing was its climate; her potential passion, its grasses and flowers.

She wanted to blossom like heather-clad hillslopes; to fly like seagulls in warm air currents where land and sky touch one another. But always down the length of her spine there were the years of solitude; her central rock strength to which in storm or turbulence she would, if necessary, return.

Sixteen

Near the entrance to Southend Pier, Lindsey adjusted her camera, setting the lens to infinity and fiddling with the meter until she had a perfect light reading. She intended to photograph each minute of the day, a day she had been waiting for. It was October and Rosie was on half term, staying at Tessa and Maureen's for the weekend.

Waiting for Lerryn to return from the sweetshop, Lindsey looked out along the estuary, taking pictures of the sea birds who were diving and swooping around a cockle boat as it travelled inland to Leigh-on-Sea. Mentally, Lindsey saw the Pennines, with high rocky outcrops, where birds would be wheeling and rising, and the horizon would be wide and open like the one in front of her today. There was nothing to stop her mind flying away over the waters of the estuary, winging wider and wider circles until she came to rest on the expanse of Ladybower.

There, she might have lived with Pete. A lifelong companion.

Thoughts can time travel, she thought, amusing herself. They can fly like birds wherever they fancy, across land and time. The wings of her mind rose up from the surface of Ladybower and, gathering height and speed, they crossed the years, until they alighted on the railings of the pier, in the present, as Lerryn arrived.

They linked arms and began to walk along the pier, close together, watching the changing pink, blue and grey skies as the day gathered itself into folds of late afternoon.

'What a wonderful time to see the pier,' said Lindsey. 'Do you know I've never been along here before?'

'It's a good place to bring a camera,' replied Lerryn. 'I came here from college when I started taking pictures. I was fascinated with all the shapes and structures, the colours and lights, and always the birds, flocks of them from the salt marshes.'

'I never really bothered with photos before I met you. But now I've got this thing, I can't stop. I got some lovely ones of Rosie's birthday party, I hope they come out well. Hang on a minute, I want one of you laughing. Say cheese.'

Lerryn's short curly hair, peeping out from under her bobble hat, fringed her smiling face. She had on a red hat, red anorak and thick black scarf, and her eyes laughed into the camera, bright and happy, telling stories.

Lindsey closed the camera case. Lerryn opened the popcorn and they ate noisily, occasionally flinging pieces to the birds who caught them on the wing. Lindsey smiled at Lerryn. 'Moss told me a long time ago that something was calling me back to London. She was right. But I didn't know that at the time and I couldn't know it was you calling me, because I didn't even know you were in London.' Lindsey watched the sky for a moment then added, 'It's been an amazing time for me since you arrived on my doorstep with a bunch of roses. You are changing my life, Lerrie, do you know that?'

Lerryn smiled, feeling very happy inside. She didn't feel a need to talk very much, and it seemed to be Lindsey's need instead. She searched Lindsey's face and then lent her a tissue to wipe off the sticky popcorn. She wanted to kiss it off, licking Lindsey's mouth in tiny, gentle licks, but in all the weeks since the scene with Aunt Harry's ceramic pot, she hadn't let Lindsey hear even a whisper of her desire, returning each night to sleep on her own, hoping that the changes she seemed to see in Lindsey were real changes, towards a shared life together.

They stopped walking and stood by the parapet as another cockle boat came into view, trailing a wide wake across which the gulls danced.

'I still hate shellfish. The very thought and I curl up inside. It'd be all pink and wriggly and slimy.' Lindsey shivered, screwing up her whole face. 'Give me a bag of chips any day.'

'Don't worry, Linz. I'll only eat them when I'm on my own. Mussels and brown rice. Yummy.'

'Stop it, or I'll be ill.'

'I've got some of your favourites in my pocket, do you want one?'

'Not buttered brazils? You are an angel. What are you?'

'I'm an angel. Here, take a couple.'

Lindsey unwrapped a sweet and curled her tongue around it, smiling and feeling like Rosie, five years old on an outing. She put the sweet in her cheek and drew the sugary saliva through her teeth.

The skies above the estuary were deepening from pink to orange, with long streaks of grey. Blue shadows were washed from the west by the wind.

'Look Lerrie, it reminds me of Rocky and her rolls of cloth and my stitches.' Lindsey pointed up to the west. 'The wind is up there shaking the sky, shaking the end of the rolls, look.'

Lindsey held both her arms high over her head as if she were the wind holding the end of her rolls of cloth in a strong grip, and shook them vigorously. In the sky above her, mile after mile of cloth-cloud flowed away from the grip of the wind. On the pier, the end of Lindsey's blue scarf came untucked and flapped as she moved. Turning and letting her arms fall to her sides, Lindsey looked into Lerryn's eyes and said, 'I love you.' Lerryn opened her arms and Lindsey stepped towards her and they closed their eyes, holding each other close. 'I love you,' Lindsey repeated. 'I want us to be lovers now.' She looked into Lerryn's eyes and winked, adding, 'We can still be friends, can't we?'

'I love you too. And, yes, we can be friends as well as lovers.' Lerryn's laughter echoed along the pier, and they linked arms, dancing in a two-step, mixing up their feet and almost tripping.

It was cold but not bitter as they reached the end of the pier. They stood with their backs to the balustrade and their hands tucked in their pockets, silently sky-gazing. A long V shape of birds came into view, and as Lindsey reached for her camera, other Vs arrived, joining on so that the sky became a lattice of intersecting shapes.

The sky was deep apricot; it was impossible to tell the colour of the birds. They looked as if they were embroidered, each bird separately, sharply edged silhouettes of deepest black. The whole V shape was sliding and slipping as if a hidden hand were pulling and pushing, but not a single collision took place.

Lindsey clicked away, then she turned to Lerryn. 'Those lovely apricot-coloured shells in your shell collection are just the colour of this sky. When I was round at your studio and I saw you cleaning the small shells, I thought you had lovely hands. I wanted you to touch me like them, like the shells. And then you took me dancing. And we still weren't lovers, but I knew I wanted you, and I always wanted someone who could dance.'

'That's wicked. Couldn't Peter dance?'

Lindsey wrapped her arms around herself and chuckled. 'Don't make me laugh. I loved him in spite of his two left feet. He had absolutely no dance sense at all, poor love. I always thought I could lose myself on a dance floor given half a chance.'

'It was a good night out, that.'

'And you didn't get me drunk, proposition me, nothing like that.'

'I don't know how I held back. I was really desperate that night.'

'You didn't show it.'

'Then miracles will never cease! Am I dreaming or did you hold me close a few minutes ago and tell me you loved me?'

'Yes, I did. You know, I started to trust you when I realised you really meant what you said about caring for Rosie as well as me. And hearing about your hidden hurts, both of us having a lot of hurt inside and taking time to find them and sort them out.'

'Are you sure about this, Lindsey? We still have a lot of hurts, things that won't surface easily, get dealt with easily. Hurts we don't know about, but they're still there. You really want me – a lover as well as a friend?'

'I'm sure. I really want you. I love you deeply, Lerrie.'

Lerryn spread her arms out, spinning around, lifting her feet and sweeping her arms in circles. As she danced she whistled and sang. Lindsey, laughing, tapped the rhythm with her feet and clapped her hands. The last remaining birds were taken by surprise, shuffling along the top of the balustrade, almost in tempo, keeping a wary eye on the dancing wild woman and her new lover.

Book Three

Seventeen

It was market day in Herton. A bright gold and blue October morning, the day after the election of 1974. The pavements were straddled by groups of people all talking about the national results: Labour: 11,456,597; Conservative: 10,464,675.

Biff walked down the High Street from the church to the market. At the bus stop people had gathered in an uneven line, like a drunken centipede, arms and legs all waving and each leg wearing a different shoe. Carrier bags and shopping trolleys, children in pushchairs and toddlers on reins, were all packed tight around the line in a jumble of wheels and colours. Behind the queue on a boarded-up shop whose lease had run out were the various party political posters, the messages following the wavy lines of the corrugated iron.

Biff bypassed the bus stop carefully, wary of being sent sprawling as she had a couple of times since starting to go everywhere with a walking stick. Her body felt lighter today, her jaunty air echoed by the glee around the market. The leaves fluttering on the trees were late turning brown; and overhead swallows were swooping and swirling, as if they'd waited with Herton people to know the result before leaving for the sun.

Grace Dundy, in her best red coat with a red rosette pinned to the collar, was waiting for Biff on the seat by the market, and Biff lowered herself down gratefully.

'Hello, Biff. We won! Even the weather is on our side today. How're you this fine morning?'

'Wonderful. All the better for seeing you. I knew you'd be wearing red. Love the rosette.'

'Wanna smell my rosette, Biff?'

'You wanton woman you,' laughed Biff. 'What would the Labour Party say? Taking their name in vain.'

'Herton's was one of the first results home, did you watch it, Biff? I'd had three cups of coffee and I was cross-legged but I daren't leave the box.'

'I know. How's the new colour telly, Grace? Bet that swingometer showed up good.'

'Good! It was bloody marvellous, 'scuse my French. You know, when they say green's so and so and red's such and such, well you could actually tell the difference. Mind you, I can hardly keep awake this morning. But I had to meet you anyroad, and I had to get me bits on the market. Besides, I always wear red on election days, don't I? Want me to do a twirl?'

'Grace, you will anyway, whether I want you to or not. You're just a devil in disguise, that's what.'

'Red for fire and red for danger, eh Biff?' Grace stood, lifted both arms, so that her coat was raised almost above her knees and turned around slowly. She had lovely legs and she knew it. 'I love flirting with you, it's so safe, you old married thing, you. Us merry widows must just languish in the wings. Oh my.' Grace sat down again, sighed and rolled her eyes.

'We were glad of a lift to the polls. It was kind of your Brenda,' said Biff, deliberately changing the subject with practised expertise.

'No trouble, Biff. When're you getting that ramp?'

'Three weeks, they said. Silly isn't it, but those two steps to the street make so much difference. Ten years we've been waiting for that ramp.'

'Not any more, eh Biff? Now that Labour's in, we might have some changes. What I love about today is that Herton people always vote Labour and now the rest of the country's realised we're right.'

'They don't even know where Herton is,' laughed Biff, 'Anyway, we're *left*.'

'I should have been an MP. Then the whole world would have known.'

'In that coat and hat, Grace, you could lead the entire revolution, up there, leaning forward on your two-horse chariot, wielding a trident.'

'You're a saucy bugger. Where's your rosette then? Here, have mine.'

'What you doing, pinning that thing on me? I look like something in the Whit Monday gymkhana, old stock class three.'

'No you don't, you look like the mayor of this town minus his chains.'

'What about our milkman, then? Moss didn't half have a go at him. He only came delivering yesterday with his float all done out in blue!'

'His wife's got a blue rinse as well. I bet she had it for the occasion. Not as effective as my red coat.'

'His bungalow's nearly finished. That's what's done it, we reckon. His own plot of land and having his house built.'

'Yes, and by the time your Moss'd finished with him, I bet he was stone-faced too.'

'He was. She threatened to cancel the milk. And she told him she was going to get the others to boycott. She's boycotted South Africa for years, she said, so what's one Conservative milkman to her!!'

Elsie Newson arrived, laden with goods. She puffed out as she sat down like the air from the top of one of her carrier bags. She had four, all different sizes and colours, bulging with square shapes and stuffed with extras to bursting point.

'Life goes on, dunnit?' she began. 'Somebody's got to keep this country going, that's what I say. Reckon things've got to change for the better for all of us with this lot in,' she continued, hardly pausing for breath and as if to say that it couldn't get worse anyway. 'Well now, Biff and Grace, what d'you both think o' the news?' But Elsie didn't wait for a reply, carrying on with, 'He got a thirty-thousand majority, this time. I was right excited, I can tell you, and my poor old dad he nearly had one of his turns bouncing up and down in his chair, writing it all down in his little notebook. I had to buy him a new one you know; he filled the other one up. Now, which bag did I put it in, hang around. I'll have to go through them all.'

'Don't bother on our account, Elsie. We'll take your word for it.'

'Oh I don't know, I've so much stuff what with all me gang to tea today. Our Debbie's brought the baby home at last, poor little mite. Jaundice. My old dad told her it was divine retribution. But she's only fourteen and anybody can make a mistake once in their life, can't they? Ooh, he is an old sod when he wants to be. I told him to watch his tongue or the divine carving knife up in the sky would swipe down and slice him. Silly sod half believed me. I know he's terrified, him being such an old sinner. Well, I'd best be going. You all right are you both?' Biff and Grace nodded, smirking. 'That's good. I'll pop in tomorrow evening and bring Moss a bit o' me gingerbread, that's if the old sod himself hasn't eaten it right from under me nose. Tell your Moss I'll be round, won't you, Biff? Mind how you go.'

Elsie trundled off, puffing and swaying with the weight of the shopping.

Grace said, 'Whew. She doesn't change. She was just like that in the reception class in Herton Infants, and I dread to think how long ago that was. Doesn't time rush by?'

'Time and Elsie.'

'Talking of her granddaughter, how's yours?'

'Our Lindsey? She's fine, thanks. Been out canvassing for the election. I didn't think she had it in her. She wrote me such a beautiful letter. Do you remember how I used to take her out to the packhorse bridge?'

'I do that. And our Rita 'n all. Isn't it a shame they fell out and us such close friends. I could bang their heads together, that I could. That's just broken my dream. Do you dream, Biff?' Biff nodded. 'I was wearing this red dress and banging me head on a wall. Nice when it stops. I woke with a terrible headache. Not this morning. Must've been yesterday. Ooh, the human mind is a funny thing.'

'Tell you what, I've got this new book from the library, all about dreams. I got a lot from it. All about seeds and plants and stuff. You plant the seeds and watch them grow and that sets you off dreaming.'

'Interesting,' said Grace, who liked gardening. It was something she shared with Biff. They swopped seeds and cuttings frequently.

'Some of it's a bit, well, you know, American. There's a whole lot of them over there, so it seems. Not that it's new. I often dream about things while I'm gardening, don't you?'

'Oh, of course I do. I do most of my thinking while I'm doing the washing or planting in the garden.'

'There you are then. Been around for ages. They're calling it a visualisation revival.'

'Geron. They do always go a bit far-fetched over there. Everything's bigger 'n better in America.'

'Moss and me were talking about it after Winnie Mandela was on telly. Moss said, "If you don't dream about freedom, you'll never reach for it, will you? But you don't just get things by imagining them. Nelson Mandela's in prison imagining freedom and don't you go trying to tell me he isn't visualising hard enough; or that there's something inside him that is stopping it".'

'Well, that's Moss's thing, isn't it? South Africa. I decided to boycott South African apples and jam on account of her. And I did love their apricot jam.'

'My heart weeps for you.'

'I know. You don't get higher wages just by planting a few money seeds under the full moon, do you Biff?' Grace paused, thinking about similar conversations they'd had over the years. Coal. Diamonds. Gold. After a few seconds Grace said, 'How do they do the visualising then? How come they can make it work? Is it like a sort of seance? Do you remember when I went to one? I did enjoy it. But I didn't get no voices.'

'There's all sorts of exercises. Things to do to make things happen. It's all in the book: you borrow it. You read it.'

'No. That reminds me. I told you the human mind was a funny thing. Mine is, anyroad. What *I* need to borrow is Moss's catalogue. I need a new string for me whirly.' She winked at Biff, loving the double meaning. 'Mind you it's been so long since I had a whirl. I doubt I could remember what to do.'

'It's all in the mind at our age, Grace,' lied Biff smoothly. 'Anyway, why don't you come round tomorrow morning? She'll be right glad to talk to you. She's stuck indoors such a lot.'

'How's her hip? Is she still in so much pain?'

Biff's voice dropped as it usually did when she confided about Moss's arthritis to Grace. Grace, as usual, leaned slightly nearer. 'Awful. Doctor's had to up the painkillers again, and they're affecting her vision. She gets blurs. The effect of the prescription. They chop and change it: try this, try that. She's addicted to her sleeping pills, but what can you do? She doesn't get that good a sleep as it is. We're quite worried about her eyes, actually.'

'Health is everything, Biff. Without your health you've got nothing. Nothing. Lucky *you're* still strong.'

'Plenty of life in me and Moss yet. Plenty.'

'If there's ever anything I can do, I'm on the end of a phone. You know that, Biff. Solid. That's what you two mean in my life. Hours and hours you've listened to me. Years and years. You passing down to the library, then? All right, I'll come part way, keep you company.'

The market was in full swing by now, though it was only 9.30. Some hadn't had much sleep; and some hadn't bothered going to bed at all. Others had slept through it all, certain their one vote hadn't made any difference, but had woken to find the radio humming with the change; Herton buzzing with the excitement, and the nation and parliament suddenly alive in everybody's kitchen. Herton and London linked for a day. It would wear off. London would return to itself, remote, inaccessible, irrelevant again.

'Oh, here's my Arthur, just pulling up with the van,' said Grace. She waited for Arthur to park: 'Hello, Arthur. That's nice. You are good. Best be off then, Biff. Be seeing you. And don't forget. I'm on the end of a phone. Thanks to my Arthur. I couldn't wish for a better son-in-law. All right, all right, I'm hurrying. There's no peace for the wicked, eh Biff?'

Biff smiled and waved, nodding hello to Arthur who was used to his mother-in-law's enthusiasm. The van moved off and for a moment Biff was alone, the market and high street bustling but empty. She pushed the feeling away. Herton was home, and its people were community, warts and all. The longing to leave and free herself from her disguise had faded to a vague sense of unease which came over her almost like a memory, now and then. At seventy-eight she had come to terms with herself, preparing for her eighties with a three-way understanding between the young, the middle-aged and older woman inside her.

Entering the library she thought suddenly of Lerryn Trevonnian striding into the grocer's shop, aged nineteen. She was now Lindsey's lover, of that Moss was also certain, but the younger generation were afraid to, what was the phrase they used in *Spare Rib*, 'come out' to Moss and Biff, so it was difficult to celebrate it all.

Lerryn was someone who might never find internal peace, thought Biff. As if she were running one of life's races in which somebody was for ever moving the finishing tape. Biff suspected Lerryn moved it herself, too, a new challenge coming from her own feelings; her mind seemed to swirl with questions, like a sea pulled by the moon. Biff started on the first newspaper, remembering the 1920s and the early 1930s when she herself had searched with the same internal pressures as Lerryn. Exiled from where she'd grown up and couldn't return to, dealing with invisibility.

She wondered what the rest of the decade would bring for Herton. The miners' long winter strike had challenged the Conservative government of 1972. There was talk about the national issues of energy, North Sea gas, nuclear power. The miners were searching for ways forward in the union, and month by month there had already been enough controversy to make Herton's men and women aware that the issues would not disappear conveniently, Labour victory or no Labour victory.

Biff read the daily newspapers slowly, the post-mortems, the analyses, the reasons the Tories were giving for losing, the swings, the floating votes, the housewives' votes.

It was Lerryn who had sent them their first copy of *Spare Rib*, with a short note: 'Thought you might both be interested in this. Lindsey tells me you both think men and women should be more radical about sharing childcare, and I know you, Biff, did so much with Lindsey when she was little. Hope you won't be offended.'

Biff had written back: 'We enjoyed reading it a lot, including the letters page where that woman said her husband and son always read it. Now I'm not at all sure about the politics of that. I think there are some things women should not show to men. But the copy you sent was certainly very, well, bland. Some of the early suffragette documents were far far more radical – my sisters certainly said so, may they rest in peace. My mother was a strong feminist, campaigning and so forth. She died for her belief in women's right to vote. And it is wonderful to know that you young women now are actively challenging all the stereotypes again. Take care. Love from Moss and me, and I am glad you sent it. Moss is going to take out a subscription.'

The viburnum tree burst into fragrant pink flowers in early December, and withstood the bright frosts of January 1975. Not until late February did the leaves appear, softening the outline of stark dark branches. The blossoms, having done their work, faded, as the tree prepared for spring and summer.

The days lengthened and dawn arrived three minutes earlier every day. Moss was cheated of a good night's sleep by the rooks making their nests in the tall trees down Church Lane. Once awake, she lay struggling with pain. Her left hip had become increasingly stiff and swollen, her bones felt raw and sharp, her muscles clenched tight so that she couldn't find a comfortable position in which to fall asleep again.

I'm like a country divided, she thought, splits and schisms chiding each other in a turbulent landscape. She shifted with difficulty towards Biff's sleeping form. She eased herself on to her right hip, curved her body as much as she could towards Biff's, and brought her left arm over Biff. In the position in which she had always loved to sleep, she found the arched warmth of Biff's back, solid and real. Like having her own rainbow composed only of sunlight, there in her own double bed. Moss knew that Biff was feigning sleep, knew why, and loved her for it.

Mind over matter, Moss forced herself to breathe slowly in spite of the pain in her hip, until she became accepting of it, so that it was not controlling her, making her afraid and angry. It was part of her body, a negative and wearisome part, but there with her for ever, or at least for the rest of her conscious life.

If she hated it, it could dominate her. It could fill her waking thoughts and then her days would be linked together by an inward-turned anger, that she who had been so active running in the Darlington fields, toiling at The Hall, loving Florence under the rhododendrons, could be prevented from moving.

Slowly she concentrated on breathing, calmness, acceptance. It took so much energy to do that, but as she gained calmness, so she gained strength. She was still the woman who lived with Biff, loved with Biff.

She breathed slowly and deliberately, concentrating. The pain became a dull blanket over her left side. Slowly, she counted each breath. In two three four five – hold – one two – out two three four five. Breathing, counting, holding and concentrating, she took herself down through the layers of wakefulness, back towards a depth of sleep.

When Moss finally fell asleep, Biff was able to relax and breathe normally again. Faking sleep was difficult these early mornings, but if Biff didn't then Moss would remain awake. Then they'd both become exhausted, and dealing all day with Moss's painful hip would be harder than it already was. Sleep was the best gift that she could give to Moss. But having slept beside Moss every night for over forty years, Biff found that faking anything at all was a work of art.

Sex couldn't be faked. True, they disagreed about the concept of old age, Moss declaring that she'd been working since she was five and had a right to say she was old; and Biff totally opposed to thinking of herself as old until she was eighty which was another two years away.

Despite this disagreement, around which they'd had a fair share of hot words, they both knew and said that they wanted to continue to make love, to have the fulfilment they'd always had. The younger generations might have words for all the things Moss and Biff had never had any public language for; but Biff would have defied any young dyke to enjoy sex more than she and Moss had.

She lay in the bedroom, listening to the rooks squawking at each other to shut up as they couldn't get a word in edgeways. She could feel Moss's warmth along the length of her back. Lovely. The idea which had been forming slowly in her mind, since she read the article in the magazine in the reference library last week, came back to her and she reshaped it during the next half hour, into images, silent words, and a plan of action. When that happened Biff usually felt full of resolve and became satisfied because she had made a decision. She had to 'get her act together' as they said these days on television. She thought back through all the years in Herton when it had taken a woman to be a gentle-man.

She would stride down the High Street just as determined as when she first cycled into Herton to escape death at the hands of the

Manchester police. She had lacked neither courage nor integrity, then. Neither would she now. Comforted by her new intentions and her old bravery, she sent herself to sleep for another hour or two.

It turned out to be a chilly April morning. Not the sort of morning that most people in Herton would choose to go shopping, unless there didn't happen to be a choice because the family had run out of cornflakes or bread or such like. Not that most men would be seen dead out in the town carrying shopping bags. For a man, most men, to go shopping, there'd have to be a family crisis such as the wife or mother going down with flu or the next baby starting to arrive ahead of schedule. Even then the wife's sisters and women friends and neighbours leapt into action very quickly.

However, on that particular morning, Biff needed to be carrying a shopping bag, so over breakfast she offered to go and get some bits and pieces including a new loaf. They worked out the list over a second cup of tea, and Biff also took back two library books under the pretence of getting them renewed. Moss obviously suspected nothing. Biff kissed Moss goodbye in her usual way, and set off up to the Square past the church, and turned left down the hill to the High Street and library.

The morning was like autumn instead of spring. For April it was a wonderful October. A mist hung in layers so that Biff thought of walks on moorlands swirling with secrets.

Biff always enjoyed the small discoveries that happened on each walk down Herton High Street, which was never quite the same twice over.

Today, it was spiders' webs with dews on them, spun around the awnings of shops. Biff realised that Moss would have missed them because they were minute and Moss's sight was deteriorating. Sometimes she missed things on television too, and occasionally said it was a relief to listen to the radio because she didn't have to deal with the dazzle. They were thankful for her hearing, which was perfect. Mercy Dundy had a hearing aid and it was a nuisance when there was traffic. She couldn't always tell which direction the noise was coming from, and noises blurred into one another. 'That's age, isn't it?' said Mercy. 'Like the curate's egg. Good in parts.'

Biff had the High Street to herself as she had planned. It was only five past nine. The junior children had started but the infants didn't begin until 9.30, so it was a few minutes too early for them to be leaving home. There were no mothers with duckling groups of bobbing children, and always one or two stragglers, webbing their way along, quacking nineteen to the dozen.

She called into the newsagent's for her copy of the local paper. The front page was all girl guides and boy scouts raising money for the Methodist chapel roof; two columns about the spate of shoplifting that had hit the town; a few column inches down the right hand side about the new health food shop called Saffron and Lentils, which had just opened at the other end of town. Biff knew no one who ate lentils except in pease pudding and she never used saffron because of the cost. She gave the shop a few weeks.

Biff reached the library and went in. Mrs Hinton, whom Biff really liked, was on duty. This made Biff feel worse about her intentions, but the time had come. Today was the day. She handed in her books for renewal. Had them stamped, put them back in the deep bag, exchanged comments about the turn in the weather, and made for the reading room.

Because it was misty outside the reading room lights were on, casting warm yellow questions into the grey daylight, which swirled in from the high windows. Overhead the same green roof glass that Biff had shown proudly to Moss over fifty years ago was still holding out against the weather and time. Biff remembered when there'd been a power cut and the place had been lit by candles until the fire department ruled that it was a hazard. It had looked lovely with the candles.

It was chilly as church in the reading room. No one was about. There was no graffiti on the walls and no one ever defaced the books.

To Biff it was almost a holy place. Certainly she felt reverential in front of so much written knowledge. A world of voices and opinions on each page. But times were changing privately and publicly. In London and other large cities there was once again an active Women's Liberation Movement, making history generating new ideas, new ways of behaving, new language. She and Moss had watched its coming with deep excitement. From the point of view of her reading she was totally up to date, though only she and Moss knew that. Yet she was not as knowledgeable as she might have been in breaking into unused houses to restore them to homes again, and had been secretly shocked when Lindsey and Lerryn had talked about squats and squatting as political actions. But the time had come to take action again. She and her sisters had set light to post boxes for the cause; her own mother had broken shop windows, generally inciting other women to violence and civil disobedience.

The time was at hand to stop chickening out. Coolly, Biff liberated the magazine from its place on the display rack, and filled the gap by moving the other magazines along. Aware of its expensive glossy cover, she put the magazine into her shop(lift)ing bag, avoiding reading the white label that she knew said 'Herton Library: not to be removed from the reading room'. There was still no one about.

She read the papers for her usual amount of time so as not to bring attention to herself. Providing she kept her head, hiding behind the status she had built up as an upright respectable older citizen of the town, she would be absolutely beyond suspicion or reproof. The reading room was filling up slowly. She read on, confident that by the time she walked out with the magazine securely zipped into her bag, no one would imagine that today she had taken a significant step to change her sex life.

Biff walked back along the High Street and up the hill towards the Square. She turned right past St Stephen's, calling hello to the vicar who called back, suspecting nothing.

At the top of Church Lane she was just in time to see the methodist minister leaving their house on his bicycle, on his rounds scooping up enthusiasm for the Whitsun Fete that would raise the new roof on his chapel. Biff looked around to see whether Father Roderick, the Roman Catholic priest might arrive, completing a holy trinity all out to get her; or even the local bobby pounding the beat to keep an eye on the red pillar boxes of Herton.

She realised, not for the first time, that she'd become a tame Peter Rabbit in an overcrowded Herton cage. To date she'd escaped being found by Mr McGregor and turned into Rabbit Pie. She half wondered whether, when she finally made it into her burrow a few yards away, Moss might have camomile tea ready brewed and send her to bed on her own.

'Hello, love. You're just in time for coffee,' Moss called as Biff entered. 'You must've heard me putting the kettle on. Give me your coat. There. Sit there and get warm. You're all damp, but the mist is lifting, going to be a nice day. How did you get on?'

'I got everything we wanted. It's cold in that library. Oh, lovely.' Biff drank from the scalding cup which Moss had placed on the table beside her. 'I can feel this warming the cockles. Wasn't that the Reverend Moore leaving?'

'Yes. I do feel a bit guilty, you know. They need so many thousands for that roof, and I really haven't given it much thought. Still, I said I'd make a cake for his Guess the Weight stall. That cheered him up a bit.'

'Why on earth should you feel guilty when you've done so much over the years?' Biff looked over at the worktop. 'Is there any coffee left in that pot? Good, then I'll have another cup thanks, love. Though I shouldn't, I'll be on the run the rest of the day.'

'I can never understand how all this coffee doesn't stop you sleeping.'

'Oh, nothing stops me sleeping. You know me, head on the pillow and I'm out like a light till the alarm goes. How are you sleeping these nights?'

'Not too bad. Mustn't grumble. I curled myself around you this morning and you were there so sound asleep and warm.'

'You'd woken up early again, had you?'

'Somebody should do something about those rooks, Biff. What a cacophany! They were having a union meeting at dawn this morning. All hell let loose by the sound of it. I reckon one of them wanted a strike and the committee disagreed.'

'I was wondering whether you might have a read of this,' said Biff, taking the magazine from the shopping bag and offering it to Moss.

'What's that then, love?' Moss took the magazine and held it at arm's length peering down her nose at the blurred title. 'Now where did I leave my reading glasses?'

'I'll get them. There they are on the draining board.'

'Oh yes. I was reading the instructions on that new cleanser. Well now, you been buying magazines? My, it feels like a posh one. Oh thanks, love.' Moss took the reading glasses from Biff, took her other ones off, put them on and read the title of the magazine, '*Health and Fitness*. My goodness, are we taking up herb tea or the long jump?'

'I borrowed it from the library.'

'Herton Library: not to be removed from the reading room,' Moss read. 'So you did. I should have put in a word for you when the minister came. Don't you feel a bit guilty?'

'I was thinking of a map you borrowed once from The Hall.'

'It was just gathering dust on the·shelf. Saved some poor skivvy from a bit of extra work. Now where was I?'

'Baiting me but I didn't bite.'

'Is there something in this that you think would help us, Biff?'

'Page forty-one.'

Moss turned to page forty-one and read slowly, the corner of her mouth winking up, and occasionally she nodded as she followed the columns.

'Aren't we a bit old for that kind of thing?'

'I was thinking we might get one. Out of our savings.'

'You're not thinking of giving French lessons at your age?'

'Now why would I want to give French lessons in this town? And to whom? Besides I can't speak French.'

'It does look comfortable. But . . . '

'I know what you're going to say, love, but I've been through all the money, and I'm sure we can run to it. I mean . . . ' Biff stopped, embarrassed that she'd used the word run, when Moss was having difficulty walking, and had to be taken to and from Methodist services on Sundays by people with cars, on a rota.

Realising that Biff was distressed, Moss reassured her, 'Don't worry. You can't get it right every time. Nobody can. Anyway, I wasn't going to say anything at all about money. What I was wondering, is what will the neighbours think when the thing's delivered?'

'They'll just think we've ordered a piece of furniture.'

'It doesn't resemble your average Herton fireside chair or three piece suite.'

'Oh, Lord.'

'Don't take the Lord's name in vain. Why don't you make me one?'

'Why didn't I think of that?'

'And I'll upholster it. I've got that corduroy skirt length that Lindsey gave me. I've been hanging on to it. I was going to get Brenda Jackson to make it up for me. Did you know she's taking in sewing on the side?'

'Perhaps she's saving up for one of these.'

'I've been keeping it and I never knew what for.'

'I could sit beside you. It's about the same height as the doctor's couch thing. I got to thinking about it the last time I came with you to the surgery, when I saw him help you on to it with that little stool of his.'

'So we'll need one of those to go with it.'

'And then I can sit beside you and massage you all over.'

'And I can too. I keep telling you God is on our side. If he wasn't he'd never have sent you this magazine.'

'Do you think you can leave God out of this?'

'The question is, can you make one?'

'I don't think that'll be a problem. They'll deliver the wood.'

'Yes, and you're always having bits of wood delivered for your shed and shelves and things. The neighbours wouldn't think a thing of *that*.' Moss turned back to the magazine and sucked her lips as she re-read the article. 'Hey, Biff. Get a load of this. It's even got a little place to put your nose.'

'*Your* nose.'

'One's nose. One could put one's nose in one's slot on one's massage table, couldn't one?'

'One could.'

'One is quite fancying a sauna as well.'

'Where on earth would one put a sauna?'

'In heaven, Biff, not on earth. I shall have a sauna in my bungalow in heaven. This one is lovely. Here, read this. It's Norwegian pine. I bet that smells good. What you don't know, because I didn't think to mention it before, is that when you were out pottering in your shed yesterday, I listened to a radio play about a Scandinavian family who had a sauna. It was so true to life I could almost smell the pine there coming from that radio.'

'Stop winding me up.'

'Shame about that corduroy though. I'd have preferred it if it had been dark green.'

Biff decided to change into her gardening clothes because the morning mist had given way to a lovely spring day. But as she made her way to the door to the stairs, Moss called her back. 'Wait a minute. Don't go. There's more, much more to say. Come and sit here with me. I'm burning with it.'

During all their years together, whenever Moss had taken on that particular tone, that change in her face, the angle of her head, Biff had been fascinated, compelled by the fire and beauty inside Moss, and drawn to her, strength for strength.

Moss continued, as Biff settled, knowing they'd talk, talk, talk until they'd talked out, layer upon layer, laying roads from the large stones below to the fine small ones that lay on top, a surface for journeying along, together, 'There are times when it's fun to be coy, glancing at you sideways, love, half saying, half revealing. Why not? After all we've talked day in day out since nineteen twenty; that's a lot of words for two women, a lot of loving, and what's a little bit of gentleness, even shyness sometimes between old friends and lovers like the two of us?'

In reply Biff reached out, laying her hand on Moss's thigh, and kept it there softly, and for a moment, eyes met, knowing, an old unspoken knowing.

'But,' began Moss again, 'but we needn't be trapped inside that coyness. Not when we've shared bath water from the same copper in the same bath. Remember? The one who had her monthlies went in second, the one who didn't got first water? No room for coyness when two women both bleed, and need each other's bodies so much that passion won't wait. Oh, we don't have the free words and names these young ones have. We don't even use words like shit, do we?' Biff grunted, shaking her head in agreement. 'And we're both a bit shocked sometimes when Lindsey comes up with some of her so called modern talk. But we do have our words for blood and need, and touching each other. My mouth has known every inch of your body. We've had our own language for all our wanting.

'I won't tolerate coyness now,' continued Moss, 'not now we're getting old. Though we don't agree what old is, what old means. Doesn't matter. We had a passion that no young woman these days could even begin to show in words. A power that kept us together, needing and wanting in one another's arms, year in year out, through thick and thin. A need so huge that we still need, a well so deep we still drink from it.

'We didn't have a well of loneliness, God bless Radclyffe, and may God rest her soul. She paid and we paid. Paid and paid. Her in public, us in private. Right or wrong, we made that decision.

'I read these young women's books, their poems, you know I do. And nowhere have I come across descriptions that go one penny in the pound anywhere near the sheer energy we used to make, with our lust and loving.

'And we still touch each other, not like we used to, my disability stops us, heaven help us, so we need a massage table, the right height, so that I can touch and be touched all over by you.

'Our trouble is we can't talk freely to anyone else. Not like the mothers used to do in my kitchen. There's no laughter and ridicule anywhere in the world quite like a bunch of married women talking about their sex lives. I never told you the half of it . . . '

'Spare me the details.'

'I always did. Poor old Frank. I used to have to make things up, just so as I'd have something to say. They expected me to talk like they did, after all, and I could hardly tell them I'd spent the night while the children were asleep and my husband was snoring his head off, with my hands all over the lodger's body, could I?' Moss reached for Biff's hand, searching Biff's face.

'I forget sometimes,' replied Biff, thinking carefully, feeling for the right words, 'I forget what tough women we are, how much passion we've made. Every day I feel the sensations of your hands on me, in me, when we were young and agile.'

'And now we're not young and you're still flexible in all your joints and I'm not. But my mind is flexible, open to the past and the here and now. Like those wonderful actresses who go on for years and years and become Dame this and Dame that, so lively you could listen to them for hours and hours on the radio, so many ideas all fizzing.' Moss fizzed the ideas, with her hands talking with them as she thought it all through, though her hands had some rheumatism now and some of her knuckles were misshapen. But her hands were still beautiful, her nails filed short and smooth. A lifetime of love and power had flowed through those fingers.

Moss continued, 'Loving you has been power and blood and tears, and getting up in the middle of passion because one of us needed the toilet, or one of the children cried. Loving you has been feeling my thighs needing you as I've walked around all day, wanting, waiting for the shop to close, waiting for the dinner to be over, waiting for the children to sleep. And then pulling off my clothes, and washing my body and folding right into you, there, clean, and smelling of need.

'And there I sat, a coy little woman making gentle jokes in some other woman's voice, about "one's dear love".' Moss paused. 'I want you, I want all our voices, I want all our loving, not bits and pieces. Not to be hiding from you like I've hidden from the whole world, God knows I've had plenty of practice, just as you have. But. But with you, no coyness, no hiding. No gentle jokes as if that's all. My need for you is as raw now as it was when I was young and pregnant, suckling Sadie on my lap and telling you I loved you. Raw need and pure lust. Blood and tears, and lava. Red hot, white hot lava.' Moss reached over to Biff and kissed her, adding: 'That's all, my love. You can go and get your gardening clothes on now.'

Eighteen

Lindsey followed Lerryn along the coast path. She couldn't speak; it wouldn't have seemed right to put human voices into the night air, unless she could make her voice sound like water, moving, restless water.

On her left, the cliffs dropped steeply in a jagged black outline down to the sea. Lindsey imagined herself in a science-fiction film as the water hurled black and silver mirrors at the rocks so that pieces splintered and flew off. Above her, the moon was a discarded tin can in a shining black puddle just floating, lopsided.

Lerryn concentrated on the path, which she knew was safe enough, worn smooth here from endless tramping feet. Momentarily, the beam from Pendeen Lighthouse crossed the path ahead of her, and in its light she turned to check that Lindsey was all right. They walked on companionably without talking.

Lindsey thought of the Yorkshire hills. She imagined them in moonlight, like these cliffs, where the sky seemed deeper than the sea.

Then she thought of her flat in Hackney and wondered if there'd ever be a time when she didn't live there among high-rise blocks and street noise, with the familiar dash to lunch with Maureen and Rocky, grabbing half an hour in the grotty grey canteen.

When Lerryn had suggested this short holiday in Cornwall while Rosie was having her half-term week with Maureen, Tessa and the children in Norfolk, it had seemed such a long way to travel for a mere five days. But now, on the coast path at night, Lindsey surprised herself by wanting to stay for a long time with Lerryn. She wondered how long was long, and how Rosie would react to the idea, and what on earth she'd do for work.

She tapped Lerryn's shoulder and motioned her to sit on a rock at the safer side of the path. In comfortable silence they watched the lighthouse beam, slow, regular and reliable. Lerryn stooped to adjust the laces on her walking boots. Lindsey fished out some fruit and nut chocolate to share from her anorak pocket and they crunched and nibbled at it.

Presently, the sea mist began to roll in, obscuring the moon. The first groans of the foghorn began as they picked their way towards the stile which led across the field to the cottage. The light from the windows gleamed like square yellow eyes through the thickening mist.

It was a two-room cottage which Harry called her Hermit's Hut. She would go there when she wanted nothing except the sea and sky, and the inevitable mist, speciality of the area, winter and summer, which would cocoon the cottage in an almost total silence broken only by the wail and mournful moan of the foghorn.

Occasionally Harry might share the solitude with one of her artist friends, but that was rare. This time the place was Lerryn's and Lindsey's uninterrupted: no phone, no electricity, and no gas. But Harry being Harry, there was plumbing and a wood stove. The place was lit by oil lamps, with candles for emergencies and to make love by.

Next morning Lerryn and Lindsey slept late and it was midday as they peered out to find the layers of mist shifting and creeping away along the valleys, and the sun struggling through. No matter that it was spring bank holiday. Cornish mists were no respecters of human time.

So in wet-weather gear they trekked out on foot, taking an inland route that led between disused mine workings to higher ground strewn with old stones from pagan times.

'I didn't realise there'd be so many. I expected the odd burial chamber and stone circle. But this is littered like stone confetti. I nearly wrecked my ankle back there. This place is strange.'

'Like you say, Linz, there are so many in this part of the world. But I brought you this way because I found one stone that I specially want you to see.'

'What's special about it?'

'It's not far now. I want you to see it first.'

They walked on and the wind was noticeably chilly as they gained height. Lindsey realised that compared to Yorkshire, they probably weren't very high above sea level but it seemed high, perhaps because each turn of the track presented a different view, a change in perspective. The moor was stark and windswept. A few stunted hawthorns all leaned inland, hanging on tight, backs to the wind, like old women bent low under baskets of twigs. The route became a narrow path between boulders, treacherous with sharp gorse and rough heather.

The track turned and there, for a moment, Lindsey thought she saw Biff leaning over the parapet of the packhorse bridge. 'Biff,' she called out. Then, about facing, completely startled, she clapped her hand over her mouth and stared wide eyed at Lerryn, who was smiling gently. Steadying again, Lindsey turned back and, looking again where Biff had been, she saw only a leaning stone with angles, just like Biff's shoulders. Trembling, Lindsey ran back to Lerryn for a reassuring hug. 'Heavens. Lerrie, hold me tight. That was one of the weirdest things I ever felt or saw.'

'Sit down then. Coffee?' asked Lerryn, unscrewing the flask top.

'Oh thanks.' Lindsey took the plastic cupful from Lerryn. 'I can hardly believe it, Lerrie. It was only an effing stone.'

Lerryn said: 'I love this place. I used to come here and think about you when I could persuade Harry to bring me up to Hermit's Hut. It wasn't often. But as I got older, she would let me come here by myself. It got me away from the hairdresser's, and from the family. A long weekend sometimes; and once or twice I had a week or ten days. Ten days is a bit too long. It's *so* solitary.'

'It's got a magical feeling, though I don't believe in all that fairy rings and moonlight stuff usually. The only time I remember being really interested in it was a programme about gods and goddesses of pagan times on tele. Now that *was* interesting. Pete and I talked about it for ages, because of course he did geology, and the programme was about sex and symbols in the stones. I was riveted actually. I can remember as if it was yesterday. The standing stones were penises . . . '

'Hang on a minute, Lindsey. Was it a man's voice, was it a male producer?'

'I've no idea. I never gave it a thought. What's the matter?'

'I can do without all those male programmes, male theories. It's like the history of art: same old images, same old symbols, penises everywhere. I can do without all that male nonsense. It doesn't give me anything.'

'Are you saying the programme was rubbish? You didn't see it, so how do you come to that conclusion? I shouldn't have told you, you're the educated one, you tell me.'

'I'm sorry. I didn't mean to put you down.'

'Good, because you had a pretty good shot at it. I shan't be able to tell you things if I'm going to get that reaction. Like I said, it was riveting. I was spellbound.'

'You were also a straight woman. You wouldn't have minded what was being said. Many straight women don't. It makes it hard for gays like me in the art world. Everyone has the reaction you just did, including the women.'

'All right, I'm sorry too. We said on the pier we'd have hidden hurts that we'd have to face up to. This is maybe one of them. I'm open to change, you know I am. I want to change. I've got a lot of straight woman still in my head, how could I not have, Lerrie. You're telling me there's a whole other set of ideas about stones and gods and goddesses and things?'

'I don't know quite what to think, because the Biff-stone mucks up all my ideas actually, Linz. Ever since I heard about stones and Celtic goddesses from Mrs Tindern, I've been fascinated. I liked the stories about goddesses best, and dancing girls and stone circles. I couldn't get remotely excited about men, men's theories, men's art, men's history, none of it. Left me cold. Of course I'd seen the Biff-stone several times before I ever saw Biff. So, next time I came here, I turned a corner and there was your granddad.'

'You can say that again. You heard me call out.'

'And it didn't fit with my ideas, not at all. And it still doesn't.'

'No it wouldn't, would it? Actually I don't remember Biff talking much about stones when he talked about history. For a start, the hills near Herton aren't littered like these ones. But anyway, Biff was more into socialism, you know, trades unions and struggles at work, things like that. Though he didn't leave the women out. Not like you say your male history wallies do. I don't know how you survive in the art world. It sounds an awful world to me. At least in the factory we're all women, thank heavens. The funny thing about these stones is you can feel how magical they are. I've never been anywhere like this before. Not even out at the packhorse bridge and that was magical in its own way.

'I can understand more about you, Lerrie, now you've brought me here. I can imagine the pagans dancing and so forth. And I bet they did a lot of the "so forth". It's that sort of atmosphere.'

'They prayed here, lots of rituals.'

'And it's not even a quoit or a dolmen, a "proper monument". Wait till I tell Nanan and Biff. They'll think I've gone to join the moonies.'

'And are you going to join the moonies?'

'Me? Catch me cutting up any sheep for rituals: I love animals!'

'Do *you* pray, Linz?'

'No. Not even when Peter was killed. Nanan would have liked me to. But Biff understood. It's a sore point, between them. I dunno. It's different when we're sitting here, among all these old stones. Maybe, maybe there is such a thing as spirit, life force. I really don't know. Do *you* pray?'

'More like connecting, meditating. I haven't found the right words yet for it. I meditate about women.'

'You mean you fancy them, more like.'

Lerryn threw her head back and laughed. 'You're dreadful, Linz. You are such a sceptic. You got any fruit 'n nut in your pocket?'

'Course I have, here.' Lindsey broke a bar of chocolate in half and smiled as she handed it across. 'I love you so much, Lerrie. I'm so glad we came here. The hut, the coast path, the moors. I even like the mist and rain. Know what?'

'What?'

'Let's go home to bed. I don't fancy doing it right here – too bloody spooky and too bloody cold. *Did* women do it with each other by the stones?'

'What do *you* think?'

'Has it gone colder since pagan times, or were they a tougher lot than us?'

Lerryn's laughter echoed on the moors. She turned to follow Lindsey, now skipping through the stones imitating a mountain goat, though she looked more like the back legs of a pantomime horse. Still laughing at Lindsey's antics, Lerryn bid goodbye to the stones and their secrets. Despite her searches, they still guarded them carefully.

Nineteen

Moss had a habit of crossing through each day on the kitchen calendar, just before she went to bed. As she marked off Hallowe'en 1975, she became aware of Biff standing behind her, annoyed and disgruntled.

Like a weather report, Moss heard herself say, 'It's such a mild autumn, who'd have thought it was almost November? I wonder if we'll have an easy winter.'

She turned to Biff for a response, but Biff was staring beyond Moss at the rows of diagonal pencil lines on the calendar. Uncharacteristic-ally, Biff shrugged, retreated into the front room and seated herself in front of the television.

Following her, Moss said, 'You going to watch more tele at this time of night? Can't you sleep or something?'

'I thought I'd listen to the film programme, see what the reviews are.'

'Are you all right? You're looking a bit grey. In fact you seem really tired.'

'You go on up to bed, love. Need any help?'

'Are you sure you're all right, Biff?'

'Don't fuss, love. Here, I'll help you up to bed, then I'm coming back down for this programme.'

They made their usual slow climb upstairs and Biff helped Moss out of her clothes and into bed, tucking her leg pillow in position so that she could go to sleep. 'Night, night, love,' said Biff, kissing Moss on the cheek and receiving a kiss in return.

Downstairs again, Biff watched television until the last weather report and fell asleep in the armchair.

Throughout November, Biff watched the weather forecasts obsessively, making sure that she caught each one during the day. In between she withdrew into a morose silence. She worked most of the day in the garden shed, tidying and retidying, mending the bird box, and repairing an old kitchen chair, scraping and sanding it, gluing the spokes back and varnishing it. She returned to the house to do the hoovering, eat her meals and do the washing up; and to collect shopping lists and library books for her solitary forays down the High Street.

'Well, at least he's still going out,' remarked Mercy Dundy during one of her regular afternoon visits to Moss.

'I could understand depression if it was awful weather and Biff was stuck indoors,' replied Moss, as they reminisced of years past when they'd been trapped by weeks of grey skies – days when the winds howled and pelted huge fistfuls of hail at the windows, mornings of low grey cloud and fine thin mists that soaked into people's clothes and shoes without hurry or drama, just with a steady determination to make the place and the people sodden.

'Yes. Seeing as he's out every day in the garden, you'd think he'd be grateful for small mercies,' quipped Mercy accepting another slice of cake. 'Not that he's got a smile for this small Mercy here.'

The well-worn joke, with whiskers on it, raised only a faint smile from Moss, who was by now seriously worried about Biff's mental state. 'Biff hasn't a smile for anyone or anything, it seems,' she sighed. 'Will you have another cup of tea?'

Christmas came and went with a visit from Lindsey and Rosie, and for a few days the atmosphere lightened, but New Year brought a deeper gloom by comparison.

Biff noticed the days beginning to lengthen, and wondered if, as promised, this really would be the mildest winter on record in South Yorkshire. There was no sign of the weather turning cold, nor of the usual frost, and she hoped like most of the pensioners that they'd get through without any snow.

Biff's self-imposed silence continued and if anything, worsened. Throughout January Moss's fears about the climate were not realised, the temperature remaining constantly above the January average, with not a whisper of a snowflake. Her fears about Biff increased, and she felt herself sliding from irritation and anxiety into anger and despair. There was no joy to be had in the house in Church Lane, only a day-long, night-long emptiness inside each woman, around each woman, and the hours of living seemed endless and useless.

At the end of January, when Moss was reaching the end of her rope and could quite cheerfully have strung Biff up from the washing line hook outside the back door, Biff announced that she had decided to take a long walk out to the packhorse bridge.

'You up to that kind of distance, Biff?'

'I'm not in my dotage yet,' snapped the answer.

'No one thinks you're past it, but it is the middle of winter, even if it is lovely and bright out there. Oh well, if you're sure you want to go that far, the least I can do is pack you up some hot coffee and sandwiches. You will be back before twilight, won't you?'

'It's not that far, there and back.'

'I know, but you said yourself that you don't stride out like you did when you were a young delivery boy on your day off.'

'I'll be back before nightfall, all right?'

'Good, or I'll be sending a posse.'

This didn't raise a laugh as it would once have done and, muttering under her breath, 'Oh don't crack your face,' Moss busied herself in the kitchen, packing Biff's lightweight rucksack as she thought best. She finished the sandwiches, wrapped some cake in tinfoil, and made up a small polythene pack with a miniature first aid kit of elastoplasts, small scissors, a crepe bandage and some tweezers. Pausing to put on the kettle she had an idea; from under the sink she unrolled a bin liner, the sort they used for garden refuse, tearing it off and folding it tightly, wedging it down the side of the rucksack. Biff can sit on it, save the cold beating up from the ground, she thought.

As Moss waited for the kettle to boil, she could hear Biff upstairs, rummaging around in the back bedroom for her walking boots, thick socks and cagoule. In the quietness of the kitchen, Moss leaned against the worktop and for a moment she wondered if Biff would come home. Was this the last trek out of the tent in the blizzard, for the sake of the others now that rations were running low? Outside, though, the garden was alight with pale sunshine, low-angled and thin but bright. It was another dry day, perfect for winter walking. Surely she could trust Biff not to do anything stupid?

Becoming accustomed to the rucksack, and with her hands in thick woollen gloves and her favourite woolly hat pulled down over her ears, Biff set out from the house down Church Lane past the fields towards the pit tip.

By the cluster of houses at the bottom of the valley people she knew waved to her and called out but instead of stopping as she used to for a friendly word, she merely waved back and carried on. She was in no mood for people. She walked slowly but steadily, following the familiar roads south-west through lightly wooded slopes towards the Pennines. Occasionally she halted, slowing her breathing because she had twinges in her chest. She didn't like their message.

Presently the road gave way to the tarmacked farm tracks along which she used to cycle with Lindsey. Carefully Biff observed the hedgerows and waysides. They were brittle and dehydrated. The leafless hawthorns were straggly. Like me, thought Biff sourly. She walked on, low in energy but determined to put the miles between herself and Herton.

This was the driest winter Herton had ever known. Biff found it unbearable, and perversely she had been longing for rain. Driven on towards the bridge, she continued as the tarmac gave way to a rough track. Biff crunched over the uneven ground, treading over old rain ruts which had dried. The soil powdered under her heavy boots. She stepped intently, grinding the tops of the ruts as if to punish them for being there. She felt an alien in a waterless landscape, estranged from herself and the world around her.

Hope seemed to have evaporated out of her life, out of her spirit. She was weary both with her life and her disguise. As the path became steeper and slowed her progress, she recognised that this was a journey of alienation.

Once, she had walked this way in the rain. She couldn't recall how many years ago. Daylight had been thick cotton wool misted with water. As twilight had fallen, and dark steel grey shaded to indigo, layered with millstone grit and granite, she had seen Herton's lights as beacons, calling her home. She remembered how she and Moss had made love for hours, with the house enclosed in rain. How they had talked of loving the rain and its wetness, each other and their wetness.

Approaching the white milestone where Lindsey had raced on her bike, Biff had to admit she was tired. She decided to have a rest and some coffee. She shrugged off the rucksack gently because of the fragile flask, and discovered the thin plastic sack which she could use for a groundsheet. It was tucked neatly, caringly, down beside the sandwiches. She held it to her cheek. Its plastic was cold and satiny. A fresh, new smell. Biff smoothed it out on the dry grass and sat leaning back against the hillside. It was her usual spot from where there was always a good view back towards Herton. She stretched out her long legs and her soft old grey cords wrinkled comfortably. She felt the cold more than she had expected.

Drinking the coffee, sniffing the aroma and feeling the warmth even through her thick gloves, she thought what Moss must have been going through living with a disgruntled porcupine of a lover all winter.

The light shone bright and glass-like across the fields. Crackable sunlight. You could harvest such sunlight into bales of glass straws, and the stubble would shred your feet through your boots. Some of the fields were bare brown earth waiting for first planting. It was possible to imagine the corn, gleaming as if with fire, and poppies scattered along the edges of the barley acres. Biff could visualise a blue sky, warm with scudding clouds, high over harvest fields, but she would rather have felt rain. Any kind of rain: squall, tempest, deluge. Was she the only one in Herton to long for rain? Odd man out, she thought acidly.

Herton people weren't that used to dry weather. They had their share of summer sunshine, and the sun shone in other seasons too. But they often dealt with rain, which made this winter so very unusual, because there hadn't been any to speak of. Jokes about life on Costa del Herton and holidays by the pit tips were part of Herton's fabric, woven into a rather leaky raincoat, not much protection against the reservoir in the sky that usually plopped and dripped throughout the year.

Biff munched her sandwiches, thinking of the long-range weather predictions for a dry summer.

Ironically, thought Biff, looking towards the colliery and the town, drying out is as dangerous as flooding. It was water, she thought, that held the bedrock together; water that fed the stones and soil; water that held the houses up. As if in sympathy, her left leg ached one of its memory aches, and Biff thought of Frank in the pit disaster all those years ago. She remembered her first meeting with Frank and his parents, before she'd met Moss, in the early days when she had felt certain that her refuge in Herton and her disguise would both be temporary.

She had loved wearing men's clothes: easy comfortable trousers with pockets, old jackets soft and warm, with pockets, shirts with pockets. When you dressed as a man you had so much you could carry by yourself, no need to clutter your hands with handbags.

Her shoes lasted longer than Moss's, shoes she could wriggle her toes in, walk freely in, run and cycle in. The advantages were obvious to her.

But.

Of all the buts, and there were many, the greatest struggle had been indoors. To keep her disguise out of the bedroom, out of bed. It had taken all her wit, intelligence, energy, wisdom and memories of Emily, to prevent herself becoming a husband, turning Moss into a wife in bed. Not to play butch and femme there was to keep open all the possibilities for loving with Moss, just as she had with Emily; but her maleness had hovered outside the bedroom door in a suit of clothes that had other people's expectations sewn into every seam, closed in every button, locked and zipped in every pocket.

They had succeeded, against all the odds, for Moss was a magnificent lover, and was capable of giving and receiving passion like warm rain in a desert, cool rain on parched soil.

Biff turned her head to face the milestone. It pointed back to Manchester, forward to Herton. She had not been facing her own milestone, she told herself. Soon she would be eighty. But instead of reaching eighty with a sense of inner power, success at what she and Moss had achieved, she had begun to destroy herself this winter.

Over the years, she sometimes pictured her body as a strong apple tree. Now she felt that she had hidden herself like an old apple stored in layers of papers, fading in a box in the corner of the garden shed. No one had done that to her. Wrinkled and sour, she had begun to rot at the centre this winter. One day someone would reach in and find nothing but dust.

Dust.

Is it the beginning of the end, then? Am I dying? Mind first. I have always been afraid of that. Always so active. Alive. Connected. A bright apple on a green tree. Dust. Ashes to ashes and . . .

For a long time Biff sat, tasting the coffee, the sandwiches – egg mayonnaise with cress, her favourite – and the rum and raisin cake. She thought of Emily and how they had loved each other, young girls who knew nothing of love except what they learned with each other, taking turns, equal. She had lain in Emily's arms, wanting to be made love to. She had been made love to by Moss, so many times. Equal. 'I am not your wife,' Moss had said. 'I will be your companion, lover, friend. But I will not be your wife.' And Emily, what had become of her? It had been too dangerous to find out. Tears ran down Biff's face and she realised that if anyone saw her they'd be astonished to find an old man crying beside a milestone. 'When they knock you down,' Emily had said, 'and they will, get up and dust yourself, and carry on.'

Biff packed the rucksack and shouldered it, thinking as she started for home, that there was no need today to go on to the bridge. You should be getting back, she told herself, time to see to that apple tree. Another season's growth.

Next day Biff walked along the garden path, marvelling at the bulbs which were tall and green and daring. If they could have talked they'd have been chiding Biff for her pessimism, with 'told you so, we just got on with life while you were disbelieving'. Under the roses by the garden shed Biff discovered the first snowdrops, with their pale green markings on white bells. Green is the colour of hope.

Biff picked all that she could find, and carried them indoors.

'We've come to the first of February, look,' began Biff.

'The most depressing winter we ever had.'

'I'm sorry I put you through it with me. I still love you.'

'I love you too, though I wondered whether I did, and what brought us this far, just as you were wondering if you loved me, and why you stayed. I wanted to reach out to you, but you kept me on the outside.' Moss handed Biff the small vase that they always used for snowdrops. It had a narrow neck, perfect for the job.

They sat in the kitchen, at the table, with the snowdrops on the tea tray. Biff said, 'So long as I had the children to link me to the future, I was all right. All the years of Sadie and Ronnie. Then Lindsey; and Rosie when she was a baby. It's not the same now. The other grandchildren in Australia might as well be on another planet. I've gone over it this winter, in my mind.'

'You didn't think we'd get through all these years together without some bad times.'

'There's bad and bad. Massage table standing there in the back bedroom, we haven't been near it for the whole winter. Bed's a wet November firework.' Biff sighed.

'Back to back like two hedgehogs. I half expected holes in my nightdress where spikes were poking through,' said Moss.

'Did you? We haven't reached for one another for weeks.'

'We didn't love ourselves,' replied Moss. 'So how could we reach out?'

'Snowdrops are pretty. They smell nice. You don't think of snowdrops having a smell, do you?' Biff paused then added, 'What held us together all these years?'

'Endurance. Love's an overrated word. Of course I can love you, when I love me. But I've been underground too this winter. I've had bad moments before, never lasted very long, not since you and I were lovers. But this time we both went to the bottom. At the same time. The very, very bottom. Deeper than Herton pit.'

'So what now?' asked Biff. 'What if it happens again, and anyway how did we get out? I don't feel as if I'm anywhere near that pit today, so what's changed, except a few tiny snowdrops?'

'We have. And now the days are getting longer, brighter, and we're ready, like animals are. Seasonal changes.'

'Why didn't it happen until now, so late in our lives? I know we were all upset and stirred up when Lindsey asked us to go and see her in London. And we didn't want to travel, all of that. But that came up before, years ago, when she lived there with Peter.'

'Yes and it was you, not me, who couldn't face it that time. You were afraid of having to be a man in London. Afraid of wanting to stay there, rip your men's clothes off, turn your life upside down, I remember that as if it was yesterday.'

'So have I lived my whole life based on fear? That *is* madness. And I'm more afraid of madness than of my body failing me.'

'You can afford to indulge that fear. Because you have a wonderful strong body, give or take a few twinges. You only gave up cycling last year. I have envied you, for so long. And pitied you, and loved you. Do you think I don't know my arthritis is fear turned inwards. You know I've read all the new stuff, yards and yards of books, you could line whole shelves with them. Do you think I'd have stayed sane if I hadn't loved you? Knowing what I know about loving Florence. We saved our own lives, you and I. You know all these young feminists talk about self, yourself, your body, your rights, your right to love another woman. But they will pay their prices too. The world is not made for women to love each other, even these days. Liberation is a long, long way away, I know that. This winter, sitting opposite you, with a deep pit shaft in the middle of our front room floor, I have done my accounts. I could write a whole tome about prices, yours and mine.'

'And you still love me?'

'I still love you. I don't know how you kept from madness each and every time you tied your tie, buttoned up your shirt, and stepped out down that High Street. There's any amount of things on tele about people who split in slices like bacon in poor old Frank's shop, and never join the slices up. How many shanks of bacon have we sliced up?'

'Hundreds, thousands.'

'I have loved you, Biff. With all my heart I have loved you. You know as well as I do that with Sadie and Ronnie, Lindsey and Rosie to care for we *couldn't* up and leave. Only the Radclyffes can move about in search of new homes. The Mosses and Biffs can't do that. I have paid with my body, and you, I watched this winter while you paid with your soul.'

'It was easier when we had the shop. I worked. I worked all the hours there were and I filled up the others with you and the children, and then Lindsey. Or I took off up into the hills. I used to think, when I was a girl, that I was a social sort of person. When I was in the mill. Always in the centre of a group, talking, all the limelight. Now, I'm a solitary sort. And I've been questioning and, well, agonising really, about whether that is really me, or something I've let happen. I don't know.'

'Which is all right when you're happy, and frightening when you're not.'

'I was never a coward. I was a survivor though. Hence the flight. Or I'd have been the next martyr.'

'And you didn't have to do that. Be a martyr.'

'No. I didn't. I wanted life. I wanted a chance to live my life.'

'And now you're going through nightmares – what did that young woman say, night stallions – they do go too far some of them, you know. We'll have no language left. Don't go shaking your head at me, Barbara Imogen Farley, we have to agree to differ sometimes – through nightmares, all winter, asking yourself what kind of a life you've chosen. I think,' Moss paused, 'I think we get one chance to change things. Just one. I ran from Darlington; you left Manchester. That was our one chance, each. We could have gone through the rest of our lives alone, me trapped in marriage, you unable to find another Emily, living on memories. And instead, we've had a wonderful long, long loving. And it isn't over yet. Come here.'

Moss remained seated as she reached out her arms to Biff. Biff stood and reached forward, bending towards her. Moss kissed her on the mouth and they held one another closely. Then Moss took Biff's face in her hands gently, kissing the soft line of Biff's jaw, and her neck above the collar. They looked into each others eyes. Carefully, Biff removed Moss's glasses, placing them safely on the table. Then she slowly kissed Moss's face, her eyelids, and the soft places just behind her ears.

Sitting in the chair, Moss was delighted and comfortable. She could look into Biff's clear grey eyes; they seemed as deep as Ladybower.

'It's good to hold you again,' said Biff.

'We haven't come through all these years to be beaten by one long winter,' replied Moss, 'even if it is the hardest winter we ever knew.'

Twenty

It was a weekend of rather mixed weather, during which Tessa's daughters, Sharon who was ten and Jean, eight, were staying at Lindsey's flat. On Saturday they all decided on an outing to Richmond Park where the Isabella Plantation was splendid with azaleas.

Ahead, the three girls seemed relaxed and happy. Sharon was the tallest, slimmer than the others. She was throwing bread for the ducks who were diving for it. Her hair was expertly plaited by her mother, tiny plaits evenly spaced sticking up from each division of her hair. Next to her, Rosie at nine seemed short and rather tubby. She'd been growing her hair and it was tied in bunches which bobbed as she ran about. Jean was the shortest, rounder even than Rosie. She loved bright colours, today she was in red and yellow. Her features were very like Sharon's and they both looked like Tessa, though Sharon was darker and Jean lighter. Jean didn't like having her hair plaited and wouldn't stay still long enough, so her hair had just been cut as short as was possible; it fitted her shapely head like a black cap and really suited her. She knew it and was preening and posing all the way round the park.

Behind them Lindsey and Lerryn linked arms, walking slowly, stopping to peer into the flowering shrubs and trees and to take photos.

'I'm so glad we came here, even if it does look like rain any minute. Look at all the colours, Lerrie.'

'Aren't they wonderful. Biff would love them. I do wish they'd visit London just once.'

'So do I. Not for want of asking believe me. I've been on at them for years.'

'I wish I was like you, Linz.'

'Meaning what?'

'Contented, not searching.'

'You having one of your restless phases again? You give yourself no peace, Lerrie. You could be enjoying the present much more, love, if you let up a bit.'

'Yes, but something drives me on.'

'You take life at such a pace, Lerrie. I couldn't be doing with it. Where have those girls got to? Oh there they are. Whoo-oo,' Lindsey called, Rosie turned, and they both waved.

'I do try to be like you. But then I'm off again, all over the world in my head.'

'Are you wanting to leave London? Travel? I thought you were up to your neck in classes this term?'

'London's home. And I love the teaching.'

'Good. I was worried that home might be somewhere else. Maybe back in Cornwall?'

'Spiritual home perhaps. But I've made my life in London, work, friends, mine and yours. They mean home to me too, and family. I'm all right. Just restless, inside.'

'I never met anyone like you before, except Biff. And he's my granddad so that's different. Bit like loving you, though, because something in Biff searches like something in you.'

They came to the willow pond where ducks landed, aquaplaning. The girls were on the other side watching the ducklings.

Lindsey let the conversation roll around in her brain. How hard it must be for someone like Lerryn or Biff, endlessly questioning things, as if a mind could be its own bone and its own dog at the same time.

She watched a leaf float into the pond from a rivulet. Sometimes it seemed to her that Lerryn was no more in control of it all than a leaf flowing downriver. It must be fascinating to be aware of all the eddies and undercurrents, but how vast and cold the water must seem around the edges of that leaf.

She didn't really understand Lerryn's needs as an artist, but she did love her. So she pulled her close and kissed her as Rosie might have done, all warm and friendly on the cheek.

There was a shriek from the girls. 'Rain!' At that moment the skies opened and a hovering cloud picked them for target practice. In seconds they were soaked. They turned and fled, pursued by the three girls, squealing and half cursing, back to the car park where they bundled into the mini dripping and laughing.

That night at Lindsey's flat Moss phoned. Lerryn took the call. Returning to the living room where Lindsey was watching television with the girls, Lerryn said, 'That was Moss. Just checking about dates for our next visit.'

'Oh, can't I talk to Nanan?' asked Rosie.

'Sorry lovie, she didn't want to be long. Too expensive. We'll phone her next weekend.'

'Oh, all right. Anyway, I'm tired. If we go to bed soon, can we have a story?'

Lindsey looked at her watch. 'If you go now you can.'

It was late when they had a chance to talk about the phone call, the story having been strung out by all three girls.

Lerryn flopped on the settee, her mind going over and over the brief talk with Moss.

'Lindsey, she knows we are lovers.'

'How can she? I've never discussed it with Nanan or Biff.'

'Because she was quite happy to talk to me, without "bothering" you as she put it, and she told me we could have the back bedroom if we didn't mind sharing.'

'So?'

'Your nanan knows. And what's more, she doesn't mind.'

'You're too hopeful. You know what a traditional place Herton is. Even if Nanan and Biff like you, we can't be too careful. I tell you, she's never given it a thought.'

'My antenna tell me that she knows. What she said was that they were going to get singles, but the room was too small, and she was checking that we didn't mind having the double bed again. I tell you she knows.'

'She does not. I don't want to come out to my nanan and granddad.'

'What's the worst thing that could happen if you did?'

'She'd die of a heart attack'

'Oh don't be so melodramatic, Lindsey. Your nanan's a tough old bird. She always offers us the double bed; and she always makes that excuse.'

'I don't want to talk about it. And keep your voice down. If the girls hear us, I'll be up half the night calming them down. Took me long enough to settle them as it is.'

'My voice isn't up. You're imagining it because you're on the defensive. I tell you your nanan and Biff know and what's more, they approve.'

'I am not going to Herton to come out to them if that's what you mean. If I thought for one moment you'd come out on me I'd cancel the whole trip.'

'Thanks very much. You're ashamed of me, aren't you? Ashamed of being a lesbian. So why have you got another lesbian's children here for the weekend?'

'Course I'm not ashamed. My friends know. But I'm not out in Herton.'

'Now who's raising her voice? Don't you turn your thunder and lightning on me – I might sizzle.'

'Sizzle? You'd be fried to a cinder in Herton. You may be a success in the art world here, Lerrie, and I'm very, very glad for you. But don't imagine all the world is like London. It isn't. Herton doesn't like gays.'

'I'm not stupid. I know that. But I'm not talking about all of Herton. I'm talking about your grandparents.'

'I don't want to confront Nanan and Biff with all this. They are ageing fast, and I don't want to cause them any worry. Any at all.'

'I'm trying to reassure you that it doesn't worry them. They are perfectly happy that we are lovers.'

'I'm tired. I've three children in Rosie's bedroom, and I'd like to fall into bed and dream about azaleas. Not worry about coming out in Herton. Now can we let it drop, please.'

It was only seven thirty on Sunday morning when giggles and cries from the kitchen woke Lindsey. Beside her, Lerryn was sound asleep. Lindsey eased herself out of bed, shrugged on her dressing gown and slippers drowsily, and went to investigate.

Three pairs of pyjama bottoms with feet sticking out were sprawled on the floor, surrounded by the entire contents of the sink cupboard, into which three corresponding pyjama jackets were determined to squeeze.

'What on earth?' began Lindsey. 'Oh, not again!!'

A bottom shuffled backwards and Sharon's head appeared. Her tiny plaits were ruffled and skew-whiff all over her head. She had an expressive face like Tessa.

'We were cleaning out Jean's gerbil and he made a dash for the cupboard again.' Sharon was grinning but her face also asked a series of questions: Are you angry? and Can you get him out? She looked down as Rosie shuffled backwards. They smirked at each other, wanting to laugh out loud but not liking to in front of Jean, still in the sink cupboard.

Lindsey straddled over the scene like the Colossus of Rhodes. Jean wriggled out and grabbed Lindsey's ankle, a typical action – she loved to reach out and touch. She had been crying and her eyes were anxious. She shook Lindsey's ankle.

'Can you get him out? He won't come out for us?'

'Let go my leg then. Let's see what we can do,' replied Lindsey as kindly as she could, remembering Houdini the newt.

Lindsey knelt on the floor as the girls pushed aside paper bags, pots, pans, and dusters. She hugged Jean briefly and looked into the bottom of the sink cupboard, wrinkling her nose against the musty smell. A tail could just be seen where the pipe went down into a gap. There were one or two tell-tale droppings.

Lindsey backed out carefully, minding her head.

'Has he had his breakfast?' Three heads shook.

Sharon said: 'He won't come out if we're all crowding him, will he?'

'I'm not leaving him in there,' said Jean, looking nervous.

Lindsey's absence had disturbed Lerryn, who called out: 'What's the matter?' This diverted Sharon and Rosie who ran to tell her. Jean sat determinedly by the sink cupboard. 'I told Mummy I wouldn't go away without him. And I'm staying here till he comes out.'

Lindsey saw herself age eight in front of Moss. It was as if Moss's voice spoke from inside her as she answered: 'He'll miss you too much in there and of course he'll come out, especially if he's hungry. Now you stack those pots and pans over by the window and stash the paper bags in here.' Lindsey handed Jean a carrier bag. 'Then you can sit and wait for him to come for his breakfast.'

Lerryn appeared at the doorway with Sharon and Rosie. 'I smell a rat,' she said, as Rosie dug her in the side with a warning elbow. Lerryn rubbed her eyes and yawned. It was ten to eight. The phone rang in the living room. Lerryn went to answer it as Lindsey leaned over Jean to fill the kettle.

'Lerrie? It's me, Tessa.'

'Hello Tessa, you all right?'

'You sound harassed, Lerrie, what's going on?'

'Oh we're all right. Jean's sitting by the sink cupboard again waiting for the gerbil to come out of the closet.'

'You'll be a long time waiting. As far as I know he's straight.'

Tessa's laughter echoed in the ear piece, as Lerryn replied in a very camp voice: 'Better late than never, dear. We live in hope.' Returning to her usual voice she asked, 'Anyway, why're you phoning? Did you hear the pots and pans being moved?'

'Well actually, Lerrie, I'm glad it's you who answered. I've rung to ask you a favour. The bag of swimming things is sitting here behind the settee. We didn't find it till we went to bed last night. It was too late to phone. But the girls'll want to swim this morning, won't they?'

'Shall I drive over and pick it up?'

'Would you? You know what the buses are like on Sunday mornings. It would take forever to bring them over to you. I'm sorry 'bout this.'

'No problem. I'll be glad to have a quiet coffee with you.'

'I'll bet. I can hear the noises off-stage.'

'Did you two have a nice day yesterday?'

'We did actually. We did sweet f.a. and a bit besides.' Tessa's laugh was low and lewd. 'Nothing like it in the mornings.'

'I wouldn't know,' lied Lerryn, enjoying Tessa's laughter. 'I'm indulging in a spot of rat catching myself.'

Tessa's tone changed abruptly. 'I'd like to do the same but there are so many I can't count. Liberal racist rats where I work, I mean. I'll tell you about it – but not this morning because the baths close at eleven.'

'It'll be a flying visit. Have you got some time in the week?'

'Yes. I tell you, the housing department is driving me up the wall. We are supposed to be giving out houses? Joke. The whole bloody structure is built on racism – and run by rats. It's wearing me down. I'm also very angry. I did a very angry painting. Strong, but I don't know if it's technically any good, you know? Could you take a look at it some time, tell me what you think? Have you got time?'

'I'll bring my diary. We can make a date.'

'I'd like that. Thank you.'

'Don't thank me. It's exciting, Tessa.'

'Yes, it is. It made me feel wonderful, in spite of what caused it.'

Back in the kitchen Lerryn said: 'That was Tessa. I've to dash over for the swim stuff. It got forgotten.'

'Tea before you go?' asked Lindsey

Lerryn shook her head. 'No time. The baths close at eleven.'

'Can we come?' chorused Sharon and Rosie, trying it on in unison.

Lindsey interrupted. 'No, you can't. Tessa and Maureen need a proper break.' Unexpectedly the girls didn't quibble. Lindsey turned to Lerryn and kissed her quickly. 'This is the home of the sunshine breakfast. Morning, Lerrie. Rise and Shine.' They hugged amidst the chaos. Lerryn hurried to dress, grabbed her diary and car keys.

'Bye, can't find my door key,' she called out. 'Will you let me in when I get back?' Not expecting a reply, she could be heard running down the concrete stairs to the street.

Lindsey sat at the pine table, thinking. 'Breakfast at Tiffany's. Nothing unusual is happening. Everything is normal, we are all right.' She handed a piece of toast down to Jean who was sitting with one arm stretched into the sink cupboard, extending a handful of sunflower seeds to tempt the gerbil.

A short while later, he was back in his cage.

Back at home on Monday, Lerryn worked all day on a dragon picture which was a representation of Lindsey.

Lerryn brought images from inside her, layer on layer, scale on scale. With long steady movements she worked colour over the silk screen with careful firm strokes of the baton. An image of fire and lightning to convey the dragon and thunder that was Lindsey when she was determined or angry. Until she became soft as ashes in the aftermath of fire; gentle as grey-white powder might be; sensuous fingers on naked skin.

Lerryn's thoughts curled themselves around her like a dragon's tail around its body. The first stages of the print finished, Lerryn left it to dry on the purpose-built drying rack, flicking the rack into position. Then she roved around the studio, a dragon moving deliberately and slowly around its lair, flicking its tail.

The studio was her place; her space. In it she could cast off a few skins and no one would know because by the time she emerged again into bright daylight, she would seem to be an ordinary common or garden dragon, the one who showed itself to the outside world.

She went into her bathroom. In front of the mirror and on the window ledge were ferns. The suite was plain white, and the floor had cork tiles. The tiles were white too and the only colour was a deep blue wall, a colour that Lerryn could look into without tiring. Her towels were dark brown and blue stripes. It was a restful room. She lit three candles and placed them in front of the mirror, and turned off the overhead light. She filled a ceramic dish with water and placed it by the ferns on the window ledge where it would reflect light from the mirror and candle flames. Then she ran hot water from the ascot, and cleaned her teeth while waiting for the bath to fill.

Three candles. One for herself; one for Moss; one for Biff. One for the past. One for the present. One for the future. One for the peat bogs; one for the mists; one for the clear wide open skies, beyond the steepest cliffs.

She stepped into the bath and lay back, chin just above the water.

The three flames wavering in the dim bathroom cast pools of light and shadow on the bathwater. The reflections of the ferns were surreal in the candlelight; and the water in the ceramic dish looked like silver.

She must be fully conscious. She put her palms flat on her belly, breathing deep and slowly, meditating without dulling her wakefulness.

An image of Moss and Biff which had been at the back of her mind for a considerable time had clamoured for attention ever since Moss's phone call at the weekend.

Three candles, thought Lerryn. One for the grandmother; one for the other; and one for the little girl who searches down the lane.

Breathing deeply, Lerryn remembered every detail of her meeting with Moss and Biff that day when she had walked into the shop in search of Lindsey. A moment of recognition had taken place. She must let their faces become clear in her memory. She must understand each line, angle; none must be blurred.

After her bath Lerryn went to bed. Outside her room, beyond the walled garden dense cloud covered the earth. But as Lerryn fell asleep she knew that the moon was there even though it was hidden; and in her dreams she felt herself cast off her skin, though no one else saw her do so. She felt herself make a powerful connection with Herton.

When she woke next morning, having slept a deep refreshing sleep, she remembered and understood each image from the hours of night.

She sat in the enclosed garden, where the wallflowers smelled of early summer. Around her the lawn was sprinkled with white and pink petals from her flowering trees. Lerryn wore her red tracksuit, and sunglasses to protect her from the glare of the paper on which she was drawing. It's 1976, she thought. I'm thirty-one and still searching for something.

The restlessness of the creativity inside her gave her no peace. Always there was work to be done; projects to be finished; deadlines and schedules to meet. Outwardly Lerryn was warm and affectionate. Internally she longed to know the women ancestors who had loved the same land, visited the same coves, watched the same cliffs, searched the same skies.

She knew there had been others like her, before her. But she did not know which of the granite cottages they had lived in, which of the neatly kept gardens they had tended, which of the clifftop pathways they had trodden.

She drew Moss and Biff, together and separately. After several sketches of Moss, she decided to concentrate on Biff, to explore the images that had been intriguing her.

She was trying to decipher coded secrets. Whenever she visited Moss and Biff she felt she was being given double messages. Some of the double messages came from Moss, that was true; but most of them came from Biff. She liked Biff. That was unusual for she usually didn't give much time or thought to the men of her grandmothers' generation. She knew that Biff's mother and two sisters Lucy and Sara had been suffragettes. As a young lad Biff must have heard and seen the campaigns at first hand. But so had other men and they didn't have the turns of phrase that Biff had: a deep respect for women that showed through Biff's words time and time again.

One of the women with whom Lerryn painted in her women artists' group was fascinated by cross dressers and had brought in pictures of suffragettes and of Radclyffe Hall, and into Lerryn's mind had come an image of Lindsey's granddad.

Lerryn had told no one of this mental picture. She had needed time to think. But now the image clamoured for attention.

As she drew, she thought of Lindsey and their years of loving. She envied Lindsey her inner peace and contentment. Lindsey was not searching.

Inside Lerryn was power and beauty and with Lindsey she revealed both. But lovers could leave of their own free will. No one was for ever. To Lerryn nothing was certain except the need to leave a record of her truths, a message to other women following her who might cut through the layers of protection and discover that she, Lerryn Trevonnian, had lived and breathed, had loved herself and her lovers, had loved the land and the sea and had worked to leave signs and signposts for the women to come.

It was late afternoon when Lerryn had finished her drawings. There were many, all varying from each other. Each was a representation of the face of a woman known as a man called Biff.

Twenty-one

Biff walked the length of the garden path breathing in the perfume from the wallflowers. She had grown them from seed that Grace had saved, last summer, planted them out into their flowering positions in mid September when they were a few inches high, and now they flourished, their deep red, almost black petals soft as cats' paws. A few had bloomed for the second year running, bushy and tall, but she preferred to treat them as annuals; they had more powerful scent, she felt, that way.

To make the morning springtime-perfect she would have liked a few butterflies flitting but none had arrived yet in the garden, still cocooned in some secret places. She stepped across the border via two paving stones, and stood on the grass peering closely and moving steadily up and down inspecting for weeds. She heard the phone ringing in the house, and imagined Moss moving with difficulty to answer it. Whoever it was knew them because the phone kept ringing and ringing as the caller waited for Moss to slowly come and pick up the receiver. It stopped.

Moss had stopped speaking to whoever it was. She was sitting at the kitchen table, absolutely still as Biff appeared at the kitchen door.

'That was Rita. Brenda Jackson's Rita. Grace Dundy died this morning!'

Biff moved towards Moss and pressed a firm hand on her shoulder. Moss reached up her own hand to pat Biff's. An old familiar gesture. They looked into each other's faces, didn't speak, just nodded, together, slowly, and then Biff filled the kettle and put it to boil on the gas stove.

'Would you like the tea out in the garden?'

Moss nodded and stood up, holding the edge of the table. Then, always keeping her hand on a wall or piece of furniture, she went outside where the morning sun was full on the bench that Lindsey had bought for them. One of the Newson boys had built a polished wooden handrail around the garden wall as far as the bench. It was a peaceful spot a few feet from a white crabapple tree that scattered its blossom as far as the wallflowers and all over the late primroses. The primroses self-seeded around the garden. They were never disturbed because they were one of Moss's favourites.

Biff carried out the two mugs of tea. Reaching the bench, she placed them beside Moss and seated herself, listening to the hum of the garden. Neither of them spoke for a while, each quiet with her own memories. Years ago, when news had reached Moss that her mother had died, she had said to Biff, 'She didn't want me to leave Darlington. She might have helped me raise Sadie. But if I hadn't left, I'd not be living here now with you. If you weren't part of my life at this moment in time, Biff, I think I'd feel utterly alone. I wonder what that would be like, again. To walk away from a family like mine was to be utterly alone.'

Biff was remembering the deaths she had lived through in her life. Her mother, her two sisters, Frank, her friend and competitor; Lindsey's Peter, and Ronnie, the child she'd helped to raise, who had never had the chance to return from war-torn Europe to peaceful Herton. There were others: people of Herton who had died in the pit disaster; several local children taken by diphtheria, polio, and whooping cough; and there had been some pensioners each winter, all of whom Biff had known by name. But Grace Dundy was the first of their friends.

'Strange, isn't it, Biff, that it has come to us now? I don't feel prepared like I did at sixty. Somehow at sixty I realised that during retirement my friends would pass away one by one. But during that whole time, it was other people in this town who lost their loved ones, sometimes younger men, heart attacks, one or two women had cancer. For ten years since Peter was killed, you and I and our friends have been untouched by death. Suddenly it's here, taking Grace away from Herton, from us, from her family. We have no preparation for death in this society. People like Grace who suffer from angina might go on for years. We all knew this could happen and when it does, we are taken unawares. It's so strange, so strange.'

Moss patted Biff's knee and left her hand there. Biff covered it with her own, knowing that Moss needed no reply. In a world of young people, fast changes, cars and hi-fi, colour televisions and satellites, it seemed sometimes that the love and understanding of people the same age was the only certainty this side of death.

Grace had told them that she had enough money in the post office for her coffin and funeral expenses, so that her daughter Brenda wouldn't carry the financial worry of it all. It was the only freedom that Grace could pass on. She owned nothing, rented her house from the coal board, put fifty pence in the savings account each week for her great grandchildren. In her cupboard by the fireplace there would be, even in April, the first stores of little gifts for the family for next

Christmas and several birthdays. Grace had a knack for choosing that small something that each person she loved would be pleased with. Twice she had been abroad with her daughter, each time by coach on the grand tour of Spain, returning with velvet donkeys with panniers. She kept them on the mantelpiece, filled with smarties for the children.

'When's the funeral to be? Did Rita say?'

'Tuesday. Methodist of course. Two in the afternoon. That's a good time for everyone. We can have an early lunch and Rita says they've laid on one of the cars to come and get us. Isn't that thoughtful of her? You know, Biff, she's a good girl. I do wish she and our Lindsey'd never quarrelled. Oh, it is one of life's wastes. It's not good, not a good thing at all. I pray for them both. What you thinking now, Biff?'

'About our deaths, yours and mine.' There was a pause. 'What we talked about before.' Moss nodded. 'When Tuesday's over, and maybe when we've had a little while to recover, we should sort it all out. Eh?'

Biff held Moss's hand tightly and there were tears in Biff's eyes. She reached forward and picked one highly scented spray of wallflowers, the richest, most velvety one she could find without moving too far from the bench, and she held it for Moss to inhale the perfume. Then she laid it in Moss's lap and leaning towards her, she kissed her in the sunshine.

The summer heatwave continued day after day, and as the water was drawn off the reservoirs, concern began to be expressed about the water levels nationally. Rumour had it that if the scorching weather continued, everyone who had a garden hose would have to stop using it. People were asked to share bathwater, and to tip the old washing-up water on to the gardens and use it to flush the toilets. The local paper reported that Ladybower was emptying rapidly.

Biff waited through the heat of the day until the shadow of the house fell along the flower borders, and the thirsty plants could be doused without being boiled alive as the droplets evaporated from the hot leaves and petals.

Evenings were the best time for Moss and Biff, because the warmth was delightful, without the exhaustion caused by the extreme temperatures mid-afternoon. During the day they both rested, had a piece of ham for high tea about five, and were cleared up ready for the six o'clock news on television. This, followed by a couple of quiet hours tidying the garden, was passing the summer contentedly.

They were more prepared now for one another's deaths.

Biff had never been to the doctor. Even when she had had two mild turns that had scared Moss and had caused Lindsey to nag her about medical treatment, she had consistently refused.

'If I die first, love,' she said to Moss one evening in June, 'then there's not much problem. You can lay me out and make them leave the coffin here until my funeral, and orchestrate everything. Our lives will be as they always have been, our own affair.'

'Some affair,' chuckled Moss.

'But if not,' Biff continued so seriously that Moss's chuckle subsided and she couldn't hide inside humour any longer, 'if not, then we shall be discovered, because when I go you won't be there and someone will find me, examine me, and though I can get away with it up top, being flat as a pancake anyway, I can't fool them below the waist.' Biff waited and Moss took off her glasses, pulled a hanky out of her skirt pocket, cleaned each lens slowly, blew her nose and smiled gently to encourage Biff to continue.

'I think we should make sure I go first,' Biff stated, and Moss looked up and sideways at her, saying nothing, so Biff followed this with: 'Something painless.' Moss winced, thinking of various horrible methods available. 'Being as I've never had a prescription in my life I was wondering about something like in films. Marilyn Monroe did it so easily, didn't she? Barbiturates and alcohol. Barbiturates are on unlimited supply to you, what's a few missing here and there. Three double whiskies, everyone in the town knows I like the occasional tot or two these days, even if I didn't drink much as a young fellow down the Colliers' Arms.' Biff smiled, remembering, and looked around the garden thinking about her next words. 'I had a headache, went downstairs for what I thought was an aspro, bit of a risk after drinking, and took your sleeping pills by mistake. No one's going to query that at my age.'

'No.'

'No, they won't query it? Or no, you don't like it?'

'No, I don't like it. It's a sin. Life is a gift from God and what you are dreaming up for us is a sin.'

'But I don't believe in your God.'

'But I do, and I would know. Don't think I haven't prayed about it. I have. Often. Sometimes I have a little prayer when you're out in the garden. It all depends on what you can live with. I can live as we have, loving you, in love with you. God knows . . . ' Biff shook her head but Moss talked past her. 'God knows all about us and is on our

210

side. And when we are both dead we will have a place to be together. It's all arranged.'

'You and God?'

'Yes. We sorted that one out a long time ago.'

'You did?'

'We did.'

'Supposing I don't like the place you've both fixed for me?'

'You will. We'll be all right, just like we have been while we are living, two lesbians here in a mining town, hiding.'

'Good heavens.'

'Yes exactly.' Moss laughed. 'You watch your language.'

'If you die first, Moss, then when I pass away, to our double bed in the sky, we will have been discovered and Lindsey will have to deal with all the consequences. Do you want her to carry the burden of that?'

'I thought about that but that's not our problem. For a start, that way round it might not even be a weight. She lives in London and it's absolutely obvious that she and Lerryn are lovers, though neither of them will say so. Mind you, Biff, I've had the feeling for a long time that Lerryn would like to talk to us about it, but Lindsey won't, so all we can do is make them both welcome and not force them into – what do the young ones say these days? – "coming out" to us.'

'Go on.'

'Yes, Biff love, I will. You're not the only one with opinions on all this. How could you be? Anyroad up, Lindsey has chosen her life away from Herton and our little scandal, which people in this narrow-minded town would love and hate, cannot hurt Lindsey in London. And it would be a way of letting her in, of "coming out" to her, which she has a right to expect of us, too. I have been thinking these long years that our deaths might release us from the trap, from the hiding, a gift to the generations that won't have to hide like we did.' Moss enjoyed a monologue from time to time and she knew that Biff enjoyed listening, so she thought for a moment then carried on. 'I read *Spare Rib* and as many books as we can get hold of, as you know. We have not led liberated lives publicly, Biff, the exact opposite and no regrets from this party here, none at all. But I would love my granddaughter to know that you and I have lived and loved like her and Lerryn. I know they don't live *together*. I wouldn't put it past them to have other lovers too, what with all the modern discussions on non-monogamy. I do hate that phrase. It's like something out of a medical text-book. Surely one of them could invent something a bit nicer sounding than that. Where was I?'

'You started with death and now you're into the young ones living it up.'

'Yes. Well, who knows what we'd have got up to if we'd been young lesbians now. I have been a lesbian since I was thirteen, Biff, and probably since I was born. So I demand a right to say exactly what I please about all this.'

'You're having a pretty good shot at it.'

'Yes I am. We have had a wonderful innings. I love you, Barbara Imogen Farley. I love you till death do us part. But only for a while and then you and I will be together again. I know that.'

'I like to hear you say it. I don't *know* it, though you make me want to.'

'Know it, Biff. Know it.'

'And if I do go first?'

'Then it will be from natural causes only. Or we shall have to pay. And the price is that we shall be separated in the next life.'

'I need a cup of tea.'

'You mean you need time to think, an hour or two alone in the shed.' Moss made it a statement not a question. Biff went to make the tea and Moss sat in the evening sunshine and prayed for a clear mind.

Twenty-two

The years come and go, thought Lindsey, relaxing in the back seat of Lerryn's old banger on the long drive to Cornwall. In the front Lerryn was driving, and beside her sat Harry, on holiday with them for two weeks, and talking non-stop.

Lindsey was free to enjoy her own thoughts, because Harry didn't turn around in case the action made her car sick. So Lindsey watched the countryside unfold, as they journeyed back to the land where both Harry and Lerryn, in turn, had been born and raised. Road signs came and went, appearing to Lindsey like years, rolling along one after the other, take this turn or that.

Can it really be four years since the summer of the drought, she thought, and are my grandparents really ageing so quickly now? Here

I am enjoying a car journey as if I never had a moment's fear since the accident. If I didn't have scars to prove it I'd not know I'd had all these injuries. That's what time can do – heal people.

My daughter was a baby when I went to collect her from Herton, and now she is old enough to go there on the coach on her own, a girl of fourteen gone to stay with Nanan and Biff. She idolises them. And her best friend is the daughter of my lost friend, Rita Gibbs, née Jackson. Anne is so different from her mother, but has the same grit. Different in what way? Let me think. Very politically minded whereas Rita always hated anything to do with politics. Wants to leave Herton whereas Rita always wanted to live there for ever. Yet loves Herton and Herton people like her mother does; and isn't afraid to speak her mind, like Rita. She stuck out to be best friends with Rosie against all her mother's off-putting. Quite a set to about that, according to Nanan. And as for Rosie, she knows to keep her mouth shut about me and Lerryn; and it's good for her to have another girl to be friends with when she's there. I wonder if Rita would let Anne come and visit us in London. Trouble is, I don't trust Rita, not as far as I can throw her. And she hasn't a single word to say to me. There are some routes you just can't return along. One way streets.

When I get back from this holiday, Rocky will be back from her trip to Jamaica; Maureen and Tessa from Spain. I'll take plenty of photos and we can have an evening at my house catching up and comparing notes. Back to work in the factory. Now *that* isn't worth thinking about!

Lindsey snuggled a cushion into the curve of her neck, leaned her head against the back seat, and drifted off into a deep sleep for the remainder of the journey.

In the front seat Harry was still talking to Lerryn, as they left behind them the bleak beauty of Bodmin Moor. Lerryn loved driving but was once again refusing Harry's offer to buy her a new car. 'No. I want to be independent of you, Harry. I already live rent free thanks to you. The gift of a studio all those years ago liberated me, as a person, and as an artist . . . '

Harry cut in with, 'So why refuse transport? This poor old thing won't struggle on much longer. It doesn't have to be a *new* car. You could have a used one with low mileage. I won't even notice the odd two thousand, dear. You know I won't.'

'No. But I would. I'd notice. Apart from the studio I have always stayed completely independent of you . . . '

Harry interrupted her again, 'Have one of my minis, Lerryn. They're both standing doing absolutely nothing in Shropshire.'

'As I was saying, Harry, I have always stayed independent of you. And that is how it's going to be. For ever and ever . . . '

'Amen? You are just like your mother, Lerryn. I don't know what to do with either of you.'

'Then don't try. You know we love you dearly, Mum and me both. You'll never change and we're used to you, but neither shall we. If you want to buy somebody a pressie, then you can get Rosie new jeans and some warm boots in the autumn. Lindsey and I will let you.'

'Let me?' snorted Harry, as Lerryn turned to wink at her. Harry continued, 'Just as you let me give to all your outrageous political causes.'

'Of course. That's different. They need the money and, besides, no one ever knows where the cheques are coming from. It still amazes me that you and my mother could be from the same family. You, the only wild redhead of the entire lot and the only one with verve and money.'

'I may be rich and wild, my dear Lerryn, but my sister is the happy one. In that she reminds me of your Lindsey. Not that I'd say this if she was awake and listening, but she's out for the count, back there.'

They flashed each other laughing grins as they listened for a moment to Lindsey's loud snores from the back seat. Lerryn concentrated on her driving for a couple of minutes, then said, 'Good job she only snores in the car, isn't it? Can you imagine me living all these years with that?'

'You'd have to build her a pen out in the garden, dear.'

'I've never once heard her snore in bed. Now Rosie's another matter, even when she was a little girl at her first school we had to shut her bedroom door on account of the noise. Heaven knows what she'll do when she wants to shack up with someone.'

'She'll think of something, don't we all?' Harry paused a moment. 'I can't tell you what it means to me to see you and Lindsey happy together. She has a propensity for happiness, your Lindsey.'

'She's not my Lindsey. She'd kill you if she heard you say "*mine*".'

'No, she wouldn't, dear. She'd humour me like you do. And like your mother. *She* knows she's the happy one of the two of us even if she is poor as a churchmouse. She chose the right man and I didn't. Pure and simple.'

'What? I thought you loved your life with Pierre?'

'Turn right here dear, through the village. That's it now, go along to the T junction, then left. I love my life and I love Pierre, but I don't have a life *with* Pierre. I have a life in spite of him, whereas my sister, your poor mother with no ha'pennies to rub together, has one of the happiest marriages in the land. Certainly west of Hayle River.'

Lerryn drove on, directed by Harry, as high hedges bordering narrow lanes unwound like flowered ribbon rolling this way and that. She thought about her mother and Harry, fifteen years apart in age. Her mother, sweeping other people's hearths until angina prevented her; her aunt, the adventuress, the amazon-sized redhead with personality to match, the full-blown stereotype of the wild woman untameable in the west wind, riding her horses with rings on her fingers and bells on her toes, if she wanted them.

She turned to smile at Harry and then returned her attention to the route for the final part of the drive.

Lindsey fell in love with St Ives. The whole town seemed like Herton by the sea. The jumble of houses and shops, the setting in wonderful countryside, felt like a home from home. It was Lindsey's first experience of that on holiday. It was unnerving and comforting at the same time. The house in which they were staying for bed and breakfast was only two very steep streets away from the Trewyn Studio, where Barbara Hepworth had lived and worked.

She had died in a fire at the studio when she was seventy-three and acknowledged as one of Europe's foremost sculptors. Later, when her studio was refurbished and opened to the public, some of the diary pages had been displayed in the foyer, in glass cases, for visitors like Lindsey to read.

Lindsey leaned forward over the glass-topped display case, her hands resting on the wooden frame, and realised that she was shaking from head to foot. She, and the large diary pages, were separated only by thin glass. The writing was enormous and the word *Yorkshire* was leaping higher than the other words.

'Are you coming with us?' The voice was Lerryn's.

'What? No. I'm not ready. This handwriting, it's so real, it's having such an effect on me. I've never seen a hand-written diary like this before. It's all such a lot to take in.'

Harry said, 'We'll go through to the glass conservatory, Lindsey, so why don't you come and find us when you're ready?'

'All right. You two go on. You've both been before and you know

Barbara Hepworth's life and work. But it's all so new to me. New connections. I'd rather be on my own.'

'Don't forget what I said to you before, will you?' reminded Lerryn. 'It's all right to touch the exhibits here.'

'I don't know about that. You both go in. I'll take my time anyway.'

Lindsey smiled as Lerryn and Aunt Harry disappeared into the gallery and she continued to study the writing in the glass cases in the foyer.

Cornwall was romantic waving waters; Yorkshire was brilliant waving fields of corn. Sentimental surfaces; underneath were the layers of rock; and under those were the tunnels and galleries which inched further and further away from the towns.

In Cornwall, thought Lindsey, absorbing the atmosphere in the foyer, tin lodes had been mined under the sea. She imagined Biff kneeling beside Frank during the great pit disaster and rescue in Herton, and noticing a crack in the gallery roof. As a Cornish tin miner, Biff might have been crouching several hundred feet under the sea. The weight of the sea above might have forced the rocks apart. Kneeling there in the open mouth of the tunnel, Biff might have watched as the rocks parted like teeth and the sea crashed down, bringing a million tons of hell, splitting the lodes like broken jaw bones, and swallowing miners whole.

Lindsey moved almost reluctantly from the foyer through the house into the gallery. It was full of natural sunlight from high windows, and it was empty of people.

There was only Lindsey, the sense of Moss and Biff, and the spirit of Barbara Hepworth.

Sunbeams sloped from the large square high windows down on to the wood and stone which gleamed and glowed.

I've never liked or understood sculpture, thought Lindsey, remembering herself in grammar school, being forced to whittle down a piece of granite-hard wood with a little knife.

Lindsey had counted the minutes in art class in wood shavings, paring the hours into quarters. Angry at being made to seem stupid and feeling herself to be one of life's artistic failures, she had tried to explain to Nanan and Biff, chipping at words, boxing them up like matches.

In the gallery a shaft of light fell on one of the closed forms. A lump of wood with a hole in it. Her mind said, Go on, touch it. She could almost hear Lerryn encouraging her. She was glad Lerryn wasn't here. There were strings across the hole. She reached to touch but

Nanan's voice said, 'Stop that, Lindsey. You don't touch art. What on earth do you think you're up to? Can't take you anywhere.' Her hand snatched itself back. Biff's voice said, 'Put it down. This is a museum, not a sweet shop.' Lerryn came back at her with, 'No. No, it's all right. This is meant to be touched.'

Her mind said, Can't think what all the fuss is about. It's only a lump of wood with a hole in it.

Her hand, in contradiction, reached out. Like a child being naughty, she looked round. Somebody might yell at her. Worse still, somebody might slap her fingers.

She was still alone in the gallery. The wood was as smooth as Lerryn's skin, curved like Lerryn's body. She stroked the sculpture, thinking of Lerryn and of the artist who had made it. Then, remembering back to the wretched art class at the grammar school, Lindsey thought of the hours it must have taken to whittle it to this perfect surface. She ran her hands lightly over it, through and round, up and over, down and round. She took her fingers away, and examined the pads on her finger tips which had begun to tingle. She touched the exhibit again, softly, then, gaining confidence, more firmly, slowly and steadily. Feeling, thinking.

She felt calm and happy, deviant and defiant. She moved round the gallery, making contact with all the pieces, reading the inscriptions and asking to be let into Barbara Hepworth's mind.

Opposite a double-form she stopped. Mother and child. She put the palm of her hand on the child's bottom, the mother's breasts. She licked salt tears off the corner of her mouth, not realising any had escaped. Rosie seemed near. There was a kind of energy coming from the exhibits, surprising Lindsey just as she had been quite overcome at the feelings in her body when she'd been for her first massage.

Outside, Harry pulled Lerryn's arm: 'I think I'm going to find a comfortable chair in the conservatory. I could do with a few minutes on my own, Lerryn. Would you mind?'

'Are you all right, Harry?'

'Fine. Thank you.' Harry paused. 'A few moments peace and quiet will work wonders. Too much dashing about.' Harry turned away along the garden parth and up the steps into the conservatory.

It was a dappled garden on a hillside with the sculptures placed in glades of light and shade, some facing forwards to the gallery, workshop and conservatory; others, tall standing forms, quiet and mysterious as dolmens, keepers of old knowledge, reaching back to hidden myths, Celtic witchcraft and wizardry.

Absorbed in the magic, Lerryn found a quiet seat, in a half-shaded corner by a small pond. She could see no one and could not be seen.

Water dropped steadily between the levels of the pond, as if naturally, down the hillside. Lerryn remembered the pond in Herton Hall grounds. She thought of her visits there; and of Moss and Biff.

From the side of the pond Lerryn could look up through old heavy branches to the summer sky, and by moving a few feet to the left or right could catch glimpses over the high garden walls, over the bay to the sea and Ireland.

The garden called her into herself, as if the great standing forms, some twice as tall as she was, were books of history that could have been written by Biff. They talked with Biff's sort of knowing. They might almost have had faces, and mouths, and Biff's shoulders. It must have been eight years ago that Lerryn had shown Lindsey the Biff-stone on the moors. Since then she had drawn the pictures of Biff, but hadn't talked about them to anyone; and no one had seen them.

But in Trewyn garden the sense of mystery about Biff deepened. If Biff *was* a woman then so much could be explained, thought Lerryn. But if I was disguised as a man, and I lived with Lindsey, let's say for sake of argument, here in St Ives, in hiding, I wouldn't want an inquisitive woman artist to investigate my life. Besides, thought Lerryn, watching a small frog plop into the pond from a lily pad, it would cause a deep rift between Lindsey and me. I would have to be very gentle, very careful, how I introduced the idea to her. *Taran-lughes*. Lindsey's anger at my searches could be lightning, flinging us apart.

Lerryn stood up and walked slowly among the sculptures. It was so peaceful and it seemed strange to think of Lindsey's potential anger – skies riven with lightning and clouds reverberating with thunder. Lerryn leaned against one of the sculptures. Some were so female. But others were impossible to label as male or female.

Aunt Harry was smoking a cigarette by the conservatory door. She stubbed it out as Lerryn walked towards her. Inside, they moved a couple of patio chairs to a companionable distance apart and enthused about the bougainvillea in full bloom on the wall behind them. Several gulls were slipping and sliding on the perspex roof. They were trying to walk over the corrugations up to the junction with the back wall. Triumphantly, one of them made it.

'Look at him. Showing off, standing on one leg.'

'I love it when they slide. Look, Harry, there goes another one.'

'They put me in mind of Pierre.'

'Meaning what, exactly?'

'He spends his entire life on slippery slopes.'

In Lerryn's head an alarm went off, like a coastguard hooter to warn of possible danger, to take care on the cliffs. She thought, Don't some people pick their moments. Not now, Harry, please, not now. Give me a break, I'm on holiday. Aloud she said, 'Uncle Pierre?'

'He's leaving me, finally. He wants a divorce.'

'Do what? I thought you . . . I thought you had it . . . organised.'

'I did. We did. But this time it's serious, whereas before, no problem. He led his life, I led mine. I gave him three sons, he had normality in the public sense. But it seems he's under pressure from the new, er, person in his life.'

'Person? That's a strange way to talk, Harry. Have you met her? Is she someone you know?'

'He, dear. It's a man. And yes, I do know him. He's seventy-two, the same age as Pierre. They look alike too: grey hair and glasses. They want to live with one another.'

'A man. Oh, why am I so stupid? I never gave that a moment's consideration.'

'People don't.'

'Well you'd have thought *I* would. Given my lifestyle.'

'I wonder that you never put two and two together, Lerryn.'

'So do I. It can't have been at all easy to cope with all these years.'

'Pierre was very discreet, Lerryn. And I always had plenty of gay friends as you know.'

'Did Anna know? Does she know?'

'She does, now. She's been so good. Listened to me for many an hour.'

'I'm glad you had someone to talk to. It can't have been easy for you, nor for Pierre. He's a lovely person. I've always been fond of him.'

'You couldn't not. Everyone loves Pierre. But I made the mistake of putting him on a pedestal, whereas he is human. He wants to settle down with Jacques and that leaves me nowhere. And I couldn't live in a threesome any more than he could.'

Lerryn leaned forward and touched Harry on the arm. 'I do love you. I will always listen to you, you know that.'

'Yes. I do know that. But I wasn't ready to say anything until now. I hoped I'd have a chance while we were away. The problem for me is that I don't want anyone else to share my home with, other than Pierre. And until Jacques came along, Pierre felt the same about me.

Obviously we haven't shared a bed for many years, but we always did live well together. Such good friends. Companions.'

Above them another gull lost its footing, flurrying off in an agitation of feathers. Harry squinted up through the perspex at the sky, saying, 'I know how it feels. If I had wings I'd take off right now, up and away, become an albatross in the south Atlantic. Fly it all out of me.'

'I've often wondered why you didn't. You could have had flying lessons years ago.'

'Couldn't stand the responsibility. Give me a good male pilot any day. And don't tell me I'm being sexist. Not right now.'

'I wouldn't dream of it. Leave me out.' Lerryn paused, changed tone and asked, 'But seriously, Aunt Harry, what will you do?'

'Do! I don't know where to begin. I'm fond of him. We've been such good friends for all these years. I could rely on Pierre. He always came home. Whether it was Shropshire, which I always regarded as a sort of Sissinghurst, or the Chelsea flat, which we both loved, you know, with the roof garden. In the sunset, I could look at the wide open sky from there and be back here in Cornwall. So much sky. Don't ever think I forget my roots. Oh, I know all those things I've said about fairy tales and so forth. The myths and folklore are not what it's about, not for me. For you it's different. For me, it was sharing that roof garden with Pierre. I had continuity. That's what is being broken.'

'Will the Chelsea flat remain yours?'

'Oh, of course. There is no problem about money. Pierre is not a mean man. He never has been, and the, er, sexual side has never bothered me. I'm not actually one of those people for whom sex is important.' Aunt Harry lowered her voice to a whisper and Lerryn leaned nearer. 'Nothing there, dear, just not interested.'

'I used to wonder sometimes, about that. With Uncle Pierre being away.'

'I'm sure there are many women who wouldn't bother at all if the world didn't dangle it like a carrot, and I do know what my images mean.' Harry laughed and Lerryn suppressed a chuckle with her hand over her mouth and her eyes grinning over the top of it.

'No, Lerryn, you are such a comfort to me. Such a comfort. I couldn't tell anyone else about all this, especially not my sister. And I know Lindsey very little really, though I am glad you have each other, even if you do both of you have your little light relief from each other now and then.'

'Harry, you are shocking. You have no right . . .'

'I know, dear. Nevertheless, you are my niece, closer to me than any of my sons will ever be, bless them, and when Pierre settles with Jacques in Paris instead of with me in London, my later years will take a turn I never in my whole life-plan made allowances for. So there you go. You might as well live life to the absolute full, because you never know what is waiting around the turn of the road. Look, here comes Lindsey. She seems to be deep in thought, doesn't she?' Harry called to the approaching figure. 'Hello there. Earth to Lindsey?'

Lindsey's face and body were wide open with pleasure, as she waved and ran lightly up the few steps towards them, saying, 'Isn't it wonderful? What a place to live and work. No wonder artists came here. It's beyond belief, this place.'

'Glad you came?' asked Lerryn, putting her arm around Lindsey and hugging her.

'Glad? It's magical. And it's definitely my turn to get us all a cream tea. Let's go and find that tiny tea shop, the one with the round tables. I'm starving, are you?'

'I could murder a cup of Earl Grey,' commented Harry, taking care not to insist that it was her turn, and they made their way back out through the lobby to the hill which led down into town.

Twenty-three

The taxi dropped Moss outside her gate in Church Lane. Moss paid the driver, thanked him, and arranged to be picked up at the same time the following week.

She wore her shoulder bag these days so that she could use both hands on the zimmer frame. Slowly, unassisted, she moved in six-inch clunks along the ramp and up towards her front door. Leaning forwards against the zimmer, she felt with one hand into the pouch on her shoulder bag for the key on its extended plastic mount which made it easier to hold. She fitted it in the well-oiled lock and turned it slowly.

The front room opened up, sunny, in the late morning. The light bright airy feel would last all day because the room faced almost south.

Moss moved slowly with the zimmer to her high-backed armchair, where she sat and rested, with her coat on. The full-blown roses filled the room with perfume. Moss still had a keen sense of smell and she closed her eyes and leaned back, drinking in the roses, thinking. The ones that she had just placed on the grave would now be opening in the sunshine. Biff had been cremated and her ashes were placed in the grave. An inscription had been added: 'Here lies Biff, lifelong companion of Moss and friend of Frank. Rest in peace. 16 February 1981.' Moss had been so careful not to put he or she.

She had made the journey weekly since Biff's death over two years ago, but today's outing had tired her more than usual so she stayed in the armchair, giving herself time to recuperate.

One minute, it seemed to Moss, Biff had been sitting in that chair watching a programme on nuclear energy and the coal industry, and the next had slumped forward.

The power of life was matched only by that of death, Moss remembered, visualising Biff's slumped form. One minute Biff had been there, the woman Moss had loved for such a long part of her life, the next she had gone, the heat gone from her body and with it the spirit, the essence of her. Gone from the room, from the rest of the house, and garden. Moss had stood out there as if she could communicate more immediately with Biff, but Biff was departed. Gone from Herton.

The shell of Biff's body had remained in the chair. Moss had pulled the body, despite all her own physical pain and discomfort, from the chair on to the floor, and had laid Biff out carefully, paying attention to her eyelids, which she closed, and her face which she smoothed with her fingers, and her mouth, which she also closed.

Then when she was satisfied that Biff was in the right position, Moss had rung both the doctor and Lindsey.

What a panic she had had when the doctor arrived! He bent as if to examine Biff. Moss did not know what he might do. She had prayed as the doctor felt Biff's neck, where the pulse used to be. Finding strength from her faith that God had always been on their side, Moss saw how easily and quickly the doctor had seemed satisfied. Was he doing his job properly, she wondered? Whether he was or not, he said he would write out a death certificate. So God had not let her down in her hour of need. She had dictated the name: Bernard Ian Ferguson.

'I'll arrange for Jones's to come and take Biff to the funeral parlour. They'll be very gentle. They'll prepare him and arrange the coffin and so forth.'

'No, Doctor. I want Biff to stay here. I want the coffin brought here, and I will keep Biff near me, like they used to do in the old days, you know.'

'Mrs Ferguson, people don't keep the body at home these days. Better to let me phone Jones's for you. I realise what a shock this is.'

'Oh no. It's not that I'm in shock, as you say, Doctor. It's what Biff and I wanted, what we agreed on. I couldn't possibly go back on my word, it would be a betrayal of Biff, of Biff's express wishes. And mine. We were both quite clear about what we wanted.'

'Mrs Ferguson, let me give you something for the shock. That'll help you. I have been worried about you for many years. Your own heart isn't good, which is why we've never been able to do anything about your poor hip, isn't it? The whole aim of funeral directors is to relieve the relatives of the deceased from further stress.'

'But it would not be a relief to me, Doctor. Believe me, I know what I want and what I'm talking about. You are very kind to me, always have been, but I want to be alone with Biff, until my granddaughter arrives from London. I'm absolutely sure about that.'

'It's not regular practice, Mrs Ferguson. Not regular practice at all. In fact it's not heard of, to keep the body at home now. People don't do that any longer.'

'I'm not people, Doctor. I'm the common-law wife of the person who is now lying there and I am almost eighty years old. I have had time, plenty of time, to know exactly what I want and how I wish things to be done. The least stress will be caused if Biff is here with me. When you are my age, you may understand how I feel. This is my home and I am certain about what I want and how I want things done. How we used to do these things in my family in the old days, as I said.

'Now I am going to phone the minister,' Moss continued, 'and I shall arrange the service while I wait for my granddaughter and great granddaughter to arrive with friends from London. I have a lot to do and I'm sure you're very busy, so why don't you leave Biff there until the coffin is ready and go and visit the people who are still alive?'

The doctor faced his dilemma and Moss's determination.

'Will you promise me something? That you will call me if you need anything, anything at all? Or if you, er, possibly, change your mind?'

'Thank you, Doctor. I appreciate your kindness. I really do. But I am all right. I'm a very tough old lady, despite my heart and hip, and I know exactly what I'm doing.'

By the time Lindsey, Lerryn and Rosie arrived in the early afternoon of the next day, the undertakers had measured Biff, still fully clothed and lying where Moss had insisted everyone left the body, and had returned with the coffin into which Biff had been gently lifted. With the lid half folded back only Biff's face was visible to friends and family.

'I've never seen a dead man before,' whispered Rosie, eyes wide and anxious. Suddenly she blurted out, 'He won't wink at me, will he?'

'Biff loved you and never wished any harm to come to you,' replied Moss. 'Just smile at Biff and say I love you. You can do that for Biff, can't you?'

Moss felt Lerryn and Lindsey stiffen as Rosie walked to the coffin. Despite her poor eyesight, Moss could tell that Rosie was shaking. Rosie looked down at Biff and whispered, 'I love you, Biff.' She was crying as she dashed out to the toilet. Lindsey ran after her. Lerryn put her arm around Moss. She kissed Moss on the cheek and said, 'If you've got a hotline to Biff, tell Biff to help us by not knocking on the ceiling.' Moss was so taken aback that she started to laugh, and as Lerryn held her she wept, looking up at the ceiling and back to the coffin. 'I know you're there, Biff,' she answered. 'You made me laugh so many times. Don't knock.'

She cried on to Lerryn's shoulder as Lerryn held her, and then realised that Lerryn had called Biff by name twice rather than saying 'he' or 'she'. This was something she herself did. Moss wiped her eyes, and was looking up into Lerryn's face as Lindsey and Rosie came back in.

'Nanan, I'm going to say goodbye to Biff now. Then can we close the lid, please. They don't do this kind of thing these days. I can't think what's got into you, really I can't.' Lindsey's voice was wavering between her 'mother' voice that she didn't know she used whenever she was defending Rosie, and her I-really-love-you Nanan-but-you-drive-me-barmy voice.

Moss looked from her to Rosie and then to Lerryn. They were all smiling tightly through their teeth like ventriloquists' dummies, waiting for her response.

'All right, if it makes you calmer. Though what Biff would say I dread to think.'

'Nanan,' warned Lindsey.

Lerryn and Lindsey paid their respects and then Moss shut the lid of the coffin.

'Now then. How about a cup of tea and a nice slice of my cut and come again cake?'

'I'm not all that hungry, thanks, Nanan,' said Rosie, as close to Lerryn as she could get with her back to the coffin.

'Nor me thanks, Nanan,' said Lindsey, putting on a smile that didn't fool Moss at all.

'Lerryn?'

'I'll have a cup of tea, thanks, nothing to eat. I think the others might quite like a little walk.'

Rosie stood and put on her coat as fast as if the house was on fire and Lindsey reached for hers. 'I'll keep Rosie company. Anything you want from the shops?' she said.

But Moss replied, 'The shopping has been taken care of.' The two of them left immediately, kissing Lerryn and Moss goodbye.

When they'd gone, Moss made tea and called Lerryn into the kitchen to drink it with her.

'There's a lot I want to talk to you about, Lerryn, but I'm not quite ready. And I can't talk to my own granddaughter, more's the pity. If I say something to you in confidence, can you keep it to yourself?'

'Twelfth house is the house of secrets, Moss. I have a lot of twelfth house in my chart.'

'I'm glad you are lovers with my granddaughter.'

Lerryn's eyes widened in surprise. Thinking rapidly she said, 'Is that what you wanted to tell me?'

'That and some other things, about my life. But I'm not ready to say them yet. Do you understand?'

'I hope so. There's so much on my mind, about you and Biff. You're both special, very special.'

'It's all I can say, until I'm ready. Now will you have some of my cake?'

Moss drank her tea, appearing to sink into private thoughts, almost as if Lerryn wasn't there. The silence wasn't uncomfortable to Lerryn. She felt sure she knew why Moss was pleased that her granddaughter had a woman lover.

That night Rosie slept with Lindsey, and Lerryn slept in the boxroom. Moss thought it was sensible and said so. She offered them a bucket on the landing, so they didn't have to go down to the toilet in the dark, past Biff. Lindsey asked her to keep the living-room light on, just in case. Moss wanted to laugh, they were such a load of jelly babies. 'Where was the true grit gone?' she had wanted to cry, but didn't. She wanted to sit up all night holding Biff's hand, but she needed a good night's sleep. So she let them help her upstairs to bed, and she told them she would get a single for herself and have it made up in the living room, from now on, because it would be hard to go up and down stairs without Biff to assist her.

Moss had been thinking that it would be better if she could sleep downstairs, but when Biff was alive it would have meant putting a double bed in the living room, and it would have been so crowded. She only went upstairs once a day, and that was to sleep; and came down each morning. Now she would live entirely downstairs, and that would help her hip tremendously.

The Methodist chapel was packed for Biff's funeral, with flowers filling each window, in honour of the grocer's delivery boy who had lived his life with the grocer's wife.

Moss felt a great sense of relief when the final part, the journey to the crematorium and the commitment service there, was finished. She felt that she had come too near to telling Lerryn Biff's secret; and she gave thanks to God in the crematorium, for having had the grace to withstand the desire to speak until the time was right. Yet something had changed in Lerryn, as Moss could tell, as she walked on Lerryn's arm, and afterwards she always thought of the funeral as marking a turning point in her special closeness to Lerryn.

On the journey home she had asked Lerryn, 'What are you thinking?'

'I was in Cornwall, actually, Moss. I was sitting in my old stone armchair, the one I told you about, remember?' Moss had nodded. 'I was watching the green and blue waves surging on to the boulders below, and the white foam flying.'

'It sounds beautiful. Is it a mysterious place?'

'It is. It's full of questions.'

They had travelled on without saying any more, each deep in her own thoughts, and both of them knew that the other was thinking of Biff.

Moss woke with a start, realising she had been daydreaming about Lerryn at Biff's funeral. She was sure that Lerryn understood why she had had to keep Biff's body at home. Lerryn had an urgent need to break open the lie. But in the years since Biff had died, Lerryn had never once invaded Moss's privacy by asking questions.

Although Moss's sight had deteriorated further, she still had some

226

vision. She had a supersensitive awareness of patterns of light and shade. She realised now that the sun had moved, or rather, she chuckled to herself, the earth had, and the shadows of the roses on the window ledge had shifted. She was too warm, still in her unbuttoned coat, so she eased herself out of it slowly and placed it on the table by her chair. She decided to move with the zimmer into the kitchen and have a cup of tea, and listen to the radio in there while she waited for her home help to arrive.

At first when the young woman from Social Services had come round offering her a home help she'd been very offended.

'Do you think I'm dirty, getting senile, that I can't do for myself these days?'

'Mrs Ferguson, you're not at all senile or dirty, and I wouldn't dream of being so rude. But we have a Mrs Gibbs available three afternoons a week for an hour and a half, and she could do your shopping, hoovering and make your bed, and take your sheets to the laundry. Those are all things that your husband used to do, aren't they?'

Moss thought of poor Frank and his three work coats and his seven shirts all hanging pressed and ready and she laughed. 'If you mean Biff, I wonder if you've read my notes properly young woman. But you're very busy and I know you mean well, so it wouldn't be fair for me to give you a hard time, would it?'

The young social worker was leaning forward, an eager-beaver body all tensed up but wanting to 'help'. Moss wanted to swear at her; or put up two fingers, do something to shock her out of being so nice, so polite, so good. But you had to be careful in a place like Herton. If you trod on someone on your way up you'd like as not meet them on your way down. Not that Moss felt she'd trodden on Rita Gibbs née Jackson, nor that she herself was now on her way down; but Rita had a bit of a name in Herton because she was old fashioned in her outlook and outspoken in her ways. However she was also one of the kindest women that Moss could hope to come across anywhere and was well thought of by several of the old people whose home help she'd been.

Moss told the young woman from the Social Services that she would think about it, and would phone her. Lindsey had bought a large face dial for her telephone and that made life easier.

So Moss made tea and sat in the kitchen drinking it, waiting for Rita and thinking of Rosie who was due to visit in the holidays, and of Rita's daughter Anne who was Rosie's best friend.

'Do you like your new radio, Nanan?' Rosie had asked, and was pleased when Moss showed her how easily she could push the buttons in, compared to turning the knobs on the old wireless. The wireless had gone to the local comprehensive with Anne, whose history group was making a forties and fifties exhibition.

'It's all "hi-tech", Nanan', Rosie had told her. 'What would you do for aggro if you didn't have me and Anne playing heavy rock whenever we're here?'

'Oh, I'd think of something, love. Between you me and the gatepost there'll be plenty of aggro in this town if this pit closure isn't cancelled.'

'Dad says there's going to be a ballot and strike, Mrs Ferguson, do you think so?' asked Anne.

'I think so and I hope so,' said Moss. She loved to sit and talk to Anne and Rosie. Anne was more like her father to look at than her mother. She was thick set and had straight blonde hair and grey-green eyes. She was taller than her mother, but wasn't likely to grow as tall as Biff, thought Moss. As she talked, her long hair fell over her shoulder and she swept it back occasionally with the back of her hand. She was unaware of being beautiful, thought Moss, and unlike Rosie, who used makeup, Anne didn't wear any, because her skin was very sensitive. The two girls side by side were startlingly different. 'The people of Herton won't put up with much more nonsense from this government,' Moss went on. 'They can't keep Herton people down for ever. It's been one debate after another since heaven knows when.'

'You don't think Herton pit's uneconomic then, do you?'

'No. Of course I don't. I agree with what your dad told you, Anne. That it's a lie like all the others to keep people agreeing with pit closures. Herton people are just as capable of doing sums as the mighty Coal Board. Like I said to Rosie, here, I've been doing sums since I was five. Now if Biff was still alive we could all sit round this table and talk it out. But me, I think of it this way . . . The government's got X amount of pounds and they can buy nuclear weapons or Herton's coal. So they spend all the money on missiles and power stations, plutonium from abroad and such like and then they try to kid us all that there's none left for coal. Of course coal's uneconomic if they spend it all on Cruise and Trident.'

'Rosie's mum's taking her to Greenham Common in December for the demo,' said Anne. 'I wanted to go and stay there with them and go too, but Mum won't let me.'

'That's right,' said Rosie. 'You wouldn't put in a good word for Anne next time her mum comes, now she's your home help, would you? *Please*, Nanan?'

'No. You two can choose your own friends, however you like. I like you, Anne, and you're very welcome here, but interfere between Rita and Lindsey I will not. You should know me better than that, our Rosie. I'm surprised at you.'

'I'm sorry, Nanan, but I bet they can't even remember what they fell out about and we just think they're plain stupid, don't we, Anne?'

Anne nodded but looked very embarrassed. 'I told her not to ask you, Mrs Ferguson,' she said finally.

'Anne, the women in my family have usually said exactly what they want when they want, give or take a few exceptions, and you don't operate Rosie's mouth for her. Go on, both of you. Out of my kitchen, I've had enough nattering for one day. Come and see us tomorrow, Anne. I'll have the scones hot out of the oven.'

'Thanks, I will. Do you need any extra shopping or did Mum get it all?'

'You can bring me some more tea bags. I forgot to ask Rita. There's a pound coin in the pot on the window ledge.'

Rita arrived promptly and began by changing Moss's single bed. She packed the bedlinen in a laundry bag, which she placed with her coat by the door, and then she hoovered around.

Meanwhile Moss was thinking of Joan Field who had been Rita's schoolfriend when they'd been together before Rita's year at the isolation hospital separated them. Rita had been held back a year in the juniors, which was when she'd met and befriended Lindsey.

The housework finished, Rita sat with Moss for a cup of tea.

'Mercy was round yesterday,' Moss said, 'and mentioned you were getting friendly with Joan again.'

'Does that surprise you, Moss? We were best friends as little girls, remember?'

'But you're so very different now as grown women. Joan's as well known for her views as you are in this town, and it's no secret that she doesn't see eye to eye with you.'

Rita was unruffled. She'd expected as much. She sat drinking her tea without appearing to mind Moss's comments at all. She smiled, thinking of herself and Joan walking around the market the other day.

Joan was a huge woman with a loud voice and a deep belly laugh. She had wavy brown hair cut short, and she always wore bright blue eye shadow which she said was to match her lovely blue eyes. Rita could hear her laughing as the image of Joan came into her mind. Joan always wore slacks and no one failed to notice her when she was out and about. Her loud banter could be heard from one side of the market to the other.

Rita, by contrast, was Lindsey's height and always wore skirts. She liked her brown hair shoulder length and took care with her makeup. She wouldn't have been seen dead without her touch of lipstick and discreetly applied mascara. No eye shadow because she thought it was common. Yes, she thought, finishing her tea opposite Moss, the sight of Joan and me together is as good as anything you'll get on television. Two very strong characters, known for our tough words.

Out loud she replied, 'Well for a start she married Steve's best mate, so our paths do cross, don't they? And for another thing she lives for Herton and her kids, just like I do. We've enough in common.'

'Does Mart Field think there'll be a strike then?'

'We all do. But we're doing everything we can to avoid it. We need a strike in Herton like we need a hole in the head.'

'Aye, well, let's be praying that the Coal Board sees sense then.'

'It could take more than praying, Moss, this time around.'

'Well, you tell Joan I'm praying for you all.'

'I will that. She did a fine thing by marrying Mart Field. Next to my Steve, he's one of the best blokes in this whole town, if you ask me. And he makes a damn fine shop steward. It's him and Joan what's brought me in on all this really. Never was one for politics and I always thought union stuff was men's talk. But Joan, she's different. Like you said, we're chalk and cheese. But she says to me, "The world isn't going to let Herton stay the same for ever, Rita. There's changes going on what's going to knock Herton, what we can't see yet. Changes in, oh, I dunno, machinery, management in the pit, even EEC policies on coal and such like. You'd better get your thinking cap on, Rita, and be quick about it, or you're going to wonder what's hit you." So I did, get me thinking cap on,' Rita smiled and patted the top of her head.

'So you've got Joan to talk to then. That's good.'

'Yes. She says to me: "I want you for my friend, you big loud mouth." So I says, "Well that's all right then because I want you for my friend too, you big softie." I don't see much of her. Don't live in each other's pockets, nowt like that. It's just that I know she's there. None of us knows what's going to happen, but somehow, all of us is getting ready. In me mind, I'm getting ready. Does that sound daft? I don't know what I'm getting ready for.'

'Doesn't sound daft to me. But them Fields were always well thought of in this town. Herton people, generations back.'

'Aye well. Like the Dundys, the Jacksons, and the Gibbses. Mind you, you've been here since the ark 'n all.' Rita paused, struggling. Then she spoke slowly. 'There's something I wanted to say to you. Years and years back, when Rosie was a new-born baby, and we had that talk, remember? I didn't mean to be rude about your grandmother. Her being Indian I mean. It takes me a long time to change. On some things I am learning, changing. That's down to Joan really. Anyway it's been on my mind sometimes. I had no right to overlook you like I did.'

'All these years it's been on your mind?'

'That and a lot of other things. Anyway I'm glad I told you. I'd best be going. See you day after tomorrow then.'

'Yes. I'm glad you told me, too.'

Rita left straight away, and by then it was four o'clock. It seemed a long time until the six o'clock news on the television as Moss sat in the armchair holding Biff's photograph in its frame.

What might life have been like if they had left Herton? Gone to live somewhere where neither of them had to hide her full identity, her full family history. Daisy never had answered her letters but had remained furious, and the gaps in Moss's letters to her mother had lengthened as the early years had flown. Then they had become too long to bridge, and they had both stopped writing. Too much longing, too much to hide on either side. But how she regretted the gap in her later years, especially when her own children had grown and flown; the cost of the isolation was the loss of the history, and Biff had always recognised and talked about that.

Moss held the photograph closer. She could not turn back the time. There was no way to do that.

'If I lived my life over, Biff, I'd still want to love you as I loved you, and for as long. But I'd want my children and grandchildren to know my mother and my grandmother. And if wishes were horses, we could have ridden away from this town, our saddlebags full of gold sovereigns, and lived a free and open life.'

She pressed the photograph to her chest, folded her arms across it, as she had folded her arms around Biff so many warm nights of loving. So many. She bent her head, unconsciously rubbing her face with the heel of one of her thumbs, as she rocked herself to sleep.

It was the middle of November and it seemed to Moss that it had been dark for hours although it was only mid evening. She wasn't used to so much talking and felt very tired. So she closed her eyes and hummed quietly to the music on Radio 3 as Lindsey did some ironing. She and Rosie were up for a long weekend; Rosie had gone with Anne to a party.

Lindsey was thinking of Rocky and Maureen who had been persuading her not to henna her grey hair. They had been talking in the factory on Friday afternoon.

'I like it grey,' Maureen had declared. 'I'm used to it, what with your dark eyes and eyebrows, it looks sort of distinguished.'

'Leave it, don't dye it. It suits you,' agreed Rocky. 'Almost five thirty. I'm switching off.' She had unplugged her sewing machine and started to pack up, as the others followed suit. 'That's it. All spick and span. I'm off for the bus, have a nice weekend in Herton, Lindsey. See you Tuesday.'

Lost in her own thoughts, Lindsey didn't notice that Moss had stopped humming, and was looking at her thoughtfully. It took Lindsey by surprise when Moss spoke. 'Why don't you call on Rita while you're here? It'd be such a good thing if you and Rita could be friends again.'

'Nanan, I've told you before, you know we can't. Please give it a rest.'

Moss glanced sideways at Biff's photograph in its frame as she said, 'I know Rita's not an easy woman to get along with, but Rosie and Anne are friends now. Surely you could let bygones be bygones?'

'I'm glad you've got a home help, Nanan. But it's not any help to me that it had to be Rita of all people. I've said before and I'll say again, Nanan, you will have to keep your rabbits in separate hutches or you'll breed a lot you can't cope with.' Lindsey hung up the jeans and started on Moss's ironing.

Moss gestured with her arms, wagging her finger at Lindsey. 'Hutches my foot. You and Rita are the devil and the deep blue sea. You want your heads examined, both of you,' she snapped.

'It's Rita who wants her head examined. Somebody should drag that woman into the twentieth century and it isn't going to be me.' She deliberately changed the subject. 'Now then, Nanan, why don't you tell me what's going on in Herton?'

Moss warmed to her theme immediately, tired though she was. 'I was driving past the market on my usual trip out, you know, and that shop behind the bus stop, the one with the jinx on it? Try this, try that, nothing works for long in that shop – it's all boarded up again. Records, singles. Oh, I don't know, all these young people and their groups. Boy George and so forth. Mind you, I do like him – such a gentle chappie. Now where was I?'

'Boarded up?'

'Yes. Posters for this, that and the other. And there, all over the top of the other posters – you know how they do, slap the things on. There were rows and rows of them – such a statement it made me quite agitated for a while, the letters so big and bold. I made the driver stop so I could get a closer look – COAL NOT DOLE COAL NOT DOLE COAL NOT DOLE.' Moss held her arms wide to show the size of the letters. 'There it was large as life and I thought, yes that's me, too. Large as life. I am going to be part of this thing. I told them all at the pensioners' drop-in. They mustn't sit back now that they're retired. This thing is for all of us. I shall go to public meetings from now on. In a taxi.'

'You're a credit to this town, Nanan,' Lindsey said, easing Moss's nightdress on to a hanger.

'I live in this community and I shall not stay silent when there are things to say.'

'As if you ever would.' Lindsey smiled gently and started on Moss's favourite blouse.

'That's right,' Moss replied, enjoying the compliment. She crossed her arms and continued, forgetting her tiredness in her pleasure at discussing her favourite topic. 'Of course it's all working men's clubs and the union, but I have a feeling about it all. Right from the ballot back in eighty-two, people in this town have been saying that if Herton is threatened with extinction they will fight back for their lives. You take a pit from a place like Herton and what have you got? Death and no resurrection.'

Twenty-four

From a distance, the block of Hackney hard-to-lets was like a ship on a night sea with lights streaming from her portholes. Nearer, some passers-by caught glimpses of rooms festooned with red, green, silver and gold decorations announcing Christmas, still three weeks away.

Lindsey wiped the pots that Rosie had washed up and took her time putting them away. She was into her grey and white phase in the kitchen. Nice new plastic drainer, matching bin and such like. She loved the place, especially as everything was bought and paid for and she'd done all that by turning her hampster wheel herself for the whole of her working life. She loved her independence and apart from worrying about Moss, she was utterly happy. She pictured Rocky and Maureen at their sewing machines. It's the people you work with that count, not the job itself, she thought. She wiped the surface under the drainer, polished it with a dry old piece of towel and laid a clean newspaper on the dry area.

Then she brought her favourite vine in from the living room and set about snipping and tidying it, letting the pieces drop on to the paper. She took three good sized cuttings, stripped off the lower leaves and placed them in a waiting bottle of water. 'Root in time for Nanan for Christmas,' she told them, carrying the bottle to the window ledge. Funny old life, she thought, her mind going over and over the recent conversation with Moss about being friends again with Rita. 'Trust it to be bloody Rita,' she muttered.

Just at that moment Rosie burst in to the kitchen. She had a habit of starting with a question. Coming up to Lindsey, and on a height with her at sixteen, Rosie put her arms around her mother and hugged. 'So can I go up on my own to Nanan's as soon as term's over then?' she asked. Her words clipped through Lindsey's thoughts, strewing them like the vine leaves dropping on the newspaper.

Lindsey put her hands on Rosie's shoulders and held her at arms length, looking at her. Rosie had very short thick black hair and dark brown eyes. Her skin was clear and smooth, the sort that people called peaches and cream. Her eyes were edged with blue liner and huge square blue earrings dangled from her ears; they clanked against her neck as she talked. She was so lively that Lindsey felt herself slow and middle aged in comparison. Neither of them was skinny. Rosie's body was lively like her personality but solid too, in jeans and a thick long jumper in blue and white stripes.

'What you looking at me like that for, Mum?' Rosie smiled, and added, 'I'm having a coke, want one?'

'No thanks. I was thinking how grown up you are, catches me by surprise sometimes. Especially since you started being able to look me straight in the eye.'

'So can I go?' Rosie sat down on one of the pine benches, drinking the coke.

'I'd rather you waited and we went up together. Lerrie and I hardly get a glimpse of you these days. We were looking forward to the journey with you.'

'But I'm missing Anne, Mum. Haven't seen her since . . . '

'Rosie, it's only been three weeks.'

'But it won't have been by the end of term and we've loads and loads to talk about. Besides, I thought you were worried about Nanan.'

'I am, but . . . ' Lindsey sat at the table opposite Rosie.

'You're not trying to stop me going to see Nanan, are you? Or Anne?'

'I'm not stopping you, love. And I know Nanan will be pleased. She loves your company, but . . . '

'But nothing, Mum. Anne's my best mate and it just so happens she lives that far away and I love to stay with my nanan. I know you don't like me and Anne being friends.'

'I never said that, Rosie. You choose your own friends, but . . . '

'But you don't trust her mother because you had a split up way back before the dinosaurs.'

'Rosie! Don't talk to me like that. I have never stopped you being friends with Rita Gibbs' daughter. I don't like it any more'n Nanan liked it when I ran away with your dad. But you'll do what you want to anyway, as I did before you.'

'And your mum before that and Nanan before that. You could say it runs in the family. Look, Mum, I don't want to argue with you. Really I don't, I love you.' Rosie came round to where Lindsey sat and hugged her tightly. 'There, that's how much.'

'You want me dead, hugging all the breath out of me?' Lindsey smiled in spite of herself. 'Obviously it's hard for me.' She looked straight at Rosie who had sat down again, opposite. 'It brings up lots of feelings and of course I worry about Nanan. Specially when the winters really set in. She seems so determined she's going to stay alive for this campaign about the pit closures. Stubborn old thing. It must be sheer willpower and faith keeping her going these days.'

'Nanan says she's held together with a wing and a prayer. I wouldn't be *going* to Herton if it wasn't to stay with her. She means more to me than anyone except you, even Lerryn, and goodness knows you've been together years. Do you know, Mum, I was thinking the other day, I can hardly remember a time when you and me didn't have Lerrie. Give or take a few hiccups.' Rosie winked.

'Lerrie and I have an arrangement about all that. She has her, er, hiccups too. You are the most right off young woman I know. How would you like to be referred to as somebody's hiccup?'

'I wouldn't let anybody call me anyone's anything, Mum. But then that's how you brought me up. Besides I couldn't stand all the broken-hearted bits when they leave in a hurry or a flurry.' Rosie looked into her coke and watched a few bubbles rise and pop.

On the table, by the fruit bowl, lay a brown paper bag of satsumas and a box of dates. Lindsey shoved the bag to Rosie and they each peeled a satsuma and began to eat, segment by segment. Rosie washed hers down with coke.

'Mum, can I ask you something?'

'Is it about going to Herton?'

'Not exactly. Nanan said, last time we were there, that at times she fell out of love with Biff. Then they just "endured", that was her word, till they fell back in love again.' Rosie peeled another satsuma and gave half to Lindsey. She waited a moment then asked, 'Do you want to be with Lerrie as long as Nanan was with Biff?'

Lindsey looked across the table at Rosie. 'I want to be with Lerrie as long as we both love each other. It seems to be working out for us, doesn't it?'

'Donkey's years, I'd say. I want you to stay together. I love Lerrie.'

'I know, love. I can't imagine life without Lerrie. But I'm a survivor, Rosie. So are you, I think. And if Lerrie and I finished, I'd recover, but it would take me a good while.'

'What's a good while?'

'I don't know. The thing is that I know I'd survive. So would Lerrie. That makes us equal and I'm sure being equal is what keeps us together.'

'You never looked for another man when my dad was killed, did you?'

'No.'

'Why not?'

'I don't know the answer to those kind of questions. Put it this way. Rocky said I was like somebody sewn up in a shroud. I had to unpick the stitches. I was starting to unpick them with the help of my friends, like Maureen and Rocky herself, when Lerryn knocked on my door.'

'Was it love at first sight then? Did you fall in love with Lerrie when you saw her there on the door step?'

'No.' Lindsey smiled, remembering. 'It was quite, quite different. It took me months to realise how I felt. Why all the questions?'

'I haven't fallen in love yet, Mum.'

'Are you worried about it?'

'Not really. Er, sometimes.' Rosie stopped then blurted: 'Mum, I don't know who to fall in love with.'

Lindsey looked at her daughter. 'We have to find out what we want and what we need by ourselves, Rosie. I found Lerrie, though I wasn't even searching when she came and found me.' As gently as possible she said, 'Yes, I am happy with Lerrie. And I do intend to stay with her for a very very long time.'

'Lerrie would hate it if I fell in love with a boy, wouldn't she?'

'Lerrie wants you to be happy and she feels that only a woman can be equal with a woman.'

'I haven't made my mind up, Mum.'

'It's your life, Rosie. It's not my life or Lerrie's life. It's yours. It's not what anybody else wants that counts. It really doesn't!'

'All right, Mum. I'll think about it. Can you spare a pound? Pay you back Saturday after I've done my babysitting.'

Lindsey fished her bag from under the table and found her wallet. 'Bit short on change. Oh well, being as it's you. How you getting home?'

'Bob'll drop me off, his old banger's on the road again. Don't worry, he's got his licence back, and he hasn't gone drinking since they did him for it. I'll be fine. No sweat.'

'I'll be in when you get back, all right?'

'Don't worry. I'm a big girl now. Got me apple and me bus pass and me hanky.' Rosie stood up, washed her coke glass, and kissed Lindsey, giving her one of her sideways now-don't-say-anything glances, which always worked. ' 'Bye then, Mum. Have a nice evening with Lerrie and give her an extra hug from me. Tell her I'll make the tea in the morning. It's my turn.'

Lindsey finished the pot plant and carried it into the front room. With the flat almost done she could at last start to save for a car. She suddenly remembered the accident, and how she'd been longing to learn to drive before then. She had been pregnant. Now Rosie was wondering who to fall in love with. She caught a glimpse of herself in the living-room mirror. She looked her thirty-seven years. Thicker around the waist, fuller in the face. Most of all, she looked happy. She heard a key turn in the lock and ran to hug her long-term relationship.

Moss's back door opened on to a small lobby with a concrete floor which led directly on to the back garden. To the right of the lobby was the door to a tiny bathroom and toilet; they were as cold as if they were old-style privvies in whitewashed blocks at the end of old-style back yards.

Lindsey had paid a local builder to make a door frame and hang a sturdy glass door so that the lobby was enclosed, but the bathroom was still freezing.

Christmas Day was mild compared to other years, but not mild enough to defrost the bathroom, so Lerryn had put on the wall heater an hour before she ran the bath, and, standing half-undressed in the hot water, she quickly pulled off her jumpers and T-shirt and immersed herself before the chilly air could get to her.

The others were in the living room listening to the Queen's speech which was one of Moss's annual rituals. However, Lerryn's alternative ritual had begun when she was fourteen, at home with her parents in Cornwall, when, despite all her mother's remonstrations, she had remained in the bathroom immersed in pink bubbles that Harry had given her, with the door firmly bolted for the length of the Queen's speech.

Until now, Lerryn had not missed a Christmas with her mother and father, but they had been treated to a fortnight in Spain with Harry, all expenses paid. So Lerryn had travelled north with Lindsey, all the way up the A1 so that Lindsey could get driving practice, to join Rosie and Moss in Herton.

It was strange to be there without Biff; and it was strange not to be spending Christmas in Cornwall.

Last Christmas had been a special time. Neither of her brothers was there because they'd rented a place near Dartmoor with their wives and families, and were having New Year instead with Lerrie's parents. So she had been the only offspring at home; and it had been wonderful. Her parents had known for the past two years about her being a lesbian. They never quizzed her, though they were never unpleasant about it either. They'd met Lindsey again since she'd 'come out' to them and had been gentle and polite to her, which was all Lerryn asked of them.

She had taken her mother and father for several drives, though her mother had had to stay in the car because of her angina. One time Lerryn had driven down the Cot Valley so that her mother could watch the sea.

Bright orange fungi were scattered in the hedgerows of the valley like unexpected candles; and beside the narrow tarmac track the everlasting water poured along its bed of rocks and pebbles, like a supernatural orchestra, water on stone and wind in wood.

'Japanese knotwood,' said Lerryn's mother, who knew every detail of the land she loved. They had stopped in a passing place for her to look at the valley. There were dark brown stems and flaming pink brown tops, twigs like squirrels' tails jumping to the sky. And white-barked birches, stunted, bent low under lichens, while the river rattled on like dried seeds in an old wooden drum. 'Can we go on?' she asked, obviously moved by the colours and the stark beauty of the place, even in December. So they did, to the parking place, with enough room for seven or eight cars, but deserted.

'Thank you, Lerrie,' said her mother. 'We always loved this place, didn't we? It's the edge of the world, I always think.'

They had returned via Sennen Cove, where she and her father had left the car to take a walk along the flat sands. The sea was washed out, pale green under low pale clouds and the thick grey wind was billowing the waves, as line upon line of them surged and crashed along the length of the beach. The waves flapped like old green and white striped pyjamas pegged out from the washing line of the shore, blown all day wet and dry.

'Your mum can't go walking like she used to,' her father had begun, 'the angina gets her, especially when the wind's like this.'

'How is she really, Dad?'

'She don't complain. Same old Sal. It means a lot to her to see you at Christmas. Means a lot.'

'And to you too, Dad? Means a lot to you too?'

'Me too. I remember you and me going fishing when you were so high,' he said, smiling at her and gesturing the height with his hand. 'You were such a bright little thing and you'd sit there in the boat so still, trailing your hand in the water from time to time. You'd be quiet for hours, lost in your own thoughts. But happy. I could tell you were happy.'

'I was. I loved those fishing trips. I was looking at all the colours in the water. You know how it changes as the sky changes.'

'I do. You can look in the water and lose all your troubles.'

'Did you have a lot of troubles to lose, Dad?'

'Not when you were very small, except money and I was trying to find it, not lose it.' As he laughed, the strong lines in his face became more defined. He turned to watch the waves pounding on to the beach. He'd always wanted the best for Lerryn – security, regular money, a safe and reliable job. He had known she wanted more, far more. Known from the way she had taken in the sea and sky sitting there as a small girl in the old dinghy.

239

Reading his thoughts, Lerryn linked her arm through his. 'I know you wanted me to be happy. You were always kind to me. I trusted you and you didn't let me down. You did your very best for me, for Mum, all of us.'

'We never meant no harm, Lerrie, sending you to that salon. We wanted you to have a trade. That's all.'

'I know that, Dad. I've no regrets. Look at me,' she looked into his face. His eyes were green-grey, reminding her of the sea. 'I have no regrets,' she repeated. 'None. And I still have you and Mum. But I knew what I wanted and it wasn't the salon.'

'Are you happy?'

They stood together in bright layers of white and grey daylight, watching the breakers. Then they turned and waved to Lerryn's mother in the car and Lerryn said, 'Mostly.'

'That's all you can ask for.'

This Christmas she was in Herton, and the primroses in Moss's garden were green clumps, tightly closed. They waited. Moss was waiting too, thought Lerryn, twisting the hot tap with her toe, and keeping the rest of her body submerged up to her neck. Herton people were waiting, and feelings and opinions were running high, though it seemed that Herton Pit was not scheduled for closure in the Coal Board's latest round of plans. Other pits locally were now on the list, and the uncertainty was angering men and women, old and young, throughout the South Yorkshire coalfield. A minefield, Moss called it. Lerryn lay back in the water remembering her drawings of Biff, which she had studied again just before this trip to Herton. Sometimes she wished she hadn't drawn them. In the first few drawings Lerryn had been aware of Biff's face looking both male and female. Gradually, Lerryn had separated out the particular lines, angles, expressions into specifically male and specifically female ones. Then she had experimented with drawings in which Biff was a man posing as a woman, and lastly, a woman posing as a man. It was this last set that had brought her to her deepest dilemma.

As she washed herself, Lerryn made a decision. She would try to find out more from Moss, as gently and carefully as she could. The drawings were etched in Lerryn's mind as if Biff were still alive and had posed for Lerryn yesterday. The eyes, the smile, the strong clean line of the jaw. Biff with a beard (it had seemed to age Biff); Biff laughing into Lerryn's face as if she shared Lerryn's secret, understood Lerryn's desire to reveal the hidden woman inside her; Biff smoking (which Biff never did); Biff with a trilby like Radclyffe

Hall, the trilby at a crazy angle so that most young dykes, propositioned, would say yes, eagerly.

Lerryn was just thinking that the Queen seemed to be taking for ever when Rosie's voice called from the kitchen door, 'It's finished, Lerryn, you can come out now!'

'Thanks. Will you put the kettle on, Rosie?'

'What d'you want then?'

'Coffee, please. I'll not be long.'

Lerryn stood up to dry herself, letting the bathwater drain until she was left with bubbles around her feet. Feeling chilled, she wrapped herself in her towelling robe, shoved her feet in slippers, pulled the off cord for the wall heater and dashed for the warmth of the living room.

'Washed all your troubles away, Lerryn?' asked Moss.

'Burst like bubbles. Anyway, who's got troubles round here at this season of goodwill towards men?'

'All the women, I should think,' retorted Moss, turning to the photograph of Biff on the mantelpiece. There was a silence. Lindsey and Rosie didn't reply. They didn't know if Biff was left out because Biff was dead or because Biff was a man. Lerryn thought she knew why Moss had chosen those words. She felt that Moss wanted to share the burden of the secret. But she dare not ask Moss in front of the others.

'What did the Queen have to say?' she asked.

'Oh the usual. She does it so well. She was very gracious,' replied Lindsey. 'Mind you, I'd be gracious on her income, wouldn't you?'

'No. The smiling would crack my face. I'd better get dressed. Oh thanks, Rosie. That'll go down well.' Lerryn accepted the mug of coffee gratefully and escaped upstairs to the room she shared with Lindsey.

She wanted to ask Moss directly, but fought the temptation. Anything rather than blow her trust with Lindsey sky high. She was almost sure now. My Goddess, thought Lerryn, how on earth did they keep it up all those years? She looked out of the bedroom window to the garden that Biff had made, kept tidy these days by some local girls, and lying dormant for the winter. Tell me what to do, Biff, please, she half whispered. She pulled on her jeans and stood very still, watching the garden. Nothing moved out there. Bernard Ian Ferguson had left no traces, no visible clues. The white crab apple tree was leafless, over twenty years old. The viburnum had sprays of pink flowers, as it did every winter when the garden was otherwise empty.

Lerryn had never seen one until her first visit to Herton and then had bought one for her own garden in Finsbury Park. Time passes, she thought, seasons pass, people are born, they live, they die. For the first time, Lerryn found herself wondering not about Biff as an adult, possibly a woman, and if so definitely a dyke, but as a child, a baby. Standing, Lerryn placed her two palms on her stomach, the tips of her fingers just touching. Breathing in, she watched the air fill her diaphragm, and her fingers move apart. She held her breath, then released it, and her fingers touched again. Slowly she let herself into the breathing exercises that she did before each art class she tutored, to relax and ground herself. Down through the layers she breathed, slow and slower, aware only of beginnings, the first breaths, Biff being born and crying out, Biff's first breaths, imagining as powerfully as she could Biff's birth. The birth of a baby girl.

The exercises over, Lerryn brought herself back into the here and now, from wherever she had been. She did not know where Biff had been born. But there must be a record. She did not know if Biff's name was his real name. Her real name? It was taken from the initials, wasn't it? Biff had said so. Bernard Ian Ferguson. Why hadn't she thought of this before? Perhaps after all, the festival had got to her, through Moss's involvement in it. Moss believed so fervently, and was so sure that she would meet Biff again. Biff's grave said: Here lies Biff, lifelong companion of Moss and friend of Frank. Nothing to give away Biff's gender. Now, reasoned Lerryn to herself, if Biff was male then there'd be no need whatsoever to leave Biff's real name off the stone, nor the gender. It did not say: May he rest in peace. And of course it could not say: May she rest in peace. If Moss believed in an after life, and there was no doubt that she did, then why had gender been left off? Lerryn had visited several graveyards in her search. Almost all the gravestones had the gender of the dead person on them, the full name, though some had nicknames as well.

Lerryn made her way downstairs even more certain that she had to know more. Later, when Rosie had gone for a bath and Lindsey had gone to bed, there would be a chance to talk to Moss while she was helping Moss to settle down for the night.

Lerryn helped Moss undress and pull her nightdress over her head. She brought her a bowl for washing her face and hands and her toothbrush and glass of water for cleaning her teeth while she was sitting in bed. Lerryn combed Moss's hair, and Moss thanked her and turned to face the photograph on the mantelpiece. Lerryn's eyes followed Moss's gaze.

'It's a wonderful photograph, isn't it?'

'It is. Not that I need a photograph. Biff's presence is with me all the time, sometimes a great and terrible emptiness, but never far away. All these years on, Biff is always in my mind. Biff was the love of my life.' As Lerryn picked up the knee pillow to tuck it in position, she realised once again that she had never heard Moss refer to Biff as he or she. That was noticeable, and was surely significant, thought Lerryn.

'Thanks, Lerryn, love. Just move the pillow down a little, will you? Yes, that's champion.' Moss winced.

'I can feel Biff's presence here. The whole house has both of you in it. Not in a sad way. It's positive. I was looking at the garden from upstairs, while I was dressing, you know this afternoon. It was already getting dusk. I was thinking about all the troubles here in Herton. How it's all building up. How Biff would have been spot on with,' Lerryn hesitated, not wanting to say his or her, 'the analysis. Like always.'

Moss heard Lerryn stumble, choosing her words. She felt closer to Lerryn on each visit; and she was sure that Lerryn cared deeply about the secret she appeared to have uncovered. Moss was also certain that only Lerryn knew of this secret – that Lindsey and Rosie continued blissfully unaware.

Out loud Moss said, 'Yes. I miss that. Biff would have been able to mesh all the details of the history together. It was a particular gift Biff had, to make people understand the history. Like Lindsey. She says sometimes she's never forgotten the lessons on the packhorse bridge but she didn't know they were lessons, just stories. Biff was such a one for stories.'

'Wasn't Biff's mother a suffragette? And two of Biff's sisters. I remember about that from one of Biff's letters. I expect that made all the difference in Biff's life really. Being part of it as a child.'

The effort of having to use Biff's name all the time was making Lerryn tired. She became conscious, minute by minute, of the energy it must have taken Moss and Biff always to be so careful without selling themselves short. Had they really decided all those years ago that for Biff to pose as a man was only to take on some of the disguise and not other parts of it? Otherwise why not say 'He' loudly, proudly, and be done with it? How much maleness had Biff taken inside herself? How had she struggled with that?

Moss was thinking about Biff as Lerryn spoke. It could almost have been Rosie, and not Biff, who had been a young suffragette in

Manchester in the early years of the century. Would Lerryn have done the same as Biff, Moss wondered? Is that why Lerryn was so in need of the truth? Tears came to Moss's eyes, thinking of herself with Florence, Biff with Emily. Young girls, loving and with a future ahead of them. Now she was old and she passionately wanted Lerryn to be on the inside of it, to know all of it, though there were things about Biff that Lerryn would never know, without having lived a lifetime in the same house, sharing daily moments and long nights.

'Manchester.'

'Manchester?'

'Yes. Biff was born and raised in Manchester. Alongside all the working-class suffragettes there. Biff lived in two different centuries, was only four when the twentieth century began. Oh I'm tired, it's been a lovely day. I'm going to sleep now. Sleep well, Lerryn. Pleasant dreams.'

'I will, Moss. And I hope you do as well. Dream whatever you'd most like to.'

Twenty-five

The alarm clock shrilled through Rita's sleep like a coal cutter ripping through the Herton black coal seam. Rita had been dreaming of crawling naked through tunnels with a chain around her body, pulling a tub of coal like one of the pictures in a school book on the Industrial Revolution. The room around her was as dark as the tunnel. Her eyes didn't want to focus. She ratcheted them open, forcing herself from the dream into the present – the summer of 1984. Dimly she could make out the fitted wardrobes that Steve had built, a patch of dull grey where she knew the mirror was. The clock shrieked again on repeat and she killed it with a blow of her finger. Dead. Satisfied, she dug Steve in the ribs and he grunted. Again, firmer.

'Uh? Time is it?'

'Four.'

'Uh.'

'Want some tea 'fore you go?'

'Ta love. Oh, nightmares. How 'bout you?'

Rita reached out and felt for the bedside lightswitch. 'Shut your eyes, I'm going to put the light on. Me, I was back in them tunnels. I can't leave them bloody tunnels. Ever since this strike started, I've been trapped down them. No lights. You know they used to have to do that, no lights?' He nodded. 'And I never get any older. I'm always nine. I don't know what it's trying to tell me. I'm right fed up of being a nine-year-old miner, that I am.'

Rita rolled out of bed and stumbled for her dressing gown. 'Shredded Wheat or Weetabix?'

'Shredded Wheat, love. It's okay, I'm awake. I'll come down for it.'

The sky beyond the kitchen window was washed dull brown with a light patch just above the rooftops. Pale greeny beige. Funny, the colours of sky just before dawn. Rita had become quite an expert. She busied herself with the routine and took Steve's jacket and boots from the airing cupboard beside the fireplace. The all-night burner had stayed on. The late evenings were still chilly even though it was June and the early morning picket duty was less intimidating if they shared the start in the kitchen like this.

Outside the pigeons woke in the loft at the end of the narrow garden. The sky deepened to light apricot where the pale blur had begun and a long shaft of pale red light moved upwards spreading until the whole dome of the sky was alight. It was like typical early morning getting ready for the shift, and Rita leaned on the sink for a moment looking out and absorbing the new day: 'Funny how you never get used to the silence, isn't it? All my life I've listened to the sounds of the colliery and now there's nothing. Only your pigeons and a few sparrows. I wonder how long, Steve?'

'As long as it takes, love.'

'Well, at least this town's solid.'

'We's'll need to be solid when they send in more pigs. They say the lot what's coming next'll make our local lads look like a troupe of ballet dancers.'

'Aye well, you'd best be off. Time's marching on. I start down the centre at eight, so I's'll see you down there.'

He kissed her as he left. He hadn't been in the habit of that, but she was liking it. He had started kissing her each time he went on duty. Ever since his best mate Mart Field got his head kicked in. You never knew what might happen. So far it had been broken wrists, cracked kneecaps, black eyes, swollen mouths, fractured jaws and Jimmy

Garth had a burst spleen. Of course, thought Rita, shoving a pile of sheets and pillowcases into the automatic, none of that was on the television news at six; nor at nine, nor at ten. She measured the powder with care, not wasting a single particle. She chose a cooler wash than she was used to, to keep the bills down, and clicked the machine on. She'd been going to get a new one just before the strike but now it wasn't possible. If it packed up again, it'd have to stay heap of the year, unused in the corner. There was no knowing when she could replace it. She didn't relish the thought of trampling the lot in the bath in cold water, but there you go. We shall do whatever we have to, she thought.

She boiled the kettle and made more coffee, looking at the jar, too, noticing it was going down too fast. She'd have to get used to it weaker. The kids had stopped asking for sweets. They had stopped asking, full stop. They were bloody marvellous kids and she felt right lucky. School was terrible, but they still caught the bus each day and hadn't started truanting like some of the others.

'I've got to get me exams, Mum. I've got to. I'm not going to let 'em get to me. I just get me head down over me books and get on.'

'You do that, our Anne. You've a right to that education.'

'You wouldn't think so to hear some of 'em, Mum. At least our town's solid, but there's two scabs' daughters from Smythe in our tutor group. You know it's only eighty per cent at Smythe. Not like here. I hate 'em. Fiona and Sarah. We used to be good mates, but not any more. Anyway they're leaving, so I shan't have 'em for ever, thank God.'

'It's just ignorance, our Anne. Don't you let it get to you.'

'I shan't, Mum.'

Rita had a routine and she kept to it day after day so that the sense of family life could go on, however long the strike lasted. Secretly she dreaded the autumn and winter when it would be cold as well as dangerous on the picket lines, when there would be no money for winter clothes, no money for extra fuel, no money full stop. But now that the women's support group had become strong and Joan Field had become the secretary, she wanted to be part of this thing, this action that was linking her home with the whole country, and other parts of the world as well.

By 6.30 she had the washing pegged out on the line; by 7 a.m. Anne and Paul were at the kitchen table eating toast and drinking mugs of tea, and by 7.30 she herself was washed and dressed. At 7.45 the young people were at the bus stop waiting for the school bus that collected miners' sons and daughters and deposited them at the comprehensive on a new site two miles out of town.

At 8 she was at the support group, sorting food parcels, writing letters and making tea for the two advice workers who ran the welfare benefits advice sessions for two hours every morning.

'Do you ever hear from Lindsey Shepherd?' The voice was Joan's.

Rita tied a clean apron around her waist and started washing up, thinking fast. It reminded her of the questions 'When did you last see your father?' and 'Have you stopped beating your wife?' It did her brain in, thinking of 'her friend' Lindsey. Rita had had a shock the last time she'd seen Lindsey, which had been last Christmas in the market. Lindsey had cropped her hair short, like one of those Greenham women. She wasn't exactly dressed in green wellies and huge Falklands-type jacket, but there was something about her that made Rita feel very uneasy.

She didn't trust Lindsey Shepherd, not since she'd abandoned her baby, though it was rumoured she'd gone gaga for a while after the accident in which her husband Peter was killed. Rita couldn't get over the fact that she herself had blamed Lindsey for the whole set of circumstances. Perhaps it had just been too scary. The mere thought of losing Steve on the M1 like that had set Rita to dreaming about crashes for nights on end. Twice she'd woken up shaking and once, though she had never told anyone about it, she had peed her own bed, in the middle of a nightmare about being trapped in a crashed car and unable to get to a toilet. When she had woken with a wet bed, she had been so glad she wasn't already married. What if she'd done that in bed with Steve? He was a kind man, but limits are limits, she had thought, realising then that she didn't want to meet or talk to Lindsey.

Afterwards, and especially after Lindsey had returned to collect Rosie, Rita wished she'd been the sort who could say sorry. She went through months of remorse, almost how she imagined a divorce might be. They had been so close, like family. They had shared secrets and told each other about things they were ashamed of. The nightmares started again. She had always been a vivid dreamer, mostly in full technicolor, and Steve was the only person she had ever met that she could talk to about *that*. Whatever was on their minds they both would dream about. Good job they didn't have extra-marital flings like a few Herton couples she could mention.

'Are you with us Rita Gibbs, or are you with the Woolwich?'

'Oh, I'm sorry, I was off in a daydream. Wonder I didn't wash these mugs with the floor sponge. Sorry, Joan, I really was miles away. What did you ask me?'

'Doesn't matter. Is your Anne going round with these parcels tonight?'

'She can't, she's got a puncture. But our Paul said he'd do it. Steve's going to help Anne with her bike.'

'There's six parcels to be delivered; and Mrs Ferguson's finished another batch of scones, so can he collect them on the way back?'

'I'll tell him. She's grand, isn't she?'

'You know Mrs Kinton in the library, who liked Biff, yes? Well, she's been saving all the papers and she goes through them for cuttings and such like and she's got a set of photographs that Rosie took at Easter. She hid up a tree near the lines. Black and white. I'm surprised your Anne didn't say. Mind you, you're not that keen on them being friends 'n all, are you?'

'Shall I tell you something, Joan? You can't pee in Herton without the whole town knows.'

'Geron with you. Hoity-toity. You've got to let bygones be bygones. That's why I was asking you, just now, when you was off in orbit, about Lindsey, because Hazel just opened a letter from one of them trades union women's groups what's sent us a cheque for fifty quid.'

'Where? Let me see that.'

'Oh, you've come back down to earth then? Hazel's fetching it out of her bag. Hazel, Rita here wants to see that cheque from Lindsey Shepherd's group. Yes, that's it.'

'Let me wipe me hands then. Here you are.' Hazel passed the letter and cheque to Rita then turned to Joan adding, 'And there's another one came first thing this morning, only I left it on the table by mistake, from one of them lesbian groups in London.'

Reading the letter from Lindsey's group Rita heard Hazel's words and remembered Lindsey's cropped haircut. Oh no, she's not is she? No, she can't be, she's got Rosie to think of. No. She couldn't be one of them and have a teenage daughter; they don't have kids usually. Hang on though. There was that woman in the papers what sued her ex-husband for custody. Didn't get it, mind you. Should think not. Whatever next. I wouldn't want my Anne around anybody like that.

As calmly as she could, she turned to Joan and Hazel. 'Is there?'

'Yes. Signed by somebody called Lucy-Anne, doesn't mean anything to us. Don't know anyone called Lucy-Anne, do you?' Rita shook her head. 'Anyway, I want to talk about all that in our next meeting. We've got support from all over. Black people. Gays. Lesbians. I want to talk about all that. Stuff we've not talked about before.'

'I suppose so, Joan, if they're sending us money. Not really part of this strike though. They muddle it all up. We don't have to go over the top or anything.'

'Like you said, they're sending us money. You don't want us to send it back, do you, Rita?'

'If I'm honest, yes, I do.'

'We need the money. We need the support. Anyway, like I said, we can discuss it when it's just us women. My place, Thursday.'

'If there's time. There's a lot of business to get through on Thursday.'

'Then we'll have to move something else to another night. We've got to make time. Hazel and me both agree it's getting urgent, don't we Hazel?'

'She's right, Rita. They've sent the money, been out collecting. Them artists have been selling paintings and such like. But *we* haven't talked about gays at all. So we've all of us got a lot of talking to do. All of us.'

'I suppose so. Hey, hang on a minute. I'm not prejudiced.'

'Like hell you're not,' Hazel interrupted.

'Don't get me wrong. I just don't like all them extremist women, look like blokes, half of 'em. And I don't see that a letter from a bunch of them sort is going to do us any good. We've got a hard enough time with the reporters and the press as it is.'

'That's why,' replied Joan, 'we've got to talk. About gays and lesbians. Now you think on. You will come on Thursday, won't you?'

'I'm not bottling out if that's what you mean. But I've got my opinions and I'm entitled to them. I'm going to take a hell of a lot of persuading to make me see things *your* way, but I'm not giving up this struggle, however much I disagree with you even if I'm the only one that sees things *my* way. Now, who's going to help me get this dinner on?'

Moss held out the plate for Rita to take another piece of cake saying, 'Go on, treat yourself. You deserve it after last night's marathon. Wish I could do more for you all.'

'You do, Moss, you do,' Rita said, giving in and helping herself. She ate and drank and then said, 'You listen to me bending your ear for a start.'

'Yes, and from what you've told me I'm surprised you and the support group haven't fallen out completely.'

'It takes all sorts in this strike. We all have to pull together, besides, when we're on that line next to each other shouting, hollering at them pigs, we're like that.' Rita held up two fingers close like peas in a pod, near Moss so that Moss could see. 'There's a deep trust between Joan and the others and me because we was born and bred in this town; there's our class and our men and our kids. I don't like all their ideas, it's true. There's eight of us and I'm the only one what's hard line. So what? Win a few, lose a few.'

'But you did agree to keep the money and write a letter.'

'I didn't want to. Majority vote. That's democracy, and I do believe in democracy, but I also feel very strongly about real families, family life as it was meant to be.'

'And what's that when it's at home?'

'I don't think that you and me should talk about all this. I mean, well, it wasn't easy for you or me when I became your home help. We've done very well up to now. I'd say we'd become friends, wouldn't you?' Moss nodded. 'So it doesn't do to poke around.'

'Meaning Lindsey?' Moss poked.

'Yes. Meaning Lindsey. I had to think a lot about her before I agreed to be your home help, just like you did.' Rita raised her eye brows in a question, and Moss could see her because she was near, as Rita intended. Again Moss nodded. Rita continued, choosing her words with utmost care, 'Lindsey and me are like a wound what won't heal. I understand wounds. I was a nurse. If the cottage hospital hadn't closed thanks to a grocer's daughter in Downing Street, I'd still be a nurse. Though I do love being a home help. Anyway, Lindsey and me are like an operation that went wrong, a long, long time ago. Now? Well, now we'd never agree about the best way to live our lives.'

'It's a shame. Maybe you're right and it went wrong and hasn't healed and never will heal, but it's still a terrible shame. I so wanted you two to be friends again.'

'Fantasy time.'

'If I was younger, I'd be out there on that line shouting with you, but I would have a few up and downers too. Times are changing, and you told me you were changing too. But it seems you've still got a lot of the same opinions, deep down.'

'Yes, well, some things don't change, not according to my lights. I want this town to be normal happy families. Like mine, for instance.'

'Gay people have rights too, and they have families too, Rita. You read the papers, you watch the television. You hold with human rights, don't you?'

'Human rights is one thing. So all right, I say live and let live. But *this* town hasn't room for gay people, it never has had. You remember Joan's sister Kathleen? She left; and to me that's no bad thing. I'm not saying she hasn't a right to her way of life, and I told Joan so to her face, but it was better for everybody when Kathleen left.'

'And supposing she hadn't got her scholarship to Cambridge?'

'No chance of that, she was bright as a button from being a day old.'

'I said supposing, Rita. Supposing she had no qualifications, nowhere to go?'

'I can understand your drift. You don't have to spell it out. She'd not be the only spinster, would she? She could find work; or she could grow out of it and get married. Lots of girls play around when they're young. They lark about like Kathleen. Then they grow up, find a nice boyfriend and do what everyone else does, they get married, have children. That's what I'm saying about normal family life. That's what I hold with. And talking about Joan's sister is as near to it as you and me should get. Because I've got a job to do and . . . '

'All right. But answer me one last question.'

'You have ways of making me talk?'

'Is this why you don't want your Anne to be friendly with my Rosie?'

'You cut bacon in thin slices, don't you?'

'Waste not want not, and I'm not frightened to cut near the bone.'

'If I thought for one moment there was anything, anything at all like that between Anne and Rosie I'd get an injunction. I'd make my Anne a ward of court. It can be done. Like you said, I read the papers.'

'I thought you'd say something like that. Yes, it was difficult for me to have you come into my house, be my home help, do intimate things for me, laundry and such like. Because I knew deep down how hard you were capable of being. But I hoped that you'd soften with time, and life's experience. I still hope that. You know how you feel, you've told me so, when the papers spread their evil lies about the miners. You want people outside Herton to change; and I want you to change. You sound like Thatcher when you talk like you just talked.'

'Me? Leave it off. They'd better not send me on no trip to Downing Street. I'd throttle her with me own bare hands. What does she think we're striking for, fun?'

'Starvation tactics, Rita. I sit here sometimes in front of the tele with your Aunt Mercy, shouting. You know like on the lines: Maggie Maggie Maggie: out out out. So I can't take it when you talk like her with your so-called opinions. Now I think we'd better call it a day, or we shall have to get me a different home help and that seems a waste after all we've been through. And you need this job.'

'I've left everything in the kitchen just like you said. So you'll be all right will you?' asked Rita gruffly after a pause.

'There's plenty of blind people do *all* their own cooking Rita; and I still have some sight left. I'm fine. I know exactly what I'm up to out there. Have you got my rock cakes?'

'I have that. Right here in me bag, thank you. I don't know what we'd do without you. Take care now and I'll be in on Monday. Half past two as usual. All right?'

' 'Bye, Rita,' said Moss as Rita let herself out of the front door.

Moss heard her walk down the path and ramp to the street, her heels clicking on the pavement.

Then she sat, shaking her head, wiping tears from her face. She turned to Biff's picture and said, 'Get a load of that then, Biff? And they say that times are changing?' There was no reply and Moss made her way with the zimmer to the kitchen where she immersed herself in activity, making tea and starting on another batch of scones for the support group.

Twenty-six

Hot July sunshine hummed in the back lane which led through the garages along the track to Lerryn's garden gate. Lindsey walked from the bus stop, taking the short cut because it was daylight. She enjoyed the glimpses of people's gardens behind walls, fences and cypress screens. The brambles in the waste patches were in flower and garish dandelions poked up through cracks in the forgotten tarmac.

She was met in the lane as usual by her old friend Archibald, the huge ginger tom belonging to Lerryn's next door neighbour. She picked him up. 'Hello, sweetheart. Who's my old favourite then?' She carried him past some rosebay willowherbs, murmuring into his ear, 'It's all cupboard love, isn't it, you old fibber? Won't that Lerrie give you any titbits? You wait till you see what I've got for you.' He purred in response.

As they came to Lerryn's gate, Lindsey knocked loudly. Soon Lerryn could be heard the other side coming along the path to let the pair of them in.

Lindsey saw immediately that the picnic rug was in place, and her favourite assortment of Chinese dishes was ready, as they'd arranged on the phone. She pecked Lerryn hastily on the cheek so as not to disturb Archibald. He didn't like Lerryn because she wouldn't let him sleep on the nasturtiums or go about his business in the rose beds. But Lindsey pampered him and he knew she would feed him. Lindsey and cat sprawled themselves on the rug. Happily eating from a container lid, Archibald started in on the fried rice.

'This is wonderful, thanks.' Lindsey spoke with her mouth full, pitchforking heaps of special chow mein. 'God, I'm hungry.'

Lerryn smiled. 'Your mouth's in the middle,' she said.

'Oops. Radar's all wrong. Oh. I feel as if I haven't eaten since the weekend.'

'You probably haven't. All those meetings. More soy sauce?' asked Lerryn, passing the bottle as Lindsey nodded, still harvesting rigorously.

'Why aren't you eating?'

'Harry fed me.'

'How is she?'

'Fine.' Lerryn changed the subject abruptly. 'Tessa rang me just now. Sharon's got flying colours for her course – so Tessa's taking tomorrow off so she can go with Sharon for an interview as a legal secretary – good money. Tessa is free afterwards, and she wants to come here to the studio. She wants to catch up she says. I'm really glad. Such a surprise – you know what her timetable is like, worse than ours.'

'I don't know how she keeps going. Did she say how Jean is?'

'All right. Decided to stay on at school. Very happy, lots of friends, doesn't have a clue what she wants to do except she won't be a secretary like Sharon and won't work for the council like Tessa.'

'And what about her and Maureen? What's Tessa's version?'

'That they've struggled for a long time, love each other a lot, know each other very well, but they hardly see each other. Tessa has meetings every night, either work or the Black women's group, and she desperately wants to carry on with her art classes. Says they keep her sane.'

'You're closer to her than I am now. All I can do with a paint brush is matt emulsion. Anyway I see Maureen every day so obviously *she* spills her heart out.' Lindsey sighed.

'What do you think is going to happen to them?' asked Lerryn.

'I don't know. They don't know. We are all changing.'

'I don't want to lose either of them. I've loved them both for years.' Lerryn paused. 'And what about you, Linz? I hardly see *you* these days. How's things in your group?'

'Progress. We found two more women to put up miners' wives if necessary. Other than that, it's all sorted out now. Rocky's got her place on that union course I told you about. Ten days. But they still won't give her the time off, so she's going anyway. Probably have to take it as holiday.' Lindsey paused between mouthfuls. 'It's been years since we ate out here.' She sniffed. 'Don't tell me that's Chanel No. 5 you've got on?'

'Harry's been doing the duty frees again.'

'You know how it upsets me if you wear that sort of stuff.'

'I'd have washed it off but I didn't have time.'

'Washing off's just as bad. You shouldn't accept it in the first place. They test that stuff on animals.'

'Just calm down a bit, take things easy. People around you can't move without you're jumping in with accusations.'

'Well, you could at least sell it. That's a mining family's Sunday lunch you're wearing.' Lindsey waved her fork at Lerryn as she spoke. 'Not to mention five hundred blind rabbits.'

'Go on then. Stick that fork in my leg and demand that I account for myself.'

'So are you going to sell it?'

Lerryn waved a small envelope that clinked. 'For a hundred per cent profit? For Herton?'

'Don't you smirk at me like that. You really are a wind-up merchant. You make me so mad.'

'You do it all by yourself. You dash around until you meet yourself coming back; and wonder why you get in a tangle.'

'Don't put me down, Lerryn. I'm doing as much as I can. I don't like you when you're smug. Anyway, what else are you trying to hide?'

'Pass me a lager, will you?'

Lindsey broke off a can from a four-pack and handed it across. 'Obviously I'm not the only one in a state. Did you know you've got your "I've-been-to-see-Harry-who's-up-to-something" body on?'

Lerryn shifted uneasily on the rug. 'Not just Harry, actually.'

She's hiding something, thought Lindsey, I'm *sure* she is. And I know it's to do with Herton. She gets that particular look about her, whenever she's thinking about Nanan and Biff. Lindsey was just about to ask Lerryn what it was that she needed to say when Lerryn threw at Lindsey the one name she least enjoyed hearing.

'Today I met up with Anna von Schiller as well.'

'Nasty smell round here. What did the ghost of Sappho want?'

'She didn't want anything . . .'

Lindsey chortled: 'Tell me another. I love your jokes.'

'Harry has to collect a valuable oil painting – just listen will you, just calm down and fucking listen – it's Anna's contact but she has to leave for the States by this weekend, and Harry can't bear to fly alone as you know.'

'Makes her arms ache does it? Can't she fly with one of her minions, help-along-cassidy?'

' . . . alone, as you know,' repeated Lerryn, trying not to throttle Lindsey who was making it as hard as she could. 'You know she hates using the plane when it's only her and the pilot. Gives her the heebie-jeebies. We could return via Manchester.'

'And where do you fit in to Harry's travel plans?' asked Lindsey, suspecting that this was part of a scheme hatched by Lerryn and Nanan. Something to do with a stopover in Manchester?

'Harry didn't exactly say so but she hinted that she'd pass over another cheque for the miners if I went to the cabin on the loch with her.' Lerryn swigged the lager, playing for time.

'Miners' families are in hock up to their necks and your aunt went and bought another holiday home. Time and money. My God. As for you, taking a convenient holiday.'

'I got a huge cheque out of Harry today.'

'And all for charity. Oh what a nice lady, and how bountiful.'

'Spare the sarcasm. It doesn't suit you. This strike is hurting us, Lindsey, hurting you and me, doing something to you. Setting you against me. As if art isn't real politics, isn't contributing to the miners' funds. I'm at a loss really. Can't quite put my finger on it . . .'

'Oh try it on Anna. She'll let you . . .'

'Don't be so crass. You don't have to sink that low.'

'Not when you're born at the bottom. There's nowhere to sink. But you've forgotten that, flirting with Anna. She always propositions you . . . '

'And I always say no. It's a game of ours by now and we both laugh and get on to the serious talking, which is . . . '

Lindsey interrupted, 'To write a cheque for the miners, I knew there was something up. What a pleasant way to raise cash. Trouble is, I know all the wrong people. Something to do with money and class, I should think.' Lerryn didn't answer immediately and Lindsey tried to calm down. When Lerryn spoke, it was gentle but very fast.

'You seem to be going over the top a bit, Linz. You're overlooking the fact that I left Anna. I wasn't seduced by the cheque book then, and I'm not likely to be at this stage in my life.'

'And what stage is that?'

'I want my work, my politics; and my relationship with you. My interest in Anna is that she's totally committed to women and art.'

'Well she could hardly be committed to the miners and Herton, could she?'

Lindsey, who hated shellfish, flicked a prawn from the special fried rice to Archibald, who licked and then ate it. He then sauntered off with his tail in the air.

Lerryn felt like crying but instead she fiddled with the ring from the top of the lager can. She didn't know what to say next, though there was so much she wanted to talk about.

'I rang Nanan today, to see how Mart Field is getting on,' began Lindsey, between forkfuls of fried rice. 'His wife Joan is thinking that they'll have to sell the house if he can't get work when this fiasco's over. So it does me no good, no good whatsoever, to hear that Harry can't miss her Scottish holiday.' Lindsey's voice became sharp and tinny as her anger mounted. 'She makes me want to spit, she really does. After all that Herton has done for her. You know how much money she's making from the Herton Foundation. You know what they charge for those courses, you couldn't even afford to go on one, that's the whole nonsense of it, and you go along with it. Mart Field had his head kicked in by Herton's boys in blue, and you want to go gallivanting with Harry!'

Lerryn was shaking but she tried to steady her emotions. She leant her chin on her hands as she talked. Lindsey was still eating as if there was no food coming for a month: a sure sign that she was tired and stressed.

'Lindsey, try to calm down a bit, please. I don't see you for days on end because of this strike. I am slogging my guts out to sell pictures for it. And I am persuading all the patrons of the arts that I meet to part with money for it.' Lerryn paused, feeling she was getting nowhere. Lindsey's body language whenever Anna's name came up was agitated and turbulent. Lerryn had explained often that there was no need for Lindsey to feel threatened. However, the combination of Anna and Harry sent Lindsey to the edge of a storm and this time Lerryn didn't feel inclined to humour her. I don't want a tempest this evening but I'm damned if I'm dancing on hot bricks around her, she thought. Who the hell does she think she is? Why can't she tread as carefully around me instead? She felt heavy as stone inside. As she spoke she had a hard edge to her voice.

'If you're in such a bad way over what's going on in Herton, then why don't you take a week's holiday and go up there or something. Rosie could come and stay with me, or she'd be all right on her own. For heaven's sake stop venting all your anger on me. I'm not one of the boys in blue and I don't deserve it. It's about time you recognised that you're not the only one fighting for this strike. I was thinking that if I go with Harry there'd be other patrons in Scotland, other places to raise money. Don't insult me by imagining I'm just dashing off for a holiday.' Lerryn stood up and was gesturing towards the picnic rug with her hand. 'Now you can finish your meal in peace because I'm off indoors for a shower. Then at least you won't be offended by the perfume.'

Somehow, Lerryn took herself from the garden into the bathroom. Lindsey could hear water running. She felt like a cloud split apart by thunder, which came from within. On the picnic rug, where she'd collapsed a short time ago, delighted to be there, hoping to touch Lerryn and hold fast all night, she now sat with her arms around her knees, her head bent over them.

The thunder died down but left her feeling churned and vapourised. Her insides were like a cloud of cold air, swirled around. She felt so lightweight that if she didn't sit still, she'd be scudded away by the wind.

The scent of Chanel No. 5 had drifted away, but the Chinese food still came towards her in delicious whiffs, practical and unromantic. She couldn't control her feelings or her whirling thoughts. Images of Mart Field and the Herton picket lines, and images of her own anger, which Lerryn called dragon-fire, blended and sharpened. She could not hold on to any of the scenes for more than a moment. They flicked and flitted as she remembered history from school and history from the packhorse bridge. Long journeys and long marches. Nanan and

Biff. Nanan and Biff. From memories to words, the names became sounds until they tapped in her head in rhythms, like a mantra, obsessive and repetitive, taking over.

Lindsey sat on the rug in Lerryn's garden, contained in the mantra as the names chanted in her head. She absorbed the warmth that came from the ground under the rug, up through the soft wool, dark blues, deep reds, and bottle green. It had long been a favourite. Harry had given the rug to Lerryn in her teens, so it was older than Rosie. From Rosie to her father, Peter, Lindsey travelled, Herton to London, back along the M1. Red tail lights zooming and strobing. White and yellow light, hospital. Grey and green light on grey water soft in springtime, fetching Rosie. Rocky saying, 'Go and fetch your baby'. Then the flat in Hackney; Lerryn's reappearance.

Nanan and Biff. Nanan and Biff. For many minutes Lindsey sat curled, unmoving, listening to inner voices. Gradually she felt herself coming down from the clouds to the earth. She was aware that Lerryn would not come to find her. Lerryn had come searching to Herton a long time ago. Lerryn continued to search, but not for Lindsey.

The air grew chilly. Finally she stood, stretched her arms and shook her shoulders and made her way indoors.

Lerryn was washing her collection of shells and pieces of stone and glass. In the large kitchen the round table was covered in a circular oil cloth, with bowls of washing-up liquid, and bowls of clean warm water, clean thick paintbrushes for the crevices and corners, soft cotton cloths for polishing. Silently Lindsey sat herself opposite Lerryn and picked up an exquisite pink and cream coloured shell. Neither of them spoke. Quietly, stone by stone, piece by piece they worked, as if the jigsaw puzzle of their relationship lay on the oil cloth in front of them and they had to build it, from the edges inwards.

Without either of them having spoken a word, Lerryn left the table, put on the kettle, made coffee, and placed the two mugs where they could each, separately, reach. She sat down again opposite Lindsey and continued with the shells.

Presently, Lindsey stood, lifted a small bowl, went to the sink, tipped it out, rinsed it, refilled it with warm clear water and returned. After a while, Lerryn did likewise. In that way they continued, neither breaking the silence, for almost an hour.

The stone began to soften. To grow lichens and flowers.

The cloud dared to move towards an uncharted continent.

'I'm sorry,' Lindsey began, looking directly across the table at

Lerryn. 'I am afraid of more changes. Afraid of what is happening in Herton, what's happening to us.'

'I'm sorry too, I don't want to anger you. I don't want to lose you either.'

'I've known you a long, long time, Lerrie. I know when you are searching for something. When you are on to something. I felt when I saw your shoulders, how you were sitting opposite me out there, that it was something to do with you and Nanan, not just Harry.' Lindsey paused, searching for words. 'Nanan has been behaving very strangely lately. Something is troubling her, something she is trying to tell me. I know she's not going senile. She's as clear in her mind as you or me. She has felt closer to you since the funeral, as if, Rosie and me, we're outsiders.' Lindsey paused. It's all linked somehow. I can feel it. It's been building up and up.'

'You can feel it?' repeated Lerryn, moving a bowl of water nearer to her. It acted like a mirror for one of the wall lamps, and dazzled her momentarily until she slid it to one side. The lighting was lovely in the room. In one corner an old black wood stove with patterned tiles on the door was also catching the light. She waited for Lindsey to reply.

'Nanan is my real grandma, my mother's mother,' said Lindsey. 'But Biff was not my real granddad, not Sadie's father. I knew that. They never concealed it. What I couldn't understand as a child was why Biff had cut off all connections with his lot, the Manchester side of the family. It was pretty obvious why Nanan cut off, on account of being pregnant at sixteen, lots of families throw their daughters out. Now the reason I got upset out in the garden was that Harry's trips to Scotland always involve a stopover in Manchester. She visits her contacts and friends there. You know that.

'So, I felt you weren't being honest with me. I was just going to ask you why you were going to Manchester, when you brought Anna into the picture. Something is going on, and I need to know what it is. I'm sure it's to do with Nanan and Biff. I wish you'd tell me. I hate being an outsider.'

'It's partly because of the crisis with the strike that I've not known how to.'

'You thought I couldn't take any more, didn't you?' Lindsey looked across at Lerryn, whose eyes filled with tears. 'You were right. *I* thought I couldn't,' she went on quietly. 'I've been in a turmoil because of Herton, feeling I shouldn't have left, should be back there, doing something, all of that. My anger at what's being done to the miners has been burning me inside, and all my time's been – well life's been one long meeting – you know all that. But there isn't a lot of point for me, Lerrie, if I lose you over this. I'm a dyke in this strike, and I've been lovers with you since you walked back into my life way back when.' Lindsey polished a smooth pebble. She was crying silently at the thought of turning her own anger on Lerryn, whom she loved passionately. 'I know that you and Nanan are wanting me to know something. And *I'm* sure I don't want to know it. But I have to, because Herton is splitting down the middle, and Nanan won't live much longer. So I think you'd better put the pieces together for me, don't you?'

'We need some tissues,' said Lerryn, smiling weakly and wiping her eyes with the palm of her hand. She fetched some from the bathroom and put them on the table.

She put the kettle on for more coffee and stood by the sink looking out into the garden at the remains of the picnic while the kettle boiled. Archibald was back, slowly picking his way among the cartons, and glancing arrogantly towards Lerryn, aware of her behind the kitchen window. He had won, this time.

Lerryn carried the coffee mugs to the table, sat down opposite Lindsey and began to speak. Lindsey listened attentively, but trembled occasionally, reaching for tissues and blowing her nose.

'I didn't think anything much about this when I was first in Herton. I just knew I liked Biff, and that both Moss and Biff always welcomed me. Open arms, literally. Then I came in search of you, and you'd just left for London, and when I walked into the shop, I remember that there was a very powerful pull between me and Biff. In Cornwall I'd found the Biff-stone, then after I met Biff again I had the same shock that you had when you saw the stone. And I thought it was important but I had no idea why.'

'And was it?'

Lerryn nodded, serious and solemn. Lindsey felt as if she was about to hear about a death or a murder, something terrible and awesome, and she braced herself.

'Many years ago I drew some pictures of Biff. I'll show them to you later. I've never shown them to anyone. I had a hunch. But your granddad was beloved of you and your nanan, and a well-known figure in Herton, so I was on very dangerous ground. Not just for me.' Lerryn rested her head on her hand and ran her fingers through her hair. It was so hard to finally say it. Had it been this hard for Biff to tell Moss? And what if I am wrong, thought Lerryn.

'I just can't get the words out, Linz. Because I might be wrong, and if that's how it turns out, I want you to know that . . . '

'That you love me. I do know that. I love you too. If you didn't love me you wouldn't be finding this so hard. Whatever it is about my granddad, whatever he has done, or not done, it still remains that you're my lover. You're shaking, Lerrie, just say it quickly, then we'll cope after.'

'I think your granddad was a woman.'

Lindsey's eyes stared widely. Her mouth hung open. She seemed to stop breathing. Then she swallowed and reached for a tissue and blew her nose. 'That makes my grandmother, the one who is still alive, and loved by both of us dearly, a woman who loved a woman,' said Lindsey slowly.

'Yes. It does.'

'What on earth are we going to do if you are right?'

'Tell the story somehow. I don't know. I've been carrying it inside me for years.'

They sat silently, holding the information like a fragile shell on the table between them. Lindsey closed her eyes, wrapped her arms around herself, and rocked slightly. Lerryn put her arms, folded, on the table and rested her head on them.

Minutes passed. The women could hear the click of digits on the clock. Lindsey opened her eyes and saw that it was dark outside. She closed the curtains and returned to the table. Lerryn opened her eyes and sat up. They didn't touch each other. It was safer to sit apart as they had been doing.

'Lerrie, tell me, what are the chances of you being wrong?'

'Almost nil. But Moss doesn't actually want to talk about it, she just trusts me with searching in the suffragette archives in Manchester. I have the feeling she would never be able to tell us directly.'

'I want you to be wrong. So that my life doesn't have to turn upside down. And I want you to be right because it's so powerful. I keep thinking about the funeral. It would explain the funeral.'

'It would explain a lot of things. I know them by heart, Linz. I've been living with this hunch for so long.'

'I want to shout and scream. Hunch? Hunch? This is my granddad on the end of your hunch. He's no fucking mackerel for the end of your line.' Lindsey took a deep breath. 'But I have been to women's discos with you where I've turned round and thought there was a man in the place. I've been taken for a man myself. Me, Lindsey Shepherd. And you have too: I remember one time in the café in St Ives. I was at the counter and you were sitting at the table and the bloke behind the counter said, "Does he have sugar?" He thought you were a man.'

'You. Me. The only one it doesn't happen to is Rosie. On account of the eyeliner and lipstick. Not to mention the crown jewels she hangs on her ears.'

'Oh my God, I can't believe it. Of all the things I've been dreading you or Nanan telling me, I never dreamt my granddad was a woman. Was a dyke.'

'Biff didn't mind you being one, or bringing me home; or providing us with the back bedroom,' said Lerryn, keeping her voice as gentle and steady as she could. She added, 'Your nanan told me Manchester, Linz, in the full recognition that I was looking for something. The way I feel about it is that if Moss wanted this whole thing stopped, she would have kept quiet. Let the family secret die with Biff. But she has done exactly the opposite. She needs this as much as I do.'

Hearing Moss's name again, Lindsey began to weep intensely. Large tears fell down her face and her nose ran. As she looked up her face looked raw and open. 'If it was somebody else's granddad, I'd be joking, happy,' she said eventually. 'Rediscovered lesbians. I don't want you to be wrong. But I wish it wasn't my granddad, my family.'

Lerryn felt like reconstituted rag-paper pulp, just passed through a shredder. Wet, cold, soggy and at the beginning of a long process. She couldn't stop crying either, thinking how glad she would be to find someone in her own family who was like her.

'What're you feeling, Lerrie?' asked Lindsey between sobs.

'Relieved that I've told you at last. Really wrung out. What wouldn't I give for this to be in my family. Substitute tin for coal and you've got my family, two generations back. Botallack; deaths under the sea. It's all there. And there might have been a Biff-person too. Turned into some family secret. Mists lifting and descending, veils of secrecy. But I know it's hard for you.'

They looked into each other's eyes across the table. Lindsey sniffed and wiped her nose. She said, 'It goes so deep, what you've told me.' She paused, trying to stop trembling. Then more firmly she said, 'Either I am proud of who I am or I'm not. I am proud that I love you, and that Rosie knows. I'm a lesbian, take it or leave it. You're very brave to tell me this, Lerrie. It must've been a hell of a weight to be carrying around. It's no wonder I love you – and I do trust you – I am very sorry about getting in a state about Anna and all that in the garden just now. I'd like to see your drawings of Biff.'

'I love you too, Linz. I'll get the drawings in a moment. Then shall we try and sleep? Are you as tired as you look?'

'Exhausted. All these emotions. I feel wiped out. Have you locked up the studio?'

'Not yet. And the back gate isn't padlocked. Will you switch on the back light for me? I'll go and see to the gate and bring the tray and stuff in.'

'And so to bed,' said Lindsey.

Twenty-seven

Overhead the sky was shining black, black as the coal that lay undisturbed for months under Herton's coal seams. No one knew that she had made her way out here, slowly with the zimmer, to the bench in the back garden, to sit in the moonlight listening to the sounds from the colliery now that it was working again. It was not that no one cared. She had prepared them all for months, in her own way, and she was certain they understood that she would never allow the Social Services people to take her out of this house and put her in their so-called part three accommodation; turn her into one of their case studies, writing her life into their files, taking her from her home.

Step by step she had walked from Darlington to this town, the town that was not much more than a village, its seams sliced by instruments designed to split it apart. Fabric faded by weathering, torn by traitors; but Herton people were no more likely to define themselves as victims than she herself had been as a young girl when her body had been torn apart by the squire of The Hall where she served.

She had taken action, made decisions, gone searching for life and survival. Like her, Herton's women had had their lives torn apart by the strike, and they had toughened and strengthened, coming through with a respect and trust of each other.

She was cold, but the sky was so wonderful, the stars like sequins. Light years of stars, generations of constellations, centuries of clusters, millennia of galaxies. There were several people dead as a result of the strike, several couples divorced, though Rita and Steve were still together, and so were Joan and Mart. About thirty people maimed and many hundreds more determined, more analytical, more aware, more connected to the struggles for liberation nationwide, worldwide.

Most of the women of Herton had never owned a dress studded with sequins like the velvet night sky; and she, Moss Stratton, had never become wealthy. But she had been rich all her life, loving and loved.

It had been difficult recently to maintain her loyalty to the secret life that she had led with Biff, in the face of Lerryn's obvious need to know the truth, Lindsey's acquiescence and Moss's own desire for the final gift from her to the younger generations, to the women she loved and respected for the struggles they were involved in. So she had given Lerryn the word: Manchester, and she had trusted Lerryn to follow it through. Her gift was the gift of that trust. She had talked to Biff about that the past year, many nights and days. She could not trust strangers whether they were feminists or not, lesbians or not (the word came more easily to her these days), with the fact of Biff's life. They might sensationalise it, trash it, ridicule it, anything, even use it somehow for their own careers. She wasn't sure how, but she would not expose Biff to the world like that.

She watched the moon moving up and across the dome of the sky. Behind the movement were the sounds from the colliery and coke ovens. Coal to ashes and dust to dust.

She had waited. For the result of the strike. Had lived by wit and willpower and was proud of having fulfilled her desire, lived it through. Lindsey and Lerryn had visited at Whitsun. Had stayed four days and five nights. They had talked about life, politics, history. Lerryn had talked about *her*story. What would these young people think of next? Then Lerryn alone with Moss had talked of Manchester, her visit last summer, feeling her words so carefully, making Moss admit nothing, lie about nothing, confess nothing. Lerryn had leaned forward and taken Moss's hand in a gesture so like Biff's that Moss had let some tears slip. She simply said, 'Thank you.' They had said nothing else, but each knew that the other knew.

So now she was ready. She did not know if she was seeing the sky, or imagining it. The distinction was a false one. She was almost blind by opticians' standards, which was why they were insisting, the Social Services people, that she move to part three accommodation. She was tired of them and their interference though she was sure they meant well. Perhaps Rita was behind it. They were all in league really, though she never revealed to them what she was thinking about them or their suggestions.

She had waited for Rosie to finish her A-level exams, although she had wanted to answer Biff's call at Easter. But she had told Biff at that time to wait a little longer.

Rosie had arrived, as planned, on Maundy Thursday, with all her revision books. Anne had been studying too. She was a year behind Rosie and doing brilliantly. During the Easter holidays they'd both been in Moss's kitchen, one each end of the table, silently poring over their books. Moss couldn't possibly upset Rosie's exams. The timing just hadn't been right, despite the fact that Moss had fulfilled her determination to live to the end of the miners' strike.

Sitting on a bench, Moss had been there when the men had paraded with their banner on the day they returned to work. Rita had been sitting next to Moss. She was the one in the support group who had arranged for the car to come and fetch Moss. So there they'd been, together, when Rita's friend Joan, who was the secretary of the women's support group, had made that wonderful speech about the wives who had given their support, and made the strike possible; who made their mark on the world. Something had touched Rita deeply about that. Moss could feel her pride, beside her. But when Joan had mentioned all the others, nationwide, and internationally too, who had sent money and messages, Rita's body had changed. Joan mentioned Black people, gays and lesbians. Rita tensed. Then Moss knew that Rita still hadn't softened, and that she did not agree with Joan. No wonder Lindsey and Rita lived on separate islands. Some things take longer than one woman's lifetime. Then, not wanting anyone to guess her real feelings, Rita had breathed out, shifted in her seat, beside Moss, and put on a smiling body again. Moss could feel that. She trusted her own intuition in such matters. She thought of Florence, passed over. What would their lives have been like if they had run away from Darlington together? What journeys had Florence made since wading into the river? Where was Florence now? Might they ever meet? Would they trust each other?

Slowly she thought of her brothers and sisters, not knowing what had become of them; and wondered if she would ever meet her mother or father. The place she was going was safe for herself and Biff. So probably her father and Frank and Ronnie were somewhere else. On another island, perhaps.

Florence had been wrong to wade into the river. She, Moss, must not take her own life. But it was different here, in the garden, at midnight in her hat and coat, on the wooden bench.

She thought of her friends, Grace and Mercy. Mercy lived with her daughter, who had moved to the next town. They had not seen one another for several months. But Mercy was being well looked after. Moss thought of her family. She had loved her daughter Sadie and son Ronnie, her granddaughter Lindsey and Lindsey's lover, Lerryn.

And, in her final years, she had had the wonderful gift of her great-granddaughter Rosie. Moss would have loved to have passed on her house in Church Lane to Rosie, but you couldn't, not if you were working-class and it was only rented.

In Moss's younger days Rosie would have been a servant like other girls from the working class. Progress was slow but there had been some. Rosie deserved her place at college, doing photography. Her photographs of the strike were so good, everyone said, especially those she'd taken of the police while she'd been hiding up a tree. Rosie's young life was opening in front of her. Opportunities. It was a good thing. Moss felt free to start the next journey.

She looked up at the sky, which seemed to be becoming closer. She imagined she must be very, very cold, but she didn't feel cold at all. She had sent her letter to Lindsey, registered. Rita had brought back the receipt. From Moss's letter, Lindsey would know that Moss had made this decision, now that she was ready. Her post office book was all in order, and so was the letter authorising Lindsey to draw it all out, and make the arrangements that they had agreed on. Simple wooden coffin. The rich people had their castles, the poor ones had their pride.

She adjusted the pillow under her head. Imagined the colours of the lands through which she would pass, and the kinds of flowers that Biff would be gardening there, where they were about to meet.

'I'm ready, Biff. Come and hold my hand while I journey.'

She closed her eyes, and left Herton, with Biff.